FIRST, MOVE THE BONES:
A NOVEL

Lawrence D. Yaklin

Dedication

To my friend from college days.

To her insights on aspirations, faith, and the fragility of life. Those were a frequent discussion topic at the student union, a far too often distraction from our studies in the library, and a serious focus of our wonderment late into the night in our dorm rooms.

Thank you and may you rest in peace.

TABLE OF CONTENTS   Page

Disclaimer

FIRST, MOVE THE BONES: A NOVEL, is a work of fiction. Names, characters, businesses, places, long-standing institutions, agencies, public offices, events, locales, and incidents are either the products of the author's imagination or have been used here in a fictitious manner. All incidents and dialogue in the narrative, and all characters—with the exception of some well-known historical figures—including those that are depicted as having been affiliated with certain long-existing institutions, along with their actions, policies or doctrine that are described, are products of the author's imagination and they are not to be construed as historically accurate or real. Where real-life historical figures, or references to actual institutions appear, the characters, situations, incidents, their actions and/or publishing of their official policies, including any dialogues concerning those persons, serve as a backdrop to the story and are not intended to change the entirely fictional nature of the work. In all other respects, any resemblance to actual persons, living or dead, events, locales or institutions of religion are entirely coincidental or wholly imaginary. It has been written for entertainment purposes only and not intended to slander, libel, or defame any person, entity or institution or has been authored with any malice toward them.

Certain references included in the narrative, i.e., timelines, buildings, towns, people, etc., are considered to be limited to historical facts of *general knowledge* held by the public and/or have been gleaned from either the Archives of the State of Michigan, or available Leelanau County, Michigan case files and local newspaper accounts that are now considered in the Public Domain. Those are referenced at each use. But some of the above may also be fictionalized and not be entirely accurate. For readers with questions regarding any of the above, they are encouraged to do their own research in the publicly available official documents.

Other references included in the following narrative are the unique individual recollections or beliefs held by persons who lived during the time(s) of the setting(s) and/or considered to be conventional wisdoms of the overall mystery, but also may not be entirely accurate. Those referenced are taken from those person's own accounts as passed down generationally are also considered in the Public Domain of discussion regarding the events described and/or are included as purely coincidental or wholly imaginary.

Acknowledgements

Special Thanks!

A special thanks to Liz Witherspoon of The Wandering Wolf Imagery for the excellent photography/photo editing and image consultation services for the cover of the book. I encourage you to visit her website, **www.thewanderingwolfimagery.com** She is available for event photography—including weddings, anniversaries, maternity photo shoots, pet portraits and more in and around the Rapid City, South Dakota area. Contact her to discuss your photographic ideas and book her services.

Also, thanks to Keira Myers for allowing me the unrestricted access to her family's unique historical archives regarding the *Sister Janina-Isadore* incident—which were passed down from her paternal great grandfather. According to her relatives, he actually served on the jury of the Stanislawa Lipczynska murder trial held in Leland, Michigan in 1919. I found those family records shed significant light onto the decades of conventional, but at times inaccurate wisdoms and folklore surrounding the mystery of the missing nun. Additionally, they were *instrumental* in crafting this *work of fiction* to reflect the mindset of people who lived through the tragedy.

Finally, accolades to the staff of the Clarke Historical Library at Central Michigan University for their help in navigating their online Digital Newspaper Archives in the Public Domain. This tremendous resource yielded many facts and direction for the narrative, but it also provided several important insights into the nature of our culture at the time of the story's setting. As an alumnus, I can proudly say, *Fire Up Chips!*

Difficulty in Researching Records, 1907 to Present

The Diocese of Gaylord was created 19 December 1970 from portions of the Dioceses' of Saginaw and Grand Rapids.

At that time, a large number of archived files concerning parishes formerly under the authority of Grand Rapids were transferred to Gaylord—that would include many of the records from all churches in Leelanau County.

From that point forward, any inquiries made to Grand Rapids re: the Sister Janina Mystery have been reportedly met with responses to the effect of: *We don't have those archives here. They have been forwarded to the Gaylord Diocese.* Requests to Gaylord for the same are routinely forwarded back to Grand Rapids, since records from the years, 1907 – 1920 were under its domain.

Beginning in the early 1970's, according to anonymous sources, responses to inquiries made to the Leelanau County Clerk's office or the Circuit Court in Leland for records reviews of the Stanislawa Lipczynska murder trial were something to the effect of: *Those records have recently come up missing and are no longer available.*

A possible explanation for their unavailability may be because they were simply misfiled. With old paper records, this often happens. Although, at the time of those inquiries, it is also possible that those in authority simply *told* interested parties that they were missing to prevent research. It is also possible that they were missing due to theft, but then returned at some later time by the party(s) who took them because of a guilty conscience, renewed talk in the public about them, or fear of prosecution.

Interestingly, one of the few counties in Michigan that the State Archives in Lansing does not maintain court case files—other than those appealed to the State Supreme Court, is Leelanau. However, there was at least one local newspaper account in 1920 saying a transcript of the testimony from trial was ordered for the appeal case and to be filed with the high court.

However, *some* of the records of interest have since been relocated upon renewed inquiries in the early 21st Century but were only given a brief and less-than-thorough review. Repeated subsequent inquiries to review or questions about their whereabouts have been either ignored or met with denials that they ever existed by the affiliated parties in the private sector, the Church, and disturbingly, by some speaking on condition of anonymity in an *unofficial* capacity. Some of the latter reportedly served in key local government offices and/or historical societies who were familiar with the mystery.

There is almost enough intrigue regarding this aspect of the story to author another book.

Prologue

Transcribed from shorthand notes provided to the author from the person to whom this book is dedicated. They are her thoughts on the research that she gathered during a summer vacation in 1974.

"...and you thought you knew this story. Those are the words I begin with. They are taken verbatim from recently discovered documents. They refer to a local mystery into which I've been looking.

Over the span of the last one hundred years, the story of the disappearance of a Catholic nun, and then the gruesome discovery of her bones buried in a church cellar, followed by a flawed criminal investigation and trial, has been subjected to the push and pull of surprisingly limited and scattered facts.

Not surprisingly, that has resulted in as many reiterations of the accepted conventional wisdoms and official conclusions of the case, as there has been alternative theories proposed. Almost all of them suffer from instances of conflation, intentional interpolations, some wishful thinking, and conjecture based on the circumstantial.

Complicating clarity, there has been both the haphazard and suspected covert archiving of the case's related documents, Institutional maneuverings, renditions of the saga that have been subjected to a wide latitude of journalistic license, and word-of-mouth recollections passed down through generations that are fraught with error.

After all this time, and all the above, the story deserves a fresh review.

Despite its closed-case status, this look at the Mystery of Sister Mary Janina will uncover substantial evidence that the story has been shaped by direct coercive actions taken by associated figures in authority, and by individuals implicated. Their reasons to have done so vary. Some were to alter the narrative due to embarrassment, or to deflect criticisms. Some were the more nefarious and overarching reasons to preserve a threatened institution. Some were undertaken to protect status and individual careers. But for some, part of the reasons for their motivations were blended into their need to save their soul.

For the latter, as a part of their everyday life, their motivations were directed by the regularity of the act of sin and the reciprocal effort to seek absolution for sin as a requirement of their deeply ingrained Faith.

My research into this story will give a new perspective on much of the above while placing it in context with key points in a religious institution's long history.

There are actually two stories. One, our story of local tragedy beginning in the early 20th century. And a larger one that was established centuries earlier. They eventually run parallel to each other, then converge and continue. And in this comparative process it will satisfy the curiosity for a segment of the population and confirm suspicions for a sub-set in that faction. But for the remainder, it will perpetuate a new cycle of speculation and conclusions to form a different composite of beliefs.

Unfortunately, in the research of the tale, it also exposed systemic xenophobia, entrenched racism and religious prejudice that existed at the time of the setting, and regrettably, from what I have personally witnessed, continues its presence long after—similar to the lingering aura of incense.

This is not simply the retelling of the black and white account of the publicly accepted facts. It is a narrative littered with gray suppositions and theories that refuse to be ignored after nearly three-quarters of a century. In short, it will create more questions for you than answers. And in many ways, that is exactly as it should be in any proper mystery.

I suspect, based on what ultimate truths and falsehoods I discovered, I will likely play my own part in the mystery.

As it is said in Latin, et tu videris hanc fabulam scire. The English translation: **...and you thought you knew this story.** *Sincerely, Ann"*

Introduction

Glen Haven Beacon-Press, 28 August 1907 (Public Domain)

Kidnapped Nun

"After three days, the unsuccessful search for Sister Mary, of Isadore convent, north of Traverse City, who is believed to be Mary Johns, of the Felician Sisters of Detroit, the investigators and local pastor believe she was kidnapped. She disappeared from the church grounds Friday with no traces of her to be found. Isadore residents tell of her to be very happy in the convent and was an earnest teacher in the parish school. In a search, none of her clothes or personal effects are missing. This strengthens the theory of kidnapping over one of abandonment of her vows."

Pinconning Press, 5 September 1907 (Public Domain)

Convent Mother Missing

"'We feel that she must be insane, and that she has wandered out into the woods, and either is hiding or is lost.' So said Fr. Bienowski, (sic) head of the convent and school at Isadore, speaking of Sister Mary, the nun who disappeared last week and no trace of whom has since been found."

Accounts vary, but most likely in either late 1917 or early to mid-1918, the *unofficial* and institutionally suppressed discovery of a woman's skeletal remains—the victim of a crime—rocked the Catholic community of Holy Rosary in the small settlement of Isadore—sometimes known as the Four Corners in Leelanau County in northern Michigan. The death was newsworthy on its own merits. But the fact that the remains found were those of a Catholic nun who had gone missing from the community a decade earlier made the story even more intriguing. That her bones were found buried in a shallow grave in the basement of the same church where she had regularly attended Mass, and adjacent to the parish's school where she had served as a teacher, added multiple layers of sensationalism.

From that point, the saga would transcend from that of a simple and local murder mystery into a regionally and perhaps internationally directed conspiracy of silence and later one of misdirected blame. The cast of characters would include a succession of Holy Rosary's serving Pastors, involvement of Bishops and the offices of an Archbishop in the leaking of details of the crime to exonerate themselves. There would also be instances of those in law enforcement and a prosecution using unscrupulous tactics. And some would speculate that the efforts to suppress discussion of the heinous act and then divert attention away from the truth of it traveled all the way up to the highest level of the Church in Rome. However, full details of it would still be secretly catalogued in compliance with ancient policy.

As the details unfolded pursuant to the investigation and subsequent murder trial, and the level of embarrassment rose among the citizens of the settlement and the local authorities of the county, there were also accusations of a rush to *judgement* rather than to *justice,* in order to avert a collapse of the Polish Catholic community. Ironically, it would be the start of a long-awaited plan to construct a new Holy Rosary Church over the spot of the old one—which was intended to strengthen the community—that would eventually decimate it.

Chapter One

Northern Michigan, 24-26 May 1969

During the Memorial Day weekend, 1969, a recently retired adjunct professor of English at a northern Michigan college, who has requested anonymity for himself and his family in this narrative, visited a flea market in Michigan's upper peninsula, west of St. Ignace, located along US 2. The man and his wife were shopping for used but serviceable household items and antiques to furnish their summer cottage back down across the Mackinaw Bridge in the lower peninsula. Their residence was located in the upscale neighborhood of Victorian homes in the highly conservative and overwhelmingly religiously Protestant, Bay View Association of Petoskey, which at the time maintained a restricted-by-covenant ownership of property to prevent other-than-Christians from living there.

While browsing the collection in the market, one item caught the man's eye—a desk in sad state of repair. He made an opening offer. "Would you take twenty dollars for this desk?

"Well, hmm, 'dats my display—to show off my best junk, eh." The operator of the outdoor market replied—hoping to squeeze a few more dollars out of the transaction.

The operator, thought to be a man named J. Simmons, who resided in a rural section of Mackinaw County known by locals as the *Simmons Settlement* was running this seasonal flea market located at the site of a vacant and decaying motel without permission of the property owner or a business permit. It was his way to supplement his hard scrabble existence between jobs in the logging industry in his capacity of what the *Yooper locals* refer to as a *pulp cutter*.

"How 'bout forty—fifty?" The man pressed without giving Simmons a chance to agree to an offer.

"Waahl, dats an antique! Story is that it was owned by the Pope—or maybe a Bishop!" Simmons exaggerated.

"I'll give you a hundred." The man had reached his limit of negotiation. That's my final offer!"

"A Hundred?" Simmons gushed. Since he had acquired the dilapidated piece of furniture at *no cost* under dubious circumstances, he was delighted in the markup. "Holy-wah, Mister!" Simmons cackled in his Yooper cadence. "Oh, ya! For a hundred bucks, do you want me to gift wrap it?"

"Ha-ha! No that's not necessary." The man said enjoying the joke.

Amused by his own banter, Simmons barked out to his son in laughter. "Milo! Help git dis desk into his pickup before he changes his mind dere, eh!"

"Do you have the key to the lower drawer?" The man inquired.

"Nah, 'fraid not! Broke off in 'da lock. Jammed shut. All sales final!" Simmons quickly added as he counted out the bills in his hand and tucked them into his front pants pocket. "But I'll drill out the lock for you if ya' want for an extra five."

"No, no. I want to be able to fix it. I'll get a locksmith to make a new key for it at some point." The man declined—realizing he had just overpaid for the mechanically compromised piece.

A few weeks later, back in his workshop, the Bay View resident began restoration of the desk. He decided to tackle the broken desk drawer lock at a later date. Instead, he determined that he could repair the side panel and bottom panel below the drawer on the left side of the desk. They had pulled away from the frame, most likely caused by the many moves the object had survived over its lifetime.

As he flipped the desk upside down to drive some screws into the oak veneer to reattach it, he noticed something that had slipped into the void between the back of the drawer and the wooden modesty shield on the front of the desk. Not wanting to disassemble the entire structure, he reached in with pair of long-handled, needle-nose pliers and was able to grab the edge of the object. He gently pulled. Accompanied by a quick tearing sound, he retrieved a wrinkled and slightly torn sheet of yellowed paper. The official looking piece immediately piqued his curiosity.

The document appeared to be a report cover sheet with an introductory paragraph. It had an official looking stamp on it in faded blue ink from the Archdiocese of Milwaukee with what would turn out to be the critical date of 2 November 1918. It also had a large red stamp on it that read: COPY.

The address line read: *To: Papal Under-Secretary, Vatican City, Rome, Italy*

The subheading: *re: Death of Sister Mary Janina, et. al.*

The *et al* notation—indicating *more than one* to the former English professor, further intrigued him.

In the body of the paragraph of the cover page, but largely obliterated by water and age, the few words still legible and relevant were *basement* and *grave.*

Finally, at the bottom, the signature line was typed as: *The Most Holy Reverend S. Messmer.*

Below that, the cc: indicating carbon copies of the original, had two entries. *Bishop, Diocese of Grand Rapids*, and *FILE copy*. The red stamp and *lack of signature* on the page confirmed that the man was in possession of the *FILE* copy.

There was an additional observation. The man noticed that in the upper left-hand corner of the cover page, there was a small diagonal slit in the paper. This indicated to him that a staple had once held the page onto others. Remembering the small tearing sound, he decided to probe deeper into the void of the desk. This time, with some additional leverage provided by a pry bar, his pliers were able to secure the remainder of the still stapled together document that lay below the drawer. He gently pulled it free. Another probe into the void and he retrieved a large manila envelope filled with materials.

First examining the document on his workbench under the beam of a flashlight, the man found that it was comprised of what he estimated to be around 80-100 sheets of both quality linen-rag letter stock and more modern, standard twenty-pound bond. The document was heavily curled, soiled, and appeared to have suffered heavy moisture damage at some point in the past. Because of that, it was now stuck together with a dried residue upon it. It also gave off the faint smell of *soured fermented alcohol*—similar to stale beer—more likely from some sort of wine or cognac spirits.

Still sealed and clasped closed, the overfilled manila envelope seemed to have suffered the same kind of damage and was in far worse shape, so it was left intact, and no attempt was made to open it.

When the man flipped the desk back to upright, a pair of small, bent, wire-rimmed eyeglasses tumbled out of the opened cavity and onto the floor. They were broken, with one glass missing. The other was shattered but held in place. As the glasses were of no use to the man, they were tossed in the trash.

Considering the rest of his finds to be unique curiosities, the man held onto them. Neighbors recall him showing them to guests at a get-together around Labor Day in 1970 or 71. The cover page, *re: Death of Sister Mary Janina, et al* and the rest of the unopened collection of deteriorated materials sat prominently on his beautifully restored desk—now with a precision working lock, in his home's enclosed sunroom overlooking Little Traverse Bay. That night, the desk would serve as a refreshment bar serving only non-alcoholic beverages in the *tea totaling* home.

"Ironic, don't you think?" One guest—a neighbor, snobbishly commented to another.

"How so?" Asked a second guest.

"John, proudly displaying pieces of Catholic ephemera and antiquities as the centerpiece of his Protestant house!" The first

Irony aside, at that party, a granddaughter of the man, a teacher from the Detroit area, who was familiar with the saga of the *missing nun of Isadore*, would recognize the possible significance of the documents. Being raised Catholic and still a fervently practicing one, she was offended by the other guest's insulting comments about her Faith but chose to say nothing. Instead, with her grandfather's permission, she would take the papers back downstate to a book conservator for restoration.

Upon completion of the two months of work, the partial, disappointing restoration was returned to the Petoskey man. It revealed that there were a total of eighty-nine pages of what looked to be portions of the *official* trial transcript of The People of the State of Michigan vs. Stanislawa Lipczynska murder trial from Leelanau County, Michigan, and related affidavits, subpoenas and writs dated from 1918 and into 1920. How any *official* court transcript or other official documents had found their way *out* of the Leland Circuit Court building or County Clerk's office remains open to speculation. The trove also included the previously mentioned *FILE* copy of the fourteen-page report of the Milwaukee Archdiocese and Grand Rapids Diocese of the *Missing Nun* incident.

Items retrieved from the manila envelope provided the most interest. Among them: Reports regarding transfers of assistant priest, an official Disciplinary Report for a Sister Angelina, dated 1903. There were several letters of correspondence between Holy Rosary Parish in Isadore and a Traverse City architectural firm. The contents of those discussed plans for building a new church—including cost estimates and blueprints with revisions. Those continued to evolve over the years beginning in 1900 but abruptly ended in August 1907.

Also, in the envelope, were several letters from anonymous sources offering what could be categorized as *investigatory services*—many with advice to give up their searches for *the missing nun*. The most intriguing and iconic, was the letter signed, *A Protestant Pup*.

There were two other items in the envelope. The first was a more modern, college ruled, spiral bound notebook. There was nothing written on its faded blue cover. But inside, penned on both sides of 143 of the two hundred pages, was a lengthy dissertation written in blue, ball-point pen—indicating the writings were authored sometime after 1945, when that kind of writing instrument became widely available.

In an unofficial comparison against available examples, in a masculine hand, the handwriting seems most likely to have been authored by Father Andrew Bieniawski—who from approximately 1900 to 1913 was the Pastor of Holy Rosary Parish in Isadore, Michigan. Unfortunately, much of the contents were still illegible due to extensive moisture damage. Though, sections that were, hint at several areas of previously undiscovered, troubling, and sensationally unimagined *facets* regarding the mystery of the missing nun. They spoke of the Priest's fond memories of a Sister Mary Janina and recalled bits and pieces of his conversations with her. Those sections would be of tremendous interest for any modern romance novelist, But again, they were largely indecipherable and now unavailable for review.

However, in the latter portions of the notebook restoration, the condition was better and revealed a more detailed account of some of the most explicit and chilling descriptions and commentaries. Described as a cryptic, personal journal or diary, it read like a guilt-laden confession—the all-important *master key* to unlocking the mystery and providing full disclosure. The writings also suggest other threads of intrigue and facts that might still be found if one were to follow the priest's footnotes.

Additionally, on the first page of the transcription, it include a curiously fascinating headline-tease. As if it were penned by a novelist, is the Latin phrase: *et tu videris hanc fabulam scire*—translated to English as: *and you thought you knew this story*.

In total, those who allegedly had the opportunity to examine the documents in the early 1970's, agreed they read with an air of believability. At a minimum, those individuals admitted that it provided additional layers of context *to ponder* in the saga of Sister Janina.

The last item found in the manila envelope was a large, men's ring. Made of high content gold, at its center was mounted an amethyst stone. Engraved on one side of the ring was a Crucifix and on the other, the initials, "A. B."

Chapter Two

Historical Perspective: The Estate of Father Andrew Bieniawski

It would be a gross understatement to say that the life and career of Father Andrew Bieniawski was colorful and controversial. After serving decades in a number of parishes—mainly in northern Michigan—he died at the age of 89 in 1964.

As per the custom, when clergy in the Church passes, the vast majority of their modest accumulated financial wealth reverts to the Church. And summarily, Father Andrew's was turned over to the Vatican. But it is assumed that a few of his personal items—mementos of his career, at the time of the liquidation of his estate, did pass on to some of his surviving biological relatives.

The rest, thought to be mostly Father Andrew's mundane office items, including a bookcase, small personal reading library, and of significance, an office desk, were donated to the local chapter of the Women's Civic League in the nearby town of St. Ignace, just to the north across the Mackinaw Bridge. The organization—which supported the old Civic League Library was housed in the city's old Municipal building at the time.

The Women's Civic League was disbanded in 1969. At around the same time, the majority of the contents of the library—including the subject desk was turned over to the City of St. Ignace where the items were held in storage in a warehouse facility in town.

From there, the well-worn and extensively repaired heavy oak desk left the facility (some say purchased—more likely stolen) and eventually resurfaced among a trove of old household items and tools at the previously mentioned seasonal flea market.

It is important to note; The significant piece of the flea market collection—Father Andrew's desk, had not originally accompanied the priest when he left his Pastor assignment at Holy Rosary in Isadore, for one in Manistee, Michigan in 1913. Office furnishing *usually* remain in the parish rectory office as a fixture for use by the next Pastor. But as it would turn out, this was no ordinary piece of furniture.

However, in late 1919, immediately after the criminal conviction of Fr. Andrew's housekeeper, Stanislawa Lipczynska, for the murder of the missing nun, Sister Janina, the locked desk was curiously and suddenly removed from Holy Rosary and thought to be shipped to the Diocese offices of Grand Rapids and placed in storage there. The single key to the desk was said to be personally delivered to the Bishop by courier. This was also about the time that Father Andrew was granted a leave of absence from his current assignment in Manistee by the Bishop, published as a "vacation."

Years later, the desk, and importantly its secured contents, along with the key to it, would be released out of storage and reunited with the disgraced priest upon his written request. However, that only occurred after the death of the Grand Rapids Diocese prelate Bishop Eduard D. Kelly in 1926 and the passing of Archbishop Sebastian Messmer of the Archdiocese of Milwaukee in 1930.

At the time of settling Father Andrew's estate after his death, a desk—reported to be the same one that originated at Holy Rosary Parish in Isadore, was still among his possessions at his last fulltime assignment in Mackinaw City.

Chapter Three

Rectory Office, Holy Rosary Church, Isadore, Michigan, circa 1917

The aggressive incoming Pastor of Holy Rosary, Father Edward Podlaszewski, rolled out a large paper—blueprints—for a new church onto the desk in the rectory office. The soon to be *former* Pastor, Monsignor Leo Oprychalski, was seated in one of two guest chairs on the opposite side of the desk.

Just a few days from full retirement, Father Leo would then leave Holy Rosary and travel downstate to Livonia to reside at an independent living facility for emeritus clergy. The elderly priest had already withdrawn from active duties and this final meeting with the new Pastor was to go over some of the outstanding issues regarding administration—including the church building maintenance schedules with the sexton-groundskeeper, and to give him a general feel for the budgets with which he would be dealing. Also of importance, Leo would go over his rolodex of contacts within the Bishop's office, who in turn, dealt with those at the Archdiocese and Vatican levels. In layman's terms, the latter discussion would be a rundown of *who's-who in leadership*, and *who to avoid* or *approach*, as was needed.

There was also one other thing to discuss with Father Edward that Leo apprehensively pondered. As he did so, he fingered a brass key that was dangling on a leather lanyard around his neck that lay under his white collar and concealed by his black shirt. He knew that at the end of the meeting, he would hand that lanyard and key over to the new pastor and only then would he inform him of the important and sensitive documents that the key secured in the bottom drawer of the rectory office desk.

Consumed by that thought, Father Leo recalled the day he first entered this office after he was installed as Pastor of Holy Rosary in 1913 when the outgoing Pastor, Andrew Bieniawski, was suddenly called by the Bishop to his new post in Manistee.

As he continued to finger the key beneath his shirt, he vividly remembered the first time he used it to open the drawer of the desk and then peruse the many secretive documents it held. Leo's stomach now churned in the same visceral way as it did when he first read the details of internal reports about Holy Rosary's most sensitive topic that had occurred six years earlier. He had been blindsided by his inheritance of the *case of the missing nun*. A *heads-up* by Father Andrew on the subject matter would have been in order but that had never occurred. The old priest was additionally appalled to have been given custody of the key by Father Andrew in a cavalier way by finding it in the clutter left lying on the desk.

Had Leo known the controversy would be placed in his lap like this, he might have even rejected his transfer to Holy Rosary and applied for retirement instead. He only knew that he would not transfer the key or the controversy to the new Pastor Edward in the same way as he had received it.

Father Leo was drawn out of his memory by the enthusiastic voice of the new Pastor. "I'm so glad I'm able to show you this before your retirement." The young Edward boasted. "I trust you will find this exciting Monsignor. It is the culmination of your ideas and answer to your prayers and ones of the leadership of this church going back at least two administrations." The priest ill-advisedly lectured his elder. "I took the liberty of talking with a local architect-builder I knew from Traverse City, and he came up with this."

Edward continued to uncurl the blueprints while he babbled. "I must say the new Holy Rosary Church will be magnificent." He beamed as he randomly grabbed items off the desk and placed them on the edges of the paper to hold it down.

One of those items was Father Leo's personalized wooden desk name plate. It was a crude, but lovingly crafted piece of white pine given to him by the parish's elementary school children upon his arrival in Isadore. The other was a decorative brass clock commemorating Leo's 40th year in the priesthood that had been awarded to him by his close friend and superior, the Bishop of Grand Rapids. The old priest was clearly irritated but held his tongue—at first. He thought. *The nerve! The brazenness of this upstart in using my personal office accoutrements as mere paperweights.* Measuring his words, he finally asked. "You took it upon yourself to go over my head and commission a blueprint?" Father Leo bristled.

"Father Edward breezed past his objection. "Well, no time to waste! I knew you were retiring soon. I went ahead after our discussion soon after I transferred in. You said yourself that Holy Rosary has needed a new church building for quite some time. I was compelled to get started after our discussion about the cold and dampness of the old structure—especially in winter."

Almost without a breath the priest continued. "…Said it yourself! Sometimes in winter at early Mass when the two old parlor stoves at the front of the church hadn't warmed up yet, you could see your breath during Consecration as you took a sip of wine from the Chalice. Your glasses would always fog up."

The old priest silently fumed at the recollection of his own amusing description being thrown back in his face. But then he was instantly chilled when he studied the details of the blueprint.

The new Holy Rosary would be structured from red clay brick and fieldstone, and heated with a new, modern coal fed gravity furnace. There would be a choir loft, and many ornate stained-glass windows imported from Germany. The building would be patterned in the trending Romanesque Revival style like many of the modern churches recently built in North America. But those details were not what gave Father Leo pause.

In light gray pencil on the scroll was the footprint of the existing church that was to be razed above grade. The foundation of the new structure in blue pencil—in fact, would almost completely encircle the old wooden structure with exception of one critical area. Of specific concern to Father Leo was the footing along the western side of the church below the sacristy, where a service entrance door was located to access the shallow *"michigan style"* crawl space cellar.

The young priest blathered in excitement about his plans. "See here? The new church will encapsulate the old." Father Leo paid no attention—still mesmerized by the troubling details of the blueprint.

"It's in a small way—like the historical succession of constructions that were common in the ancient world." Father Edward continued to lecture in oblivious joy to the well-schooled senior priest. "Like the ones that took place over time at the location of the Church of the Holy Sepulcher in Jerusalem—first just a freestanding memorial over the simple tomb of our Lord. Then to accommodate the growing number of pilgrims and worshippers, a rotunda was built surrounding it in the fourth Century under Constantine. Just last century, under the rotunda, a protective Edicule was erected over the spot to protect and to venerate the fragile structure. We are essentially doing the same kind of thing here."

Father Leo sat patiently drumming his fingers on the desk—waiting for Edward to run out of steam. As he did, the old priest silently summarized the young priest's thoughts with his own knowledge of ancient history. *...In the old world, the new construction was often over the old—a Christian monument to cover a pagan one—a monument of the victor to cover the site of a foe's bloodbath. A structure to conceal—to erase history—like this desk before me conceals what's inside."*

"Look here Monsignor." Father Edward gushed like an enthusiastic child on Christmas morning. "With exception of a reconstruction of the western foundational wall, hardly any new below ground excavation will be needed. Just the service door entrance. We'll put a coal chute there for the new modern furnace. That'll require some *digging.*"

The word *digging* made Father Leo wince.

Edward noticed but paid little attention to the Father Leo's distress. He continued. "Without the required extra work below ground, the architect says..."

Father Leo had heard enough and angrily spoke up. "I well know the history of *this church!"*

Edward was taken aback at Leo's abrupt objection. The old priest struggled to pull his chair closer to the desk and leaned over the drawing. He slowly placed both of his hands on it, bowed his head and squinted his eyes as if pained. Without looking up, he shifted the bearing of the discussion.

"Father, it has been two weeks since I last received the Sacrament of Penance. Will you hear my Confession?"

"…Um, certainly Father." Edward haltingly replied, as if his lungs had just been depleted of air. "Yes, I can hear your confession."

"We can discuss the new church building afterwards." Father Leo added. "That is—if you still want to."

"Why would I *not* want to?" Father Edward asked with noticeable trepidation.

"How familiar are you with the history of the Church?" Father Leo hauntingly asked but received no immediate answer, and then continued. "There are many aspects to consider at the crux of this matter." Father Leo prefaced his discourse. "Tradition. Justice. The Institution we serve. The *individuals* we minister to. Our roles as confidants of those and their crimes surely committed but then measured against the exacting of punishment. You must consider *Confession* versus *Absolution—Sin* versus *Forgiveness*." Those last two comparisons gave Father Leo another pause, and his mind drifted back to just a few days after he was installed as Pastor of Holy Rosary in 1913.

It had been twenty minutes since the last person had left the Confessional box. Father Leo, newly arrived as Pastor of Holy Rosary, had spent the previous two hours on this Saturday afternoon hearing the usual assortment of trivial sins from his parishioners who had felt their Catholic obligation to regularly receive the Sacrament of Penance. The confessions had been to the sins of, among other things, engaging in gossip, a disagreement with their spouse, drinking too much, taking the name of the Lord in vain and others. The tired priest had already forgotten the details of most and issued his absolution out of rote memorization.

Leo was sure he had heard the last confession of the day. After all, it was a beautiful and clear late September day. Folks were out enjoying the remainder of it. The ones that had received the Sacrament could now do so without the burden of guilt on their souls which had just been lifted by him.

In fact, penitents always came away from Confession with Father Leo with renewed optimism and joy. They seemed to like his style. It was well known throughout the priestly grapevine and the many parishes in which he had served, that if one had a choice, Father Leo was the one chosen as confessor because he was always light on issuing penance. His reputation was that he was filled with pastoral compassion rather than assigning blame or shame, so the sinner could feel better about their situations. Though, truth be told, among all the duties of any priest, this was Father Leo's least favorite. Having to be emersed in so much personal information about everyone was uncomfortable for him. So, he usually never probed too deeply about the sins he was hearing.

Through the slightly cracked window which provided light and fresh air in his cramped confines of the priest's cubicle of the Confessional, he could hear a jay squawking in a nearby maple tree on the south side of the church. The late afternoon sunshine penetrated his space and worked to relax Father Leo. He dozed off for perhaps ten minutes in his cramped, oak lined cocoon.

The sound of the heavy woolen curtain being pulled to the side of one of the confessional boxes suddenly awakened the priest from his slumber. Then, the sound of the curtain closing and in a familiar pattern, first one, then the other knee of the penitent settling onto the squeaky wooden kneeler signaled him to slide open the latticed screen partition between them. The priest waited for the person to start.

Several seconds elapsed. The priest cued the penitent. "You may begin."

A deep and shuddering breath preceded the person's first words in a barely audible whisper.

"Bless me Father, I have…for I have sinned." Then they paused.

The priest had experienced this sort of thing many times before. Most likely the details of the sin was of serious nature and the person was laden with guilt. Leo would need to be especially attentive for this obviously troubled soul and provide the utmost pastoral care to draw out every sinful detail of the transgression. Only then would he fulfill his priestly duty as Confiteri—a confidant—which would then allow him to administer the full absolution that the person sought.

"Go on." The priest encouraged. He could hear another deep breath from the penitent.

"...F-For...For I have sinned. I've, uh, I have done something...some things..." The person stammered in an extremely secretive voice.

In a reassuring tone, the priest responded. "And you are here to seek God's..." But he was interrupted before he could say the word, forgiveness.

Having gained more courage, the person in the confessional box—a man, cleared his throat and raised his voice from a whisper to more of his full voice. "Uh-hugh, I seek your absolution under the Veil of Secrecy provided by the Sacrament in the Confessional."

The language coming from the man in its official sounding context disturbed Father Leo. And more importantly, at the same time, he immediately recognized the voice. This dumfounded the priest and now caused him to hesitate.

"Do I have your absolution?" The man brazenly inquired.

"I, uh." The confused priest mulled a response. He was trying to make sense of why this most unusual conversation was taking place now. After a few seconds, Father Leo regained composure and continued in his litany of the Sacrament. "Please tell me of your sin."

"I, uh, I am responsible for the Sister Janina incident." The man quickly said in a manner as if to gloss over the specifics and significance of his admission.

"Again...You what?" Leo asked. The full weight of what he was now dealing with in this confessional conversation became alarmingly apparent. Immediately the recollection of everything the old priest knew about the well-known saga of the missing nun of Holy Rosary rushed to the forefront of his mind. In one sentence, a hidden truth surrounding the guilt of the mystery that had hovered over Holy Rosary since well before he became its pastor, had just been laid in his lap.

The penitent continued in a painstaking drawn out fashion. "I...caused...Sister Janina's..."

"Disappearance?" The priest interjected. "Am I to understand that you—that you did something that resulted in—our missing nun?"

"Yes." The man said meekly. "My actions—she—we. I couldn't let her. I would have had to...Please give me absolution." The man's scattered words offered little explanation.

"Please stop! STOP!" The priest ordered. "You can't ask for absolution without first telling me your full confession to the sin and that you show remorse and true sorrow for your sin. Deep sorrow. If you indeed have had a role in Sister Janinas disappearance, I must hear that from you." The priest sternly warned.

"Yes, Father. I seek your absolution and forgiveness." The man reiterated.

"Absolution from me and forgiveness from God—they are two different things. But I don't see how I can even begin to give my absolution for this without knowing the details. I have not heard them yet. This requires considerable discussion." Pleaded Father Leo. "This is not just a simple matter. You are aware there is the legal and criminal matter outside the church. There has been continual police investigations even though it appears to be a cold case. The burden is upon you to turn yourself in and do the right thing. I cannot insulate you from justice. Only after that can I absolve you of your sins." The priest lectured.

There was no response by the man in the confessional box.

"And I must be satisfied with your assurances that you are truly sorry. As I am a representative for God, I must hear both—the details and sorrow. They are required for God's forgiveness." Then the old priest added in a verbal faux pau which revealed to the penitent that he knew to whom he was speaking. "You should know this as a priest."

"But you cannot say anything about this! Do I have your vow regarding the secrecy proviso of the confessional?" The man responded—understanding that his identity was now known.

Father Leo was flummoxed by the stubbornness he was hearing. "I have no choice in that." He angrily assured. "But first we need to discuss this—fully! And then you—YOU must go to the authorities and turn yourself in before we can even begin to discuss absolution!"

"I understand." The man coldly answered without conviction.

"Please, let us pray together now for direction." Father Leo launched into reciting the Act of Contrition on behalf of the person. "Repeat with me, Oh, my God, I am most heartily sorry for having offended thee..." But then he paused when the only voice he could hear was his own. The man had quietly slipped from the Confessional box and made a quick exit out the back of the church before the priest realized it.

And with that, the burden of the knowledge of a potential crime had been squarely placed on the priest's shoulders. Leo stepped out of the confessional and looked out into the empty nave and transept of the wooden building. Beads of cold sweat formed on his brow as he contemplated what to do—knowing what he should do under his moral responsibility for secular justice and human compassion for Sister Janina, versus what he was obligated to do by his vows.

Over the next several months, Father Leo would be able to piece together a fuller narrative of truth about the missing nun story from additional sources, casual inquiries by him, rumors, speculations, and hints—some coming to him through what was known by insider clergy as the priestly grapevine. Still other details came to his knowledge by way of the confessional of local parishioners in the know. The rest he would glean from the documents locked away in his parish office desk drawer that was secured by a key—the one that was always close to him, hanging from a leather lanyard, under his high collar and concealed by his black shirt.

However, on this late September afternoon, after experiencing the failed confession, Father Leo dejectedly walked down the main aisle and out the main entrance of the church. He turned and looked up to the steeple of the old wooden building. Cumulus storm clouds were beginning to gather overhead. He could appreciate the parallel of this impending thunderstorm that would descend upon the town within the hour, and the moral one now

Father Leo's troubling memory evaporated, and he returned to the present. All the while, Father Edward had remained motionless before his mentor.

The captive audience of one now had Leo's undivided attention. The elder took a deep breath and began. "Historically, to answer your question regarding whether to build a new Holy Rosary Church, I must make sure you understand the significance of its benefits to both the greater Church and this Catholic community in Isadore, versus the problems it will create for *both*. Before you can proceed Father Edward, you must have a firm grasp of the sometimes-contradictory policies of the Church. You must consider the centuries of Vatican thought on things that were set in stone like the Papal Bull on *Invalidum aeternum ego ita praedicate* of the Magna Carta and how that has shaped it. You must consider how we have historically treated *sinful behaviors* of the priesthood deemed by the hierarchy to be *cottidanius*—that is in English; *daily, ordinary, customary,* or even *normal*. And how those are largely protected by the *Encyclios autem de Confidentia,* and sometimes covered by the *Ineditus Secredito Encyclios.*"

Father Edward's brow furled upon hearing the terms—indicating his ignorance of their meanings.

"Oh, that's not all!" Leo expounded. "You will have to weigh your decision to build or not to build based not on just *some* of them, but *all* of them. And to complicate your deliberations, you will temper your decisions with a keen eye toward the history of the *sometime whims and wishes* of the succession of Pontiffs—which tend to disregard the individual and perpetuate their own *self-importance.* Then you must measure that versus the powerful *political* counter forces within the Vatican who are relentlessly pushing for reform but only occasionally have had successes. You should do some research on that. I think you'll find it instructive."

Father Edward finally looked like he was beginning to form a question, but Father Leo was not done. "And there is always the matter of deference to your immediate superiors—the Bishop—the Archbishop—those in the clergy who are on a "fast track" politically or affiliated with the more powerful of the Religious Orders." Father Leo's additional layers of caveats in his mysterious explanation halted Edward's pending query and his mouth produced no sound. Specifically, it was the flurry of *Latin* terminology amid policy, that to Father Edward, as someone had coined in a vernacular saying, *was all 'Greek' to him.*

"Hmm." The teacher peered at his student over the top of his glasses. "I can see you did not pay particular attention at seminary when they covered the many applicable historical doctrines, dogma, and policies for when situations like this come up, my young, ambitious, Father Edward. So, I will now for you." Leo posed the leading question. "That is, if you'd like?"

There was still no reaction from Father Edward—with exception of a flush of crimson embarrassment rising under his collar, up his neck to his cheeks and his brow, which remained furled.

Father Leo let out a brief laugh. "Ha! By the lack of your earlier enthusiasm and your catatonic state, I'll take that as a *yes.*" Then he added with an additional layer of sarcasm. "And you thought you were just trying to put together some new mortar, brick, and stained glass for Holy Rosary. No, there is much you will need to know before deciding to turn over that first calamitous spade of earth. Please take a seat behind my—that is *your* desk. But first, let us administer the Sacrament of Penance—*to each other*—but only after I tell you this." The old priest's tone turned serious.

In anticipation, Father Edward braced himself against the edge of the desk.

Leo drew a measured breath. "First, *move the bones*, Father."

"Wha? What was that? Father Edward questioned, as he was unsure of what he had just heard.

"Father, you must first *move the bones* before any construction." Father Leo repeated.

The young priest stood dumbfounded. An impasse of immense proportions had smothered the room.

Father Edward did not know it at that moment, but his enthusiasm for a project that he had championed since his arrival at Holy Rosary Parish was about to unravel into confusion, turmoil, and deepening controversy. In the coming days, weeks and months, his initiative for a major capital improvement for the parish—the realization of a 30-year hope for a new church building was about to be delayed and superseded by a revelation of deepest intrigue—the weight of which would burden him as it had his two predecessors.

Then Edward would blunder with a poor decision by attempting to eliminate the evidence of a crime so he could achieve his building goals—consequences be damned. But he would also compound that mistake by including someone else in his coverup who was not bound by a Sacrament's *proviso of secrecy*. That person, the current sexton of Holy Rosary, was reportedly one of several sources to leak the privileged information to others in the community.

In yet another twist, an additional source of the leak was reported to be from a young woman of the Holy Rosary Parish. She had become intimate with Father Edward and became pregnant.

Deepening the crisis, in his futile attempt to mitigate his own personal troubles with the Church for conduct that violated his vows of celibacy, Pastor Edward told the young woman in confidence about the bones buried under the church. Versions of the story say that he revealed this during an occurrence of the Sacrament of Penance between him and the young woman. She however would not maintain the Church's traditional secrecy for this kind of scandalous transgression and would immediately pass the critical information on to a relative, who would in turn contact secular authorities.

Going forward, the *Mystery of Sister Janina* and its law enforcement investigation that had stood dormant for several years would be reenergized—albeit in piece-meal fashion.

Chapter Four

Historical Perspective of Conduct: Holy Roman Empire, Rome, circa 1215 CE

Innocent III, Prelate of the Holy See—head of the Holy Roman Empire, along with every other leader of major countries or tiny principalities dominated by Western Christianity during the first thousand years of the Church, were never known as defenders of liberty for the individual. It was a rule of the few over the many—the educated of the Institution over the uneducated masses. Rare are any surviving stories from that time of successful efforts of the individual speaking out in the cause of freedom and reforming their societies or reducing the dominance of the Church. All efforts were universally crushed—usually with brutal force by the ruling classes. That is, until the publication of the Magna Carta—the first document of civil rights.

The beliefs held and practices used prior to the Great Charter by the elites were not historically unique. If certain freedoms were allowed to proliferate for the individual, it would eventually upset the balance of power between the Church and the ruling Lords who controlled the populations bound to the feudal systems of Europe. If individual liberty were allowed to become a significant rallying cry of human desire, the results would be an overall reduction in the Church's absolute authority in matters of religion within its territories and over the people in them. It would also drastically affect its wealth and power.

"Invalidum aeternum ego ita praedicate." (Invalid forever I so declare) the Pope groused between his clenched teeth after reading his official copy of the Carta that had just been delivered to him by way of the Charge d'affair of France. Per contemporaneous notes found in Vatican archives, then to complete his great displeasure, the Pope dismissively waved the document over the flames of a burning candelabra that sat on his desk in his Papal residence. Then he tossed it to the floor where much of it was consumed by the fire. Thus, the Magna Carta would go on to be renounced by Innocent III in his Papal Bull published in 1215 at the Fourth Lateran Council.

With its official stance now in writing, the Church had irrevocably ignored the growing call for human empathy, dignity, and recognition of rights for the individual. In essence, Innocent's Bull put the faithful back in their place.

Near the same time of the renunciation of the Great Charter, and per some historians, entirely intentional, there was now an urgent need within the Church to monitor the populace for outbreaks of free thought or calls for societal reforms in order to keep those ideas in check. Thus, Innocent III subsequently demanded the application of *private confession* by all within the Faith with his establishment of the Sacrament of Penance. Although, there had always been a responsibility for believers to seek forgiveness for their sin as cited in the words attributed to Jesus in the Gospels, the formal Sacrament would now be at least a once-a-year obligation for the laity, and of even more importance to Innocent, all levels of the clergy would also be required to participate in the Sacrament.

In the tight confines of the Basilica's Baptistry—located along the Porta Sancta of the edifice—just north of the tomb St. Peter, Innocent outlined his appeal ad nauseum to a small contingent from the College of Cardinals. "We are obligated to provide council and absolution for the many sins the faithful commit in their daily lives. To do that, we must know all human transgressions to prevent them from entering the gates of Hell. This is not only for the laity but especially if sin is committed by our clergy. Confession will redirect them in their pastoral duties and thereby prevent the Church from following the same path." The Pontiff continued. "And we are to engage the clergy at all levels to root out heresies—and with all swiftness." He then asked for comments. "Are there any objections?"

There were none. The Pope's entourage all wagged their heads in the negative.

Innocent's thinly veiled warning left no doubt as to how the College of Cardinals should control the Sacrament of Penance in the parishes within their regions.

Arguably, Innocent's unpublished purpose of the Sacrament's vigorous application was never to prevent the faithful from entering *the Gates*, but it was to find out in the many churches' confessional boxes what problems might be developing at the grass roots levels in the movement toward free-thought and independence—two things the Church was not going to allow to proliferate without a fight.

Additionally, the formal Sacrament was intended to be a confidential matter. But institutionally, the reality was that Confession would always be a highly non-discreet forum with layers of oversight. Innocent's aims would mean that the knowledge of all transgressions—venial—that is common, along with those that were more serious—that is mortal, were to be shared up and down the Church hierarchy—with disciplinary action to be taken if necessary.

In the clandestine flow of information back to the Diocese, then to the Archdiocese level and then to Rome, the more serious incidents would be recorded in official Vatican Archives. That would be unavoidable with the Institution's traditions to record, copy and preserve documents. It was thought that by Innocent's Papal decree, the intended sequestering of some of the most damaging information in the official archives would work in concert with the pacifying nature of the passage of time. Over generations, and the delegation of the knowledge of them from one Pope to the next, the Church's wrongdoings would seem less so.

For a time—perhaps the next four hundred years, Innocent III's accompanying *Encyclios autem de Confidentia* for the clergy—to maintain *confidentiality*, would mostly achieve its aims but would not be without periodic challenges by reformers from within and breaches to its strictures which failed to be successfully checked.

Eventually, Innocent's Encyclios and its resulting long-practiced policy would be laid bare for its inherently corrupting nature. But that would take time—centuries. One can point to a series of events occurring around the same relatively short span of time, along with the evolution of society to have caused that.

Cited by historians, the invention of moveable type, printing and the more rapid disbursement of news, the height of the Renaissance with its increased education, openness, and literacy, and through the 16th century at the same time of the Protestant Reformation, would all converge to be the major reasons that would undermine the ancient Papal *confidentia* policy. Thus, no longer would universally ignoring criticisms and/or controlling the publication of documents regarding them, or completely banning access to sensitive archives, then expect the passage of time to cause the more problematic issues to fade away, work as it had always done in the past.

Going forward, the next succession of Popes would need to employ other, more subtle, and flexible methods to protect their beloved Institution as a first priority, rather than their old standards of a heavy hand and/or absolute stonewalling. They would expedite actions regarding internal transgressions with a variety of methods meant to mitigate the problems, including the extensive use of personnel transfers, payments of stipends, and obfuscation of their complicity by allowing leaks of incriminating information from the Confessional. They would also attempt to rein in their biggest problem, the unwieldy paper trails of Institutional transgressions in a decentralized way—housing them *away* from the Vatican.

Chapter Five

Holy Rosary Parish—Polish Settlement of Isadore, Michigan, circa 1900

The always charismatic Father Andrew Bieniawski, Pastor of Holy Rosary Catholic Church, *publicly* interacted with most members of his small parish in the same manner. For the men, women, and children—at least the *female* children, his *ecclesiastical* approach to them had a *secular* informality brimming with good nature that had remained consistent since his arrival in Isadore in 1900. All were greeted by him with a ready smile, a handshake, and often accompanied with a hearty pat or two on the back, and quite often a meaningful embrace.

Although with his young *male* charges—those boys that were enrolled in the parish school or served him as Altar Boys, he could be harsh, strict, and a taskmaster. To others—those of non-Polish immigrant backgrounds who resided nearby but were not officially members of the Holy Rosary Parish, but who also occasionally worked the parish grounds for him as *chore boys*, he could be equally as difficult, and largely uncaring.

The Priest's hands-on nature to the *favored* under his ministry was interpreted by most of the parishioners to be that of a deeply caring cleric expressing his love for his growing flock—in the traditions of Jesus himself. In his public display, Father Andrew's sermons during Mass often included specific verses from the New Testament that highlighted the tenderness of the Savior's love for his followers. One of his favorites was a portion of a verse from Galatians, which seemed to ring true for many of the orchardists on the peninsula who attended Holy Rosary: *but the fruit of the Spirit is love.* However, away from an audience, for the young men of the Faith, his applied verse seemed to be *spare the rod and spoil the child.*

Furthermore, Father Andrew's close interaction with his parishioners—to know the details of their lives, in both casual interaction and through formal Confession, was not only sought out by him because of his desire and solemn duty to be their spiritual mentor, but also because he was duty-bound to apply a forcefully encouraged Church policy to do so. That policy had hastily emerged several hundred years earlier under a concerted Papal effort to change from what was the norm of ancient times—that being the same kind of relationship as that which existed between kings and their subjects—which was distant and without compassion. With the establishment of the Sacrament of Penance those many centuries before, the Church's relationship with the faithful became intimate and would forever be ingrained in their existence. However, for most parishioners and priests, they soon recognized that intimacy at that kind of level had the great potential for abuses. As each group—clergy and laity—are both biologically predisposed with the same human emotions, urges and temptations, fostering highly personal and/or physical interactions between the two would often strain the vows of celibacy and purity and regularly threaten spiritual well-being. But the level of that depended on the priest, the individual and the culture of the society and leadership within the various Diocese.

For most laity, they would share a mutually positive experience in their Faith in closeness with the clergy—though some would still find it uncomfortable. Others in the minority would outright criticize the informal interactions—advocating for restraint and clear delineations of roles, as they saw the relationships as overtly unrestrictive and improper. And for an unfortunate few, they would completely misunderstand the reasons and function of the intimacy to their spiritual and sometimes physical detriment.

Specifically, in the conservative farming community of Isadore, in the beginning of his Pastorship, Father Andrew's initial intention was to redirect his flock back to a more pious and stricter adherence to Doctrine. He would put full efforts to dissuade the citizens from their frequent participation in drinking, dancing and the accompanying sins of the flesh that had a propensity to follow. By his observances, the men were the biggest culprits in this. They did most of that kind of carousing—and nearly all of it occurred outside his parish grounds and local community. What Andrew considered *all manner of debauchery*, took place in the saloons, dance halls and hotels in nearby Traverse City, and the towns of Provemont and Leland.

Unfortunately, those locations were all well outside Andrews's influence and authority. Thus, he quickly evolved away from his wholesale efforts to reform the mindset and practices of the *adult* men as it would require time and effort—both of which he had limited supply—and would most likely fail. "I cannot teach old dogs—even the ones trained to fetch in the Polish language, any new tricks." He had told his flock in one of his first Homilies at a High Mass soon after his arrival.

So, Father Andrew would instead play the "long game." He would concentrate his efforts onto the school age *young men* of the parish, who were far more impressionable. He determined that in just the few short years he expected to be at this assignment at Holy Rosary, with his firm tutelage, they would inherit a righteous moral leadership of the church community and he would get the credit. He would achieve his goals of developing a parish of which his superiors would be proud, and his demonstrated leadership skills would lead to a promotion and transfer to *anywhere* more sophisticated.

Chapter Six

Historical Perspective: Administration of Complaints, Papal Summer Retreat, Rome, circa 1495

It was another sweltering summer in Rome and Pope Alexander VI was in the third year of his reign as leader of the rapidly expanding and influential Catholic Faith. He had retreated from the Apostolic Palace near the Basilica to his personal villa on higher grounds southeast of the city. His intentions were to stay there for the months of June, July, and August to escape the heat and stagnant, raw sewage laden atmosphere clinging to the lowlands near the Tiber River—which would seasonally suffocate the Vatican compound.

A full two and a half days after the Pontiff had arrived at his summer retreat, Bishop Giuseppe Llanzolani—who had been appointed by Alexander to his position of Visiting Nuncio to placate influential members of the Borgia family to whom he was related, had finally coaxed Alexander into entering his office to do some work. Though, the Pope remained disinterested. Apparently, affairs vital to the wellbeing of the Church did not seem to demand his serious attention.

With this lax attitude, Alexander had thus far successfully ignored the relatively few, but looming problematic aspects of his rule at a critical point in history. He did so in a naive hope that they might fade away with inaction in light of the tremendous, good news and wealth that had been coming into the Institution since the discovery of the New World across the Atlantic Ocean. The serious topics that the Nuncio wanted the Pontiff to address were the accusations of *genocide* and *slavery* committed under the authorization of the Church.

Since his elevation to the Papacy, Alexander had followed tradition. The established protocol for handling serious internal problems was that a Pope would set them aside for future, well-thought-out investigation, and consideration, while continuing to gather the reports of them in the *official* Vatican Archives with its limited access. This usually resulted in years—sometimes decades of deliberations, slow reaction and sometimes none at all in the large and bureaucratic Institution. It was Alexander's prerogative to unilaterally continue this strategy.

However, of late, the Pontiff could see that the policy of consolidating written records of the most egregious transgressions committed by the clergy into a single archive—increasingly accessible by more and more learned historians over the last several Papacies, had exposed a security risk for the Church's most sensitive topics. Recently, small breaches in security of the archive by a growing number of suspected internal *Protestant Reformers* had resulted in publications that were an embarrassment to the Church and threatened it's future.

Though, like a petulant and prideful child, the Pope was not keen on accepting advice, timetables, or suggested revisions to established traditions to resolve pressing matters of responsibility—especially when they came from the likes of his rivals in the College of Cardinals. But in this case, he reluctantly agreed with them that something had to be done.

So, beginning with this visit to his well-fortified villa, and going forward, regardless of whether the Pontiff was in residence or not, there would now be a small unit of the loyal Swiss Guard stationed on the grounds year-round. Specifically, one or two of them would stand guard outside the Pontiff's inner office. They were there to protect his newly created important, and secretive Papal archive. No one, with exception of the Vatican Secretary of State and sometimes a visiting Papal Nuncio with expressed permission, was allowed in the Pope's internal office or access to that archive. And they were only given entrance under constant surveillance of the guards—and only a day in advance of any Pope's visit. The other exception was during the time between the death of a Pope and the election of a new one. The *Camerlengo*—or interim Pope, could access the office at his discretion to perform necessary administrative tasks.

Finally, seated at his Papal desk, a small mountain of parchment lay in front of Alexander. He began to rifle through the stack. Of the utmost interest to him were the documents that showed the recent sharp increases in the Vatican's wealth. Those revenues were due to decisive military victories over the defending native tribes that had taken place in the Americas following Spanish and Portuguese discovery. The conquests had garnered unfathomable riches from the decimated warring nations. Alexander preferred to refer to those historical windfalls as tributes paid to the Church—*and him*—after religious conversions of the natives. The fuller truth of the matter differed greatly.

Interspersed between the reports of military triumphs under the banner of Christianity, along with the cataloging of confiscated gold and silver, there was ample evidence of outright annihilation of the New World native populations. In fact, not all the spiritual transformations of indigenous peoples were due solely to the notion of a superior Christian God. Historical accounts showed that many were reluctantly brought to the Faith only after a great loss of blood. And here they were, reports in ink on parchment—all in explicit detail, for the Pontiff's review. Alexander expected those.

However, as often happens in a highly layered bureaucracy, the Pope's instructions to forward only the most serious reports to the new Papal archive at his villa, were misinterpreted farther down the line of administration. In the stack of papers before him, he was dismayed to also find accounts of clergy involvement in what he considered more minor offenses. Things like creating illegitimate offspring, debauchery, a *single* murder, a suspicious disappearance, abandoning vows, malfeasance, and others that had customarily been catalogued but held and handled at lower levels of administration in places like the Archdiocese and Diocese levels were also included for his review. He had not expected those reports to be sent to him.

And on this day, they all seemed to arrive at the same time at the Papal vacation retreat—much to the Pope's chagrin. "Must I do everything?" the exasperated Pope complained to his Nuncio, who stood attentively at the side of the Pontiff's desk.

In that moment, Alexander VI decided he was not about to be bothered by problems generated by what he considered his underlings. So, he took the parchments of the most recent complaints and combined them with the trove of more troublesome historical case files that had just been moved from the official Vatican Archives. Then he shuffled them into a uniform stack. He slipped the lot into a bulging calf-skinned portfolio—one that the Vatican's tanners had created on his orders for just this use. He bent over in his chair and stuffed the heavy bundle in the lower drawer of his desk.

Completely filling the space, with considerable effort, Alexander managed to close it.

"Well, then, Nuncio Llanzolani, that unpleasantry has been *dispensed*. Now, what of the new financial reports? I think I should like to commission a new and grand mural for my Papal apartment in the Vatican when we go back to Rome at the end of summer. I hear good things about the young painter, Raphael Sanzio. Issue an invitation to him."

The Nuncio wagged his head imperceptibly at the dismissive action of the Pope. But he handed him the requested documents. "Here they are, Your Holiness."

Chapter Seven

Holy Rosary Parish, Rectory Office, Isadore, Michigan, Spring Semester, circa April 1905

"Father, I have received complaints from one of our families. They object to the corporal punishment you have given one of their children." Flatly stated Sister Angelina, one of the teachers at Holy Rosary elementary.

"Let me guess. The parents of Johnny Szarnowski." Pastor Andrew sarcastically responded.

"Father, respectfully." Sister Angelina prefaced. "I will not name the parents as they made their complaint to me under condition of anonymity. I do not even know the child's offense as he is not in my classes. And they wouldn't divulge that to me either. I only bring this to your attention…"

"Hmmm." The priest was unimpressed with the nun's protocol of loyalty and posed a rhetorical question. "Sister Angelina, the Szarnowski's would prefer I use their business diplomas from the University of Detroit to spank their child?"

"I do not know." The nun conceded. "But Monsignor…Well, perhaps for some of the children—the *boys*, a gentler hand might be beneficial for them for minor offenses. I feel Master Szarnowski might benefit…"

The priest interrupted. "I'm not sure, but didn't we have a discussion about this kind of thing before Sister? I could swear I explained my position to you the last time we chatted about it. If so, I wouldn't think I'd have to have the same discussion again! And yet here we are. This troubles me Sister." Andrew drummed his fingers on the desk. "If we have been here before, and you were in my place, wouldn't you consider your showing up at my door again as insolence? Wouldn't you think that sort of thing might be reportable to Mother Superior of the Felicians? Maybe the Bishop? The Auxiliary Bishop? Certainly, it's a *confessionable* venial sin—if it has occurred. Shall I put on my stole to administer the Sacrament of Penance to you?"

"That won't be necessary Father." Sister Angelina bruskly assured him.

Father Andrew continued to be irritated by her defiant attitude. "Well, that is your choice Sister. But—but wait!" The priest then tugged at his collar and the top button on his black shirt and pulled out a leather lanyard from under it. He located a brass key dangling at the end of it. Then he bent over—still seated in his chair—and inserted the key into the lock mechanism on the lower left drawer of his desk, roughly yanked back on it and reached in. Pulling out a large manila envelope, he bent back the metal clasp securing it, opened it and fished out a file folder. He dropped it heavily on his desktop and flipped it open with disdain.

"Ah yes. Here it is. *Disciplinary Report—October 1903. Spoke with Sister A.* Um, that would be you!" Father Andrew feigned surprise at the fact. "Hmmm, it says here: *regarding discipline for boy students. Sister A. assured me that she would defer to my authority.* Yes, well, it's all right here. I thought I had the feeling of déjà vu."

"Yes, Monsignor." Sister Angelina's attitude immediately changed. She had no idea that the priest had kept a record on her like this.

The priest then returned the Disciplinary Report back into the file folder— shuffled it back into order by banging it twice on the desk. He roughly jammed it back into the manila envelope, clasped it shut and plopped it back into the drawer. After he roughly slammed it shut, he reinserted the key in the drawer lock, and gave it a firm twist.

Sister Angelina slightly jumped at the sound of the key locking its mating mechanism. To her it was the sound that would *forever* preserve her negative personnel file and sinful behavior. *For how long and for who's future review?* Sister Angelina pondered. She began to fathom the chilling concept of every level of the Church knowing about her work performance. She shivered at the thought. Father Andrew noticed her reaction.

Having dramatically made his point. Andrew suddenly realized that the use of his desk and its locked drawer as a *prop* for his reprimand of the nun, was an homage' to his predecessors in the Faith. Whether it was a secured desk drawer, or a locked strongbox, Andrew knew from Church history, that similar internal, limited-access archives had from the beginning been employed by the hierarchy to get compliance from subordinates or cloak certain documents and their secrets. He had just borrowed their tactic.

The Pastor then slipped the key and lanyard back out of sight under his collar and shirt. With the smuggest grin, he leaned back in his chair, all the while maintaining eye contact with the nun. His elbows rested on the arm of his chair—tapping the ends of his fingers together before his lips, waiting for her response. The meeting would not end until Andrew was satisfied with the nun's submissiveness.

For quite some time, Sister Angelina had stood silently before Pastor Andrew after he had dramatically produced and then resecured her disciplinary report in his desk. Finally, the Priest spoke. "Sister, the Altar Boy, Johnny Szarnowski's sneaking into the sacramental wine is not a minor offense, *Sister!*" Father Andrew's voice was pitched with anger— emphasizing the word, *sister*.

"Well, I agree with that Father." The nun's voice wavered. "But boys will be boys…"

The priest erupted. "You don't have the *credentials* to know anything about *boys being boys. However, I DO!* You are a cloistered *woman!*"

"Yes, Monsignor." Angelina contritely replied.

"Also, yours is not to agree or disagree with me, *Sister*. Look here! The agitate priest pulled out his desk lap drawer and retrieved a gold ring with an amethyst stone mounted at its center. He placed it on the index finger of his right hand and pointed to his collar. Then he tapped at it with a fingernail. "See this? Do you see this?" He asked.

The retreating nun nodded yes. She was able to clearly see the ring and its ornate engravings on either side. But she was confused by the priest's wearing of it.

"I wear this collar, *Sister*! It signifies that I am a priest—specifically a Pastor—*your* Pastor. This ring signifies I am *your* superior. I did not get this position by chance or by being weak or lax or letting the *boys be boys*—succumbing to modern secular liberalisms. *It's just a taste of wine, you say?* But a taste of wine often turns into glasses of wine and steins of beer and bottles of whiskey. And without discipline, the *boys that are just being boys*—that are predisposed to the dangers of falling into alcoholism, soon turn into men and become slackers and elbow benders at the Dew Drop Inn in Provemont on Saturday nights. And then they are too hungover to come to Mass the next morning. They become lax Catholics and have another generation of failed families." The priest ranted. Sister Angelina took another step back out of fear. When his ire had slightly subsided, the priest exhaled deeply but continued to tap at his collar and spoke tersely. "The church, the school, the parishioners—they are *all* my responsibility—but *especially* the boys. They are *my* responsibility—not yours."

"I understand Father." Sister Angelina demurred.

"If not now, you will!" Warned the priest. "Sister, I'm seriously thinking of putting in a request for an additional nun from the Felician Order of Livonia to be the Mother Superior of the convent and principal of the school—*and* your supervisor, albeit under *my* direction. Your duties would then return to that of a *teacher only*—not a disciplinarian—not the maker of educational or church policy."

"Father, I was only trying to offer a suggestion—constructive criticism." Sister Angelina tried to defend herself, but the priest would have none of it.

Andrew bristled but held back his anger to a simmering state. "Sister Angelina, there is something else I want you to see." He prefaced.

"Yes Father."

"Over there." Andrew pointed to the other side of the room. "Do you see?"

"The bookcase?" The bewildered nun asked.

"No, to the left. Do you see it?" He insisted.

"The door?"

"Yes. Go through it! And make sure you shut it behind you on your way out! Oh, and make sure you take your minimally informed suggestions and constructive criticisms with you." Andrew directed.

The nun spoke no more. Her face flushed. She nodded her understanding, turned, and briskly walked out of the Rectory office and sharply pulled the door closed behind her.

For a moment, Pastor Andrew sat silently before roughly pulling the index finger ring off his hand and thrusting it back into the lap drawer of the desk—slamming it shut. The desk and its contents had now become to him the object of his frustrations—a cumbersome, wooden stumbling block in the path of his career advancement. A repository of petty administrative paperwork and his own failing ambitions as represented by his ring.

Still seated in the oak executive chair, he roughly pushed away from the desk—causing an ear-piercing squeak from the rusty wheels rolling across the oak floorboards. For several more minutes, he remained there stewing in his irritation. In the moment, he wasn't sure if it was more from the nun's affront of his authority of the parish, or the fact that he had to take off the ring and accept his environment.

Andrew had forgotten how long it had been since he had the ring commissioned and made by a jeweler in Milwaukee. He had done this in anticipation of him being first given a dispensation to wear it by his Benedictine Order. And he had done this *across the lake* rather than have a local jeweler create it, as there would be questions and rumors—both of which he would rather avoid or have to explain to his sometimes volatile and meddling Bishop. Besides, he was sure he would soon be able to proudly wear it after receiving a new, prestigious assignment—a result of the recent transition from the late Pope Leo XIII to the new Pontiff, Pius X in 1903. He envisioned his elevation to an Auxiliary Bishop position, as he was philosophically more aligned with Pius than he had ever been with Pope Leo.

However, when the opportunities arose, the promotion had not occurred, and he remained in what he had openly referred to as *the Isadore wilderness*. The dispensation from his Order to wear the ring had not been issued either, so it remained in his desk. He could only think that someone in the hierarchy must have black-balled him. He had his suspicions of whom but was powerless to affect anything.

"Instead, I have been sentenced to be a baby-sitter for loggers, apple and grape pickers, and beer drinking, Polka dancers in Isadore." The priest groused. "The Bishop says: *I am best suited for this assignment, as I speak their language.*"

"That's the qualification? Because I speak Polish? Everyone in the Milwaukee Archdiocese speaks Polish—except for the Swiss Archbishop! No, its *political*. Ugh! The clash of *personalities*. Someone's toes got stepped on, and *this*..." The dejected priest waved his hand around the room. "*This* is my—*my punishment*."

Out of frustration, Andrew snatched a crystal goblet off the top of the credenza that sat behind his desk. He reached behind the set of books of his personal library that lined the shelf below and grabbed the nearest bottle of his private reserve of fine imported French wine. He popped the cork and poured a goblet of Bordeaux Cabernet Franc to the brim. Then in an attempt to relax, he drained the vessel with one hearty gulp.

After a refill and another slug of wine, the quickly mellowing Andrew reasoned that his lashing out at Sister Angelina was probably unwarranted. The nun was just trying to do her job to the best of her limited ability. His barely restrained fit of anger told him that he was suffering from job burnout and frustration over his lack of movement up the hierarchy of the Institution. The nun didn't deserve to have that taken out on her because of his bad mood.

For a moment, he thought to retrieve the negative reports on Sister Angelina, rip them up, and then incinerate them in the large ceramic ash tray that sat on the corner of his desktop. He *thought* to do so. He had once read that Popes often did this with reports they did not like. But he was no Pope. So, out of compliance to established protocol, since the earlier reprimand had occurred, and records of it had long since been transmitted up the chain to someplace in the Bishop's complex in Grand Rapids and a copy forwarded to the Felician Order of Sisters in Livonia, Andrew reconsidered, and the nun's file would remain under lock and key in his desk.

However, the pragmatic priest would not wallow in self-pity for long, or dutifully accept his fate. He would eventually follow-through on his warning to Sister Angelina. He would soon start the process of first showing a need and then fight through the administrative paperwork of requesting an additional nun for his parish. He knew it might take a year, as personnel was in short supply. But if all went well, he could expect the additional nun to be in place at the start of the 1906-07 school year.

Andrew vowed that from the *get-go*, the new sister would be told by him, in no uncertain terms, that she was to *run herd* on Sisters Angelina and Josephine and insulate him from the petty day-to-day. This would free up more time for him to focus on the overall direction and growth of Holy Rosary—which included the completion of his plans to demolish the old and build a new church. Andrew felt that a new church building was paramount to show his leadership qualities as a man who got things done. And it seemed to him to be the *only* opportunity he had to impress whoever was in charge of his career and deliver him from Isadore.

Furthermore, with the additional personnel at Holy Rosary, it should afford him more time for some of the few leisurely pursuits that the area offered, and that he greatly enjoyed—like hunting and especially fishing. It would also clear time in his schedule to attend social gatherings with other area community leaders.

Andrew theorized aloud in his growing inebriation as he took another gulp of wine. "There will finally be some *idle time* for me—regardless of what St. Jerome warned: *Keep always busy so that the devil will find you always engaged.* Then he settled back into his regular amiable mood—fingering the key dangling from the lanyard beneath his collar and shirt.

Chapter Eight

Historical Perspective: Increased Utilization of Secluded Archives for the Most Troublesome Incidents. Castel Gandolfo, Southeast of Rome, 23 August 1640

Pope Urban VIII sat in the inner office of what was now the new Papal summer palace at Castel Gandolfo. Before him was a new, large, and ornately hewn desk. It was an impressive piece—complete with a Papal Seal made of tightly grained Lindenwood inlayed into the wide planks of the desktop made of old growth oak felled from the Black Forrest. It had recently arrived at Castel to replace the original desk in the office furnishings—an inadequate holdover from previous Popes, moved from the old summer palace a few miles away.

Urban had found it to be insufficient for his needs. The over-one-hundred-year-old piece had reached the capacity of its limited storage and was riddled with powder-post beetle damage. The Pontiff thought it also rather plain and determined it was beneath the grandeur of what his new summer Papal Palace demanded. Thus, it had become fuel for last night's bonfire on the veranda below Urban's second floor office balcony.

The new desk was a recent gift from the Zunft—the collective term for the ancient Woodcarvers Guild of Bavaria upon Urban's elevation to Pope. Made by the master carvers of the lineage of the revered Lienberger Family with help of local metalsmiths who cast the desk's bronze locks and single key. The gift was meant to curry the Pontiff's favor and gain his support for the southern Germany regions as they struggled to repel the advances—both territorially and ideologically—of the Protestant Reformers, in the conflict that would become known as The Thirty Years War on the European Continent.

However, the desk and similar tributes to Urban had not persuaded the Pontiff away from his official position, which had thrown the Vatican's support fully behind the opposing French factions in the protracted war. His policy was to the detriment of the Catholics residing in the southern areas of the German State.

Although blunting the growing Protestant Reformation in any region on the continent would normally be a major religious concern for the Pope, resulting in him authorizing military and financial aid for protection of the faithful, in this war's complicated dynamic, the Vatican's more immediate need was *political.*

Urban's priority was to thwart the Hapsburg Empire. He feared their increased strength if he provided help to their German region. It would promote their expansion of territory and influences, and eventually threatened to lay claim as the true regional authority over the Holy Roman Empire and the Papal States, rather than his established seat in Rome. Thus, he decided to ignore the struggling members of the Faith within the Zunft and the German region. The result of his inaction was that they continued to languish under Protestant aggression and many reported atrocities. This was despite Urban's repeated unofficial assurances issued by the Vatican through the Bavarian Archdiocese to provide it. It would never come.

Vindictively, many factions of the suffering Catholics in the Guild of Woodcarvers felt abandoned and furthermore insulted by the Pope's lack of appreciation for their offering. They would hold onto a perpetual grudge. The elders of the Catholic, Johan Faulhaber family—who were a tradesman of weavers in the Guild and had provided funding toward the creation of Urban's new desk, would even swear a family vendetta to someday atone for the Pope's inaction. According to them, his vacillation had resulted in three members of their family perishing due to French Protestant mercenaries in the nearby Alsace region. However, their efforts to exact that vendetta and expose the Church's inaction would only be attempted some three centuries later.

Thus, for the administratively undisciplined Urban VIII, his new, larger, and locking, perpetually guarded desk at Castel continued the established protocol of a secret file stationed away from the official Vatican Archives in Rome. The new desk would not only allow for an out-of-sight, out-of-mind repository—a *secretum consignation* for the many serious things the administrative clergy would rather knowingly avoid, outwardly deny, or simply ignore. It would now also be the hidden compilation of records used for disciplinary purposes within the church body. Those stored records would be used as *compromissum*—the compromising personal details about the subordinate individual clergy who had strayed from their vows or established doctrine or if they had acted contrary to the wishes of their superiors. It would act as an enforcement for them to comply with expected behavior under church standards.

Urban reached down his collar and retrieved a key from under his cassock. The shiny bronze key dangled from a freshly tanned leather lanyard draped around his neck. He yanked back on the drawer pull of the desk, and dropped the old, and well-burnished calf-skinned dossier of reports into the over-sized lower left drawer and slammed it shut. Then he slipped the precision-made key into the lock and gave it a satisfying twist to secure it.

The Pope then called to his nuncio to bring around a coach to take him back to his residence in Vatican City.

Chapter Nine

Holy Rosary Parish, Summer 1905

After his last *discussion* with Sister Angelina, Father Andrew decided, going forward, he would refrain from getting overly involved with the daily grind of the parish and focus most of his *time* and *attentions* on the greater, long-term good of Holy Rosary while reserving an adequate amount of the remaining of each for himself.

To do this, Father Andrew remembered his edict to Sister Angelina. *The boys are my responsibility and require a strict discipline to insure they grow up to be responsible and pious men.* However, as Pastor, Father Andrew's personal demeanor and conduct would turn out to be an example that nearly always was the complete antithesis. Perhaps it was his perception of his own lofty privilege, but he rarely *walked the walk that he talked.*

Despite his preaching, Andrew's own physical interactions with parishioners—the females—especially the prettier ones, privately drew criticism. The observant felt that it was a bit too *forward in appearance* for the likes of the majority of the faithful. They found it to be hypocritical as they were often chastised by Andrew for the same kinds of behavior in his church sermons.

Additionally, Andrew frequently condemned excessive drinking. However, it was well known that Father liked his drink of choice, finer imported wines. This created another ambiguity. The Pastor was also known to chum around with some of the more influential men of the parish and surrounding communities, where they gathered for occasional card games—usually gambling at poker. Those get-togethers in town or at deer camp usually were *beer-and-a-shot* affairs. Father Andrew was even seen at one annual parish Christmas bazaar sipping wine with a couple of the members of the Ladies Auxiliary who were noticeably tipsy. His unstated message to the parish implied that *one should do as I say, not as I do.* This created a problem that few in the community had the courage to address.

To explain; The norm for Isadore and Holy Rosary—similar to most tight-knit communities to control problematic behavior, was a well-established, albeit unofficial, but highly effective *grapevine of rumor* that was utilized by most of its citizens. The path of gossip regarding someone's errant behavior usually took the same course. It would first travel throughout the parish's ordinary citizen. Then it quickly reached the level of the various church organizations and their leadership. At that point, usually the widespread salacious gossip regarding things that qualified as less-than-criminal, tended to tamp down and mitigate the wrongdoing of every individual in question. Though, for the gossip regarding Father Andrew, out of respect—but mostly fear, that kind of critique never reached his ear. If it had, it could have served as an indirect way to modify *his* behavior.

Thus, the lack of any early intervention with the priest created a looming scenario for the spiritual leader of the community that was much more serious than simply fodder for discussion at the local tavern. It threatened his priestly vows and the spiritual well-being of at least one of his parishioners, his housekeeper, Stanislawa Lipczynska. Father Andrew's continued openness to engage in the pleasures of life and physical contact—with Lipcznyska in particular—was received by her as a sign of personal attraction.

Stella, as she was known by most, was a plain and largely ignored member of the congregation who had been widowed many years earlier. Her first language was Polish, and her understanding of English limited. She was described by some as a zealous *"church lady."* She usually went about her cleaning duties in the spirit of silent volunteerism, although could be critical of the other church help if their performances were not up to her standards. Though, she was well aware of Andrew's friendly behavior with other parishioners, she was surprised and overjoyed when the Pastor also lavished attention upon her in the same manner he did with nearly everyone he encountered. By that show of attention, she was inextricably smitten by the dynamic priest.

With the false signals she received and others that only she *perceived*, she began to purposely spend extra time around the priests' rectory office. There were considerable efforts on her part to come up with reasons to be in the same room as him. She would often create additional work for herself if it meant being near him—like the tedious job of dusting the Pastor's bookshelves—regardless of the fact that she had done so just a few days earlier. She scoured every imaginable crevice of his office and living quarters to spotlessness, just to extend the time in his presence.

In addition to the *time* element, Stella created many overtures to the Pastor. In her off hours, her obsession of the priest continued as she would bake fresh batches of the labor intensive *chruściki*—a kind of Polish cookie, or *kremowka papieska*—a decadent, cheesecake-like dessert that was lovingly wrapped in waxed papers and would often appear on the Monsignor's desk to greet him at the start of his workday. Stella believed her efforts were meant for Father Andrew alone. She would bristle and complain to her friends if he offered them to anyone else—even if it were to visiting dignitaries—including other priests or the even the Bishop.

Reciprocally, Father Andrew had shown true compassion for Stella—something few others had for the easily irritable woman. After the death of one of her close friends, he had been especially attentive to the woman through her period of mourning. This only worked to further beguile Stella.

Fully appreciative of the attention and niceties Stella paid to him, the priest felt obliged to extend his thanks to her generosity in other ways. Beyond simple blessings and commitments to pray for her, their frequent proximity and the unavoidable human desires of male and female companionship—in addition to Stella's willingness to cross the boundaries of a priest/parishioner relationship—eventually urged him to do more.

In short order, a standing weekly *date*—for lack of a better word—took place in either the Pastor's Office or sometimes in his personal quarters in the rectory. This was always scheduled on a late Sunday evening when the parish's activities were done for the day and the church grounds were usually quiet. Their *date* was intentionally chosen for this time because the pair calculated that per the Catholic tradition, the faithful were to refrain from work or activities other than essential or farm chores and remain inside their homes in prayerful contemplation on Sunday evenings, rather than be out and about. Thus, they could be confident that the town and church property would be deserted, and their activity less likely to be observed.

Stella would arrive at the rectory well after dark. Father Andrew would either uncork a new bottle of sacramental wine to share or pour from one already opened from the supply that had been used in that morning's Masses.

"It's a shame to let it go stale." Andrew would justify. "Once the cork is popped, it rapidly loses its *terroir*—that is, its distinct character."

Stella listened in fascination to the educated priest's explanation.

"This one is not the normal type of Sacramental wine that we use in Mass, Stella—normally a local Riesling from a nearby vineyard on the peninsula—a serviceable wine. What I mean by that, it is only considered *serviceable* prior to its greater purpose for Consecration into the Blood of Christ."

The older woman nodded in agreement.

"No." Father continued. "Tonight, this one is an excellent Sauvignon Blanc originating from an ancient Italian vineyard situated in the foothills just south of Rome. The Gandolfo—they call it. It is the site of the Pope's summer residence." Stella felt extremely special for being allowed to share the exclusive vintage with the priest.

It was these types of interactions—ones suggested through anonymous accounts—that created a growing friendship. Coupled with Stella's barely contained attraction for the priest—along with the wine's effects, slowly progressed to what more than a few speculated was a predictable and inevitable conclusion each Sunday night.

Those that were suspicious of the pair started to pay even closer attention to any errant behaviors. Their ears perked up when the priest and housekeeper were in proximity to eavesdrop on their conversations. A few witnesses recalled with certainty that during the time frame of 1905-06 when the alleged rendezvous occurred, Stella was said to be present in the church at the next opportunity to receive the Sacrament of Penance. That was always the next Saturday afternoon. Additionally, she was observed to always wait till the end of *confession hours* to enter the space in the empty church. It was thought that she did this so no one else could possibly hear any of her admissions. Additionally, that by doing so, it insured she was not rushed in her private time with the priest.

"We are all creatures of our created conscience." Father Andrew would counsel Stella in a low volume from his cubicle through the latticed screen of the Confessional.

Stella would listen intently—enamored with the priest—even in her sinful remorse and in her limited ability to understand his educated prose.

"Stella, sometimes I wish I was a Protestant—a *Born Again.*"

"Dlaczego miałbym to powiedzieć!" Stella said in shocked Polish and performed another Sign of the Cross for the perceived blasphemy.

"Why would I say that you ask?" Andrew translated. "Well, the *Born Agains* interaction with the Almighty, with regard to the battle against sin and the upkeep of preparing ones soul in order to enter the Kingdom, is far less onerous than for our Faith!"

"Jak?" Asked Stella.

"How?" The priest translated. "It is our laborious daily *dance* with temptation and sin. We and they have the *same dance partner*—Satan. In both our factions of the Christian Faith, there is sin, then denying or justifying our sin. Then, with the inevitable advance of our guilty conscious, we reluctantly admit to sin, under the weight of remorse. It is the same for both Protestant and Catholic, Stella."

Andrew began to lecture. "For *us*, we are obliged to regularly seek forgiveness like we are now doing so in the Confessional—ostensibly in private—admitting to our transgressions surreptitiously. All the while, knowing that our sin could be shared institutionally—seditiously leaked by those who break their vows in this Institution! But we are obligated to cling to that thinly veiled trust of secrecy like a child."

Stella did not talk but exhaled heavily when she considering the awful possibility. *What if what I speak in the Confessional is later discussed by unknown people in the Church? Surely, Andrew—my priest—my Pastor— my friend, wouldn't tell them—would he?* She thought.

Andrew continued. "For us, confession is followed by performing penance for sin, getting absolution with our well-intentioned affirmation to avoid the temptation of it. But then, as we are weak and imperfect creatures, we soon invite temptation of sin to be our *dance partner* again. How can Satan refuse our invitation? And as we step out onto the dance floor with the Evil One, with that, the cycle repeats."

At this point in receiving the Sacrament, Stella was bewildered, but Father Andrew forged ahead in completing his comparison.

"And for the Protestants?" The Priest posed the question. "They can simply and myopically, perform a self-centered public expression to *accept Jesus as their **personal** Savior*—as if he rose from the dead for just them—a single individual and not the entirety of mankind as *we* believe. It is sufficient for them to do this kind of repentance *only one time*! Just *one time* to assuage their cumulative sin that burdens them at the present and will surely continue to amass in the remaining interim of their earthly existence. However, over the span of that time, in their process of *folly*, by their single declamation, they are given the leisure in their conscience the ability to dispense of *their* sin—the same as ours—regardless of it having been committed yet or not—without any lingering remorse to confuse their daily chores." The Priest almost sputtered. "While ours, dear Stella, remains steadfast until the Sacrament of Penance takes it away."

Stella had no response to Andrew's explanation, and he continued. "Until your—my—*our* most recent and grievous sins..." Andrew struggled to redirect his counsel to that of a priest providing counsel to a sinner. "I believed I was fortunate to have been taught and lived under the mores of our Faith—with its constant attention to preservation of one's soul through the regular application of the Sacraments. Though, I am now envious of those who live under the *Protestant* way—without its ominous cloud overhead constantly reminding me—*us*—*sinners* of our regret. But again, those of our Faith are required to perform this regular ritual. I am bound to participate in the process—as are you."

Andrew concluded the Sacrament. "Your penance is waived today, Stella. My observations are to be your–*our* counsel. In nomine patris et filii et spiritus sancti. Amen"

And with that, the lament-filled instructive course on Christian theology between the priest and the housekeeper would adjourn. Then another Sunday evening *date* would occur, and time would be scheduled for the next Saturday afternoon's confession. That is because, convention holds that the heart does what it wants—despite readily available sounder judgement.

No one really knows if the regrettable sins of the flesh occurred between the two—although, the rumor was very strong. But whether they succumbed or not, at a minimum, the *suspected* sins would be the gossip of the community for another week. And neither Andrew nor Stella would envision that the *near occasion* of their *sin* was brewing a destructive scandal.

Despite their efforts to keep things confidential, there are always the keenest of observers in any congregation that would begin to suspect *something* and had the courage to do something about it. Most however, couldn't let themselves believe that anything could possibly happen between a simple—and by most counts, a plain woman, and the handsome, charismatic Pastor. After all, he had his vows to honor God above all. And she was outwardly a pious and fervently strict Catholic. Yet eventually, the tight knit community—where one's business often becomes your neighbor's business, could not suppress the volume of *whispers* that rose to a level heard by some of the church elders.

Chapter Ten

Holy Rosary Parish, Isadore, Michigan, Winter 1905-1906

As rumors usually do, the salacious gossip about *the priest and housekeeper* had reached some of the church elders. It had done so by way of the Columbiettes—the affiliated Ladies' Auxiliary of the local chapter of the Knights of Columbus. A few of the *good ladies* of the group had passed on the secretive information to their husbands. In turn, it is thought that many of the Knights then discussed the findings with family and friends.

Many of those discussions took place at a local bar in the nearby settlement of Provemont to the north of Isadore. There, the gossip along with the drinks flowed among the fraternally inclined men. Predictably, the questionable rumors shared by the elbow-bending patrons, would be subjected to the same process as the ingredients in their favorite alcoholic beverage—beer. They would both be *fermented* into something much stronger. All agreed that someone needed to confront their priest.

The highly suspected—but unconfirmed inappropriate interaction between Father Andrew and Stella continued until it would abruptly end one evening in the winter of 1905-06, when there came a knock at the Pastor's office door.

A member of the local chapter of the Knights, a man who in this narrative is only identified by his first name, Robert, reported to be an old friend of Andrew's, paid an unscheduled visit. At the urgings of his wife, he had agreed to investigate the alleged misconduct and to confidentially speak with the priest.

"Father." He began in a serious tone. "I'm glad you're working late tonight, and you were able to meet with me."

"That's quite alright, Bob." The priest answered at ease. "But our regular K of C meeting is not until next Thursday. Please take a seat and make yourself comfortable."

"I wish I could, Andy." Robert replied. "This is not comfortable for me. It's a more serious and *personal matter.*"

"Should I put on my stole to hear your confession?"

"No, Father." Robert returned to formality. "It is not *me* that this matter concerns. It's *you*!"

The priest blanched—the direct affront catching him off guard. He did not know exactly what Robert was prefacing, but he had an inkling of what was to come.

Robert continued. "Let me start by saying this. We've been friends for years. We've hunted ringnecks together—fished together—attended deer camp together for years. This is not easy for me."

"Go on." The priest cautiously advanced the conversation.

"It's about you and the rumors I've been hearing, Father—I'm not saying from whom—but it has been rumored that you and *Stella*, the cleaning woman, have been…" He faltered for a moment but reasserted. "You two have—that is—have been spending *time* together late on Sundays inside this office—even your quarters."

"Robert!" The priest attempted to tamp down the tension and the flush raising under his collar in the face of this sudden accusation. "You sound like ol' Stosh! Always worried about the *appearance* of this or that. Always going on about what something *looks* like."

Andrew affected Stosh's voice. *I don't think it's appropriate for you to greet the women of the parish with an embrace. It's not right. The children seated on your lap—people will talk!*

"Andrew!" Robert tried to interject.

"No, no, Bob!" The priest became defensive, now fully understanding the purpose of his visit. "I have always refused to go into any discussion with Stosh about *appearances,* and I will tell you what I always tell him. I will not address any *specifics*—especially since I know from whom you are getting the accusations. You can pass this along to *that person* the next time you see *her*—later this evening."

Andrew leaned over his desk, laying his hands flat on the oak surface, and locked into direct eye contact. "She is just a lonely old woman—strictly platonic! And beyond that, there is nothing I'll say about the subject matter or the inferred accusations. You are not my confessor—not my spiritual authority. I am not obliged to do so with you. If you were the Bishop…? Well, then that might be a different matter."

"I understand Andy." Robert reasoned. "But for the sake of our church community, I'm sure you know of the consequences of *scandal*—even if it be false, and what that *rumor mill* can do to our community. I've seen it before—there was an assistant priest a few years before you came here…"

"I'm fully aware of the history of the church." Father Andrew inadvertently patted the top of his desk—knowing the full transcript of the incident about the assistant priest that Robert had mentioned was all contained in the desk below his hands.

That fact was oblivious to Robert, and he continued. "Since the new Pontiff—well, there's a renewed effort to return to *traditional values*, and with it, I've seen an increased close scrutiny of all of us—including you, Andy. Let's not stir up a hive of bees for Pope Pius X."

"No one knows that more than me, Bob." The priest schooled. "Call it what it is. The Pope has *informants*. They act to serve a warning. *Don't step out of line*. I get it." Andrew starkly admitted. But there is something else I am well aware of. I tally the Sunday collections each week. The totals have been on the increase for many months. Many Catholics are moving to the area. The Poles are coming by the dozens crossing the big lake from the Milwaukee area. Meanwhile the *grubi* in the Czech settlement to the northwest at Bay Harbor and St. Wenceslaus Parish in Suttons Bay are languishing."

"In contrast, we are a thriving Polish Catholic Community—due in no small part—I must say—to my unswerving determination." The priest bragged. "Just this past month, I procured several large *anonymous* donations and several renewal pledges for our Capital Improvement Fund from orchard owners in the area for our long-awaited new church building. *That* is what outweighs every other concern for the Vatican." He lowered his voice and leaned forward in a secretive way. "We are in a good position, Robert. We have many more plusses than minuses. We, the *Polish*, have been blessed."

"Indeed, we have been of late." Agreed Robert. "But the rumors?" He weakly argued.

"They are just that." Andrew flatly summarized. "This is not the first time that *detractors*—both externally and internally—have criticized the Catholic Faith to bring it down. Go back centuries in the history books. For nearly two millennia, they have failed. Failed, because we have a unified stance in the face of lies. From our Popes on down to the bishops, to the priests, to the altar boys—as far as I know—we are to treat the naysayers and their vile as it is—idle gossip from jealous gossipmongers. I will treat *this* reiteration of it in the same way."

Robert tried to speak, but before he could, Andrew held the floor. "And here's something else I know full well, Bob" He *pontificated.* "Giving legitimacy to it—whether by casually discussing it in the *Dew Drop Inn* or with your spouse or addressing it in some kind of official complaint—as you would have me do—will only enhance it. That act alone—regardless of facts—will undermine the Greater Church and succeed in bringing it down after two thousand years of failures. Not on my watch! It'll remain under lock and key." He then inadvertently patted the top of his desk.

If the two had been playing cards, and Robert had been more observant, that second pat on the desk would have been what poker players consider a kind of "tell." The *unintended disclosure* would have tipped-off Robert to the fact that under lock and key in the desk drawer, were just the kinds of *legitimacies* to the rumors that the priest—for his own survival and on behalf of the Church policy, was desperately trying to keep under wraps.

However, Robert was now in full retreat and could not respond to the *dressing down* he was receiving from his spiritual authority.

"Robert." Father Andrew instructed. "Let me give you an analogy. Gossip—it is like the cherry blossoms of spring. They appear on the peninsula. They are observed. Everyone talks about them with fascination. But if left alone and allowed to fade on their own, they fall to the ground and decay. And if they are allowed to wither, the fruit that grows in their place brings a harvest of plenty to all." He paused for effect as he leaned back in his chair. Then he brought his hands up in front of him to a loose praying position—his elbows resting on the arms of his chair. Tapping his fingertips together, he waited for Robert's response. "Does my soliloquy register with you?"

"Yes Father, it does." Robert reluctantly admitted.

"Furthermore." The priest continued after turning the tide of the conversation and getting his friend's confirmation. "I am a public figure and always the first one to be a target for criticism. Jesus himself was a public figure and was wrongly accused of so many things that led to his crucifixion!" The priest chuckled. "Bob, you're not planning my crucifixion are you?"

"Certainly not Andrew!"

"I'm relieved to hear that. Then, is there anything else you'd like to discuss?"

"No, no." Robert expressed his regret. "And I'm now sorry to have brought it up. I'll talk to the wife. I'm sure you can understand why I mentioned this."

"I can be sympathetic to your worries, but they are unfounded old friend." Andrew said in a relaxed manner. "Now, let's just pretend this whole conversation didn't happen. Would you care for a glass of wine?"

"No, no thank you, Andy."

"Perhaps something stronger?"

"On second thought, yes! That would be good. But I doubt you have anything like that in the office."

"Oh *contraire*, Robert!" The priest then removed his starched white collar—wringing wet with his nervous sweat. That incriminating fact thankfully went unnoticed by Robert. He then unbuttoned the top two buttons on his black shirt, reached inside the front of it and pulled out a thin, deer hide strap which was draped around his neck. It was his Scapular Necklace from the Benedictine Order—called the *jugum Christi*—or to the laity, it was known as the *Yoke of Christ*. On it was tied a brass key.

Robert had never seen the priest expose these before—even in deer camp. However, as an historian and fan of the previously mentioned Pope Leo XIII, he knew that Andrew had taken his priestly vows as a member of the Benedictines. They were the Order that had developed the tradition of the Scapular. He felt privileged to witness the intimate personal revelation.

"Oh, this?" The Priest acknowledged his friends fascination. "I was awarded this about a decade ago when I visited the Vatican. That's when the Pope established the Benedictine Confederation."

The priest then removed the scapular from around his neck, grasped the key dangling from the string, bent over while still seated, and unlocked the bottom drawer of his desk. He reached in and pulled out a large stack of official looking papers and with a thud, placed them on his desk.

Still rummaging through the drawer—the priest's attention focused there, Robert took liberty to scrutinize the documents—noting some of what was written on the top page of the stack. Even upside down to him, certain words jumped out: *Complaint. Confession. Transfer. Stipend.* And at the top of the page, a name he recognized as that of the former assistant priest at Holy Rosary who suddenly left under questionable circumstances a few years back under the guise of being granted a brief *vacation*. To date, he had never returned to the parish.

That was the extent of Robert's observations before Andrew again looked up and roughly shoved the stack back into the bottom of the drawer with one hand while presenting a bottle of Polish *Starka* to his guest with the other. He wheeled his swivel chair around and snatched two crystal glasses from the credenza behind his desk.

"Whiskey?" Asked Robert.

"No." Andrew replied. "Much more interesting! For centuries—I think—in the old country, they distilled it. It's a regional spirit derived from rye. It is neither a true whiskey or vodka and has a stronger alcoholic content. You will sleep the sleep of a baby after a shot or two."

Robert took his filled glass and toasted his host. "To friends."

The Priest modified the toast. "To *loyal* friends."

The pair nodded agreement, clinked glasses, and then downed the contents.

After a couple of slight coughs expelled which were needed to acclimate each to the high proof of the liquor, they quickly had another. Soon after, the Starka's effects mellowed the tense ether that had existed in the room. Each man leaned back in their chair. The priest put his feet up on the desk after another refill of their stout glasses.

"Speaking of ol' Stash." Andrew reminisced. "Bob, do you recall the prank we pulled on him in deer camp a few years back?"

"Which?" Robert droned in a grammatically lax response from the drink. "We *done* so many to the ol' duffer."

"Yeah, that's true. You r'member, the time he brought what he called his, recently *self-taxi-der-mized, big ol' trophy buck* to camp to brag and show off?" Andrew clarified in an equally relaxed *singsong*. "He was *sooo* proud of it."

Robert started laughing, for he knew the story that was coming.

"Remember?" Andrew chuckled and progressively slurred. "Someone took that trophy mount while Stosh was 'sleep—in the dead of night—stumblin' through the woods and rigged it up somehow so just the head and neck was showin' from 'b-hind a tree—jus' visible 'nuf it was from Stosh's deer blind. Someone else told Stosh that the day 'fore he had seen a big bruiser near his blind n' to be on the lookout. It was all Stosh needed to hear to get him out of bed and into his stand by first light on opening day."

Both men giggled like schoolchildren.

Robert picked up the story. "Can you 'magine his 'citement at seeing what to him was the twin—spittin' image of his trophy—peekin' out from the 'b-hind the big hemlock—a perfect shot, jus' 35 yards away?"

It was Andrew's turn in the telling. "First shootin' light, I could hear *pop* after *pop* racking through his bolt-action *ought six*. God bless the ol' fool."

"Oh, you shoulda heard the cursing in Polish, echoing through the woods, Father. Words even I have never used." Robert added.

"I'm sure that was right after he discovered the reason the buck wouldn't fall was not because of a poor shot, t'was 'cuz he had shot up his new trophy!" The priest bellowed.

"Haaa!" Roared Robert. "Ol' Stosh was redder 'n a beet when he got back to camp with the remains. Gotta hand it to him, he sure was a good shot. Hit that mount every time he pulled the trigger!"

The priest guffawed until he nearly ran out of breath. Then he sighed as he attempted to pour another round of shots. His growing inebriation caused him to wobble and dump one glass' contents onto the desktop. Much of it streamed off the edge and trickled into the open drawer, soaking many of the documents inside.

This time, with two hands, the priest carefully refilled the vessels and handed one to his friend. "Ahhh, such a gentleman." Andrew said. "Never complained or got angry at anyone—although he wanted to. He had no idea who done it. Do you know, he asked for forgiveness from *me* for swearing so much in the woods. He apologized to *me*! Can you imagine?"

"Such a good sport about it all." Conceded Robert.

"That is a man of Faith and *loyalty,* Robert." Andrew said in a pointed manner.

"Yes. That he is." Robert agreed when his laughter had subsided. "By the way, who was it that hatched that prank and put his deer mount out there anyway?"

"Why, it was me, Robert." Andrew smugly admitted. "I suppose that is *my confession* for tonight. Too bad you can't give me absolution or penance." The priest jokingly lamented. Then he added with unusual seriousness. "And in keeping with the veil of secrecy in the Confessional, you can't tell him—or *anyone*."

Robert nodded his understanding, and the priest poured another generous shot of spirits for each man. Pleasantries progressed late into the evening. People reported hearing crude harmonies of old campfire songs being crooned by the two old friends from as far away as the other side of the church courtyard. The earlier tension in the office had evaporated into the air like the alcoholic vapors of the Starka!

Unfortunately for Andrew, at some point later, by either Robert who may have reconsidered his commitment of confidentiality to him, or by way of Robert's wife and/or members of the Columbiettes, word of the rumors got to the Bishop in Grand Rapids and possibly others higher up. Andrew soon received a concerning phone call from his superior. He vociferously denied the rumor, restated his defense to the Bishop as he had to Robert, and fortunately the incident was not pursued.

Chapter Eleven

Holy Rosary Parish, Early Spring, 1906

After the uncomfortable surprise meeting with his friend from the Knights, and with his recently renewed determination to concentrate on the over-arching aspects of his duties as Pastor, Father Andrew also re-pledged to honor his vows. He decided it was best to consciously avoid personal interactions with Stella and return to the formalities of his position. The Sunday night "dates" ended abruptly. He applied his own advice to his situation based on the precedent established by the Vatican as how they historically handled such internal matters for a member of the clergy: *Ignore the criticisms. Set aside the controversy for later consideration. Allow it to wilt over time.*

The priest had every intention to correct his behavior—which was starting to weigh on his conscience—even if it was only the behavior that was occurring in his heart and mind. He would rededicate himself to the business of *pastoring,* from which he had *slightly strayed*—according to him. But always the bureaucratic administrator, he made note of his meeting with Robert of the Knights, and his intended course of action, and locked it away among his personal papers in his desk drawer.

Andrew had also unilaterally determined that the Sacrament of Penance, that he highly encouraged his parishioners to participate in on a regular basis in order to redirect their Faith, would not be required for *him*. He decided that he could abstain from an uncomfortable *Confession* to another priest, or an even more involved one to the Bishop. After all, he reasoned. He well understood his sins, knew he was sorry, and could administer his own form of absolution. He had met all the requirements. He confidently thought. *I'm good! No need to involve the Vatican process of documentation beyond my own personal notes. Sacrament of Penance, absolution, forgiveness—on **their** terms? That be damned.*

Soon however, Father Andrew's interests would again be pulled in a new—but again, *lurid* direction. Very soon, the new nun from the Felician Order in Livonia, Michigan would arrive in Isadore. His requested Sister Mary Janina—also known as, Sister Mary Johns to some, would join the other two nuns at the parish to teach the burgeoning number of children who had enrolled at the parish school.

Andrew—a slave to his creature carnal weaknesses, holding the most powerful position in the community, and coupled with a false sense of how insulated he was from accountability of his decisions and actions, couldn't help but be attracted to her.

Chapter Twelve

Northern Michigan, Spring, 1906

The rumbling and swaying created by the passenger train's Pullman car as it rolled over the tracks as they progressed up from Detroit, on to Saginaw, then west to Reed City and Manistee, had worked as a sedative for one of its passengers, Josephine Mezek.

Josephine, now known as Sister Mary Janina after taking her Perpetual Vows while in residence with the Felician Order of Livonia, had fallen in and out of a restless sleep. On the final leg of her journey from Manistee to Traverse City over the frost heaved rails of the Manistee and Northeast line, she had gone from trepidation to sheer excitement about beginning her new teaching assignment as School Principal and Mother Superior of the convent at Holy Rosary.

After arriving at her destination at the train depot in Traverse City, there would still be an hour or so of a rough horse and buggy ride to the remote Polish Catholic community of Isadore, located in the middle of the Leelanau Peninsula. Always the optimist, Sister Janina would try to make the best of the time in her remaining uncomfortable journey. The time would also allow her to reconcile the events of her life to date.

Janina pulled up on the collar of her heavy wool coat to escape a light breeze in the rail car. Thinking back to when she was a child, a minor draft like it would have never bothered her. Her previously long, thick hair had always insulated her neck from any chill. Though, now a nun, with her hair mandatorily cut to a modest length, what was left of it was always hidden under her coif and veil while she was in public and offered no protection.

Deep in thought, Janina fingered her rosary beads and thought about the many changing aspects of her new life. She prayed that a doctor's recent diagnosis was correct. His prescription was that the crisp, pine-scented air of northern Michigan would benefit her chronic tuberculin condition. She was confident that the change of atmosphere would also ease her plaguing depression and improve her frail state. She also hoped that her new home—a room on the second floor of the school building—would be a stable and comfortable one for many years to come. It would be the first dwelling she could call a real *home* since she was a child living in the suburbs of Chicago.

Though unknown to her at the time, Janina was about to be exposed to a new life, with a set of new, mature *sensations* that she had never encountered before. She knew the joy she exuded today over her prospects were in distinct contrast to her previous simple and mostly sad life. However, among the joy, in the days and months ahead, there would also descend upon her unimaginable complications which would lead to her demise.

Chapter Thirteen

Historical Perspective: Early Life of Josephine Mezek, circa 1880

Josephine Mezek was the youngest of seven children to an *outwardly* devoted Catholic couple in the Chicago suburbs of Skokie, Illinois. However, *inwardly* they were largely inattentive parents—a father and mother who regularly drank to excess and were abusive in their neglect.

Josephine's father, a common laborer, had died two years earlier at the age of fifty. He had succumbed to pneumonia while on the job in an unheated slaughterhouse on the west side. Her mother—laden with the burden of providing for seven hungry mouths, fell further into drink. That was followed by a complete mental breakdown. She was committed by the courts to an institution at the age of forty-seven.

Due to the sheer number of children and their universally indigent nature in the poor parish, the nuns, priests, and religious brothers charged with educating them had little real personal knowledge of any of their family circumstances and took little effort to find out. If fact, after Josephine's mother was committed, she continued to attend school for a time. The elderly, Sister Mary Catherine Blasko, her teacher, for a month, was none the wiser. However, the crotchety nun, still expecting full participation in church-school-family activities, would eventually find out more about Josephine's home environment.

After a particularly poor turnout at the Sunday Mother-Daughter parish breakfast the previous day, Sister Catherine—a stickler for conformity, made each child in her classroom stand at attention and explain to the class why they were absent from the event.

"Josephine Mezek, I did not see you or your mother at the breakfast. Why?"

"Sister, my mother has been sent away."

"Sent away?"

"To an institution—for a rest."

"What about your father? He could have brought you!"

"Sister, my father died last year."

"Be seated." The nun barked her order to obscure the embarrassment of her ignorance. She quickly jotted down a note regarding Josephine that she would later give to the principal of the school. Without a break, she proceeded to the next student.

"Margita Pleva, why were you not at the breakfast?" And so, the cold-hearted interrogations continued until all thirty-eight children had responded.

The next day, Josephine was met at the door of the school by the city truant officer and escorted to the Orphan Asylum of Chicago—after a stop at her home to gather two of her siblings—both boys under the age of fourteen. The older four of her siblings—ages 15 to 20 years, were left to their own devices.

On a cold and dreary midwestern morning in March of 1882, Brother Lucazk Bieleska, who was the interim Rector-Administrator of the terribly overcrowded orphan facility, transferred Josephine, then age 9, along with twelve other children—but not her two brothers—to The Sisters of Charity, House of Providence, located in Detroit on West Grand Boulevard. The institution was established to shelter what was described as *destitute children and unfortunate women*. After just a few weeks, Josephine was then moved to The Order of the Felician Sisters of Livonia, where she would remain for the next few years until taking her final vows to become a nun.

The young Josephine, buffeted by all the recent tumultuous events of her life, if at the time were to be evaluated, would have been diagnosed as suffering from clinical, long-term depression. She existed in a void, where she was effectually numb to feel much of any emotion.

"Whatever is God's will." Was Josephine's ready response. "Anything must be better than what has already happened." She was often heard saying.

Although still burdened with joyless emotions, Josephine's ever-present dimples and fair skin with vibrant light blue eyes belied her inward grief and sorrow. She poured herself into her studies at the nearby St. Albertus School to excel in memorizing her prayers and complete assignments. Unlike most of the wards of the institute, she relished the challenge of her strict and cloistered life as it finally gave her a narrowly defined purpose.

In her pious existence, Josephine would do things like internally debate with her own hunger at mealtime in ascetic contemplation. *Should I eat this slice of bread with my soup, or should I save it and give it to the homeless?* She would ask herself.

This debate and others like it were prompted by her exposure to limited experiences in the nearby neighborhoods. For example, that morning she had witnessed several hungry vagrants panhandling at the corner of Schoolcraft and Levan near the Convent. She rationalized that her plight was not so bad by comparison and decided she would save the bread for them and slipped it under her blouse.

Josephine's unusual lunch behavior happened to be observed by the principal of the school, Sister Mary De Salle. She pulled her aside and questioned her. "What do you have in your blouse, young lady?"

Josephine slowly pulled the crust of bread from her blouse—a shower of dried crumbs fell onto the linoleum tiled floor.

"It is not for me, Sister." She pleaded. "I was saving it for the homeless." She innocently looked up to the usually stern Mother Superior waiting for judgement and punishment.

The confrontation resolved itself, as it usually did with most encounters with Josephine. Sister De Salle found her response to ring with honesty and compassion. She was unable to criticize her actions or punish her Christ-like motives. Gently patting her on the head and lovingly running her arthritic fingers through Josephine's lustrous long curls, she ushered the girl along to catch up with the rest of her class and allowed her time that afternoon to complete her mission of charity to the homeless. The tender-hearted nun even contributing two more loaves of bread from the pantry for her to distribute.

Afterward, Josephine prayed. She prayed in thanks for not getting in trouble over the bread. She prayed to find any other ways to help those less fortunate than her—albeit that was a low bar to clear as the needs of the poor were so great. But it was also a high bar as her resources were limited.

If fact, Josephine—in a near-fanatical compulsion—prayed on virtually every thought and action she contemplated. She seemed to have a running conversation with God—for direction—for whatever perceived wrong she might have entertained or have committed. Continually asking for forgiveness was her way for atoning for whatever wrong that must have caused her to be sentenced to this existence.

On her fourteenth birthday, devoid of any celebration, Josephine's deliverance from her dismal lot was put on a path to redemption when the Mother Superior took an increased special interest in her. She summoned the girl to her office with intention to speak to her about her future outside the protection of the orphanage.

"Josephine, I can see you are filled with the Holy Spirit. I have a sense that God has special plans for you." She flatly stated with conviction.

"Um. Oh?" The girl barely uttered coherently—taken aback by the nun's statement—one obviously backed by her extensive experience and what would be considered by most as the Mother Superior's expert assessment abilities.

Sister De Salle–outside of her desire for all of her female charges to contemplate entering the Sisterhood, had special concerns for Josephine. Mother Superior could see she was pretty, bright, and had a personal chemistry about her that attracted boys. Some, she had observed, had already made inappropriate juvenile overtures to her. The nun knew that in just a few years, that would include overtures from men as well.

To her credit, Josephine always interacted with both the boys and girls in a friendly but strictly platonic nature. Despite her purity in the present, her budding feminine aura loomed as a future source of sinfulness as determined by the elderly head of the Felicians.

Sister De Salle had seen other young girls like Josephine—and many not nearly as pious—fall to the pressures of the lowest common callings of male dominated society placed upon young women of her station. She knew that if the girl were allowed to mature and remain in the laity, her virtue would never last. The odds for her success in secular society were so clearly stacked against her.

"Have you ever thought about becoming a nun, Miss Josephine? Devote your life to Christ?" Sister De Salle began her presentation.

Josephine leaned into her words—at full attention.

"You would be the bride of Jesus." Mother Superior boasted on her behalf. "There is no greater calling for a young woman. Your future—destined for glory—to serve at His right hand. It would bring purpose to your life and respect and maintain your purity. Would you think about it over the next semester?"

Upon completion of the Sister's much-respected words, Josephine immediately felt a welling within her heart. It was as if the weight of her entire previous existence was lifted from it. A path to a bright future was cleared. She could see it in perfect clarity.

At that precise moment—most likely a simple coincidence—the sun beamed through the window of the Mother Superior's office and cast its glow on the girl. Josephine took this as a sign.

Sister De Salle was also surprised by the way the brilliant sunlight—generated in the depths of a dismal winter, had bathed her young charge with its warming and affirming luminance. Although reluctant to accept this as a sign from the Almighty, she none the less, appreciated The Lord's timing—if it was to be categorized as that.

"Yes! Yes, Mother Superior!" Josephine nearly shouted her response. "I—I don't need to think about it. Yes, please. Yes! Help me become a sister like you. I have thought about it a lot lately." The girl rambled. "I love the Lord with all my heart. It would deliver me. It would make up for..." Overwhelmed, she began to cry in joy and could not complete her thought.

Sister De Salle was pleased and nodded. She knew this was the right decision for the girl. But she still had lingering concerns about what she perceived as the girl's perpetual naive nature—which would not serve her well in a harsh world outside the convent. Despite Mother Superior's serene smile, there was an ominous foreboding under her veneer that would not leave the old woman's mind.

"Very well, Miss Josephine. Or should say, *Novitiate* Josephine. We will begin your training in the coming semester—your last one with us. She warned through her pursed lips. "And may God bless you and your decision."

Chapter Fourteen

North of Traverse City, Leelanau County, circa May 1906

It was a particularly rough stretch of two-track that tossed Sister Janina from left to right on the buggy seat. It jarred her from her reminiscences. She determined that she had spent enough time on that. It was time to relegate her unfortunate past to history and focus on the present.

"Driver, how much further to Holy Rosary?" Janina asked the young man on the reins of the horse drawn cart.

"Hour." He replied in an introverted single syllable and with a slight bow to her.

"I'm sorry, I don't know your name." Janina confessed. The young man nodded but didn't respond. Surprised she needed to further explain, she added. "Could you tell me it?"

"Gruba." The embarrassed, pudgy, and unkempt boy mumbled.

Janina questioned herself. *Did he say Gruba or Grubi?* She thought his response odd and curiously coincidental. *Is his name also his condition?* Janina knew from when she was a child, that *gruba* is sometimes a Polish slang term for *fat*. But the nun knew that the word, sometimes spelled and pronounced slightly different as *grubi,* in Czech, Slovak or Croatian, can also mean *filthy* or *rude.* She remembered years ago in her immigrant neighborhood of suburban Chicago, that the parents sometimes chided or lovingly teased their children as that. She recalled her mother saying that word to her father—sometimes *gruba,* sometimes *grubi.* He was also a stocky person from what she remembered of him. When he arrived home from work at the slaughterhouse—his clothes covered in grime—she would call him the latter word and make him change his clothes at the door.

Perhaps, it is just this boy's nickname—but an apt one in either language. She concluded her thought.

Janina had been picked up by Gruba at the train station in Traverse City that afternoon at the instruction of the Pastor of Holy Rosary, Father Andrew Bieniawski. As soon as she stepped off the train and onto the platform, the young man had approached her with a letter of greeting from the Pastor that contained instructions for her to accompany him back to the town of Isadore—several more miles to the north.

Based on her observations, Janina at first suspected the boy was either mentally or emotionally challenged—or both. Perhaps he was not fluent in the English language. She recognized his compromised persona as one she had seen often among the many homeless men she encountered on the streets of Detroit near the Felician Order while she was performing her charitable community works.

Silently, she compassionately said a prayer for the boy. *Dear Lord, may you grant this special soul and his personal plight your Grace and Mercy in all our interactions. Amen.*

Janina also noticed the boy clutched an additional envelope in his calloused fist. On it were penciled instructions—apparently written by Father Andrew—for the young man to give to anyone in authority to open and read and provide help in case he ran into trouble. Additionally, the priest's meticulous hand-written notes included a physical description of the person he was to seek out and transport—as if those details would be needed. After all, she was a woman in a nun's habit. The overwhelming odds were that Janina would be the only one attired that way on the train platform.

From the time Sister Janina had made connection with the young man at the station, she had quickly lost track of time. The travel north in the horse cart over rough gravel roads and sandy, rutted two-tracks had consumed her. She estimated that they were still about a half-hour away from their destination.

Over the remaining time, Sister Janina studied Gruba as he drove, while he kept his eyes on the difficult terrain. She thought it odd that he had only spoken the one word to her since they met—merely responding to her additional questions in more slight bows at the waist to show reverence to her trappings.

Sometime later, the other two nuns stationed at the parish along with a few of those more prone to gossip in the community, would go into more details about the young man and others like him who frequented the area. Speculations were that he was thought to be an orphan—perhaps a migrant—a sometimes orchard worker and fieldhand who was also occasionally seen around the church grounds doing odd jobs for the Pastor.

Father Andrew had taken the underprivileged youth and others like him under his strict wing. Under his coordination, the youths sometimes also

69

lived in foster family situations as they became available. Collectively, they were known as *chore boys*. Few of the residents of Isadore took the time to get to know them or even their names.

Janina increasingly studied the grimy young man as the journey progressed. His extreme quietness along with the rapidly advancing dusk of the northern Michigan woods gave her pause. At the same time, a biting, early spring northern Michigan breeze cut through her veil and sent a chill down the back of her neck. There were few things Janina missed from her life before becoming a nun. But on that short list, her long and thick, brown hair descending down to the middle of her back that helped to insulate her from winter weather was one of them.

As Janina struggled to keep warm, an early memory again surfaced. In her early life, Janina's understood that her tresses, in addition to their insulating properties, had always stood out as a feature of distinction among the other schoolgirls housed at the Felician Order. But since her vows, the hair had been cropped, and she soon discovered that her personal identity no longer mattered. Her *collective* identity instantly became just another in the *sisterhood.*

The unanimity of the Felician Order's standard garb consisting of floor-length, drab, brown, woolen habit, stiff brimmed veil, and tight, white, oversized collar was intended to remove any individuality and feminine attractiveness. Though, even for the generally plain in looks—but exceptionally charming Sister Janina, she understood that no uniform would ever completely suppress her feminine charms.

Another icy blast buffeted Janina. As she again ran her hand along the back of her neck to warm it, she thought. *I will make sure that longing for a full head of hair is the only one I ever have.* Her guarded optimism regarding *longings* would turn out to be prophetic, but wrongly so.

Regardless of her outward appearance, it would be Janina's overt kindness, smile, and her uninhibited, infectious laugh—most of the time starting with a slight impish giggle, that would perpetually challenge the dour accessories of her physical image. Furthermore, parishioners, and almost all in the community who began to interact with her on a daily basis would marvel at her beaming joy and would be unavoidably attracted to her. That attraction was universal among the children she taught in the school. It was shared by *nearly* all the women—except for a few who harbored an illogical jealously toward her. And of most concern, by virtually all the men of Isadore—chief among them, would be the Pastor of Holy Rosary, Father Andrew.

Chapter Fifteen

Holy Rosary School, Isadore, Michigan, January 1907

The winter semester of the 1906-07 school year at Holy Rosary Elementary was in its first week. Pastor Andrew had heard many excellent evaluations about Sister Janina's progressive teaching methods during the previous fall semester—especially in teaching proper English to the majority Polish children who mainly spoke their native tongue at home. She had accomplished noticeable results among even the most challenged students. Although some of her methods in regard to instructing the boys in her classes were a bit too lenient for his tastes.

At Parochial schools, it was standard practice for the Pastor to visit each classroom at the start of the new semester to review student report cards from the previous. Their teacher would also be under review to gauge the academic progress.

"Good morning Father!" the class would stand and loudly shout to greet Father Andrew as he entered their overcrowded room. Thirty-six children stood at attention, as did their teacher.

"Good morning to all of you! Be seated class." Father Andrew would gently say to relieve some of their stress. The children would find—at least for the girls, that even in criticisms of the lower performing students, he would usually be mild mannered and supportive.

"Kazandra Petruska." The priest called call out a name. After scanning that child's grades and written notes penned by Sister Janina off their individual goldenrod colored index report cards, the child would then stand and straighten to attention like a soldier in a military inspection.

"A *D* under *pays attention in class*." The Pastor would gently chide. " I will expect at least a grade higher by the next semester. Wouldn't you say that is a goal you can achieve, Kazandra?"

"Yes Father."

"Good! You can be seated. And say hello to your mother and father for me when you get home tonight, will you?" The priest would conclude the child's review.

"Yes, Father Andrew!" The child would respond with relief for having escaped *Divine Retribution*—at least in her mind, and then plop back onto the pine boards of their desk seat.

"William Konesko!" Father Andrew's demeanor would change.

"Yes, Pastor!" The boy would timidly respond.

"Stand up straight—no slouching!" Andrew's inspection proceeded. "A *C-*

minus under *pays attention in class*. William, I will see you in the hallway after I am done here."

"Yes, Father." The boy would tremble. Tears would well in his eyes as he knew what would soon happen to him.

At the end of the class review, the disciplinarian priest would take a standard wire coat hanger from the room's coat rack and twist it into a makeshift switch. In the hallway, witnessed by the teacher and the other underperforming horrified students, he would then administer a stinging swat or two to the boy's backside. There was never a gentle corrective chiding when it came to the boys of Holy Rosary School.

And so, it would proceed like that, in that very different manner, for the *boys* versus the girls. When he was finished, Father Andrew and Sister Janina would remain in the hall for his private assessment of *her* performance.

"Well done! All in all, I'd say you are off to a very good start at Holy Rosary, Sister!"

"Thank you Monsignor." Janina blushed. "I am pleased with their progress after one full semester. The smartest are excelling and the ones who usually lag behind are also showing improvement. But I wonder if spanking is appropriate for some..."

"Father Andrew interrupted—forcefully asserting his authority. "I have been doing this longer than you, Sister!" He looked down with all seriousness at her over the top of his spectacles. He wanted to make sure—right here and now—that he didn't give rise to another upstart nun like Sister Angelina telling him his business.

"I understand, Father." Janina acquiesced.

Hoping he had made his point, Andrew quickly returned to his upbeat mood. "Yes, you are fitting in nicely at Holy Rosary. You deserve a reward." He joked—but it was tinged with an unsettling note of sincerity. "Would you care to join me for a glass of wine Sunday evening?"

"I beg your...I'm sorry?" The Sister was caught off guard by the invitation.

"A glass of wine." The priest repeated as if there was nothing unusual about his invitation. "Just my way of saying thanks to you for all your tireless work. I know so often the teacher's successes tend to be overlooked. Only the complaints seem to reach my *desk*." Andrew thought back to his reprimand session with Sister Angelina—the report of which was secured there. "Would you join me?"

"I…I suppose that would be ok." Janina haltingly accepted.

"Excellent! See you Sunday around eight. Oh, and that will be in my quarters." The priest casually confirmed the details. "And keep up the good work, Sister." He said as he reached out and purposefully and most inappropriately half-hugged her, while he stroked Janina's bicep with his hand.

The contact between them startled Janina in a way she had never experienced before. In a split-second her trust of Father Andrew had changed from one of complete confidence to a cautious on-guard. It caused her to rethink and decline the priest's offer.

"Oh, I don't know what I was thinking." Janina nervously blurted out. "I…I told Sister Angelina I would go into Cedar with her to visit her sick friend."

That was true. Janina had made those prior commitments. "But I guess I can cancel with her. She'll be disappointed but will understand your invitation."

The prospects of Janina discussing the nature of his invitation with anyone caused Andrew to politely withdraw it.

"That's quite alright!" He blanched. "Please stick with your prior commitment. We can't disappoint Sister Angelina. It's probably best not to mention my invitation extended to you but not *to her*. It would hurt her feelings."

"Yes, you are right. I would feel awful if she were hurt." Agreed Janina. "Then it'll be our little secret." Father Andrew accepted her excuse and nonchalantly replied. "Perhaps another time—and soon!"

"Yes!" Janina replied cheerfully overcoming the uncomfortable exchange, but secretly hoping that time would never come.

Chapter Sixteen

The Persistence of Temptation

Father Andrew did not sleep well that night. In his fantasies he wrestled with the thoughts and emotions of adolescence. Aroused by the schoolgirls of his youth and the desires he fought hard to suppress, in his subconscious visions it felt like he was a teenager again. It had been years since he had such a dream.

With the awakening for the new day—and throughout his regular ritual of morning prayers, Father Andrew's dream did not fade away. The vivid details of this one stuck with him. And unlike during his formative years when he experienced such dreams, this time he would not experience a self-loathing and then mentally flagellate himself for such impure thoughts for someone who was being groomed to enter the priesthood. Throughout this morning, he continued to ruminate about what his dream might mean.

In the details of the fantasy, he was a young man again. He was lean and athletic. A girl in his class at prep school approached him with a seductive smile on her face, but then in what dreams usually do, the scene had changed, and the girl's face had transformed into that of Sister Janina's. He also remembered that during his euphoric state of unconscious, the scent of lilac and the chemistry of the young woman filled his senses.

Later, throughout Andrew's officiating of the morning Mass, he was barely able to focus on his sacred duties. His Homily was disjointed and was abruptly cut short due to his lack of concentration. He found it difficult to keep his eyes away from Sister Janina who sat in the third-row pew with the other two nuns of the parish.

After Mass, Andrew anxiously paced back and forth in his stuffy office struggling with the sinful thoughts planted in his mind by what he believed to be the Evil One—Satan—tempting him. He would never admit to the possibility that that his own *free will* played as much a role in his deliberations for contemplating misdeeds as the influence of the Devil. For an experienced priest—not just a misguided and impressionable youth, he put little effort to prayer to push the impure ideas out of his mind. Thus, it was a foregone conclusion that lust would win out and he would willingly succumb to it.

That afternoon, Andrew waited inside, near the church's back vestibule, with door slightly ajar. He was waiting for the opportunity he knew would present itself for his prurient interests. Soon he heard the sound of human presence—the creak of someone seating themselves on the plank of the old pine picnic table in the oak grove outside the church. Then he waited for the faint sounds of someone reciting a Rosary and then the Marian prayer as his signal to initiate his lustful ambitions. He had about ten minutes to make one final decision to act or to not before Sister Janina would be done with her regular prayer time and head back to her personal quarters above the school.

Predictably, Andrew surrendered to the enticing choice. He exited the side door of the vestibule and approached Janina. His approach would not be as the head administrator—the Pastor of Holy Rosary, but more like a predator approaching its prey.

"Sister?" Andrew gingerly spoke.

Janina looked up—surprised to see Father Andrew hovering over her—uncomfortably invading her personal space.

"Monsignor, good afternoon." Janina startled, but then beamed her usual temperament.

"Hello, Janina." The priest surprised himself—both by dropping the prefix of *Sister* from his greeting, and by the lecherous sound of his words escaping his mouth. "It is a *lovely* afternoon. I—I was wondering." He stammered like a schoolboy. "I was wondering, if later after your evening vespers with the sisters—wondering if you might like to finally share that glass of wine with me at the rectory—in my quarters?"

Janina raised one eyebrow. She was at first unable to answer because of the nature of the forward sounding request, but more surprised to hear it coming from her spiritual superior—for a *second time.*

Andrew continued his invitation. "It is a wonderful vintage—the wine, that is—supplied by a local grower on the peninsula. He has guaranteed to supply us—the church—free of charge—with enough to meet our needs for Sacramental use in Mass until next spring—saving the parish a considerable amount of money rather than having to purchase it out of church coffers." The priest over-explained. "We will be able to repurpose those funds to fixing the roof of the school." He prattled in a nervous cadence. "Since you and the sister's will eventually benefit, I thought it appropriate you should celebrate with me our good fortune."

"Father." Janina cautiously answered. "I have never drunk much wine in social settings before."

The priest drew upon his knowledge of history to allay the nun's trepidation—but his true intentions leaked out in his speech. "It is no *sin* to enjoy in moderation what God has provided. Without the alcohol produced in wine, mead and beer, the polluted water of communities in ancient times would have wiped out the population with cholera and dysentery a long time ago."

The priest's joking assessment of the state of human existence made the nun break into a small smile. Her dimples belying her reluctance to accept Andrew's invitation.

"I will see you around seven-ish?" Andrew prodded.

Janina still provided no definitive answer. "Well…"

The priest persisted—encouraging her with the raise of an eyebrow and a cock of his head—a non-verbal push.

"Ok." Janina's meekly replied.

"Very well. See you at seven." The priest pulled on the fob of his pocket watch. He slipped it from his trouser pocket and checked the time. There would be four more hours to wrestle with his impeding sinful thoughts and action, but his decision had long ago been made.

That first of what was to become many late Sunday *rendezvous*—for lack of a better word—between Father Andrew and Sister Janina concluded without incident. Both had maintained decorum based on their religious station. Though Janina was extremely nervous during the roughly two hours in Andrew's quarters.

"I should confess, Father—that is, *clarify* my earlier confession." Janina spoke after Andrew placed a crystal goblet of pale-yellow Liebfraumilch in her tiny hand as she explained her earlier declamation.

"Call me Andrew. It's fine in a private setting like this—just the two of us." He purred.

"Okay…*Andrew*." Janina tested the sound of addressing him by his first name. "I told you before that I have never drunk much wine in social settings. Actually, I have never drunk *any* wine—ever!

"How is that?" Andrew questioned. "Never in a social setting?"

"Never!" She confirmed.

"Well, that is not a *confessionable* offense in my opinion." Assured the Priest.

"Father—er, Andrew, *even* at Mass. When I place the Chalice to my lips when receiving the Sacrament of Communion, I never let the consecrated wine touch my lips. Do I need to make confession for that?"

"*Each time* you receive Communion, you never drink the Blood of Jesus? Not a drop?"

"No, I'm afraid of what it might do to me. I know it has been Consecrated into the Blood of our Lord Jesus Christ, and it is a Sacrament for our salvation, but it still has *alcoholic content*. Is that a sin? I am afraid of the effects it might have on me. I've seen far too many who are weak and cannot stop themselves from drinking more and more. During my time performing community outreach with the Felicians on the streets of Detroit, I saw that most of those we tried to help were there because of alcohol. It ruins so many lives. I'm afraid that I might be one of the weak ones to fall under its addiction. My own parents..." Janina did not finish her sentence.

"Hmmm." Andrew contemplated Janina's fragile and thoughtful nature—but only for a moment and continued to fill her goblet.

"Well, no one is going to get you drunk here, Janina." Assured Andrew. "A little wine—*in moderation*—never hurt anyone.

"I suppose that's true. I'll trust you on that." Janina reluctantly conceded.

"Of course, you will!" Confirmed the Pastor. "And I'll take your admission about you not partaking in the Blood of our Lord during Communion as your *confession*. But I determine that no penance is required this time. However, next Mass, I will expect you to at least wet your lips." He laughed but with a somber lingering stare at her that acted as an unspoken command.

Janina's initial smile melted under his authority, and she nodded. "I will Pastor—er, Fath—er, Andrew."

Andrew *did* speak the truth about the modest amount of alcohol they would consume that evening. It alone would not be the cause for both of them to fail in their vows. The alcohol would have to be mixed with other factors. One was the unquantifiable and undetectable chemistry between them. But even that in addition to the wine would not be the primary catalyst for their coming transgressions. Those by themselves, under any circumstances of their interaction, would never have been sufficient for them to stray.

No, it would be a critical combination of *all* of the above, repeated weekly over the summer—along with the Pastor's barely restrained desires and disturbing machinations—coupled with the *newness* of the mature feelings that were coursing through Janina for the first time in her life, that would be the ultimate recipe for disabling their defenses and place in jeopardy their religious vows of chastity.

Chapter Seventeen

Complaints and the Rumor Mill, circa Summer, 1907

Gossip Heard From the Barstools of the Dew Drop Inn, Provemont, Michigan

"In spring, a young man's fancy turns to…Well, I guess that goes for a middle-aged priest, too."

Father Andrew's new *desirous* attentions for Sister Janina did not go unnoticed. To the keenly observant cleaning woman, Stella—the eyes and ears of the parish's *rumor mill*, the truth of it was obvious. The arrival of the new nun—coupled with the priest's overt efforts to avoid *her*—were *cause* and *effect*.

Stella's mind descended into the basest of comparisons between her and the nun. Her conclusions were stark. Sister Janina was younger, prettier, overtly friendly, and far more vivacious than the aging and plain woman she saw in her mirror. The nun's feminine characteristics—despite her heavily concealing habit, still exuded a quality that had lured many of the male parishioner to her. Most devastating to Stella and consequentially to the parish, the sister's *chemistry* had also worked to the detriment of Father Andrew's recently quelled libido. Under the housekeeper's watchful eye, she noticed that the priest came to within an uncomfortable distance of Janina whenever he was in the room as she played the piano. Under the guise of watching her hands on the keyboard to learn the selection, Stella could see Andrew wasn't watching her hands.

Stella felt abandoned, thoroughly betrayed by Andrew, and filled with anguish. She could not conceal her anger regarding Sister Janina to anyone who would listen to her rantings.

The housekeeper's complaints were not resigned to just verbal critiques. Additionally, the old woman would often physically accost Janina over minor tribulations by grabbing at the sleeve of her habit to admonish her like one of the schoolchildren.

"Tardy, loud and undisciplined students!" She would berate Janina. Then there was the matter of the young Sister' *breezy* attitude in her teaching methods—which created clutter in the classrooms that Stella would have to clean up. That would cause additional conflict and heated arguments between the two. Janina's every action was now subject to unwarranted evaluation by Stella and their confrontations were observed by numerous people in Isadore.

Chapter Eighteen

Holy Rosary Parish, 18 August 1907

It had been a clear and quiet late summer day—an unusual stretch of cooler weather for August. It had finally reached the time of year when it was comfortable to linger outside without being bothered by the persistent nemesis of all who resided in the north woods—black flies and mosquitos. Sister Janina and the other two nuns had decided to spend the summer at Holy Rosary rather than returning to the Felician House downstate as was the tradition between school years. They believed the cooler climate would benefit their health.

Janina sat at the weathered pine picnic table in the oak grove on the north side of the church deep in thought and prayer. She meticulously maneuvered the beads of her rosary through her delicate fingers, muttering the prayer that each bead represented. That prayer was The Novena of Petition—approved by Pope Leo XIII in 1887. She had memorized it as a child and regularly recited it during particularly trying times. This was one of them.

"…O God come to my assistance. O Lord, make haste to help me…"

She was startled mid-prayer by a firm hand on her shoulder.

"Janina, can we talk?" Asked Father Andrew.

Her ever-present smile was absent in her response. "We are already." She looked up at him, waiting for him to continue.

For the past three months, Janina and Andrew had avoided each other. Since the time that their *collegial friendship* had crossed the line from that of platonic confidants into forbidden territory, Andrew had avoided entering the school for fear that he might bump into her in the hallways and then be compelled into an awkward conversation. He purposely walked in the other direction if he saw Janina and the other nuns walking the campus of the parish.

Janina was also uncomfortable around Andrew. She now sat in a pew near the back of church during every Mass she attended. This was to avoid making eye contact with him, which would result in the exchange of the emotions they both felt, ones that she feared would be apparent to any in the church community. She began to attend the crowded Sunday Noon Mass, so she would feel more hidden. She even refrained from taking Communion if there were no assistant priests helping to distribute the Eucharist and Andrew was the only celebrant. Thus, she never went to early Mass, as that would most likely be the case.

Father Andrew—still standing—swung his right leg up and rested his foot lightly on the plank bench of the picnic table—remaining an appropriate arm's length away from her in case anyone was observing them.

Before beginning the conversation, Andrew turned to scan the wide-open windows that ran along the nave of the church. Satisfied there was no one inside who might overhear, he launched into a chatty nervous banter of small talk.

"Did you like what Stella made this evening? I found it to be rather bland—and perhaps a bit spoiled. Of course, I'd never tell her that. She is so sensitive to my criticisms lately. But I'm not sure venison stew gravy should look like that." He tried to elicit a smile from Janina with a small play on words. "It was a *gray* color alright, but I wouldn't call it *gray-vee!*"

Janina's stiffened expression softened to some extent at Andrew's attempted humor. His outward good nature *toward her* and to most of the amiable parishioners were qualities that drew her to him. But like others who encountered the Pastor when he was in his *disciplinary mode*, she tread lightly around him. She saw him as a complicated man comprised of a much different outlook than her own approach to life.

Where Janina gave others the benefit of the doubt and attempted to always seek the *best* in the *worst situations,* Andrew's position of power in the community seemed to have him first see the worst of the worst in people and circumstances. His attitude was one of, *I have the plan for you. And as I am your superior, do as I say, and you will be a part of it. But if you are not with me, don't get in my way.* That personality difference between the two would be the determining obstacle for what they now faced.

"It wasn't my favorite meal...I *confess*." Janina haltingly agreed. She would have liked to retrieve the word *confess* if she could, but it seemed to escape her lips on its own will. It's implications cast a shadow on their conversation. "But all-in-all, it wasn't so bad." Her small talk was now losing enthusiasm. "Far better than some of the meals I had in the orphanage." The mention of *meal* suddenly made her recall the *crust of bread* incident from when she was a child. She wished this problem in the present was as simple as that one had been in the past.

Both Andrew and Janina knew that there was no need to extend the pleasantries. Each knew it was not the focus of this long-delayed discussion. The issue that would finally be addressed, had been like a brewing storm cloud advancing across the horizon. It would soon overtake them and all in its path.

"Dear—um, I mean, um, Janina." Andrew stumbled through his salutation. Contritely, he continued in a soft whisper. "I am so sorry for what has happened between us. I never meant for things to progress to what they did—the embrace—the kiss...and." He paused not able to speak the exact word of the sin. "The *intimacy*—and the desire to want *more!* Rather, I should feel shame and guilt, but I do *not!* I know I should be filled with remorse, but I am not!"

Andrew exhaled deeply at the admission. "Huhhff. And I should have reached out to you—come forward with this much earlier than the months that has passed since we..." Again, Andrew paused as he futilely searched his mind for another way to describe their transgression. "I am ashamed of my weakness. Satan has tricked us by his deception." He asserted in a way that appeared to be his belief that he had played no part in their sin.

"Andrew, STOP!" Janina replied in earnest—aware of how he had crafted his admission with zero amount of blame placed on him and *all* on the Devil. "It is as much my fault as *yours*." She redirected his share of the guilt to him but took full responsibility for hers. "I am accountable for my own actions. I also embraced and kissed and..." She could not say the words either. "I have sinned. I cannot assign blame to the Devil himself and that the unsuspecting *me* was lured into that sin. I am a person of free will. That is what I believe despite the Church's stance that Satan is always lurking to bring us into sin. Or that God predetermines *all* and it is only by his Grace alone that we are forgiven. My deeds DO count—both positive ones and negative ones. And I am liable for choosing them. I will not blame Satan to relieve my guilt. No, I am responsible for my sins. This one especially—as are *you*."

Andrew was impressed by Janina's acceptance of her guilt, but equally stung by her honest assessment of *his*. She continued. "Like you, I admit. I have difficulty feeling any remorse for our actions. I have relived our night together many times—every night since. And each time it fills my inner self with joy. I cannot make myself feel otherwise either—no matter how much I pray. I am *not* sorry. I know that my lack of sorrow, in of itself is also sinful. I should request a transfer."

Feeling another wave of guilt, Andrew offered. "No, no, I will put in for a transfer. I don't know what has gotten into me. I have abandoned my vows. To fix this I will leave your life and then there will be no more cause for *you* to sin again. Distance and time will extinguish any lingering passions. Time will make us forget."

"No, the solution cannot all fall on your shoulders." Janina argued. Though she knew that *distance between them* was ostensibly the only solution if they both intended to remain in the Church and to reestablish their vows. Though, between the two of them, she knew it was Andrew who *held the cards* to make that happen swiftly with her transfer.

Heartbroken, Janina futilely belabor her point. "The people of this parish need you. I am just one teacher. You will still have two others. You can replace me."

Ultimate understanding had become apparent to both. Andrew would *not* accept Janina's request for transfer so she could remain at Holy Rosary to teach. That was her true talent. The gallant thing for him to do, and one he could orchestrate without a lot of scrutiny from the parishioners in Isadore, was that he would leave his pastorship at Holy Rosary and take whatever opening was available under the pretense of submitting to his vows of service. He knew there were plenty of other parishes in dire need of a priest in the State or even across the lake in Wisconsin. He reasoned that it would be the expedited solution. Naively, he thought he could handle any questions about the move, and no one would bother Janina. He figured he had all the connections to make something happen—and soon. Despite the imperfect logic of his impending decision, he still yearned to reach out and embrace Janina.

However, what she said next, made him instinctively recoil and reconsider. "I must seek the Sacrament of Penance for my sin." Janina whimpered. "I will go to another nearby parish to confess to another priest, Andrew. I don't see how I can do that with you. Perhaps I can go to Traverse City, or to St. Wenceslaus in Suttons Bay."

Andrew suddenly feared their scandal would become the talk of the *priestly grapevine* that existed throughout the parishes. If word of it got back to the Bishop, he would be called in to explain gossip concerning him—*again!* He must rethink this whole thing.

"The people of this parish need you." Janina repeated. "It's not just about you and me." Janina forlornly drooped her shoulders, stood, and started to walk away. Her words turned out to be prescient. Indeed, it was not just about the *two* of them anymore.

Andrew moved to stop her from leaving, but after she took a few steps, Janina halted and turned back toward him. A wave of surprise and fear swept across her face. She gasped and reached for her abdomen.

"What is it? Are you ill." Andrew asked. He rushed to her.

Janina's maternal instincts then suggested something was happening. Her moment of upset was not just a simple case of nausea from the venison stew. Although unsure of what it felt like, she feared it was the unmistakable sensation of a *quickening* in her womb.

"Oh, Andrew…" The words escaped Janina's lips in a gasp. Not knowing what to do and gripped with fear, she turned and quickly spirited away to the Convent—leaving Andrew in a state of bewilderment.

Unknown to the pair who had been deeply immersed in their discussion, there was an eavesdropper who had heard every word and saw every physical interaction between the two as it had transpired in the oak grove. The intimate details and truths revealed to that witness deeply offended and angered them.

Chapter Nineteen

Sunday Overnight, 18 August 1907

Father Andrew spent another restless night in utter anguish mulling over what he should do despite earlier indicating to Sister Janina that he would transfer. *Transfer?* He considered. To the contrary of his earlier optimism, he knew there would be questions from his often stern and difficult Bishop that he would need to address. He would have to craft answers that skirted the edge of truth. And there was already the file on him from the Stella incident. There would likely also be questioning of Sister Janina based on the rampant rumors circulating. The Bishop might just as likely demote him as transfer him—possibly defrock him from the clergy, or at worst, excommunicate him from the Faith altogether. The possibility of that core of his existence being stripped away terrified the normally unflappable priest.

A myriad of solutions ran through Andrew's mind of how to possibly circumvent the normal procedure for church scandals like this that might side-step his superiors.

He could contact his old friend in the Milwaukee Archdiocese who had considerable political connections. Maybe with his help, he could get assigned as the Headmaster of the Campion Preparatory School and Seminary in nearby Prairie du Chien, Wisconsin. He theorized that move might be personally helpful as the all-male society would suppress his recent sexual failings. That was one option—albeit a complicated one. Though, it was not one for which he was overly enthusiastic. So, he would put it on the "back burner" for now.

Should he just resign? *Resign?* No good. He would still have to concoct a story that left out the specifics. More importantly, what would he then do with the rest of his life—his ambitions? Yes, what about his career?

Should he admit that *he had feelings for Janina* and leave the priesthood altogether on his own? *Ask her to marry him?* No, that would require her to also abdicate her vows. She had never indicated that was something she wanted to do. He had never even asked her for her thoughts on that prospect. In retrospect, it was a chivalrous consideration that did not receive as much attention by him as it should have.

As time dragged on during his night of decision, the darker facets of the potential consequences of Andrew's failings—the specter of scandal and his personal embarrassments slowly flooded his thoughts and drown out the more gallant responses he would consider. By daybreak, he had made a choice. It would not be one that would be in the best interest of Janina.

True to his self-absorbed nature, it was a panicked response that would benefit only him. And he would need to act upon his decision very soon.

Chapter Twenty

Historical Perspective: Legacy of the Pontifical Celibacy

In the early Church there were several married Popes while in office. An *apocryphal* account—one not included in the Canonical Gospels in the New Testament, is a claim that Peter, considered to be the first Pope, was betrothed. In addition to leaving his trade of fishing at the moment of his recruitment by Jesus, he also immediately left his wife and family.

Marriage was reportedly also common among the bishops and priests for the first thousand years of the Church. Eventually it was decreed that the priesthood should remain unmarried and ordained to be celibate. That edict emerged from the Second Lateran Council in 1139 AD.

Some historians would later speculate that under the guise of emulating Jesus—who was reportedly unmarried by the Church's accepted accounts—the real and *unpublished* purpose and benefit to the institution by having an unmarried clergy or legitimate heirs, would be that property and wealth of a priest would not pass to those rightful descendants upon their death, but to the coffers of the Church.

Though, that ban on marriage would streamline financial succession, the edict of celibacy that went along with it would regrettably not reform *personal behaviors* in some segments of the priesthood. Especially during the scandalous period for the Church in the 10th Century and again during the 15th and 16th Centuries, there were a series of Pontiff's who were accused of what might be coined *extra-clerical* affairs with men and/or women during their papacies—some producing illegitimate offspring.

Chapter Twenty-One

The Week Prior to Sister Janina's Disappearance, Monday, 19 August 1907

There was a knock at the Rectory office door.

"Come!" The Pastor called.

Andrew's friend of twelve years, Robert, took off his hat and entered the room. He had a grim look on his face and stood quietly until the priest offered him a seat.

"No, this should not take very long." Robert stated flatly.

"The priest was suddenly awash with a sense of déjà vu. Robert shared the same feeling.

"Father—my friend, Andrew." Robert, began. "I am again *torn* to be here with the same problem we discussed several months back."

Andrew said nothing. He brought his hands to his mouth—palms together—his index fingers to his lips as if praying.

Robert proceeded. "I have just been informed by whom I consider to be an unimpeachable source that you and—forgive me—Sister Janina have been seen together. And per them, it was overheard that you and she—have—forgive me." He took a deep breath and blew it out forcefully. "Have been *intimate*."

"Who would say that?" Father Andrew blustered. "Who would know that?" The priest was flushed with embarrassment. Thoughts raced through his mind. *Someone had to be eavesdropping on our conversation last night. It had to be either Stella or perhaps a chore boy. Either could be around the church—or more likely IN the church at that time of night— lurking near the open windows closest to the oak grove. Though, Stella would be the only one to qualify as an* **unimpeachable source**.

"We have had this discussion before." Robert spoke in terse terms. "I wouldn't think that after the last time, I would have to be here in this office *again* discussing the same thing, Andrew—Father! Perhaps I should just refer the matter to the Bishop. They're the legal authority for this kind of stuff. It really shouldn't be my concern. I'm your colleague. I should've never gotten involved. I should've told the wife, NO!"

Mention of *the Bishop* made Andrew's blood run cold and he faltered. "R-Robert—old friend." The priest quickly regained his composure. "I appreciate your concern and also the fact that you came to me directly to confront the issue rather than the Bishop. There's no reason to involve him."

"I suppose you're right." Reluctantly agreed Robert.

Andrew spoke in measured breaths. "I can assure you, that what you heard from your *unimpeachable witness* was the misguided fantasies of a person with a deep streak of jealousy. That *person* suffers from delusions going back to when I first came here to Isadore! That old woman has a fascination with me." He began to lecture. "It is not uncommon for lonely old women in a church to attach themselves in a fantasy of romanticism to the pastor or a priest." Andrew quickly turned the tables on the discussion. "Or even someone like you—a man in the Knights of Columbus. A man in *uniform*, Robert! You know what I mean."

Unfortunately, Robert did. He, and not to mention his wife, had seen the fawning of certain women of the parish toward *him* because of the trappings of his group of Knights and it's official uniform, with its plumed chapeau, cape, and ceremonial sword worn on formal occasions.

"It is common human behavior." Maintained Andrew. "It comes with the territory Bob! But I'm glad you came to me first before discussing this with anyone else. You have not done that have you?"

"Well, just the wife." Robert assured. "I find the accusations too sordid to mention to anyone else—just to her *in the privacy of our marriage,* Andy."

"Just like the *Confessional!* Good." The priest verified with an unnecessary comparison. "Does my explanation make sense?"

Robert took a deep breath and contemplated for a moment before answering. "Yes. Yes it does." He reluctantly agreed—although less enthusiastically in light of the fact that this was the second version of his previous discussion with the Pastor. "In context of the comparison, yes it does. But I'm sure you realize that I thought I needed to come to you when the accusation surfaced. Just locking it away—the accusations—the evidence—chucking it in a drawer somewhere to ignore it is not the way I handle anything."

A shiver ran up Father Andrew's spine at his friend's coincidental but also intuitive mention of a *drawer.* If Robert disdained the locking of things away in a drawer as his way of handling problems, it was the exact opposite for Father Andrew. He instinctively glanced down to his locked desk drawer which secured many of the Parish's files regarding the church's most sensitive issues and his notes regarding all of them. That included the contemporaneous ones regarding his own personal issues. "I agree with you. I do too." Andrew stated in a complete falsehood.

At that moment he thought to immediately retrieve any of the mentions of him that were stored in the drawer and set them ablaze to destroy the paper trail. But he knew that it was a futile effort. Based on his earlier phone conversation with the Bishop, even though no official reprimand had been issued or disciplinary action had been taken against him, odds were that an official incident report regarding his suspected inappropriate relationship with Stella had been created and was on file somewhere. He shuddered at the thought.

Andrew had long ago accepted the fact that the Institution's historical penchant for bureaucratic documentation and efficient distribution within had already included him. The name of Pastor Andrew Bieniawski would live in perpetuity in an unflattering way in either the Bishop's Diocese office in Grand Rapids, or even somewhere higher up. He again cringed. So, what would be the point of destroying his own notes? For the foreseeable, they would remain locked away in his desk.

"Robert, I'm glad you came to me with your concerns, my friend." Andrew calmly belied the undercurrent of anxiety running through him. "Speaking of *drawers*, I still have another bottle of Starka." He said as he started to retrieve the key from around his neck to unlock the desk drawer. "Have not had a drink of it since the last time we…*chatted*. Shall I?"

"No. I came in here hot under the collar and could *use* a stiff drink—but no!" Robert sharply declined.

The priest chuckled—still trying to soften his friend's mood. "Robert, it's been awhile since we went fishing. Whadya say? Get away from the pressures of the day-to-day, and spend an afternoon on the water? Good conversation! Enjoy the creation of our Lord? I hear the perch—*the big ones*—are starting to bite at dusk on south Carp Lake near the mouth of the inlet creek.

The idea appealed to Robert initially, but then was tempered. "Um, yes. Well…Hmm. I suppose. Maybe Friday afternoon. I already have my boat waiting at the launch."

"I'll have a chore boy drive me and whomever else wants to go. See you then." Andrew cheerfully said. He leaned forward and quickly penciled the event onto his desk calendar before Robert had a chance to change his mind.

His business over and *tentatively* satisfied with the Pastor's answers, Robert rose from the chair, bid the Father a good afternoon, and left the Rectory. The firm click of the door latch signaled the end of Andrew's passive strategy for dealing with his growing *problem*. His strategy would now have to become an active one. Unfortunately, and *sinfully*, it would be one that would only be comprised of options available within the darker choices before him.

Andrew leaned back—his elbows on the arms of his chair, palms of his hands together—his index fingers placed to his pursed lips—not to pray this time, but to plan.

The priest fully understood that he had pushed his personal conduct to the limits of acceptable behavior. He had given himself—like the old axiom says, *just enough rope to hang himself*. Now, in his mind, he had no choice but to unravel that rope and render it threadbare and useless. Going forward, Andrew would reorder his previous considerate, balanced, and proper thoughts concerning the welfare of Sister Janina, to a distant second place of importance to him. Rising to the forefront, would now be his own greater ambitions—ones that would be in complete alignment with the historical edicts of the overall preservation of the Church. That would be his physical reaction to address his *problem*.

As far as his guilty conscience was concerned, that was another matter. At some point, as a requirement for his continued participation in the Faith, Andrew would seek a *veneer of forgiveness* and a *limited absolution*. Those would be sought by him for what he had already done and for what he was about to do. In the false belief that by receiving the Sacrament of Penance, it would deflect the blame away from his own free will as being the major influence of his poor choices, seeking formal confession for him would allow him to assign blame for his deeds to that of his Faith's more plausible and traditional nemesis—Satan.

Chapter Twenty-Two

Holy Rosary Parish, Tuesday, 20 August 1907

Early that morning, Pastor Andrew tried to be in the vicinity of the nun's quarters at the back door of the school building, waiting for Sister Janina to exit. He paced back and forth for nearly twenty minutes. "Good morning Sister." He addressed her in a formal tone when she finally appeared.

Deep in anguished thought, Janina was surprised by his presence in the twilight of the early dawn. Regaining her composure, the nun acknowledged his greeting and forced a smile. "Good morning, Andrew..." She rephrased. "...Monsignor."

"Sister." He said in an unemotional and loud enough voice to appear completely appropriate in case either of the other two nuns exited the building while they stood there. "You look detached."

Janina did not respond, and the priest hurried through the rest of what he was there to say. "This Thursday afternoon—*late*, meet me in my office at the rectory. I would like to discuss with you *your 'situation'* and let you know of my decision."

Sister Janina was still mostly numb and introspective from the events of Sunday evening and agreed without putting much thought to it. "Yes, Father." Andrew would not speak to her again until the Thursday appointment.

The next morning, Wednesday, Andrew had planned to leave the parish on a last-minute trip. His ruse was described to the parish volunteer secretary as a *consultation* with an old friend—a priest assigned to the Milwaukee Archdiocese. It was in fact, to address his astute *premonition of oncoming guilt* that hatched the previous night in his convoluted mind. As a man with *some* sense of remorse for what were his past and what would be his future actions, in essence, he was making this trip to seek *absolution **before** the sin* in a formal Confession and be afforded the protection of the important *secrecy clause* of the Sacrament. He had specifically chosen the Milwaukee Diocese for both as they had precedent in dealing with Andrew's type of *problem*.

To make his journey to Wisconsin quicker, rather than travel by train downstate through Chicago and up to Milwaukee—which would take at least a couple days, Andrew used his considerable Grand Rapids Diocese business connections to book passage across Lake Michigan on a ship.

Mainly used for freight commodities, the wooden Flint and Pere Marquette #1 anchored in Ludington, traveled round-trip nearly every day to Milwaukee and back. His lake excursion would be a short one. He would be back in time for his scheduled appointment on Thursday with Janina and his fishing trip to Carp Lake on Friday afternoon.

Unfortunately, late Tuesday afternoon, word came to Andrew from the parish volunteer secretary that the freight master of the F&PM #1 had called to tell him that his reservation aboard the ship had been unavoidably cancelled.

"Why?" questioned Andrew.

"They provided no *official* reason." The secretary said. "But he confidentially let me in on the reason. The Bishop's Office in Grand Rapids had contacted the parent company soon after you booked passage and requested the cancellation."

Andrew was now sure that the rumored details of his *situation* had leaked. "Robert!" He surmised in a huff. "Maybe Stella. I doubt if any chore boy would think to contact the Bishop."

Despite the complication, Andrew forged ahead with the immediate likelihoods of his scheming. He determined that he would seek absolution *after the fact—someday.* "That's the traditional way the whole *sin-forgiveness* thing has always been done anyway." He justified in a forlorn fashion. "I sometimes wish this need for confession, absolution and forgiveness wasn't so ingrained in the Faith. I'm a slave to it, just like everyone else in Isadore—in Holy Rosary."

With a deep breath, Andrew further rationalized. "I think a rescheduled trip across the lake at a later date is in order—when things have calmed down. It's only a minor disruption. It'll be ok—for me. After all, the Archdiocese across the big lake has a track record on something like this…Well, maybe not *everything* like this."

Chapter Twenty-Three

Historical Perspective: A Priest's Dual Life, State of Wisconsin

Milwaukee Daily Free Democrat News, circa 1856

"The Most Reverend Archbishop, John Martin Henni, announces that Fr. Canoni de Vivaldi would leave his assignment as spiritual mentor on the reservation of the Winnebago Nation for an extended leave of absence from the priesthood and then be scheduled for reassignment."

By historical account, the Archdiocese of Milwaukee had previous experience in dealing with a priest with designs on the women of the Faith. Its own charismatic cleric, Rev. Canoni de Vivaldi, surprisingly left the priesthood and then the Church altogether to marry a Protestant woman around the time of the run up to the American Civil War.

Then after decades, the much-traveled Vivaldi—feeling remorse—and under the requirements that he make a good Confession for his sins and be given absolution—was welcomed back into the Church, again as a priest. The caveat was that his assignment was to be the desolate areas of Patagonia on the southernmost part of the continent of South America.

Somehow though, in his old age, Vivaldi still found his way back to the United States to serve out the remainder of his days in the Milwaukee Archdiocese. Although, that was in a small parish on the quiet prairie of western Minnesota.

Chapter Twenty-Four

Holy Rosary Parish, Rectory Office, Thursday Evening, 22 August 1907

Definition of Interpolation:
"The insertion of something of a different nature into something else."

Pastor Andrew sat at the desk in his office—impatiently waiting. There was a light *tap, tap* at his door. He had sent word to the convent earlier that morning as a not-so-subtle reminder to Sister Janina that he wanted to see her before she retired for the night. It was critical that he speak to her, to build his resolve to carry out his nefarious plan.

"Come!" The Pastor called out.

Sister Janina, eyes lowered, slowly entered the office, and stood before Andrew. After wrestling with what to do over the last several sleepless nights, she knew there was no choice but to tell Andrew what she had felt in her womb at the end of their private conversation outside the church.

Janina knew her intuition would rock the Pastor to his core. It would complicate everything in their relationship—even more than the priest-nun disgrace it already was—but he had to know. She never imagined he would be anything but supportive.

Janina began to speak but couldn't get the first word past her trembling lips. Andrew interrupted. "Sister Mary Janina, I'll get right to the point."

Janina was taken aback by him addressing her by her full *title* rather than by her first name, as he had done in every private setting since soon after she had arrived at Holy Rosary. His expression was unusual. His tone was surprisingly stern for someone with whom she had been intimate. It was cold and austere. He did not even invite her to sit. Everything about him was so unlike the tenderness he expressed to her just a few evenings earlier.

"I am concerned by your behavior with some of the laity." Father Andrew prefaced. "It has come to my attention that you have been seen—let's say—a little too *congenial* with some of the men of the parish—even with some of the visiting Jesuit Brothers." To Janina, he spoke as if he was some third-person observer—one who purposefully had left *him* out of the conversation.

"But Andrew? Um, Father?" Janina was totally confused by his demeanor. Was she here to mount a defense of the gossip the cleaning lady had been spreading about her? She was well aware that Stella had spied on her repeatedly and orchestrated a smear campaign of her reputation to show her displeasure of her. She knew it was just a matter of time before those ridiculous rumors would make it to the priest's desk. But surely Andrew her knew her better than to put any stock in her accusations—especially now amidst their *reciprocal* relationship.

"Andrew!" She interjected, still in confusion. "Yes, it is true I am friendly and always chat with many parishioners—both female and *male*. It is a daily occurrence. It is my nature, but strictly platonic—*unlike...*"

The priest interrupted her without giving her the opportunity to say the last word of her sentence—the word, *you*—which would have implicated him. "That is not what I hear. Perhaps it is best you address me as Monsignor or Pastor. To whom have you spoken of our *problem*?"

Janina's jaw dropped. "Andrew...Uh, Monsignor? Problem?" She replied—deeply hurt by the priest's insistence of formality and by use of the word *problem* for what should be *relationship*. "No one."

"Then why are these people coming to me with their *observances*— officials within the Church?"

Janina stumbled through a response. "There is no one!" Janina knew from where the *reports* emanated. "We both know of *the one* who has an axe to grind with me, and jealousy for me—for some reason." She explained— not knowing of Andrew's more intimate past with the other woman. She lowered her voice. "I am devoted to you. Have only *been* with you." She whispered. "Andrew, why do you accuse me of this after what we both feel—what we have been? After our talk the other night, I do not understand your change toward me." She whimpered as her tears welled.

Father Andrew forged ahead in his indictment without acknowledging the truth of her statement. Proceeding as coolly as if nothing had ever happened between them, he lectured. "I am disappointed Sister. The *reports* I have heard."

Reports? Janina thought. Andrew's uncaring response was like some parent scolding a child over a poor *report* card—which she had witnessed him do many times when reviewing underperforming male students. However, she was baffled that this attitude was coming from him and directed toward *her*. It was a complete contradiction to his normal caring nature that he had always shown before to any and all females. Now he was harshly treating her like one of the boys—like one of his *chore boys*— like one of his *grubi*.

To the astute Janina, she could see that Andrew was in the full throws of denial. Furthermore, she was convinced it was an *orchestrated* one. His repudiation of her felt like a carefully contrived show of bluster to now deny the existence of their relationship. She could see his narcissistic attempt to disavow his participation in it in the face of parish rumors. Shocked into silence, Janina could not bring herself to mention her suspected pregnancy. Not now!

The Pastor continued his critique. "Your accusers are not just some *rumor mongers*. They are individuals who believe in maintaining the overall strength of Holy Rosary and the Faith. They seek to keep the integrity of this parish above reproach in appearance as well as to help maintain the morality of our faithful. Not to mention, they are on constant vigil to rebuff those in the community who are critics of the Church—the ones who are anti-Catholic."

Then Andrew deftly borrowed a well-worn line of complaint from his housekeeper. "Your accusers fear you *have turned many a head away from God.*"

Sister Janina stood mortified by Father Andrew's disconnect from reality. Her mouth agape, the color drained from her unblemished cheeks. She was unsure if she had even taken a breath since he began cataloging his charges against her.

Andrew had no desire to listen to anything Janina might say—that is if she could have. The quivering nun was incapable of verbalizing anything.

Satisfied that his narcissistic ladened outburst had exonerated him in his confrontation with Janina, and that the exoneration was enough to last until he could get his required absolution through the Sacrament of Penance, Father Andrew excused Sister Janina. "Go! Attend to your duties, Sister." He dismissed her with a wave of his hand.

As Janina backed away, coincidentally, that wave of Andrew's hand caught a ray of the setting sun piercing through the office window. With a degree of prescience, the ray landed onto the gold ring that adorned the index finger of his right hand. The brief, narrow glint of that amber sunlight reflected off the large amethyst stone mounted in its center, and it refracted into Janina's eyes. If she had not already been entirely mortified by the previous interaction with Andrew, she might have taken note that this was the first time she had ever seen him wear the ring.

If Janina had the time to reflect, she would have recognized from her knowledge of the trappings and history of the Church, that a ring like his was only worn by a Pope, sometimes a Cardinal, infrequently by Bishops, and rarely by priests who had received special dispensation or granted special authority by higher-ups due to their favored status politically or due to connection to powerful families associated with the Vatican. This ring— especially as newly worn by Andrew—signified a complete change in his alliances—from what was that of a *parochial* approach to his *flock*, to that of a fealty to the powerful authority of the Church, its traditions, and rigid orchestration of their politics. It symbolically and perfectly explained Andrew's change of personality. But in Janina's present state of emotions, she did not make the connection.

Janina quickly turned and left the office—not pausing to even close the door behind her. She ran out of the rectory and across the parish grounds— her head bowed in contrite embarrassment. In utter anguish, tears trailed off her cheeks and gasps escaped from her mouth. She had abandoned her intention of telling Andrew about the potential of a baby—his baby, growing in her womb.

Chapter Twenty-Five

Historical Perspective: The Wearing of an Index Finger Ring in the Church

Wearing of an ornate ring on the index finger by monarchs of principalities and certain other heads of state, while forbidding it to be worn by anyone else, was a long-standing tradition to show who was the recognized leader. Often performed in the public forum, *kissing of the ring* was a ritual and reminder for all others to show deference to the individual who adorned it.

But occasionally, subordinates in the domain—usually those who were on the fast track politically, or with familial connections, sometimes also wore rings of this nature. For the most cases, those individuals did so with approval of the entities in power within the political structure.

Yet, the wearing of a ring was sometimes done so in passive defiance of the leadership rather than lodging an official complaint or confrontation— which could be financially or socially dangerous or even deadly. It showed the *wearer* to be an influential insider—though usually of a competing faction—and it served as a warning to other lesser members the aggressive application of their favored status. It also proclaimed their personal aspirations to move up within the organization. Specifically, in the organization of the Church, the usual aspiration of a ring wearer, was ultimately the Papacy.

Though, in practical matters, wearing a ring had limited successes in any reformation efforts. The smattering of abbots, bishops and priests who applied the ostentatious adornment to themselves—worn by them to show a kind of *Zealot* piety, were just as likely to wear them as a ruse to *imply* piety—much like a discreet wink of an eye.

Chapter Twenty-Six

Holy Rosary Parish, Isadore, Michigan, Friday, 23 August 1907, Early Afternoon

After her unsettling meeting the day before with Pastor Andrew, Janina existed in fog of disbelief. Although she was present at that morning's daily Mass, she "sleep-walked" through her morning duties with an ashen face and disheveled appearance. Her inattentiveness raised more harsh criticisms from the ever-observant jilted housekeeper.

"You are not much of a nun—or teacher!" Stella groused.

"Stella!" Admonished Sister Angelina. "Have mercy! Can't you see that Sister Janina is ill!"

Stella's confrontations with the non-reactionary Janina gave concern to Sisters Angelina and Josephine. They wondered if she might be having renewed health concerns with her chronic condition of tuberculosis.

"We can cover your duties. Why don't you rest." Angelina pleaded with her.

"We can ask Father Andrew to summon a doctor if you're not feeling well." Sister Josephine chimed in.

"No!" Janina briefly exited from her fog. She sternly warned both. "Do not bother him on my account—for *anything*." She demanded. "Besides, I have promised I would set up the decorations for the Bishop's visit this weekend." Then the tears that she had been able to hold at bay during her workdays while in public, now began to trickle down her cheeks. Pulling out a handkerchief—one that she always carried hidden in the sleeve of her habit—she brought the cloth to her face and dabbed at her eyes and nose just as a muffled sob of despair escaped through the white linen. She turned and aimlessly walked away—not responding when the Sisters called after her.

Although unresponsive to anyone as she retrieved the decorations from the church cellar, Janina's ears continued to "burn" through the stifling afternoon from the increased idle gossip being spread about by Stella to anyone who would listen.

"I have no use for Sister Janina." Stella complained. "She is frivolous, scatter brained, and I believe she has…" Stella crafted her criticism to make her contention less graphic. "The Sister has *turned the head* of the Pastor." Then without evidence, she also included more accusations for those who would find that indictment to be unbelievable. "And most likely she has turned the heads of the other fine men in this parish—like your husbands and sweethearts with her *ways*. Someone should do something about it." She jawed her demands.

"Sounds like you are jealous of their *friendship,* Stella!" That was the assessment of one of the other two cleaning women, as she stopped scrubbing the old wooden floor of the church sacristy to criticize her co-worker.

"Friendship?" Stella angrily responded. With her arms crossed defiantly and rapidly tapping her foot she pontificated. "If it were only that, I would *not* be! I tell you she has turned the head of our Father Andrew. And to what end? The scandal!" She scoffed in what many would say was a self-righteous, double standard of projection onto another. But then she paused for a moment—suddenly reliving her own scandal with the priest. However, her jealously overcame her hypocrisy and she continued. "That woman is no nun. This will ruin Holy Rosary unless something is done."

Chapter Twenty-Seven

Holy Rosary Parish, Isadore, Michigan, 23 August 1907, Later Afternoon

With some coaxing, Father Andrew was able to convince his younger sister, Susan, and according to some reports, but not the official ones, his housekeeper's daughter, Mary, to accompany him on a fishing trip that afternoon/evening to nearby Carp Lake.

Although conventional wisdom is that it was reported to be Ted Gruba, all accounts would later say that one of the *chore boys* was told by Andrew that he would be the driver to transport the group by horse cart up the sand two-track north of the parish, then along the narrow high ground skirting the marsh that led to the southwest end of the lake. There they would meet Robert—Andrew's friend from the Knights of Columbus. He had agreed to go on the trip after his tense discussion with the priest that had occurred earlier in the week.

Robert kept his wooden rowboat near the mouth of Victoria Creek at the south landing of Carp Lake throughout the summer months. His skiff was large enough to comfortably hold four people without the fear of capsizing. But five? That seemed unlikely. The party would fish for yellow perch known to congregate in small schools in the *cabbage*—the seaweeds of late summer—clustered in about 10 to 15 feet of water on the southwest side of the lake. Near the shoreline, the boat would be protected from any westerly winds. However, on this humid August day, the lake was eerily absent of any noticeable breeze. It was an oppressive, stifling, and ominous atmosphere which perfectly matched Father Andrew's dark thoughts.

Near noon or 1pm, Father Andrew's party was ready to head out from the parish. The grounds of the church were quiet—with exception of the periodic rise and fall of the buzzing sounds emitted by thousands of cicadas in the oak trees. Sisters Angelina and Josephine were about to retire to their rooms for a nap per their usual schedule after their late lunches. Janina was scheduled to remove decorations from the church cellar in preparation of the Bishop's visit.

An hour or so prior to the trip, Andrew had instructed his chore boy to dig in the low ground on the border between a nearby standing corn field and an orchard next to a recently tilled field after its potato crop had been harvested. The area was now more of a swale—devoid of sod, where he was sure the boy would find a few dozen nightcrawlers to be used for bait. Not wanting any miscommunication, Andrew had painstakingly told the boy it was imperative for him to turn over a wide area of soil there— perhaps three by six feet—to dig deep past the late summer dry earth nearest the surface and down to the level of moist peat and sandy loam. As per usual, after the *chore* was completed, the *boy* had not washed his hands of the caked-on dirt. Father Andrew reminded him to do so before they left.

As the horse cart rumbled away from Holy Rosary, Andrew and driver were up front on the wooden bench seat and the two girls sat in the back of the flatbed. They balanced themselves on the rough trail, precariously perched on top of several planks of pine stacked on top of a rolled-up and heavily soiled canvas tarp.

To amuse themselves, the girls giggled and made faces at the driver behind his back. He either did not notice them making fun of him, or he did not let on that he knew. As he and his like were the frequent butt of jokes of not only children and adolescents, but several adults in town, he paid little mind to the chattering girls.

Father Andrew slightly cocked and turned his head and frowned to let the girls know he disapproved. He didn't want them to upset the fragile ego of the boy and risk him somehow not being able to concentrate on his duties that afternoon.

Upon reaching the end of the high ground of the trail before it descended to the lake, Andrew had the driver stop to let him and the girls out—not wanting to risk the rig going further down the sand trail to the landing and get stuck in the muck. He told him to be back near 7 pm to pick them up. To aid the boy, he gave him his pocket watch and told him which hand needed to be over the seven on the dial to indicate the pickup time. The boy put the watch in his pocket and turned the horse cart around and headed back.

Andrew shouted before he was out of sight. "Grubi, just do as I told you. It's all right there on the note I gave you."

Sliding down the steep terrain, and upon arriving at the boat landing, Father Andrew felt a rush of fearful adrenaline run through his veins. His friend was not waiting at the landing as he had said he would be.

Robert's wooden skiff was off to the side of the landing, turned over to prevent it from filling with rainwater. Andrew started to panic. *Well, if Bob doesn't get here soon, I'll just—I'll just have to take the girls out myself a few hours to catch fish—to get to dusk—to cover the needed time. No problem.* He thought. But yes, there was a problem.

Andrew lifted on the boat to turn it over and was met with resistance. He discovered that the heavy craft had a chain running through a hole in the breasthook at the bow. The chain was wrapped around a stout willow and secured with a keyed padlock to prevent theft. "Robert has the key." Andrew gasped and thought. *We can't just stand here for hours. That would be suspicious to the girls. They would talk. If we start walking back, we'll get there just in time for...*

Frantically, Andrew began to go over the details of his plan to see if he had an alternative. It was too late to call it off. They'd never be able to catch up with their cart. He wrestled with a myriad of implausible ideas for a minute before he thought of something. "Maybe—just maybe..." He said as he reached under the starboard side of the boat and felt under the breasthook. There, just like one would place an extra key to the house above the door frame, hidden on a tiny hook was Robert's spare key to the padlock.

"Well, we're starting a little late, but that's good." Andrew babbled to the girls. "We should be on the spot at just the right time. The perch bite is usually better toward dusk anyway. We'll just fish till dark, or we get a bucket full of fish—whichever comes first." He then let out a sigh of relief and wiped his brow. But now he was worried. He was sure that Robert had second thoughts about coming on the trip to spend collegial time with him.

Had he reconsidered and followed through on his first idea of turning the whole affair over to the Bishop's office? Andrew would never know for sure, as surprisingly, the two would never again speak to each other about the matter.

However, if he were a betting man, Andrew would've wagered that the lingering aura of scandal that would plague him for the rest of his life was because Robert had, in fact, relayed his suspicions up the chain of church hierarchy.

Chapter Twenty-Eight

Friday, 23 August 1907, Around 8pm. Beginning of Investigation

"Father, Father! Sister is missing!" One of the volunteer cleaning women shouted as she rushed Andrew's fishing party. The party, consisting of Andrew, his sister Susan, and the driver of the horse cart. Absent from the group, per most of the later accepted reports was Mary, the daughter of the housekeeper. In the confusion, no one noticed, but some would later question why she had not returned with the group. Others would, in retrospect, cast doubt that she had ever made the trip at all. Eventually that was the accepted story. The initial claims that she did not accompany the party were suspiciously said to be promoted by Stella.

"Janina is missing?" Andrew gushed his question in forced amazement. Then he repeated a corrected statement—realizing he had made a huge Freudian slip. "Sister is missing? *Which* sister?"

"Sister Janina!" The woman blurted out a string of the known facts. "We haven't seen her in hours. She's not in her room. The back door to the school building and the nun's quarters is unlocked. No one in town has seen her. She didn't tell anyone where she was going!"

In another *tell*, Andrew slowly turned to his driver to see if he had a reaction. He showed none. But the priest did observe that his hands were again caked with partially dried soil when he returned the priest's pocket watch to him. The silence of the volunteers now waiting for Andrew's response was only interrupted by occasional splashing of the perch the party had caught. Many were still alive in a bucket of water that sat on the flatbed of the horse cart. Andrew then turned back to the frantic woman who had now been joined by a rapidly growing contingent of concerned parishioners.

"Father, we should search the grounds—make a thorough search?" Someone offered.

"Yes, that's a good idea—before it get too dark." Andrew agreed.

Andrew instructed the chore boy who had dismounted from the horse cart but still held onto the horse's reins. "Grubi, go to the storage shed and get several oil lamps so we can search for Sister Janina."

The diminished young man blinked several times—obviously confused. He furrowed his brow and looked off back in the direction of the sand two-track from which they had just come. To Andrew, his puzzled look said; *we are now going back toward Carp Lake to find Sister? But why?* Andrew, seeing his confusion, redirected his order to him. To make him fully understand, he stood directly in front of the boy and held him steady by placing both of his hands on his shoulders and looked into his eyes.

"Get the oil lamps from the shed and bring *them here* so we can all see each other." Andrew spoke slowly. That slightly clarified the order for the boy. He bowed at the waist—confirming his understanding and led the horse cart away to the stable. Soon he brought back several oil lamps. He lit each and distributed them among the growing search party. He then receded from the glow of the lanterns to the outer edges of the group and melted into the darkness where he returned into his usual ignored existence.

As the night advanced, the group scattered and combed every building and thicket on the church grounds. Then they extended north to the church's Mount Calvary Cemetery. Returning to the parish well after midnight, Father Andrew met the dozen or so volunteer searchers in the oak grove next to the church. He raised his right leg and rested his muddy boot on the seat bench, folding his arms and resting his elbows on his raised knee. Then he realized that he was in the same pose—in the same spot as he had been when he and Sister Janina had their intimate discussion a few days earlier. Without looking up, he said. "Get some sleep everyone. We shall start out again at first light. This time we'll go deeper into the swamp."

"Um, Father, what about the property to the west—the corn field?" Someone in the group offered.

"Yes, I suppose that should be done too." Andrew agreed. "But I'll talk to the owner in the morning and have him get his migrants to comb the corn field, apple orchard and potato field for any sign—while they harvest." He added even though he knew the harvest of the potatoes had already been completed and the corn was at least another month or so before it would be ready to harvest. "They'll be able to cover more ground than us." He advised.

However, and later considered an important omission in the continued search, Father Andrew did *not* contact the owner of the orchard and tilled field adjacent to the parish as he said he would. In fact, the conventional wisdom was that little search effort was ever conducted on the *orchard portion* of the property—either by ordinary citizens or by law enforcement. It was a failure of the haphazard investigation.

"I think we should bring in a bloodhound from the Sheriff's Office." Someone suggested. "They have a team of them in Antrim County. They're trained to track down lost people."

"Oh, well, hmm." Andrew responded—seemingly caught off guard by the excellent suggestion. "Yes, that's another good idea." He agreed with a false enthusiasm. "With a bloodhound we'll be able to look more deeply into the swamp area or corn field with it. Those seem to be the more likely areas." Andrew directed.

Several in the search party would later wonder how Andrew had determined that the odds of finding Sister Janina in the swamp or corn field was greater than any other place. At this point of the investigation, Sister Janina could be anywhere. Though, at the time, several in the crowd nodded at the sound reasoning of the priest. Apparently, it was a mass assumption that those were the hot locations to look based on Andrew's assessment and authority in his normal supervisory capacity.

"And in the morning, we'll do another thorough search of the parish grounds to make sure there are *no signs*." Announced Andrew.

Again, many nodded, but one man who was on the scene as a volunteer to search, and who would later be one of the twelve chosen to serve on the jury for Stella Lipczynska's murder trial, thought it odd and suspicious the priest would phrase his thoughts in that way. Years later, reflecting on the events of that day, Juror #7 told his family that upon hearing Father Andrew's words, *"...to make sure that there are **no** signs,"* he remembered thinking it would have made more sense if the Pastor had said, *"...search to see if there are **any** signs!"*

"See you all in the morning. Let's all pray for Janina's—*Sister* Janina's safe return." Andrew again corrected himself.

The group folded their hands, bowed their heads, and waited for the priest to begin prayer. However, he did not. Oddly, the Pastor did not begin to recite any petition of prayer as one would think a priest would do in a situation like this. Leaving the group befuddled, Andrew simply turned away and walked directly to his quarters without further comment.

The search party—a bit confused—mumbled to each other. A few remained to initiate their own prayers and then they too drifted back to their homes.

Chapter Twenty-Nine

A First Cache of Questions

Pinconning Press, 19 September 1907 (Public Domain)

Who Can Solve Them

"Every effort is being made to solve four systeries (sic) which have agitated the Grand Traverse region, but no results have yet been obtained. The first of these is the missing nun from the Isadore convent. On Friday, August 23, Sister Mary disappeared while the priest in charge of the convent and church was out fishing."

Pere Cheney Messenger, 21 September 1907 (Public Domain)

To Solve a Mystery

"...no results have yet been determined for the missing nun of the Isadore convent. On Friday, 23 August, Sister Janina disappeared while the Pastor in charge of the Holy Rosary convent and church was out fishing. An alarm was issued, and much effort has been undertaken to find her. A detective was called in to search but only to give up. Tracks of the woman have been found in swamp and cornfield. A bloodhound was said to have found traces, but still

she is no where (sic) to be found. There for (sic) successfully eluding any of the several search parties. "

Saline Observer, 10 October 1907 (Public Domain)

Sister Mary Again

"That Sister Mary, the nun who disappeared from the Isadore convent August 23, voluntarily left the institution is the final conclusion in the case which has mystified upper Michigan for many weeks. Detectives have searched for her in Chicago, but the hunt has finally been given up and the sister will be permitted to pursue the course she has chosen. 'The sister has tired of her job. She is safe.' A letter containing these words was received by Fr. Bienowski, (sic) in charge of the convent where the nun lived for many years. It was written in a masculine hand and postmarked at Chicago. "

In the aftermath of the disappearance of Sister Janina, discrepancies in the accepted story have emerged that have never been properly explained. In no particular order, here are a discussion of many of them.

Law enforcement of Leelanau County spoke to the Pastor of Holy Rosary, but that was only days after the nun had disappeared and after at least one or more parish-led searches that had yielded no results. Why were authorities not alerted earlier? By most accounts, this led to a thoroughly uncoordinated search for the missing nun and may have been done so on purpose.

From the Preliminary Hearing for Stanislawa Lipcznyska, early 1919. Father Andrew testified.

"I call up John Nolan (Deputy Sherriff of Cedar) to come to the parish. And when I called him up, he says he will come and he did come, but he makes excuses. He says, after some time he says, he doesn't feel like putting in any more time, because he don't know where his pay will come from. "

"I offered a reward of $500 if anyone could find Sister. I brought

Father Andrew stated that on the day of Janina's disappearance, he had departed from Holy Rosary earlier in the afternoon on horse drawn cart driven by a *chore boy*. Which chore boy? The assumption was that it was the Sexton, Gruba. However, there appears to be confusion and questions regarding that chore boy's identity in official statements, court documents, later published stories, and per Andrew's own contemporaneous notes. The questions specifically regarding the *chore boy*, Gruba—*Theodore* Gruba, will be addressed later.

But, for the discussion of *chore boys*—in general, one has to consider that Father Andrew's template for identifying them was inexact. Historical analysis seems to show that there could have been more than one of them in or around the parish at various times. He routinely disregarded them beyond their worker status or made the effort to distinguish them by their individual names. Per his documented references to them, he often confused them with each other. Andrew's desk notes indicated that to him they were an interchangeable lot of *grubi*—the derogatory term. Most who fell into that category seemed to come from nearby St. Wenceslaus, the Bohemian-Czech, Suttons Bay Parish.

Also, with Andrew on his fishing trip, was reported to be his younger sister who lived in town. Curiously, this *Susan*, was hardly considered and barely mentioned in any investigations or beyond that of being a passenger that day.

In conflicting accounts, also accompanying Andrew on the fishing trip was the daughter of his housekeeper, Mary Lipczynska. Some later dismissed accounts say it was actually Stella and not her daughter that accompanied Father Andrew. Other accounts do not mention either Lipczynska taking the trip.

Accepted as fact was that someone in Father Andrew's fishing party recalled that Sister Janina had retired to her quarters on the second floor of the school for an afternoon nap about the time they were leaving the parish. Secondhand accounts from an unidentified witness later stated that they were told by the fishing party that at least one in the party had seen *someone*—presumably, Janina, draw the shades of her window as they drove away. Later, no one could verify which member of the party had made that statement.

Questioning the above aspect; How would someone remember such a small detail for the second or two it would take for it to happen and then assume it to be the nun? How could that be the sole piece of evidence that was used to establish that she was indeed in her room that afternoon? This uncorroborated detail was anything but definitive. Still in other conflicting accounts—later the accepted ones, say that Janina was seen in the vicinity of the church cellar retrieving decorations at the time of the party's departure. Though later, in testimony at the Preliminary Hearing for Stella, both Andrew and Mary Lipcznyska contradicted the above account by stating under oath that they had seen Janina and the other two nuns wave goodbye to the party as they left the parish from the porch of the Pastor's residence.

Andrew was reportedly scheduled to meet his friend Robert and possibly others at a southwestern boat landing of Carp Lake. Some reports say the party did not launch from that landing near Victoria Creek but at another popular landing at another location on the lake. One story says the fishing trip was to nearby Lime Lake. In fact, no one would ever attest to *seeing* the priest at any of the landings. We would later read in Andrew's contemporaneous desk notes, that Robert did not show up at the lake. Still other renditions of the events of that afternoon, never mention anyone named Robert or a friend of the Pastor's.

One rarely pursued conspiracy theory is that the person identified as Robert never really existed. The Pastor's friend with whom he confided was really someone else. To date unidentified, it has been alleged that the man had managed to be empaneled on the jury of the Lipczynska trial in 1919. Anecdotal comments after trial say that behind those closed doors, the man was the strongest advocate to convict when the sentiment among the jurors was that Father Andrew should've also been considered.

Another question arises. Was Gruba, or another chore boy—a *grubi*—also scheduled to fish with the others? As they were considered *workers* and not necessarily close friends, likely not. If not, then where was he or they during the time of the fishing trip? Who besides the priest could vouch for his or their whereabouts that afternoon? One would think perhaps Susan, but there is no record of her confirming that. In fact, as you will read later, during court proceedings in the Lipczynska case, even the priest had trouble identifying him or them.

In fact, for the entire timeline of the fishing trip, from Friday afternoon to evening, no one would come forward to disagree with any of the Priest's claims. Andrew's exemplary reputation would alone exclude him from any initial consideration in the disappearance of Janina. What he said would be taken as *Gospel.* This would later be seen as a sloppy failure of usual protocol for law enforcement investigators in the initial phases of the mystery.

Later, after Janina's disappearance, one of the other sisters with whom Janina shared the second floor of the school as living quarters, reported that the back door to the building—normally locked during the time of their afternoon naps, was left ajar. They had never recalled that ever happening before.

There were no signs of break-in at the school/convent residence. That evidentiary conclusion should have pointed the focus back to the large number of people who regularly frequented the parish grounds and would have access to the buildings. But why were the other sisters, the sexton-groundskeeper-chore boy or *boys*, the volunteers, the church guild, the ladies auxiliary, and the members of the Knights of Columbus not be more thoroughly questioned on this aspect? Surprisingly for most in those groups, they were never questioned at all. And for the lesser number of individuals known to possess a master key or individual keys to the various parish buildings, they also appear to have not been questioned. It seems after taking a count of known keys, none appeared to be missing. So, the focus of the investigation turned elsewhere.

So, who *did* leave the door unlocked and ajar? The accepted assumption of investigators was that it had to be Sister Janina. Though, that would always be dismissed as a too convenient explanation for the many discussions about the disappearance that were happening around the dinner tables of Isadore.

Additionally, there was no sign of any struggle in Janina's room or near it. That did not entirely exonerate some of the town drunks, passing vagrants or migrant workers—always an increased number of them around town during warmer months—from snatching her. At first thought a plausible theory, the few interrogations that did take place with the *usual suspects* rounded up when crimes of break-ins or burglary happened, provided no leads.

The investigation then offered another theory. Sister Janina, knowing her condition and being despondent, decided she would take advantage of the priest being gone, and slip away from Holy Rosary. One conspiracy theory was that she walked away from the parish, but an unscrupulous person who lived nearby abducted her, killed her, and buried her on adjoining property—perhaps in a barn. This was followed with letters to the parish—suspected to be written by the real killer, urging Father Andrew to abandon his search. The tale continues that only years later, after the case was considered cold, the murderer returned Janina's remains to the easily accessible church basement.

Per reports of several parishioners, the night of Sister's disappearance, Pastor Andrew immediately organized and headed a search party comprised of concerned citizens to thoroughly cover the grounds, surrounding parcels, the cemetery, and nearby outskirts of woods and swampland. Reports were that it revealed no evidence from initial searches. But was that true?

One rumor at the time, but never verified, was that early-on someone recovered portions of a garment—thought to be part of the nun's brown woolen habit from either low ground adjacent to the trail to the lake, or perhaps from the low grounds on the edges of an orchard that had recently disturbed soil. Another was that a pair of muddy shoes—women's shoes—were retrieved from the edge of the swamp. Neither of those taken as evidence were ever positively identified as having belonged to Janina but thought to be similar to what she may have worn. Despite the uncertainty, they were used for scent identification when bloodhounds were brought in for two searches.

Neither of those searches led by the canines revealed positive results. However, in one recollection, the bloodhound(s) found no trace of Janina in the area near the basement entrance of the church. That conclusion was offered by Father Andrew and never challenged. Another unidentified witness claimed that the dogs were kept away from the entrance of the basement and instead directed to search in a nearby corn field.

It is important to note: Per Father Andrew's testimony at the Preliminary Hearing, he states that he and *"the boy"* searched the church cellar.

As the fear of a simple disappearance slowly turned into a potential crime, additional law enforcement investigators from Grand Traverse County were finally brought in to expand the search. Father Andrew was also able to gather around 300-400 volunteers from the community for a search. Those effort also surprisingly found nothing to provide a solid lead.

At this point in the investigation, the process began to change from one of following plausible theories to one of exploring the implausible.

Cheboygan Democrat, 4 October 1907 (Public Domain)

"Miss Francis Elmina Cox, the dramatic reader and desciple (sic) of Browning, who was recently here, was detained by the Frankfort police for 24 hours, because they suspected her of being the nun Sister Mary, of Isadore convent. The Priest had to go and swear she was not nun wanted. "How can you expect a country constable to differentiate between an enthusiastic desciple (sic) of Browning and a distracted Polish nun, anyway." Father Andrew was quoted as saying.

Some men of the town reported that for several nights immediately after Janina vanished, they *might* have heard the voice of a woman singing religious songs in the swamp, but they were superstitiously afraid to investigate. That nonsense was quickly dismissed as unsubstantiated fantasy—likely concocted on the bar stools at a favorite local pub. Still, no renewed probing of the swampland was initiated after the report.

As news of the disappearance spread, an array of psychics, mystics and some described as *crazies* descended upon Isadore. The entourage produced a series of outlandish theories and worked to slow down and eventually stop the legitimate investigations. Authorities felt that if the saga had reached this stage, then their time and efforts were going to be wasted.

Then a few weeks after the disappearance, it has been reported that one or more anonymous letters circulated in the community—all claiming to be from Janina or those that knew of her whereabouts. Their uneducated prose said things like. *"I'm doin' good and no body should worry."* One stated, *"I'm fed up and left to return home to Chicago to get married."* And *"I left the sisters cuz I was tired of bein a nun."*

These letters were dismissed at the onset because, after all, Janina was an excellent English teacher. The atrocious grammar sounded like nothing she would ever compose. And many would question the motives for someone sending letters of this nature. Were they sent to halt the active investigation? Was it a prank? There was much anti-Catholic sentiment in the surrounding areas and throughout northern Michigan as a whole. It could have easily been someone of that thinking to do such a thing for their own amusements and to assign ridicule. The most famous letter coming into Isadore may have come from someone of that mindset. The letter that said, *"Give up lookin'"* was signed, *A Protestant Pup*. Overall, the reasons for the letters have never been satisfactorily explained.

There was also the publicized out-of-town excursions Father Andrew reportedly made in order to find clues. The Pastor stated that he had made inquiry in both Detroit and Chicago areas to see if anyone had seen the nun. Later at the Lipczynska trial, he testified that his outreach had included Janina's living relatives. He claims to have written letters to the Mezek brothers to see if they might know the whereabouts of their sibling, the former Josephine Mezek. Oddly, both stated that they never received any letters and that no one ever contacted them to discuss their sister. This would later raise serious questions as to the veracity of Andrew's efforts and that of law enforcement investigators as well.

The Northern Clarion, 29 August 1907. (Public Domain)

Mystery of Nun

"...At this time, she is about 33 years old and most say she has had little contact with the world outside of convent and quite naive. (sic) The rumored idea of any love affair for her is preposterous per the Diocese in Grand Rapids and the priest in charge of the church in Isadore."

Pinconning Press, 12 Sept 1907 (Public Domain)

Leave The Convent

"Filled with an indefinable fear that that (sic) mysterious something which caused the disappearance of Sister Mary John, the nun, from the convent at Isadore, nearly two weeks ago, would work to harm them, the two remaining sisters at the convent have left."

At the height of fear and confusion in Isadore, both Sister Josephine and Angelina announced they would leave Holy Rosary out of fear that Sister Janina's fate could also be their's. This left the parish and school in chaos. Amid their decision, within two or three months after the disappearance, the head of the Felician Order of Livonia came to Isadore to see things for herself. It was reported that Sister Regina found a pair of damaged steel-rimmed glasses buried in the dirt near the entrance of the church cellar. They were thought to be the same kind as Janina wore. In other conflicting accounts, it was two or three *years* later that the glasses were found.

Later at Stella's trial, Sister Regina would testify that she immediate brought the discovery of the glasses to the attention of Father Andrew and that he took possession of them. In rebuttal, Andrew would refute Sister Regina's testimony of ever receiving the glasses. After weeks of sporadic searching with no true leads after Janina's disappearance, under guidance of the Felician Order of Livonia, they officially listed Sister Janina as missing and *presumed* dead.

A memorial Mass was scheduled for the repose of her soul at Holy Rosary, officiated by Father Andrew. Most of the town—including a large number of non-Catholics packed the old wooden structure. Many observers—especially the members of the parish who were close to Sister Janina, commented that the Mass and especially the Homily, which would eulogize her, was especially devoid of fond personal remembrances or emotion expressed by Father Andrew. They commented that the ceremony was pitiful for someone whom the entire town regarded so highly and loved.

After the Mass, rumors persisted, as one might think. Going forward, talk of any new leads or theories were quickly dismissed as hearsay. In Isadore, the issue became the town's embarrassment and inappropriate to discuss in polite society. But privately, lingering questions remained.

The community was angry that the mystery had now ground to a halt—becoming what everyone feared—an open-ended tragedy. Any new community discussions—usually between patrons at the local pubs, would raise serious questions of thoroughness on the part of law enforcement.

It was a gut-feeling of a large number of parishioners of Holy Rosary and residents of Isadore, that it was almost as if law enforcement had high suspicions of who might have been involved, based on rampant gossip that pointed to the top. But they shied away from those conclusions and worked feverishly to try to find another plausible explanation that would satisfy the community's curiosity. That effort spectacularly failed.

Many residents thought the investigator's quick dismissals of consideration for those few suspects, was based on thinly veneered exculpatory facts, and worse, personal friendships or their associations with the Church. Folks uniformly accused the authorities of either corruption or incompetence.

Thus, the conventional wisdoms in Isadore began to be what many of the more astute of the community considered to be *wrongly accepted facts* in the case.

Finally, where was Stella during the critical hours of 23 August? As a generally anonymous individual most days, no one could pin down the times when or if she were on the grounds or inside any of the buildings on the day Janina disappeared. No one would ever come forward to offer explanations with any amount of conviction.

Chapter Thirty

A Few Weeks After the Disappearance of Sister Janina, Sept-October 1907

A Flawed Confession for Both Priest and Penitent

Historical Perspective: The Sacrament of Penance—The Tradition of Vatican Expectations.

The Church maintains that conversation between a priest and a penitent in the process of the Sacrament of Penance is confidential and revealing it to anyone is prohibited in every circumstance. A priest violating that protocol is subject to automatic excommunication. The penalty is also applicable when a priest hears the confession of another member of the clergy. It is subject to scholarly debate whether a penitent in the process of confession is held to the same restrictions and whether they can divulge what they might have learned from a priest during the process.

"…And now she is gone! I drove her away with my words." The woman in the confessional box wept as she spoke in anguish in a thick Polish accent.

"Yes, she is *gone!*" Father Andrew reiterated the technically correct, but not completely accurate description of Sister Janina's whereabouts. He did so also in Polish.

"I fear I will burn in Hell for my transgression—my *words* against her and…" Stella would not finish her sentence. "I cannot help but believe that I have eternal guilt. I had viciously spread rumors regarding her—and *you*…and…" Again, the distraught woman failed to use words that would acknowledge full responsibility. Though, with the mentioning of the priest, it drew Andrew into the Sacrament's mechanism and parameters. He was alarmed and concerned by that but would try to shape the process in his favor. He peeked out his confessional cubicle door to see if anyone else was in church and were near enough to hear.

"I am filled with sorrow, Monsignor!" Stella was inconsolable.

"Now you mustn't blame *anyone*." The priest whispered, then paused, not only for effect, but to confuse who the guilty party was in this Confessional space. *Was it her or him?* He thought. *Does this alter the dynamics of this application of the Sacrament of Penance from me giving absolution and forgiveness to Stella or does it now include it for me as well? Can I give absolution for both of us?* He mulled the possibilities. Then in a linguistically and meticulous way he proceeded to craft his words to limit his exposure of guilt and not make any verbal admission to the woman.

"I'm sure there are other *factors* at play that are not yet discovered." Andrew continued. "There are probably ones that you may never know about regarding her *disappearance*." He omitted incriminating additional information and supplanted certain words with others that would obfuscate the truth. "The *Church* may never be able to reveal the ultimate truth." He authoritatively told the woman.

"Stella." Father Andrew then spoke as a friend using carefully selected words that skirted along the edges of truth. "Sister Janina would be the first to tell us that in some ways her own actions led to her *disappearance*. You've been known to observe it as well." He reminded the tearful woman. "You've pointed it out to others."

"Yes, and I am sorry!" Bawled the woman.

But it takes two to dance! Andrew thought of the trite phrase. *One, being Janina, and **two**, being **me**.* Though, he held that thought to himself.

The old woman listened in confusion but said nothing as the priest spoke in mild condemnation of her. "You are guilty of violating the Ninth Commandment: Thou shalt not bear false witness against thy neighbor.

Sister Janina, on the other hand, is possibly guilty of *impure*...pardon me, that is*, improper* thoughts and actions." The priest had just uttered a *Freudian slip* of self-incriminating verbiage by bringing up the subject of *impurity*. The mention of the word caused his voice to purr in unsuppressed arousal. It made him wonder. *Where did that inflection come from? It must be Satan!* He thought. Then he remembered his private times with both the confessing woman before him and even more so with Sister Janina. He tried to correct his preface to provide some acknowledgment of his own actions. "We are *all* responsible for what we have done." He said to Stella.

If one were to analyze Andrew's *epilogue-of-sorts* expressed to the woman before he gave absolution, it could be described as a convoluted, denying, *third-person* condemnation of his *own* actions. All of it was utterly confusing to the woman in the confessional box. He struggled to continue. "The *impure—improper* thoughts and actions are the kinds that cast the *late*—that is *missing* Sister in an *impure* light—I mean *improper* light and cause death...of the *soul*." He struggled with clarity in a sentence that was fraught with what one could call more self-confession-able verbiage—another "tell." Stella remained silent and unsure of the course that her Sacrament of Penance had just taken. "Do you understand, Stella?" Andrew summarized.

"Yes, Father." She replied. But clearly she did not.

"And I should advise you that you have my word as a friend and consistent with my vows of a priest that what has been said by me and *you* in our conversation in the confessional is only between you, me...*and God*." Andrew's voice grew serious to make the maximum impression to the woman. "There can be no revelation of our words outside the Confessional, or we are subject to Excommunication.

The seriousness of the explanation of the consequences caused the old woman to shudder. For the remainder of her life, she would never reveal any of her involvement or knowledge of the mystery of the missing nun to anyone *outside* of the Sacrament of Penance.

Chapter Thirty-One

Holy Rosary Parish Grounds, October-November 1907

Missing Sister Mary Search Called Off

"Sister Mary Johns or Janina, that nun who disappeared from the Isadore convent and school on 23 August has voluntarily left the Church. That is the official conclusion in the case that has baffled upper Michigan for many weeks. Law detectives have searched for her in the surrounding areas and even near Chicago where she was born, but the hunt for her has finally been halted. The nun will be allowed to follow the new life she has pursued."

"I'm sorry, I have to tell you something you will find troubling." Father Andrew prefaced his bad news to his protégé and chore boy.

The young man looked at the priest. It was clear he did not fully comprehend.

"At the end of this month I will no longer be able to honor my commitment to you. Since the, um, unfortunate disappearance of Sister Janina, the parish is in turmoil. The other nuns have left. Attendance at Mass has been down. The collection plate is empty. I'm not sure what to do…Well, that's none of your concern. It's beside the point." Andrew spoke in a flurry of confusion.

An initial wave of panic swept over the young man's face. This was a normal reaction by him to anything out of the ordinary—complex instructions, or when asked to perform a difficult task given to him by the Pastor. To brace him for what was coming next, Father Andrew reached out his left hand to hold the boy by the shoulder. He cupped his chin with his right hand to lift it upwards so he could look him straight in the eyes.

"I'm sorry." The priest tried to console. "I'm afraid I cannot continue to provide you a stipend from the church coffers or even one from my own resources—which have now been limited."

The boys diminished capacity showed when he heard the unfamiliar vocabulary of the priest. It was clear he did not comprehend in the least. "That is to say, I cannot keep giving you money." Andrew bluntly stated. "There will always be odd jobs like I have had you do in the past around the parish, but I cannot expect you to do those for free. And the shelter in the lower level of the convent or other buildings will be closed to you. Again, I am sorry—*so sorry*."

Andrew looked deeply into the young man's eyes for reaction. There was little thus far. "I know this is sudden to you, but I have known this was coming for the last few weeks. I am grateful for all the assistance you have provided me over the years—in *everything*." He emphasized with a knowing bob of his head and the rise of his eyebrows in a non-verbal way of impressing his point. "But I fear that my time at Holy Rosary could come to an end at any time, and I wanted to be fair to you with notice well in advance. What else am I to do?"

Still no discernable reaction could be gauged from the young man after hearing the news. Though, to Andrew, that was predictably expected from the socially and perhaps mentally inept individual whose first language was probably Czech. But soon, tears began to well in his eyes.

Andrew continued to explain the reasons in a futile attempt to soothe the young man's obvious anxiety. "Therefore, I cannot continue our *arrangement*—you remember our arrangement? The *secredito*?" Andrew used the Latin term to question him, and then moved to bolster the boy's now withered self-esteem. "You are still a young man—a strong young man. You have served me well. I hope I have trained you well. You will find work. I will pray for you."

Finally, the young man showed some kind of reaction other than tears. He bowed at the waist and nodded. But it was clear he was distressed at the avalanche of news.

Seeing that his words had penetrated the chore boy's pitiful veneer of ignorance, and had struck his core, the priest became more ebullient. "There is much work in the orchards and vineyards and logging camps! I have forwarded your name and reputation as a hard worker to some of the local orchardists. I'm sure if you contact them you will be able to find enough suitable work and shelter to sustain you. Here! I printed the name and addresses of the orchard owners—with my reference for you on the outside of this manila envelope. There are six dollars in it for you. It is all I have."

Then Andrew went on to meticulously instruct in the manner he did with most complex orders he gave the boy. It was done in a manner that the priest expected the boy to comply with his directives. "If you run into any confusion—on the back side of the envelope—see my handwritten note? It explains to whomever that you are applying for work with them. Show that to them—just to be clear." The boy looked down at the envelope as if he were waiting for it to speak out loud to him.

"Look, I've made arrangements. You'll be able to stay for the night in our old hunting cabin, just up the trail a few miles. You know where that is. It is near the landfill—the dump. The keys to the camp are above the door. It's my spare set. You'll find the key to the front door of the cabin on a ring with several others. They are ones to the parish buildings. It's an old bronze key—well, you'll be able to figure it out. Just put them back when you are done using the cabin. I'm sure no one will mind for the night—or even a day or two if you stay there." Andrew paused to make sure his explanation was clear. "And I have to ask you for your set of keys, *Grubi*." Andrew rephrased his offensive address. "I mean Gus."

"You *do* understand me?" Father Andrew waited for a response. He suddenly remembered how he had gone through this same arduous procedure of explanation and assurances the time he had sent him to pick up Sister Janina at the train station in Traverse City. Then he remembered when he had recently given him even more detailed instruction when he asked him to take care of his *problem*. With that memory, Andrew was hit with the full weight of what had transpired since that day in August. He shuddered and shook his head in disbelief of how he had let things go so wrong. The priest had run out of words and simply looked down at his *grubi*. Then tears welled in his own eyes.

Finally, the young man responded as he usually did, with another bow at the waist. But when he raised his head and reconnected eye contact with the priest, it was accompanied with a deeply furrowed brow and an ominous narrowing of his eyes.

Andrew stepped back in mild shock upon seeing this expression from his subordinate. Was it the first glimmer of anger? He could not be sure as he had never seen the boy with this look before. "God bless you, *grubi*—that is…" Andrew paused as he grasped for the boy's real name. *Gus? Or is it, Fred?* He thought. He then realized how insensitive he had been to not only this chore boy but others of the same ilk. *They have been all just a class of grubi to me.* The priest pondered while he made the Sign of the Cross over the boy. "As a last form of administering to your spiritual needs, I can hear your confession" He urged.

The boy turned and started walking away. Andrew misinterpreted his movement as heading to the church for receiving the Sacrament. "No, right here!" He shouted out. "No need to go to the confessional box. If you would care to, I can hear confession right here!"

However, the chore boy was not heading for the church. He was leaving the parish grounds. Looking back over his shoulder, glowering at the priest, his former benefactor and friend had just abandoned him. The boy forlornly shook his head at the priest for several seconds in what could best be described as *menacing dejection*. He turned away again and quickly strode away.

Father Andrew watched as he mounted the seat of his horse cart. After it rolled a few feet it stopped, and the boy quickly dismounted. He walked to a nearby tool shed, flung open the door and retrieved a filthy and worn green canvas tarp and a shovel from it. He tossed them onto the flatbed of the cart and remounted. Then he harshly slapped the reins and quickly drove away. Over his shoulder he again gave another frightful and uncharacteristic scowl at the priest before disappearing into the dusk, down the wooded, two-track that headed north out of town. It was the same two-track he drove while taking Father Andrew and his party to Carp Lake for his fishing trip that late Friday afternoon in August—the day Sister Janina disappeared.

Unsettled by the out-of-character show of what Andrew perceived as the boy's simmering vengeful demeanor, he worried, but then rationalized in a whispered peptalk to himself. " I don't know. He has always shown his fierce loyalty to me—over many years developed under my authority. Why would that change now—despite the bad news?" Andrew silently continued his thought. *He should be filled with gratitude for all the room and board I have provided him. I doubt that other nearby parishes would have done the same—even with his own kind. He won't do anything. Yeah, I'm pretty sure he won't."* Though a glimmer of doubt in the back of Andrew's mind would never be erased.

Andrew's concerns shifted momentarily. Focusing away from his trepidation concerning the boy, for the next several minutes in the fading sunlight of the day, Andrew remained in the church yard where he launched into an internal debate with his conscience. He attempted to convince himself that his original decisions and actions concerning Sister Janina were right for him to take. Though he also tried to soothe his onerous guilt. Having wrestled with it for the umpteenth time, he returned to the more present concern of what the chore boy might now do in the aftermath of him being sent away.

There was an uneasy feeling that settled in Andrew's heart. He had just severed the boy's only lifeline—his sustenance, his shelter, his way of life for the last several years. It was foolish of him to think that a simple letter of recommendation and a few dollars would suffice as a *parting gift* or be enough to satisfy his immediate needs. To think that his meager actions of recompense would somehow placate the boy—now former servant—who had now been set adrift, was naïve and a self-serving misunderstanding of the boy's fragile existence.

In addition, the insult of Andrew's *under*whelming financial compensation to the chore boy was only surpassed by his pathetic offer of absolution for him in the Sacrament of Penance. It reeked of shallowness. In retrospect, it was a wholly unsatisfying course of action or option to offer.

Andrew continued to theorize in the chill of the dark woods of Isadore— hoping for some other conclusion, but his summary was unsettling. And now it was also too late. His chore boy was long gone.

"A man will do what he has to when facing starvation." Andrew prophesized in a whisper. "I pray it is positive." Even when saying it aloud, he doubted his own optimism. Regretfully, he was sure there would have to be other considerations for his *grubi.*

The priest continued to stand in the church yard well past dark—long after the chore boy's horse cart had disappeared into the woods. The ominous atmosphere of the encroaching night fed into his worst thoughts. He spent another sleepless night as he contemplated his next action.

Andrew arrived late and disheveled at the next morning's early Mass. He had not slept well. However, when he walked out of the sacristy to begin Mass, he was slightly relieved to see the chore boy seated at the back of the church. Andrew theorized. *The boy also had the night to think over the situation. He probably has cooled off by now. It'll be fine.* He observed that the chore boy even dropped an envelope into the collection basket as the usher passed it front of him during the service. This was unusual as Andrew knew he had never made an offering like it before.

Terribly distracted from his priestly obligations of the Mass, Andrew continued to dwell on the boy's action. *I'm sure he is giving small alms for all the Grace he has received here at Holy Rosary.* The priest was proud of his protégé's giving nature. He figuratively patted himself on his back for the good job he had done in the catechism of the young man and grooming him into the Faith. However, he would soon find out that his evaluation of the boy's state of mind would turn out to be completely wrong.

During Communion, as was common, the attendees at the back of the church were the last to receive the Sacrament. In fact, the chore boy would be the last person to approach the communion rail. He kneeled and patiently waited as the priest moved down the line administering the Eucharist to the parishioners. When it was his turn to receive the Host, the altar boy placed the gold paten-communion plate under his chin, but the chore boy's eyes remained closed, and he did not react. The altar boy slightly tapped him on his Adams Apple with the paten—as he was taught—as a signal to the recipient to open his mouth and stick out his tongue. But even after being poked in the neck, the chore boy remained still. Andrew nodded to the altar boy to repeat the prompt, but this time after the jab, the young man opened his eyes and raised them to Father Andrew. His look was so fierce, both the priest and altar boy reacted by taking a step back.

With his hands folded, palms together in the position of the *Anjali Mudra* as in eastern religions, the chore boy raised his index finger on his right hand and pointed in an accusatory fashion at the priest. Still glowering at Andrew, he rose from the rail and turned away without receiving the Sacrament. Lacking any reverence, in a near run, he headed down the main aisle and exited through the narthex and out the main doors at back of the church—flinging them open with a bang as they slapped back against the frames. Nearly all of the sparse crown attending the early mass turned to watch the boy's dramatic exit and then in unison turned back to Father Andrew for his reaction. The priest—seriously shaken—could barely complete the rest of the Mass.

At the conclusion of the service, still fully clothed in his vestments, Andrew grabbed the collection basket and hurried back to the Rectory office. He locked the door and hunkered down in the chair behind his desk. Quickly rummaging through the envelopes, he retrieved the one that the boy had placed in it and tore it open. There, was the same six dollars that he had given him the night before along with Andrew's letter of recommendation. It was a defiant refusal to accept Andrew's terms of separation, if there ever was one.

Later that morning, after his heartrate had slowed, Andrew finally got up the courage to leave his office and ventured back over to the church. He gingerly descended the stairs of the sacristy, to the basement where the chore boy had sometimes resided when he had no other place to shelter. Grubi's things—spare though they were—were gone.

The priest looked around the space to see if he had left his set of parish keys, but they were not to be located. That worried Andrew. If they were still with him, he had access to every building—including the Rectory office and his personal quarters. *He could show up at any time to surprise—to exact revenge.* The thought chilled Andrew. *Maybe he left them in the tool shed.*

But then Andrew decided that it didn't matter. Even if he had left them somewhere at Holy Rosary, last night he had told the boy that another spare set was above the door of his hunting camp north of town. The entire situation had now become critical. He needed to *fix things* with the obviously angry young man. He must take the time out of his busy daily schedule to go to the hunting camp. He needed to use all his powers of persuasion to make sure there would be no future problems with his chore boy.

As Andrew made his way to the camp, he calculated. If he were able to locate the young man, Andrew would draw from his experience in counseling—controlling the situation—smoothing things over with him. Or, if he had to *figuratively* lean on him, he would use the full weight of his authority to bend the chore boy to his demands to eliminate any repercussions. He knew the boy had always succumbed to him in the past. Andrew summarized. *If grubi is vengeful, I am confident I can reason with him—make sure he is going to be ok with everything now and into the distant future. If not, well, I will have to deal with it as the situation develops.*

Chapter Thirty-Two

Considering the Housekeeper, circa 1914

There had been an approximate forty-year period of Polish-Catholic families leaving the Archdiocese of Milwaukee to migrate across Lake Michigan to northwestern Michigan and the Grand Rapids Diocese. Thus, many still had relatives in Wisconsin. One of them was the housekeeper of Holy Rosary at the time of Sister Janina's disappearance, Stella Lipczynska, who over the years had occasionally returned to the Milwaukee area for family reunions.

After Father Andrew left for his new assignment in Manistee in 1913, Stella was forced out as housekeeper at Holy Rosary by the new Pastor

Leo. He determined that she was unfit for the job. From there she moved back to Milwaukee, but then later returned to Michigan temporarily to set up housekeeping for Father Andrew in Manistee. Upon his urging, she then moved back permanently to serve the Pastor in the same capacity.

Living again in the Grand Rapids Diocese, Stella could see that the persistent rumor mill of the simmering scandal of Isadore had followed Father Andrew and her to his new assignment and she too was constantly under accusation.

As with most of her generation, as a devout Catholic whose eternal salvation was a lifelong ingrained priority, absolution for even the slightest of sins was sought on a regular basis to continually be in good Graces with her Lord. That was done through God's intermediaries—the priests. Stella believed, like most, that if God should call her *home* at any moment, with continual absolution, she would avoid an uncomfortable stay in *Purgatory* after death in her journey to Paradise.

At some point, during one of her trips back to Wisconsin, Stella must have felt the luxury of complete anonymity—or so she believed. Continuing to be deep in guilt—convinced her treatment of the nun had caused at a minimum her disappearance, or potentially because her actions had caused her death, she decided that it was time to unburden her soul a second and possibly a final time in her life for what she considered her sinful actions.

Although she had previously confessed with Father Andrew shortly after the disappearance had occurred, she came away from that experience feeling that the confession was more or less a counselling session for both. This time, for her, receiving the Sacrament of Penance would be an easier admission of her sins to a priest in a parish that did not know her and would not recognize her voice—as it would most likely be if she made confession in any parish in or near Manistee or Isadore. She naively miscalculated that the people of the State of Wisconsin and the Milwaukee Archdiocese was so far away, they had not heard of the tragedy.

On a Saturday afternoon, Stella knelt in the confessional box of St. Adalberts Church on the southside of Milwaukee to receive what she hoped was a dispassionate Sacrament of Penance. However, in doing so, she would initiate a years-long process that would eventually implicate her and convict her for the murder of Sister Janina.

The latticed screen slid open and without thinking, Stella began to speak a mixture of English and Polish in her thick accent.

"I'm sorry, please choose a language." Interrupted the priest, reported to be, Father Wenceslaus Kruzska. "Can you articulate in English?"

"No, I do not know how to *articulate*—only tell you my sin." Stella explained as best she could.

"Yes, that's what I want you to do. Let's start again." Encouraged the priest.

The woman calculated her response. "If I tell you, is this a secret? Will I be forgiven?"

"Yes, if you are truly sorry." The priest parsed her questions. "Yes, and this will be our secret."

"Tak—yes." Stella was satisfied with his response and began. "Bless me father for I have sinned. I am sad with guilt over the nun who vanished in my old church. Many years, I spread gossip about her and then she is gone. I told others she was having a romance with my friend. Told others that she was a bad nun and loose morals. Then she could not be found in Holy Rosary. Some are saying I caused her to leave the church…"

Father Kruzska at first yawned, but then his ears perked up at the description of the circumstances. He remembered hearing a story like this a few years back. The gossip surrounding it had readily traveled through the local Diocese and to his Archdiocese when it had occurred. Coincidentally, and shockingly, the confession of this woman had struck a nerve of painful embarrassment for *him*. His mind drifted away from the woman's plight to what was his as he sighed heavily and remembered.

Several years earlier, a parishioner in St. Adalberts had accused him of being intimate with a woman and fathering her illegitimate child. Upon the revelation to his superiors, he was suddenly transferred out of the Milwaukee Archdiocese for temporary assignment about eighty miles away in what he considered the backwoods area of Ripon, Wisconsin.

Although at the time he had vigorously denied being the father or straying from his vows of celibacy, there appeared to be record of him or someone on his behalf paying for maintenance of the child and mother—funds thought to be from the Archdiocese coffers.

Years later, Kruzska was still in the process of what he considered serving out his punishment as a transient assistant priest between Milwaukee and Ripon. Someday he hoped to be able to get back to Milwaukee and St Adalberts on a permanent basis. But on this Saturday afternoon, exhausted from yet another trip from Ripon back to the big city, he was completing his lengthy stretch in the Adalberts church's confessional box as an extra "ear," due to the crush of parishioners wanting to receive the Sacrament in advance of Easter.

"...Some are saying she is *dead* after all this time! If she is *dead* now, is that my sin, too?" Stella bawled in despair. The woman's sharp question drew Kruzska out of his memory.

"*Is* she in fact dead?" Asked Kruzska.

"Tak, I think so now. It was years ago that anyone has seen her. No one has heard from her—even her living relatives—her brothers. My friend told me so." Stella continued to leak details.

"Your friend?" The priest suspected the penitent was trying to obfuscate the truth. "Is that friend *you?*"

"No, a friend." Denied Stella.

"Who is your friend?" Kruzska insisted.

"I cannot say. He told me in confession—in Michigan."

"In *Confession?* Is he a priest?" Kruzska persisted.

"Tak...Yes." Stella finally admitted.

With the admission, Father Kruzska reconciled all the information. He remembered hearing the details of the tragedy across the lake. He even personally knew some of the players in that church scandal. There was a priest, a missing nun. a housekeeper, a parish groundskeeper. He even knew a couple of people in the local law enforcement and some in the Grand Rapids Diocese. Kruzska knew there were potentially others involved in knowledge of the tragedy. Would that point to a cover up?

At the time, he had dismissed the rumors of how the suspected priest had tried to arrange a cross-lake journey to Milwaukee to meet with someone in the Archdiocese but was denied by authority. The reason? For a confession? A possible transfer? *Well, good luck with that and getting a plum assignment!* Kruzska groused to himself. And now, based on what he was hearing in his confessional, he was sure *this* was the *housekeeper* in question.

"Then your friend should be here confessing, not you!" Advised the priest. "You cannot receive the Sacrament of Penance in his stead."

"What is *stead*?" the confused woman asked.

"For someone else! You cannot admit to sins committed by *someone else* or get forgiveness *for them*! What made you think you could do that?" The perplexed Kruzska demanded.

"From him." Stella sheepishly answered. This appeared as new information to the woman as she had been led to believe her previous confessional experience with Father Andrew had been a sort-of communal, bi-lateral absolution with her spiritual mentor. "But I have had it before. With Father—my friend."

Kruzska now had a crystal-clear picture of what was being presented to him. He was dismayed that this woman had been misled—that her previous confession had been flawed. To him it sounded like the confessor priest had orchestrated the Sacrament to confuse blame for his likely culpability in what could very well be a criminal act. "I do not know the complete circumstances of what you are confessing, but I think I know most of the details." He assured the woman.

A chill ran up Stella's spine. *On wie? He knows?* She thought. She remembered fearing that her sins might be shared with others in the church when Father Andrew had alluded to it in her earlier confession with him.

"I cannot absolve you of your sin." The priest flatly stated. "And I'm sorry, but your previous confession with *your friend* was compromised."

"What is compromised?" Stella asked.

"It was no good! Absolution and forgiveness was not truly given." The agitated priest barked.

Stella gasped and wailed before muffling her outburst into a handkerchief.

Father Kruzska raised his voice over the din of her crying. "Until you admit to *your* sin, what *you* have done, be sorry for *your* sin and complete penance for *your* sin, only then can I forgive you for *your* sin. But even before that, I must first confer with the Archbishop's office or at least Bishop Kozlowski.

"No, I don't want you to tell anyone else." Stella whined.

"I must!" Kruzska argued. "Meet me again next Saturday during confession hours and I will advise you of his decision."

"But what if I die during the next week?" The frightened woman bawled.

"We will *both* pray that you do not. Our Lord has compassion for those who have been led astray—a lost sheep. And I believe you have been by your friend. Try to stop crying. Listen! In the Bible, do you remember the parable about the lost sheep?"

"Tak." Stella croaked through her tears.

"Good! He—Our Savior will leave the flock to seek out a single lost sheep." Kruzska paraphrased. "You are like that lost sheep. I am sure He will be there for you if you happen to *pass* this week. But let's pray that does not happen. I will see you next Saturday." The priest heard a rustle, the confessional door opening and closing, followed by rapid footsteps away from the confessional across the tiled floor of St. Adalberts.

Not wanting to confirm the person's identity, although he was ninety-nine percent sure he knew who it was and trying to honor his vows of secrecy for the penitent, he remained in his cubicle for another few minutes to make sure the woman had left the church and to further pray for her and her *friend*. Then he said an additional prayer for himself, since the woman's circumstances of scandal were a little too similar to his own that still plagued *him* with guilt. *Perhaps I should get a confession for myself— just to be safe—just in case the Lord calls me home.* He thought.

But first things first. Father Kruzska *would* immediately get an appointment with his superior, the thorough Bishop Kozlowski, who would confer with his superior, the equally meticulous Archbishop Sebastian Messmer. He was sure The Most Reverend had already been apprised of the entire Michigan controversy. Kruzska reasoned, by being a diligent priest and providing full disclosure, even though it be old news to his superiors, it would keep *him* from being involved any deeper in *this* controversy. "I don't need another one." Kruzska murmured. Hopefully— eventually, Messmer would look favorably on his forthrightness, provide guidance, and authorize him via the Bishop to give absolution to the poor woman the next Saturday as he had promised.

Kruzska also knew that this new revelation would most likely prompt additional action by the Archbishop to manage the renewed controversy. He would be insulated from that, but Kruzska could wager that this suspected priest, Father Andrew, would be *required* to make that postponed cross-lake trip to the Milwaukee Archdiocese when he was "whistled for" regardless of travel conditions for an in-person *discussion* with His Excellency. His fate? The result would be a required *vacation* for the beleaguered priest—just as it had been for him when he was banished to Ripon for running afoul of doctrine and his vows.

Chapter Thirty-Three

Historical Perspective: Pope Pius X, circa 1914

It was an idyllic summer morning on the Apennine Peninsula. Unsteadily stepping out onto the balcony of his office in the Papal summer residence, the Pontiff, Pius X, could sense he was nearing the end of his Papacy. He looked out onto the pastoral beauty of the uniformly tilled grape vineyards in the valley below and breathed in the faint scent of the blossoming Fiori di zucca—the zucchini, that were planted in terra cotta pots on the veranda below him. For a few moments, he smiled and pleasantly listened to the buzzing honeybees that were visiting them.

As the Pope absorbed the splendid setting, he calculated that he was one of only a handful of men to have ever witnessed this scene as an occupier of the Papal Palace at Castel Gandolfo. By his count, there had been twenty-three. It had only been since the early 1600's, during the reign of Pope Urban VIII, when this current structure was commissioned to be built on land donated by the devout Gandolfo patriarch. Pius X had been fortunate enough to see a decade of such summer mornings during his reign.

In further reflection, he knew that fact offered him a particular amount of privilege and an unprecedented level of discretion in directing the largest institution of its kind. It also burdened him with its centuries of documented history.

Dwelling on the beauty, Pius also thought back to the beginning of his Pontificate. Upon his elevation to the head of the Holy See by the College of Cardinals in 1903, he remembered that day he had also stood unsteadily in the Room of Tears—just off the Sistine Chapel in the Vatican in Rome. He had been given the traditional alone time in that space—where all

Popes were allowed to fully comprehend their new godly responsibilities bestowed upon them by the tradition of Apostolic succession. During the time he would draw upon his predecessor's spiritual strength and to give him composure before he greeted the crowd from the window above the Vatican Square.

Pius was relieved that today's *mental* preparations of administration would not be nearly as frightening to him as that momentous first day. After all, he had now accumulated nearly eleven years of experience in his position. But the *physical* preparations this day would be similar to the ones that had occurred his first day as Pope and had every morning since.

With the utmost reverence, assistant priests helped him into his daily vestments adorned with a fine, sheer, and lightweight cassock chosen because of the summer heat, a fanon detailed in gold fillagree, and a pallium with six gold crosses. Finally, they placed a white silken zucchetto on the top of his head.

While he was being dressed, Pius' mind drifted. Returning again to the first day of his Papacy, he recalled how a similar bevy of assistants in the Sistine Chapel had gently applied their hands to his already aged body to slowly undress him from his Cardinal vestments—laying him bare—with the exception of his scapular medal.

Joining the scapular medal around Pius' neck that first day, would be something of greater importance imposed by an institutional loyalty. It was a *secretum*—or *secret accoutrement* of the Papacy—an ancient bronze key dangling from an oiled leather lanyard. It was the only key to the intricate lock mechanism of the Papal desk that sat in the internal office complex at Castel Gandolfo. It was the same key that had been passed down from Pope to Pope since Urban VIII.

The memory then quickly faded. Pius's mind fast-forwarded back to the present and he turned to look at the locked desk behind him. When the assistants had completed their work in dressing him in his vestments, they helped to reseat the frail Pontiff in his gold-leafed trimmed and now wheeled chair. It was a sturdy repurposed oak desk chair which had been lowered a few inches to allow for an added base with caster wheels. The chair would allow the Pontiff to easily slip his legs under the short-in-stature desk while he worked.

The attendants receded from the office, bowing to the Pontiff on their way out. Then the Papal Nuncio to Pius entered to help the Pontiff address that day's schedule of matters. The stack of papers carried by the Nuncio was exceptionally tall this morning.

The Pontiff, upon seeing it, gave an irritated sigh. Additionally, he immediately noticed the ring on the index finger of his Nuncio's right hand.

As a Spanish Dominican, Bishop Renatto Ximina Cardenas, had reportedly been granted special permission by his Order to wear the ring of gold and silver, with a large amethyst stone mounted at its center.

To Pius, the adornment of such a ring worn by his subordinate— historically, reserved for the Pope alone, was considered by him to be a less-than-subtle, ostentatious affront to his supreme authority. Pius resented his Nuncio, but he also understood the politics of the situation. He knew the Nuncio's family was a rich and powerful patron of the Vatican.

"Your Holiness." Bishop Cardenas reminded. "You have approximately one hour before you have been scheduled to make a brief appearance from your window for a few dozen well-to-do tourists who would appreciate your blessing."

"I would prefer no personal greetings! The Pontiff said in a way that was more of an order rather than a request.

"Of course, Your Holiness." Agreed the Nuncio. "I will have aids inform them that your schedule unfortunately will not allow that today. They will be disappointed of course, as they were promised by their tour guide. But if you bless these Marian medals, I will have the tour guide distribute them to the group."

Cardenas held about a half-dozen examples of them in the palm of his right hand and extended it to the Pope. Pius stared at the silver trinkets with some ire. To him they paled in comparison to his Nuncio's index finger ring he felt was being waved under his nose. He dismissively gave a nearly unrecognizable Sign of the Cross over the medals and then directed his subordinate. "And make sure that Vatican tour guide is reassigned to another duty. I'll not have a glorified assistant priest assign my valuable time or set my schedule."

"Understood, Your Holiness." Cardenas dutifully replied. Without mentioning them, he then placed the burdensome stack of official complaint forms he had held in his other hand onto the desk in front of the Pontiff.

No explanation was necessary for Pius. The unwieldy pile was more of what he had been told to expect on the day of his elevation to the Papacy, *An increase in the volume of problematic matters of clergy misconduct for the Pontiff's review.* Another sigh escaped Pius' mouth.

"These are just the ones from America" Advised the Nuncio.

"America? South?" The Pope asked.

"The United States, Your Holiness." Admitted the Nuncio.

"Yes, yes." The Pontiff gruffly replied as he recognized the names of the Bishops and Archbishops along with the official seals of the various Diocese and Archdiocese that were clearly stamped on the cover pages of the documents.

The increasingly harried Pius would react in a passive-aggressive way targeting the Nuncio. The young priest before him was well educated, punctual, all business. Those particular aspects—normally assets for a person tasked in service of the Leader of Christianity, would be thought of as beneficial. But for some reason the Nuncio's efficiencies combined with him being a well-known proponent of reform, in addition to his ring, gave the Pontiff an additional undercurrent of irritability.

While he continued to fume over the work on his desk, Pius remembered when he was an enthusiastic young priest fresh out of seminary like Cardenas. Like his Nuncio, back then, he was just as ambitious, healthy, vibrant, and fully committed to a life of serving the Lord. Then over the years, the reality of institutional responsibilities, layers of bureaucracy ingrained in the 1900 hundred-odd years of church hierarchy, and its legacy of difficulty staying focused on their Saviors' simple mission, had worn his Papal Infallibility to a mere *Mortal Fallibility* with the ails of old age. But he was still in charge of the entirety of the Church—still responsible for the day-to-day of the flawed human condition of his faithful. For the past eleven years, it had weakened and also tainted him. And he hated that he was about to take out his frustrations on someone who reminded him of himself.

"Give me the hour to review these. In the interim please prepare a cappuccino for me." Pius impolitely barked.

The Nuncio's brow furled in a frown. "Your Holiness?" The Bishop questioned. A cup of coffee was a duty that should be relegated to someone else—perhaps one of his many valets—a kitchen staff volunteer, but not him. Cardenas' unsuppressed reaction made it clear to the Pontiff that he resented being treated as some menial errand or chore boy.

Unfazed, the Pope insistently flexed his administrative muscles—albeit emaciated ones—to show who was in charge. "With two sugars." The Pontiff dug in.

The point was made. "Yes, Your Holiness." Cardenas retreated from the office. The door closed behind him.

It was a shallow victory for the Pope. He had exerted his authority, but there was still the stack of paper and problems to deal with. He slowly leafed through the forms—reading the first line or two of each complaint that had been submitted over the first quarter of the current year. The specifics varied, but the nature of each were primarily rooted in the same areas of concern—human moral failings. Another exasperated breath escaped his lips.

Thoroughly disgusted by the task and that the café he had ordered was not appearing as soon as he would have liked, the Pontiff tugged at the starched collar of his outer vestment and pulled the oiled leather lanyard he wore out from under his cassock. He rubbed the patinated surface of the bronze key dangling from it between his finger and thumb. He knew that this was something that had also been done by countless other Popes over the last four centuries.

Pius pushed back on his wheeled chair, leaned over, and inserted the tarnished bronze key in the lock mechanism on the lower left drawer of the ornate desk. He turned it with difficulty due to his arthritic hand. The tumbler in its antique mechanism squeaked and opened. With difficulty he grasped the black metal pull and struggled to heave against the weighted drawer. When he had opened it far enough, he reached in and struggled to withdraw a large, well-worn, and increasingly overstuffed leather-bound attaché.

Pius thought to shout out to the Nuncio for assistance but did not out of ornery defiance. Finally, he had extricated the unwieldy portfolio. The aroma of old leather and musty, decaying parchment inside it reached his nose. There was also the faint smell of burnt ashes coming from something in the trove. The acrid stench, combined with his own displeasure, perfectly matched the contents of what the leather portfolio contained.

Despite his first inclination—which was to responsibly address the controversies detailed within the documents Cardenas had dropped on his desk, he delayed action and grumbled aloud. "Why should I be tasked with these new and most likely trivial individual problems, when there is the more pressing matter of guiding the entire body of the Church?"

Instead, Pius decided to ignore the lot. He would restack the newest set of papers he had just received from the Nuncio and wedge them into the leather attaché on top of the others. But then he paused.

At the very bottom of the stack in the attaché, he noticed a tattered codice—a bound document that he determined to be the oldest submission to this archive. Filled with curiosity, he retrieved every document from the leather portfolio and pulled that one from the bottom of the pile. Then with surprising unconcern for the age of the item, he unceremoniously flipped back the brittle velum cover of the entry. He could see that this was the essay that was emitting the burnt scent from it received from fire damage. Ashes from the parchment now whisked away in the turbulence of the cover being pried back. It floated in the sunlight penetrating the room along with centuries of dust. The thought occurred to Pius that this was possibly the first time this composition had seen the light of day since its archival. The fragile piece had been penned in medieval black iron-gall ink and its inherent corrosiveness had eaten away at the manuscript—making it nearly indecipherable. Though, a date was still legible on the remaining shard of the unburnt portion. It read 10 August 1216. To Pius' amazement, he was viewing the historically important Papal copy of the Magna Carta.

Now even more curious, Pius began to leaf through a few more of the missives, working his way up the stack from oldest to the newest. He noticed some were in folders, some were loose. But each was stamped with official Papal Seals and a series of similar ones from Diocese and Archdiocese, showing their progressions through the chain of command before reaching the Vatican.

Thoroughly engrossed, the Pontiff thumbed his way up the archive, reading articles that caught his fancy—the earliest all penned in old Latin. They were the unvarnished discussions about things that were to be privileged information—ones to be reserved for the eyes of the 256 Popes who came before him. Now, he would be the 257th to know of some of the scandalous details secured in the calf-skinned attaché.

For the next hour, Pius read about things like a rogue feudal Lord and the Cardinal of the Alsace Loraine region of Gaul in the year 854—accused of poisoning a rival by serving strychnine to him in a wine cup at a formal reception.

Then there was a massive report on the growth and decimation of the Knights Templar orchestrated by the Vatican. Written in a lengthy dissertation, it traced their early Vatican endorsed mission from the early 1100's through the termination of their ring of leadership in the year 1309. It included a casual hand-written catalog of confiscated ephemera once held by the Templars—reportedly ones found in the ruins of Solomon's temple in Jerusalem. It also contemporaneously noted that this was the primary reason why the Church had embarked on the campaign to eliminate the Knights, per the anonymous author of the note.

The Pontiff's jaw dropped when he read what was the guarded human materials inside a specific ossuary the Knights Templar had excavated from the destroyed temple. The contents of which, if ever revealed, would rock western civilization, and question the entire legacy of the Church.

Pius read about a series of deaths in Spain and Portugal of so-called heretics during the time of the Inquisition. Justified as efforts on the Iberian Peninsula authorized by the Vatican for seeking confessions under extreme duress, the narrative was surprisingly dispassionate for something that documented gruesome tortures.

After those, the rest of the contents would seem to be mundane in comparison by the Pontiff. But the sheer volume of the trove of mystery and intrigue held in the attaché seemed unending and held Pius's attention. Thus, he read on.

Finally, Pius was reaching the top of the stack. He leafed ahead to concentrate on more recent cases. They were from the latter 19th and early 20th Centuries.

At the top of the volume, Pius came upon one, that to his surprise, had been submitted to him the previous year, 1913, but at the time he had ignored it. Now he read it with full attention.

An Archbishop, explaining in far too much detail to be preserved in this manner by the Vatican, discussed an incident of the disappearance of a nun assigned to a parish in the State of Michigan in the United States. That had occurred in 1907—early on in his reign. He struggled to remember ever hearing about it before.

Now presumed dead, the missing nun—despite rumors promoted at the

Diocese and Archdiocese levels that she willingly left the Church—had yet to be located. Pius shook his head in disbelief by the looming specter of complications on the horizon for the future Church. He regretted being derelict in his duties and not getting involved earlier.

If that nun's body were ever discovered, the Institution would be under severe scrutiny and potential criminal prosecution as an accessory to a crime. He hoped he was not the Pontiff if and when that ever occurred. Knowing his own sense of mortality, and of his end's certainty, he doubted he would be.

Pius' interest waned and he went on to lightly scan the remainder of the archive. It was more of the same kinds of human imperfections. There was malfeasance of the Sunday collections, pedophilia, affairs between priests and women of the parishes—including nuns. Each offense was followed by the Church administration of a confession by the perpetrators, aided by the shroud offered by the veil of secrecy of the Sacrament of Penance which worked to mitigate the scandal. And more importantly for the Church, each transgression was followed by swift transfer of the offenders to other parishes—or to a pensioned retirement which removed them from any lingering criticisms in the public forum and calls for needed reforms internally.

The Pope took another deep breath of determination, folded the leather flap on the attaché and dropped it heavily back into the bottom drawer of his desk. He struggled to shove the drawer shut. Inserting the key in the lock, he turned it with a defining clink of the tumblers. That sound signified yet again what the only response of the Church would be for the volume of problems cataloged in the desk. That was the well-established practice of Papal inaction to close-out the entirety of the matters. And, importantly for Pius, the 400-year tradition of secret archival would continue with one of his loyal Swiss Guards placed outside the Papal office 24 hours a day— every day of the year—whether the Pope was in residence at Castel Gandolfo or not.

Pius returned the greasy lanyard holding the bronze and patinated key to under his cassock. With difficulty, he righted himself from leaning over the drawer, and at the same time attempted to scoot his chair back under the desk apron. The motion caused his zucchetto to fall off his head and under the wheels of the moving chair—leaving a grimy stain on its surface.

"Cardenas!" The Pope called out for assistance.

The Nuncio was at the ready outside the Papal office and immediately entered and approached the desk. He noticed that the papers he had given Pius were no longer on his desk and understood the action, or lack of action that the Pope had taken to dispatch them. He had expected nothing different. Cardenas also saw that the skull cap was missing from the Pontiff's head. He came around to Pius' side and leaned down to pick it up off the floor. Briefly brushing at the grime on it with his right hand—his index finger ring providing heft to his efforts, he saw that the stain was not about to disappear from the fine white silk.

"Let me get you a clean one." The Nuncio offered.

"Do not bother." The Pontiff answered in irritation. He grabbed the zucchetto from Cardenas and firmly slapped it back on his head. "Now help me up from this chair."

With the dirt stain clearly evident on the head of the Holy See, the Nuncio could not help but see the symbolism it offered. All who would come in contact with Pius today would see the stain. The Cardinals, Bishops, Vatican staff, the public—they would see it, but no one would have the nerve to mention it. They would all speculate on when it had occurred and what it might mean. However, to the observant—to the *reformers*—they would see the grimy stain appearing across the pure silken white on the head of the Church, as also emblematic of the guilt on the Institution.

Chapter Thirty-Four

St. Joseph Parish, Manistee, Michigan, circa 1914 - 1915

> **From a handwritten note addressed to Father Andrew, dated September 1915. It was found in the collection of documents discovered in his desk a few years after his death. The note was signed, Rev. Lempke. Lempke has been identified as the same priest who heard the deathbed confession of the Milwaukee Bishop Kozlowski.**
>
> *"Guilt will make its visit to a person and place its incumbrance upon him at the time of its own choosing, not theirs."*

Father Andrew, although conflicted, was not a man without at least some sense of conscience. That *mindfulness* was an inherited trait that is ingrained in nearly every person of the Catholic Faith. He knew from his dealings in hearing the confessions of his parishioners and feeling the torments of their guilt, that it would eventually visit him too. He was well aware at some point; self-reproach would become too big a burden for him to shoulder and it would affect his long-term future.

However, there is one aspect of his Faith that the priest would rely upon—even in the throes of his own unaddressed sin. Andrew would rely on the inevitable security provided by the balance of ones *sin* and its redemptive counterpart, *absolution,* that was rooted deeply in his Faith's doctrine and mindset. It gave him the cool, calculating persona to continue to pursue his life's agenda regardless of his guilt.

Over time—approximately eight years, Father Andrew had been able to suppress the guilt, so it remained dormant in his mind and soul. However, of late, rumors about him and the Sister Janina incident began again to circulate—especially among his fellow clergy. His Pastorship in Manistee was now in turmoil like it had been in his last years at Holy Rosary. Attendance at church and offerings were down. Circumstances dictated that it was now the right time to follow through on his quest for *absolution*—if not *forgiveness,* in order to resurrect his career and give him his own flawed peace-of mind. He would again attempt to get that through the Sacrament of Penance.

This would be his second attempt to give himself a fresh start with a renewed soul. In his earlier visit of remorse at the time he was leaving Holy Rosary, he did not get that in the Confessional with the incoming Pastor, Father Leo in 1913 and he was denied his trip to the Milwaukee Archdiocese to attempt to do the same just a few months earlier.

So, this time, Andrew placed a hurried long-distance telephone call to is old friend, Father Antonin Lucchesi—his one-time fellow seminarian. He did so for a specific reason. That reason was the frequent precarious state of Antonin's memory—more likely now considered *dementia,* helped along with too frequent partaking in sacramental wine. After the slow routing of the call through Chicago, then onto Milwaukee, then to the Campion Preparatory School in Prairie du Chien, Wisconsin—where Antonin was a senior clergy, someone finally picked up the telephone.

Andrew could hear someone in the background—likely an assistant or secretary—prompt Lucchesi. "Say Hello!"

The old priest complied. "Ohhh, hello?" A bewildered voice came through the receiver of Andrew's handset. He smiled as he listened to the familiar cadence of his old friend.

"Is this Father Lucchesi?" Andrew cheerfully greeting him.

"Oh, Yes. To whom am I speaking?"

"It's your old seminary friend, Father Andrew Bieniawski!"

After a bit more time and additional clarification, Father Lucchesi finally recognized the voice and person on the other end of the call. What Andrew could hear was the desired condition he was seeking when he placed the call, but it was also a bit sad. The diminished Pastor—now Pastor *Emeritus* at Campion, had held onto his appointment over the years, not because of his merits, but because of his deep family heritage and connections within the Church. He had favored status among the elite despite his limitations academically and administratively. He had always been notoriously absent minded—even before signs of alcohol-enabled dementia. That fact was what Andrew was counting on.

It was common for every action by Lucchesi—his decisions and especially any publication authored by him, to have constant oversight prior to release by the Archbishop himself, The Most Reverend, Sebastian Messmer—a man of strict adherence to doctrine. It was an absolute policy that anything coming from his administration must be above reproach, at least *in appearance* for the Institution of the Church. Rumor among the clergy in the Milwaukee Archdiocese was that even Father Lucchesi's sermons were to be approved by the Archbishop's office before they reached the pulpit. And then to be read *verbatim* by him.

"Antonin, it is good to speak with you again after all these years." Charmed Father Andrew.

"Where are you calling from?" Father Lucchesi questioned.

"Northern Michigan! Long distance!"

"Modern technology is wonderful." Conceded Lucchesi. "I had a telephone installed at the parish office last year. I just spoke to the Archbishop on the phone yesterday—or was it on Tuesday? They seem to call a lot. We are organizing a parish festival and picnic."

"Yes, technology is wonderful, Antonin." Father Andrew agreed despite the fact that the telephone was not a very recent technological invention at all. It had been around for many years and Andrew was certain Lucchesi's parish office telephone had actually been installed about a decade earlier. He shook his head at the state of his friend's memory. "But to the purpose of my call. I'd like to meet with you."

"Oh, yes. That would be wonderful. Will you be coming to the picnic? It's a week from Saturday. Where did you say you were calling from again?"

"Northern Michigan."

"Oh, I'm sorry. To whom am I speaking?"

"Father Andrew Bieniawski—your old friend from seminary."

"Oh, that's right. I wrote it down. I have it right in front of me. If I don't write it down, I'll forget it completely." Antonin chuckled.

"I'd like to meet you Antonin." Father Andrew pressed his point. "I can take the ferry from Ludington to Manitowoc. We'll pick a date in the next few days. It'll be good to see you—to discuss *some things*."

"Oh? What would they be?"

"It'll be better to discuss in person—*confidentially*, Antonin."

"Where do we meet?"

"Manitowoc. I'll be coming from Ludington on a ship. Well, never mind for now. I'll have the Archbishop's office remind you of the date and time. I'll place a call to them to set it up right after I get done speaking with you, my friend."

"Very well. Thank you for calling…Uh…"

"It's Andrew."

"Oh, yes. Yes, of course. Now you say you'd like me to do what?"

"Just wait for the Archbishop's office to contact you."

"Yes, yes. I suppose that would be alright."

"I will let you go for now." Andrew concluded the call. "Bless you, Father."

Father Lucchesi did not answer. Andrew heard him place the receiver down—but not on the phone base to end the call. Andrew wagged his head in pity as he heard Lucchesi's footsteps retreat from the phone and fade away. The call remained active until Andrew hung up.

Father Andrew leaned back in his desk chair—his elbows propped on the arms—fingers tapping together in a faux position of prayer. So far, his plan to secure some sort of absolution and more importantly a termination to any discussion of his culpability in the Sister Janina matter was going as planned. Via an *out-of-Diocese* confession, Andrew believed he would effectively wipe clean his conscience, and more importantly, blunt any legal or criminal inquiries into the controversy of the missing nun.

Andrew pondered. *I'll meet with my old and forgetful friend, get his absolution, and Antonin will forget the whole thing with no records of the details surviving in the Church hierarchy.*

He summarized aloud. "The passage of time and faded memories…Faded memories and the passage of time." He repeated like some kind of mantra.

Chapter Thirty-Five

Ludington, Michigan, circa May 1915

On a raw and blustery day on Lake Michigan, the now confident Father Andrew stood along the starboard railing on the deck of one of the two freight steamers of the F&PM. Without thinking, he whistled the melody to a *secular* tune. It was one he had heard at last year's deer camp from an Edison Amberol cylinder recording that had been played over and over by one of the rowdier members of his hunting party. The song was highly inappropriate for any *celibate*: My Best Girl and Me, by Edward Favor. To the beat of the tune, he tapped his brilliant index-finger ring adorning his right hand on the metal rail. Since his call with his friend, Father Lucchesi, he had decided he could once again wear it.

As the large ship slowly entered port and tied to the dock in Manitowoc, Andrew scanned the crowded pier and searched for his friend who would likely be accompanied by a church assistant to guide the aging priest. He was glad to be leaving the ship. The rough crossing, due to high winds, had given him a case of nausea. However, to his dismay, Andrew's anxious stomach became immediately worse by what he saw.

There, waiting for him at the end of the gangplank, was Father Lucchesi.

Alongside him, was the Archbishop of Milwaukee, The Most Holy, Reverend Sebastian Gebhard Messmer. He was accompanied by his personal Diocesan Secretary, Father Renault Alarie—who out of deference stood two steps behind the Patriarch. Andrew knew of him. He was devoid of personality. Like his surname—the French meaning, *All Powerful*, he was in his capacity as documentarian and enforcer—being inseparable from Messmer. He carried a thick, calf-skinned attaché with the Archdiocese's Seal.

Andrews heart sunk. His plan had backfired. The *grapevine of the clergy* had betrayed him. He immediately suspected the Bishop's office in Grand Rapids. They must have been informed that he was scheduling a trip to Wisconsin, and they had communication with their peers across the lake. He also suspected that the initial leak of his circumstances came from the highly intuitive Father Leo at Holy Rosary. *So much for the veil of secrecy of the Confessional.* Andrew thought.

On this trip, Andrew would not be receiving his sought-after time in a friendly confessional with a sympathetic and the forgetful ear of his fellow priest, where he could—although reluctantly—tell *all* of his sins. Now there would have to be a less-than-full accounting of his transgressions— not to Lucchesi, but to the Archbishop. He would have to artfully concede a limited knowledge of Sister Janina's disappearance—but nothing more, in order to escape harsher punishment.

With his friend Lucchesi removed from Andrew's equation, there would now be no end to the scandal. It would be fully documented at even higher levels of the Institution. Like a metaphor he well understood, it would continue to *dog him like a beagle tailing a rooster pheasant, waiting for it to flush in panic, and then be dispatched.* More importantly, there would be no absolution—no forgiveness. There would be no fresh start for him or his priestly career—whether in Manistee or any parish. What Andrew would instead receive on this trip, was a *dressing down.*

Andrew, in his naiveté, should have known the Church's history in dealing with problems like his. He should have recognized that the church hierarchy was playing the *long game* on his situation. They already knew the particulars and were waiting for Andrew to break down of his own volition—his own guilt—and then seek them out. Then they would prescribe the solution that he must follow. They did not need to expend their energies in pursuing the facts prior to that. If they did, it might show to the secular world they might be complicit in the mystery. No, they knew Andrew, in time, would come around to their authority.

A last gush of air escaped to deflate Andrew's lungs to complete his total feeling of dejection. Archbishop Messmer extended his hand to the priest in order for him to kiss his ring. Before he bowed to do that, Andrew plunged his own right hand into his front pants pocket and managed to slip off his index finger ring before the Archbishop saw it. Andrew would never again wear it or be filled with the perceived importance and insulation from accountability that it would have afforded him.

Chapter Thirty-Six

Offices of the Archdiocese of Milwaukee, circa 1915

"Should I start you off?" The Most Holy Reverend, Sebastian Messmer, Archbishop of the Archdiocese of Milwaukee asked in a condescending tone. He did so, not only to get to the heart of the matter and dispense with pleasantries, but more so to establish his supreme authority over the priest—to let him know who was in charge now—should he have some misconception that he still had any choices in the matter.

"No, I know. Bless me Father…" Began Father Andrew.

The priest could now see that his plan to seek absolution from the Archdiocese in Milwaukee rather than his direct superior within the proper jurisdiction, the Bishop of Grand Rapids, was like that of a child trying to avoid punishment from one parent by complaining to the other in order to triangulate the discussion and obfuscate his misdeeds. He had witnessed this often in dealing with the schoolchildren and parents during his time at Holy Rosary. It had never worked for them. He now wondered why he had thought it would work for him in this case.

"Father, what do you *personally* know of it—the circumstances of the disappearance?" Messmer continued to process the information given to him by Father Andrew. "How had this unfortunate incident been allowed to happen under one's Pastorship?" He crafted his initial question as if he and the priest were both disinterested third persons.

Soon however, he would systematically lay much more blame onto Andrew than anyone had dared to articulate to date. The Archbishop artfully gleaned more insight into Andrew's thinking, actions, and failings, while reserving both his spiritual judgment, any possible absolution for past transgressions, and most importantly, what would be his prescribed *direction* for the priest going forward.

Unsurprisingly, as it had been the tradition of the Church going back centuries, that *direction* by the Archbishop and Church—lacking punishment—would be without any input or involvement by law enforcement. At this stage they would not be informed of any of the facts the Archbishop would find out from the priest. Despite the human tragedy of a missing person, disclosure to them would rank a distant second in importance to that of the Church's priorities. In some ways, it would not be considered at all.

The Archbishop sat patiently, his hands folded in his lap, listening to Andrew recount his saga. Occasionally, he would reach for the crystal copita that sat on the edge of his desk and take a sip of sherry from the vessel. His ornate Archbishop's ring on his index finger would *clink* against the glass each time he did. Andrew thought it done on purpose by Messmer as a not-so-subtle way of reminding the priest to whom he was speaking. Out of deference to Messmer's authority, Father Andrew had declined any drink.

Finally, near the end of the priest's lengthy admissions, the Most Holy Reverend Messmer sat in judgement over the transgressions committed by Andrew—the ones for which he *must* accept responsibility. Those were limited to the *disappearance* aspects of Sister Janina, as those were already in the public discussion. But Andrew had not confessed to *everything* at this juncture. Andrew was taking a calculated risk that Messmer didn't know the full extent of the mystery. But if he were a betting man, he should have wagered that someone from Isadore had already leaked the *final* tragic outcome about Sister Janina and those facts had already been well distributed, including to Messmer.

However, to this point, Messmer had not divulged in what he may have already known. He hadn't attainted his level of authority without skillfully developed political connections both inside and outside of the church or maintaining his unreadable demeanor. The fact was, he had already been able to gather his own set of information regarding the wayward priest from his clandestine informants scattered in various parishes throughout the Midwest—including the Diocese of Grand Rapids. He was well aware of the rumors but had keenly separated them from verifiable facts—waiting for Father Andrew's confirmation of them.

For Father Andrew, he was convinced the disappearance of the nun from his parish a few years earlier had been contained to the Grand Rapids

Diocese. Although salacious, he thought it a local matter. Now he had made the foolish miscalculation to bring it to within the purviews of the Archbishop's larger realm with his much stronger connections to the greater Church. And never shying away from a challenge to administrate, Messmer would *take the helm* of the missing nun saga and would steer the course of it for the Institution he served. And in turn, *his* superiors would be thoroughly apprised—*in writing*.

Chapter Thirty-Seven

Continued Undercurrents of Accusation and Activities, circa 1913-1916

Starting with Father Andrew's departure from Holy Rosary to his new assignment in Manistee in 1913, to approximately 1916, talk of the unsolved mystery began once again to freely circulate among townsfolk of Isadore. With the principals of the legend now absent, tongues were looser and wagged without fear of their conversations getting back to the former Pastor, where they would surely have to face his ire. Largely though, the controversy again reverted to a state of only simmering concern and cold case status for law enforcement and in the public forum. However, not so for the Church, where behind the scenes conversations and events continued to evolve.

Then sometime in mid-1916, new information surfaced in the *public's knowledge*—albeit originating from outside the area. The Sister Janina mystery started to percolate again with the hearsay tale about an alleged kiss between Father Andrew and the missing nun.

The story emerged from the Detroit area and made its way back to Manistee and Isadore. It came from one of the former *chore boys* of Holy Rosary, Theodore Gruba, and another young man identified as E. Berkowski—sometimes referred to as, Victor Berkowski—also now living in the Detroit area. Both were reported to be orphaned and each had served time as Sexton-groundskeepers under Father Andrew. The young men told either relatives or friends still residing in Leelanau County that they had witnessed incidents of Father Bieniawski being *intimate*—kissing Sister Janina and possibly another of the nuns at Holy Rosary. It was also well-reported than neither young man cared much for the strict priest, so some listened to their claims with considerable skepticism.

When the accusation was brought to Bieniawski's attention in Manistee, he threatened to sue the gossip mongers for slander—emphatically denying their story and making a challenge to the accusers to prove their contentions. They never did. However, Andrew was forced to respond to persistent follow-up questions from concerned parishioners in Manistee as to why the young men would make their accusation.

The priest responded dismissively in a lengthy dissertation. "It comes with the territory. As Pastor and spiritual mentor for the parish in Isadore, I made many enemies because when I arrived there I made it clear that my priority was first and foremost to stamp out the frequent drinking and dancing orgies in the parish and nearby communities. My efforts left no question in anyone's mind. I demanded piousness from the young men of the parish, so they would refrain from such debauchery when they became adults. The gossipers are nothing more that young ingrates. They should be thanking me for the strict instruction they experienced from me when it comes their time to meet our Lord. That is, if they have learned the lessons I taught and applied them to a life of virtue."

That would be Andrew's only response to the accusation.

Chapter Thirty-Eight

Evolving Around the Same Time - Other Events Help to Renew the Controversy

In early 1914, Reverend Edward Kozlowski was named Auxiliary Bishop of the Archdiocese of Milwaukee. However, just over a year after his appointment, he became ill and died in August 1915. In attendance at his deathbed, was Rev. Joseph Lempke—who would hear his final confession, and the Provincial of Milwaukee, Mother Superior, Mary Veronica.

"…and for your penance." Father Lempke paused. "Well, for this final confession, I will not give you any, Bishop Kozlowski. I'll leave that up to our Savior—whom you will meet this day, to assign it to you should He find that you require it."

The Bishop smiled weakly and slowly closed his eyes. "Thank you." He managed to express through his shallowing breaths. The time was near.

"In Nomeni Patri Et Fili Spiritus…" Father Lemke began his final blessing prior to administering the Rites of Extreme Unction.

Then suddenly, the dying man's eyes opened widely, and he tried to lift his head from the pillow. "Oh, wait! There is one more thing." The Bishop urgently grasped at the sleeve of the priest. The priest and Mother Superior were startled by his sudden burst of energy.

"A few months ago, I heard of a confession that was told to one of my priests. It continues to haunt me! It *haunts* me!" Kozlowski pleaded with intensity.

Father Lempke and the Mother Superior looked at each other and silently agreed that this must be a delusional outburst—a final expression of the Bishop coming from the depths of his twilight of consciousness.

Father Lempke gently took his hand and spoke softly. "Yes, Bishop. Go on."

With a brief, renewed clarity, Kozlowski explained. "Until now, I have said nothing about it. Nothing! I honored the vow of secrecy of the confessional. But as I hopefully pass into the loving arms of our Savior today, I hope He will allow me this variance in my vows in order to give final justice for a wrong done to another one of our faithful servants—a nun, who became missing a few years ago."

Sister Mary Veronica now leaned in with full attention and tightly gripped the rosary she held in her hands.

Koslowski took a laboriously deep breath. "Our friend, Father Kruska—I suppose I can identify him at this point in order for you to follow through for justice for the nun. Kruska had heard a confession of a woman who knew of the intimate details of the *disappearance* of that nun. She was there at the time it happened. That woman is still alive and serving at a parish in Michigan as a pastor's housekeeper. He is somehow involved too from what Kruzska told me, but he suspects others also know. You know how word travels internally around here."

The Bishop paused to let out a faint laugh. "Ha! I think there are more in the Diocese that knows about this story than the law." His breathing and voice grew erratic, and his pulse quickened.

"Bishop, take your time." Father Lemke tried to calm the struggling man, but he would not be.

"It has always been said that the nun abandoned her vows and left the Church." Kozlowski paused and winced with pain but forced himself to continue. "That was the convenient conventional wisdom. Easier to accept from our standpoint—the Church. The penitent woman was allowed to be convinced that the sister left the Order because of *her* doing—*her* gossip—*her* treatment of her. But not any of *our* doing."

The Bishop shuddered again and continued. "It's been seven years since her disappearance. She has not come forward or been found." Kozlowski's breathing shallowed. A tear trickled down his ashen gray cheek. "And from what I have heard over the years, from various rumors and alleged meetings and sources within the Church, I believe the sister is dead."

Father Lempke and Mother Superior again looked at each other. But this time, the explicit lucidness of the Bishop's words gave them chills.

"And worse! Much w*orse!*" Kozlowski almost cried. "She is buried on parish grounds where she served—in Michigan. They say in the church cellar." The Mother Superior gasped at his contention.

Then the Bishop's words then grew urgent. "By passing this information along to you—in my confession to you, Father, I waive *your* vow of secrecy and give you permission—no, I *order you* as Bishop and your superior, to pass this along to *both* the authorities in the Church and to law enforcement to investigate. Hopefully, they can piece it together for the full truth." The Bishop—still grasping at the priest's sleeve was insistent. "I confess my hearsay knowledge of this to not only unburden my soul, but so that the sister's remains can be found and give *her* soul eternal rest."

Kozlowski had finished but would only relax after Father Lempke had given him his solemn word he would follow through on his wishes as ordered despite the fact that it would break *his* vows of secrecy. "Rest

Monsignor. Rest. Now, I will administer the Rites of Extreme Unction for you." A few minutes after the Rite was completed, the Bishop passed.

As witnesses now laden with the burden of carrying out a pledge to a dying man, both Father Joseph Lempke and Mother Superior Mary Veronica would, over the span of the next three years, quietly corroborate the Bishop's revelations through their own inquiries and then along with other sources confirming the same, incrementally notify those that would pursue secular justice and re-open the cold case of the Sister Janina mystery.

Chapter Thirty-Nine

Renewed Interest in the Sister Janina Case – Behind the Scenes Activities

Late in 1916, the following item appeared in a local newspaper.

Provemont Courier, Friday, 27 October 1916 (Public Domain)

"Messrs. Ed Kelly and Theodore Gruba of Detroit are visiting friends in this vicinity and Isadore."

This innocuous blurb, noticed by only a few attentive, regular readers of the publication, would reignite conversation in what had been a nearly ten-year stagnation of the case and refuel the rumor mill of wild speculation surrounding the Sister Janina mystery. From the above single sentence, under the heading of community events in CEDAR, the public discussion and fascination would quickly go from one of a third column, page one— just above the fold, filler, to a front-page headline.

Although he was not identified as such in the news clipping, those of the Holy Rosary parish who knew Theodore Gruba from his time in Isadore, soon found out that his traveling companion, *Mr. Ed Kelly* was in fact, the

Auxiliary Bishop of Detroit, Reverend, Edward Dionysious Kelly. The real purpose of their visit was a fact-finding mission.

Unaware that word of their arrival in Isadore had appeared in the local paper two days earlier, Kelly, Gruba, the current sexton of Holy Rosary, Jacob "Jake" Fleis, along with the current Pastor of Holy Rosary, Father Leo Oprychalski, gathered in the rectory office of the Isadore parish on Sunday evening, 29 October 1916.

Auxiliary Bishop Kelly began. "Gentlemen, let's begin with prayer."

All in attendance stood shoulder to shoulder, folded their hands, and bowed their heads. Kelly continued his thought. "Then I shall administer the Sacrament of Penance for *all of us*. "

The two laymen looked up nervously—first at Kelly, then at each other. Pastor Leo showed no reaction as he had been prepped that this was to be the procedure.

Kelly recognized their unease. "Confession will not need to be *individually*. We all know each other and why we are assembled. At this time, I'm not interested in how many times you took the name of the Lord in vain or argued with your spouse. So, we will do this *collectively*. That includes you, Father Leo. " Leo nodded in agreement.

"We in the church administration all know the many facets of this tragedy have not been forthcoming." Admitted Kelly through his sigh. "I am not here to lay blame but to gather additional information and somehow see if we can chart a course for the greater good of this parish and the Faith we ascribe to. And by this communal confession, the Church's goal is to hopefully provide closure and final blessing to the late Sister."

That would be Kelly's spoken reason. His unspoken purpose as directed by his superiors, was more so to reinforce the continued management of the tragedy and to suppress unpleasant facts from escaping the control of the church hierarchy and rapidly spread into the public.

"Are we in agreement?" Kelly asked the group's permission, but only in rhetorical fashion. With no objections, he proceeded. "Good. Let's begin. In the Name of the Father, and of the Son…"

Unfortunately, for Kelly, the local "chatter" provided by the *society ladies* of the Columbiettes regarding his and Gruba's sighting had already been passed onto their socially connected husbands, who would alert investigators and further unravel the truth of their visit with their own conversations and snooping. Thus, Kelly would ultimately fail in his efforts to suppress the renewed scrutiny of suspected scandal, but it would offer extensive insight into the internal Church's knowledge of the events of a decade earlier. Subsequently, it would shed embarrassing light onto their continually ongoing efforts in managing the controversy since it had occurred.

In another miscalculation by Kelly—having thought his meeting was clandestine, the two *vacationers*, Kelly and Gruba, made the mistake of lingering in the area which would accelerate the conversations about them. They would further err by attend public functions where they would be identified. Reportedly, the identification and a specific conversation concerning the pair during a well-publicized event, was said to be overheard and documented by a man, a Mr. G. S., who would later serve as Juror #7 on the murder trial of Stella Lipczynska.

Provemont Courier, 17 November 1916, Notice, Column One, Front Page

"Dance in the Provemont Hall on Thanksgiving Eve, Wednesday, Nov. 29th. Don't Fail to Come."

Overheard conversation between male attendees at the above:

"My wife read in da Courier 'dat Gruba's buddy is a priest."

"Nah, I 'tink he's a Bishop 'er something."

"Think Gus is gonna join the seminary?"

"Teddy? Nah, I don't make it that Gruba is priest material. He never had a good word for Father Andrew when he lived here, so I can't imagine he would wanna be one. Besides, that guy with hims no priest. He's got no white collar."

"Priests don't have to wear a collar all the time. Ol' Father Andrew didn't a lot of the time."

"Well, maybe..."

"Speakin' of Bieniawski, I heard Gruba tell his pal, 'Ya know,

It would be persistent eavesdroppers and several other *busy-body* observers like the above, who would soon find out the real reason of the *vacation* trip for Kelly and Gruba. Although, their stated purpose, if asked, was just a pleasant visit with old friends, it was in reality to investigate a new report that had circulated in the Church and made its way to Kelly's Detroit Archdiocese. There had been a grisly discovery in the cellar of Holy Rosary. However, beyond idle gossip regarding the pair and speculation in and around Isadore, their visit would not immediately prompt any release of that new information to the public.

Thought to be the next year, 1917, or by some accounts in 1918, when Pastor Edward Podlaszewski had taken over the duties at Holy Rosary, there would finally be Church confirmation of Sister Janina's bones and their reinterment under suspicious circumstances performed by the Sexton, Jacob Fleis, and Father Edward. Yet, this news would also continue to remain sequestered within the Church—*for a time*.

According to many, it was Fleis or someone in his family in whom he had confided, that would eventually leak the contents of the discussion between him, Auxiliary Bishop Kelly, Gruba, and Father Leo, and the later activities he and Father Podlaszewski had conducted. That news quickly progressed *internally* to Father Andrew's parish in Manistee. In a matter of days, confirmation of the gory details had made it to the Bishop's office in Grand Rapids. All clergy familiar with the matter suspected a leak in the Confessional—a violation in the vows surrounding the Sacrament of Penance. Based on the accompanying story that the breach of vows originated in Wisconsin, word quickly traveled cross-lake to St. Adalbert's in Milwaukee and ultimately to the Archdiocese Office where Archbishop Messmer was briefed.

Truth be told, the Archbishop's briefing, was most likely just a duplicate of what he already knew. His knowledge was so detailed beyond others in regard to Stella's confession, Father Andrew's attempted confession(s), Father Podlaszewski's involvement and more, that he was undoubtedly the only person who would be able to navigate the mounting negative publicity for the Church.

Thus, it would be Messmer who would take command of the situation rather than Auxiliary Bishop Kelly of Detroit or Bishops Richter or Gallagher of Grand Rapids based on the leak happening during instances of the Sacrament of Penance having been administered in his domain. By that, all would defer to Messmer's superior administrative skills over the next several critical months and throughout the rest of the Sister Janina incident.

However, it would still be quite some time before anyone would tell law enforcement investigators of the find. When they eventually did, the story returned to an active concern in the public and would soon enter the courts for prosecution.

Pere Cheney Messenger, 18 May 1918 (Public Domain)

"As a plague of what is suspected to be the Spanish flue (sic) the same malady that was first detected at Fort Riley Kansas several weeks ago, has begun to afflict soldiers in training at Camp Grayling and kill several to the southeast of Grayling, a single nun, missing for 11 years has been rumored to be found deceased by unknown cause in the Leelanaw (sic) County town of Isadore north of Cedar. She was found by the priest of the church buried in the cellar of it. The former housekeeper Mrs. Lipcryznski (sic) has been ordered for trial in the likely murder."

Chapter Forty
Holy Rosary Parish Grounds, Isadore, Michigan, circa 1917-18

"Come with me!" The Pastor, Edward Podlaszewski told his Sexton, Jacob Fleis. "Do you have your set of keys to the grounds?"

"Yes Father, what are we doing?" The Sexton inquired.

Father Edward did not answer his question but hastily added. "…And bring a shovel."

Each carrying an oil lantern, the two quietly exited the church rectory office—making sure no one else was on the grounds—and were slowly led by the dim light emitted to the back service entrance on the western side of the church. Fleis struggled to find the right key from his large collection hanging from a small chain on his belt. Finally, locating and inserting the correct one into the mechanism, the jingling noise made only heightened their shared anxiety. After more coaxing, the rusty lock snapped open. The two cautiously descended down the incline of the dirt floor below the church sacristy. Fumbling through the shrouded space hunched over in the low headroom, Fleis pulled the rusty hinged door closed behind them. The haunting screech made by it gave Father Edward a chill that ran up the back of his neck.

"There!" The priest pointed to an area several feet inside the entrance near a pile of lumber and wooden crates filled with Christmas decorations. The sexton kicked several loose boards away from the spot, paused and then thrust his spade into the sandy loam. He pulled back and thrust a second time and stopped when he met a resistance that felt unnatural to him. He looked up and stepped back, unwilling to dig further.

Father Podlaszewski held his lantern closer. He was shocked by what he saw. Remnants of brown frayed wool poked up through the dirt. He made the Sign of The Cross and began muttering the first thing that came to mind. It was a line from the Devotion to the Blessed Virgin Mary—which coincidentally per Catholic doctrine, gives a person three hundred days of indulgence from the distresses of Purgatory for their sins if they recite it. Podlaszewski knew he would need to claim those days—and then some—for these clandestine efforts to deal with this disturbing discovery.

"…To thee I come; before thee I stand, *sinful and sorrowful*. Oh, Mother of the Word incarnate. Despise not my petitions, but, in thy mercy, hear and answer me. Amen."

When he had finished, he again made the Sign of the Cross and directed the sexton to keep digging.

That night, he and the sexton would disinter the remains and immediately reinter them in an unmarked grave in the adjacent Mount Calvary Cemetery. Suspiciously, the priest did not divulge the discovery to his superiors but would only months later to a young woman—a confidant—an intimate.

Chapter Forty-One
Conflation

Definition of Conflation:

"The merging of two or more sets of information, texts, ideas, etc. into one—a normal occurrence over long periods of time or can also occur by intentional design."

Over the course of a century, it is common for the particulars of well-discussed stories to evolve. Elements of fact can often be mixed with opinion or outright changed to the apocryphal—either by overt actions, by simple misspellings and/or errors in transcription of documents, etc. Such is the case in nearly all levels in the disappearance, death, investigation, trial, and conviction in the Sister Janina mystery.

As an example, let's consider this for one of the primary characters, Stanislawa Lipczynska—the accused and convicted murderer. If one were to check the multitude of newspapers accounts and official documents regarding the case, they would find that there are no less than a half-dozen different spellings of the woman's last name. There are also at least two different versions of her first name.

This common occurrence of misspelling a person's name prior to more modern and accurate methods of fact checking and documentation, would tend to make one believe the old *wives tale* of when immigrants came to America and were confronted by officials at Ellis Island. Folklore is ripe with anecdotal efforts of officials trying to create entry visas for these foreign groups by translating their surnames into English from pronunciations that originated in the Cyrillic languages of eastern Europe. Lipczynska's misidentification is easily explained as the difficult spelling and pronunciation of her name—a totally innocent byproduct of *Conflation.*

Additionally, at the same time, newspaper coverage in the late 19th and early 20th Century was well known for its *yellow journalism*—a term coined to describe the industry's tendency to *color* their stories with unverifiable aspects to increase sales. The murder of a nun would qualify as a story worth sensationalizing with *conflating* certain aspects of the mystery.

However, there is another person of interest in the case who in hindsight has been put forth as a confusing combination of witness, suspect, and source of alibi. Questions in our decades-long mystery concern the variations of fact, spelling and misidentification of this person. Have they been weighted with purposeful disinformation that has resulted in *conflation* of their involvement in the story—not as a totally innocent byproduct, but as a nefarious act?

To discuss, in every account of the Sister Janina story, there is the mention of someone who was the *chore boy* of Holy Rosary Parish—a groundskeeper, handyman, errand boy—sometimes referred to as the Sexton of the parish in Isadore at the time of Sister's disappearance in 1907. When a surname has been used, that person has been identified as, *Gruba.*

Per cross referencing newspaper accounts across Michigan from that time up until the 1960's, there are several mentions of a Detroit area resident named, Theodore Gruba. He is thought to be the same person as the frequently mentioned *chore boy* of Holy Rosary. Per accounts, Gruba, was an orphaned youth living on or near Holy Rosary parish grounds in 1907.

Possibly due to his young age at the time of the nun's disappearance— which would be approximately 10 or 11 years-old, he was not considered a suspect in the crime, but he had the potential to be a key witness to corroborate Father Andrew's movements and efforts and should have been regarded as such.

In what was believed to be the sound alibi put forth by Father Andrew, he vouched for Gruba's whereabouts on the afternoon and evening of 23 August 1907 as the driver of the horse-drawn cart that transported the priest on his fishing excursion to and from Carp Lake. Though thought to be a failure of investigators, he was never seriously questioned at the time. Some accounts say that soon after the nun's disappearance he left the area and was never heard from again. But there is ample evidence to refute that claim.

In fact, Theodore Gruba continued to reside in the Isadore area until 1911 when he moved downstate at the age of 15—some two years prior to Father Andrew's departure from Holy Rosary in 1913 to his new assignment in Manistee.

Frustratingly though, as the years progressed, the person identified as the driver—the chore boy, seems to in some key instances, have been changed in its spelling from Gruba, (spelled, G R U B A) to, *Grubi,* (spelled, G R U B *I*).

Increasing the frustration, the word has sometimes been spelled with a capital first letter—indicating a person. Sometimes it was all in lower-case—confusing the reference as to whether it was a person's name or a similarly spelled slang term used for him or for someone else. This dilemma in research—especially in later renditions of the account, are most prevalent in mentions gleaned from Father Andrew's desk notes. The person, Gruba, would also be misidentified by the priest in testimony in court proceedings. Some or all of the above variances point to prime instances of *conflation* that has muddied the truth. But how and for what reason or reasons?

To unravel some of it, let's first examine the possibility that *conflation—over time* has confused Gruba's involvement in the story by narrowly focusing on *coincidental language.*

For Father Andrew, as Pastor of Holy Rosary, his outreach and frequent interaction with the local population also included with those of other nearby communities, and with the unknown number of transient migrant laborers from the surrounding farms, orchards, and lumber camps—many of whom spoke native languages other than Polish—although many of them were also majority Catholic. There is also some evidence to show that from time to time, these outsiders offered their volunteer work to the Holy Rosary parish grounds. The work was menial—things like excavating cemetery plots for the funerals of parishioners, periodically moving outhouses, or snow removal after heavy lake-effect events off Lake Michigan onto the Leelanau peninsula during winters. As a results of their work, they were usually quite filthy.

Those transient workers and migrants sometimes received compensation for their efforts—that usually amounted to temporary room and board for their efforts from the church at the direction of Father Andrew. The person known as the *chore boy*, Gruba, often was afforded the same—sometimes housed in simple accommodations in parish buildings or with parish families on short-term basis. It was a common sight to see some of the above mentioned periodically attending Mass and receiving Holy Communion at Holy Rosary. Though to the regular attendees, they were seen as a grimy lot and customarily confined to the back of the church during Mass.

Like many tight-knit and segregated ethnic communities of the time, residents of Isadore rarely interacted with those who were outside their own sphere and even more rare for them to know the transients/chore boys by name. They held the outsiders in suspicion and referred to the group in derogatory fashion.

Thus, collectively from the perspective of the more upstanding and permanent Polish community, any foreigner or outsider was often disparagingly called things like, *niechluj*—meaning a pig, sloven, dirty, a slut, *nieczysty*—dirty, unclean, or impure, or *czarny*—meaning black, dark, a Negro, or more often in the common vernacular of the time and area, they used the offensive, "N-word."

But there was also use of the word, *gruba,* or sometimes, *grubi*, that was a borrowed slang term used to describe them. The word *gruba* in Polish is an adjective that generally means *fat* and sometimes *slovenly.* To the English speaking, the foreigners were often referred to as *grubby.* However, in the Czech language, and also in Slovak and Croatian, *gruba* or sometimes the nearly identically spelled, *grubi,* is a term for *unkempt, filthy*, or *rude.*

It is not a coincidence that just a few miles to the northwest of Isadore near Good Harbor Bay, there was a settlement—largely comprised of Czechs. Established in the 1850's, like the Polish of Isadore, this gritty group of homesteaders usually only associated with themselves and also left their marks on the area with landmarks named for them—one notably, Bohemia Road. (Bohemia, at the time a province in Czechoslovakia) There is also the parish of St. Wenceslaus which was also a largely Czech-Bohemian settlement only a few miles away from Isadore at Suttons Bay.

Thus, we have a picture of competing segregated communities, each with a fierce sense of loyalty to their own. That made it likely that slang terminology for referencing the others—sometimes as insults, sometimes as simply a general reference, flowed back and forth with regularity between the ethnic and religious factions.

Returning to our question: Has a key *person of interest* in the story of the missing nun—*Gruba*, been altered over time in the public forum in numerous published accounts and been *conflated* by folklore retellings into someone else—some new truth? Was it the *person, Gruba*, or was *gruba* or *grubi,* the *condition* of Andrew's chore boy? Or was it in reality, Father Andrew's slang terminology used to identify someone else?

From the onset of the disappearance of the nun, was the community wrong in assuming that the person, Theodore Gruba, was the individual who accompanied Father Andrew on his fishing trip? Frankly, after a century, it is still unclear. But there are theories to consider that point to that as a strong possibility.

Regardless of Andrew's true meaning(s), in his statements soon after Sister Janina had disappeared, it placed the person, Theodore Gruba, at the scene.

He had been used by Andrew to establish the priest's alibi, placing him in the middle of events of 23 August 1907. But in the numerous reiterations of that alibi over the years and specifically a decade later to investigators, there reveals a progressive confusion of *Gruba's* identification to that of a *grubi,* by the priest. Knowing Andrew's general involvement in the tragedy, a betting person could say that this was intentional to muddy the facts.

To explain; Gruba, just a boy in 1907, could easily have his recollections and testimony dismissed as unreliable. Whereas Gruba, now as a man in 1918 and 1919—over ten years later, or other chore boys who had served the priest and were now adults, had to be taken more seriously. Thus, they were not the types of persons whom Andrew would want around to recall unflattering stories about him that were beginning to circulate or to challenge his uncorroborated contentions. Why?

Chapter Forty-Two
The Priest's Reasons to Keep the *Invisibles,* Invisible

Let's consider the above in a different way by looking at the court proceedings leading up to the murder trial of Stella Lipczynska.

In 1919, almost twelve years after the disappearance of Sister Janina, from the Preliminary Hearing of Stanislawa Lipczynska, Father Andrew testified, "only *Fred* Gruba and my younger sister accompanied me on my fishing trip."

FRED? Yet another discrepancy in identification?

In a review of all available documents and writings, the name, Gruba, referring to the *chore boy* of Holy Rosary Parish, has been interchangeably identified by the priest and others as, Ted, Teddy, Theodore, Gus, one of the orphan boys, the chore boy and now Fred. And let's not forget the previously discussed possible *conflation* and/or coincidental language usage and the similar spelling of Theodore Gruba's last name to the slang term, *grubi.* It is dizzying.

Though, it is also possible that the above transcribed name, *Fred,* in Father Andrew's testimony, was simply a typographical error in the unwieldy volume of the approximately 200-page Preliminary Hearing transcript.

Perhaps what Father Andrew really said was, *Ted*. A casual read of the transcript reveals many typos in the cross examinations and numerous recalls to the stand of the priest and the nervous Mary Fleis nee Lipczynska—daughter of the accused murderer. Humorously, at one point in the hearing, aware of the possibility that the extensive, confusing, and at times choppy testimony would result in difficulty for the court stenographer, one attorney urged Mary to "get to the point, because this all has to be transcribed later."

But, if this is not a typographical error, and Andrew used the wrong name of *Fred* to identify who accompanied him on his fishing excursion in 1907—especially since the fishing trip was *the* exculpatory factor in eliminating him as a suspect in Janina's disappearance—one would question why it was not something he would remember.

This returns to our earlier contention. It paints a picture of Gruba/Grubi and/or the other subservient male orphans of Holy Rosary serving as chore boys, as just an afterthought to the priest—*afterthoughts* deemed as undeserving of his considerations. They were a disregarded lot of *invisibles*, viewed by Andrew as useful agents for his dirty-work, and then as anonymous scapegoats.

This was true in 1907. Gruba served as an alibi *when he was a boy*. But, at the time of the Lipczynska trial, circa 1918-19, now as a young man and based on the negative press already generated by him and another *chore boy-invisible,* both held the potential to undermine the priest's alibi, and might further implicate him. Why would they do that?

Review of the facts show that many of those who were housed and worked at Holy Rosary as chore boys during his tenure as Pastor, describe Andrew as a tyrant. The boys frequently disobeyed orders or slow-walked the completion of any given by him or his housekeeper—challenging their authority. However, he held supreme authority over them and their existence. They eventually had to comply with his demands—even if they were unpleasant or *unlawful*. Not surprisingly, the prevailing dismissive attitude held by Pastors toward their *chore boy types* was not an unusual scenario.

The history of these sometimes misnamed, but generally ignored and disrespected lot at Holy Rosary and other churches predates Father Andrew's assignment that started in 1900. For the Catholic Church in general, starting soon after the Civil War and increasing throughout the late

1800's, orphaned children—at least for the *boys,* was handled in a different and uncaring fashion compared to the girls of the same plight.

Like the young, Josephine Mezek, orphaned girls often found their way to the protection of the convents, like the Felician Order, where they were generally given quality education and a gentler hand. The boys, however, were customarily sent away from their home regions to be housed at whatever accommodations were available at the time within their Archdiocese or other nearby ones in the Midwest. From there, those deemed of *priestly material* were sent to seminary for further disciplined instructions in the Faith and indoctrinated to become priests.

However, those from the rougher, uneducated edges of society, deemed lacking the quality of spirituality, or sometimes those originating from *other than* an ethnically exclusive parish—in this case Polish, were often disbursed to various churches to become *chore boys* under the direction of the Pastor, Mother Superiors of the convents, and housekeepers of the parish. If they performed satisfactorily in their labors and grasped somewhat of an education, they received room and board—sometimes at the parish, but often with temporary housing with foster families. It was often a harsh existence until they reached at least 15 years of age and could go out on their own.

Two examples to illustrate this happened early in the assignment of Father Andrew at Holy Rosary. A pair of youths named Victor Berkowski and our Theodore Gruba were sent from the greater Detroit area to an orphanage at Manitowoc, Wisconsin, where they soon became chums—sharing their self-described *misery.* After a while, Berkowski would be transferred out of Manitowoc and sent to Isadore to be the charge of Father Andrew. The two boys would again be reunited when Gruba was also sent to Holy Rosary. Neither young man would ever have anything good to say about the harsh supervision under Father Andrew.

Gruba was eventually considered to be the main chore boy or *sexton* after Berkowski left the parish for downstate sometime around 1905 or 1906— apparently to live with relatives. However, during the boy's time at Holy Rosary, per either Gruba or Berkowski, the priest had a violent temper and would often cuff them about the head if they didn't perform to his satisfaction. This story comes from the contemporaneous comments of the man known as Mr. G. S.—Juror #7 in the Lipczynska trial. According to his descendants, he was told this by one of the chore boys in a post-trial conversation occurring sometime in the 1920's.

It was contended that Berkowski believed the authoritarian priest had a dual personality. "He was sweet to them who agreed with him. And to them who took him to be a priest who took his charitable vows seriously." He stated to a local Leelanau County newspaper reporter who sought him out looking for commentary post-Lipczynska trial. "But if you crossed him, he was a son-of-a-bitch. And when parents would approach him to complain about the treatment or problems with their children attending the school, he would 'bawl' them out." Berkowski added.

It is not surprising that both boys hated their time at Holy Rosary under the supervision of both Pastor Andrew and Stella Lipczynska. The priest and housekeeper controlled their every move. "We were disciplined if we didn't come quickly enough when we were 'whistled for.' It was a kind of *slavery* under Father and that old woman." Said Gruba.

In 1917, when the general consensus was that Sister Janina had "left the Parish voluntarily," Berkowski stated something to the effect of, "As for the Sister's disappearance, when I heard about it, my first thought was that Father Bieniawski had something to do with it. I'd bet five dollars on that!"

It was also Berkowski who claimed that at one point, as *one of the invisibles*, he had been able to witness "Father Andrew kissing Sister Janina one time while she was playing the piano." This was something that the priest vehemently denied.

Sources disagree, but potentially also coming from Berkowski and/or Gruba, was the accusation that Andrew had accumulated funds he later used for Stella's appeals process and promised *stipends* to certain individuals by withholding some of the pay from some of the other chore boys and migrants who worked for the parish. It was also alleged from an Altar Boy at Holy Rosary that Father Andrew occasionally pilfered money from the collection plate on Sundays for the same uses. These concerns were voiced, post-murder trial and years later to the same Mr. G. S., Juror #7, per his family's folklore.

However, in contrast, Berkowski said that both chore boys, the parents and other children generally liked Sister Janina. They had no ill will for her. He said they tolerated the other two nuns.

As mentioned, Theodore Gruba left Holy Rosary for the Detroit area in 1911 when he was about 15 years old. That was about four years after Sister Janina's disappearance.

Finally, let's also consider the following: It's an assumption. There exists some possibility that the priest, both Lipczynska's and the other two nuns, were *never* speaking about Theodore Gruba—Andrew's chore boy/sexton of Holy Rosary at the time when referring to the person who took the priest fishing. They were only repeating what the priest had said. None of them actually ever witnessed their chore boy, Gruba, leaving or returning from the trip.

However, by the time of the renewed interest in the missing nun's story around 1916, it was already well documented that Gruba and anyone under the priest's authority fitting the description of a *chore boy* did not like him. Yet, Andrew still needed *him* or *them* to substantiate his alibi of being away from the parish on the fateful afternoon and to attest that he conducted a legitimate search for her. Thus, in writings, the mention and identification of Gruba—spelled with an *a,* evolved into the spelling and references of *grubi*—spelled with an *i.* Historians believe this was conducted by Andrew in order to obscure identification of this key witness.

The reason(s)? By 1918, innuendo had already begun to surface in news accounts and through a persistent rumor mill that pointed to Andrew's suspected central involvement as a prime suspect. For a murderer or mastermind of one, one would think that they would put effort to hiding the identity of anyone who had carried out the deed on his behalf. Thus, researchers note the priest's evolving progression of pronouncements about the crime after the discovery of Janina's bones. He now steadfastly maintained that the disappearance of the nun was likely due to an outsider, vagrant or drifter. His stated beliefs helped keep his official *chore boy(s)* from consideration and/or from formally accusing *him* of the crime.

Andrew's hope was that they would not offer evidence—real or imagined—that was the result of his confrontational relationships with them and expressions of their lifelong grudges against him. It was a fine line for the priest to walk when recalling the *invisibles* of Isadore and discussing the crime. Now as adults, Andrew knew he no longer had power over them or the ability to suppress what they might say.

But all the variables in the above theories do not make it a simple, *cut n' dried* matter. There are additional considerations which make one rethink the above and the depth of involvement of the chore boy, Theodore Gruba. We will discuss that next.

Chapter Forty-Three

The Preliminary Hearing of Stanislawa Lipczynska Before the Hon. C. W. Nelson, Justice of the Peace, Leland, Michigan, circa 1919

Father Andrew testified that on the day of Janina's disappearance, Stella and her daughter Mary remained at his residence. He recalled that it was about 12pm or 1pm the last time he saw Stella and all three nuns wave good-byes to his party as they left the parish.

He claims he was only informed of Sister Janina's disappearance when he returned from his trip.

Fr. Andrew: "It was getting on—it was getting late about 8 o'clock or so in the evening. I immediately told the sisters to look in all the buildings and nearby corn field (for her)."

Attorney for the Prosecution, C. L. Dayton: "At the time of the disappearance, did you search the church basement?"

Fr. Andrew: "Oh yes. I searched the basement with the boy."

It is assumed the priest was referring to the chore boy, Gruba. Though, in this exchange he did not specifically identify him. In a failure of cross examination, the attorney never followed-up to clarify which chore boy either.

From Testimony of Mary Fleis nee Lipczynska at the Preliminary Hearing

According to the transcript, in addition to affidavits claiming the defendant did not like Sister Janina, Prosecutor Dayton pressed Lipczynska's daughter about Stella's access to a likely weapon thought to be what was used to kill the nun. According to medical examiners, death by one or more blows to the head was "due to a heavy object—*like a shovel.*"

However, Mary's plain-spoken answer to the Prosecutor seemed to unravel his tack, refute his contention, and point to *another* person who had access to and ability with that kind of implement.

> *Dayton: "Your mother worked the garden a little by herself? Weeding?"*
>
> *Mary: "Weeding?" I do not know what that word means. Only in Polish."*
>
> *Dayton: "Did she work in the garden?"*
>
> *Mary: "Wyrywanie chwastów. Yes, pulling weeds."*
>
> *Dayton: "Did she spade the garden?"*
>
> *Mary: "Spade? I do not know...Shoveling?" The boys must do the shoveling."*
>
> *Dayton: "Who?"*
>
> *Mary: "Gruba. He was the boy for the shoveling."*

After his vacation to Isadore with Auxiliary Bishop Kelly in late 1916, and with the renewing public interest in the mystery of Sister Janina beginning in 1917. Suddenly the potential key witness, Gruba—Father Andrew's *chore boy,* was not to be found.

At the same time newspapers reporters began making another round of inquiries and investigators renewed their probes into the mystery, they sought out Gruba for an interview. Curiously, he was no longer in the country. Per relatives and friends, Theodore Gruba had suddenly moved from the Detroit area to Canada to pursue his lifelong dream of adventure in the wilderness. Reports were that sometime in early 1917 he showed up in Valhalla, Alberta, Canada.

There were three possible reasons for Gruba's departure from the United States at this critical time in late 1916 or 1917.

One; He could have left for the north woods due to true wanderlust that had fallen upon him as reported by family members in Detroit.

Two; The United States had remained out of the European conflict of WWI that had started in 1914. However, many suspected it was only a matter of time before the U. S. would enter the war. Knowing this, and because he was of military age, Gruba left for Canada to avoid the military draft. In April 1917, The U. S. finally declared war on Germany and conscription of American men commenced.

Three; This is the most likely and intriguing of the scenarios. If the reports of Gruba and his associations with the Auxiliary Bishop of Detroit and others of interest were in the Isadore vicinity in late 1916 are true, he like others were aware that facts of the case were slowly leaking out into the public. Gruba may have also suspected or had been given prior knowledge of the ramped-up criminal investigations that would soon be coming in 1917 and 1918. He didn't want to be around for them or the court proceedings that would be coming in early 1919 where he could be forced to testify to his and the priest's knowledge of the crime—potentially contradicting Father Andrew under oath.

Perhaps Gruba's absence was a combination of all the above. None-the-less, he was unavailable for any input on the Isadore matter, where he might face criminal prosecution as an accessory—or even as the prime suspect. However, his absence may not have been by his choice alone. There is a suggestion there may have been *heavy encouragement*—perhaps with financial compensation provided by the other key players in the investigation, or directly from the Church, for him to leave the country for an extended *vacation* as a move to thwart justice.

In fact, there would be no mentions of Gruba in Isadore, or the Detroit area again until after 1920, after all court proceedings regarding the Sister Janina incident had been completed, Stella Lipczynska was serving her term in prison, her appeal had been denied, and WWI was over. However, long after he was in the clear—years later—in the 1940's and into the 1960's, he would again occasionally be mentioned as a visitor to the Isadore area in one Leelanau County newspaper.

Suttons Bay Courier, 7 August 1947 (Public Domain)

"Mr. Theodore Gruba of Detroit was a town caller this week. He spent several years in Isadore and left about 36 years ago."

"Mr. Theodore Gruba and family of Detroit passed thru here Friday, enroute to Raff's Fishing Camp north of Northport. He is a former resident of Isadore, having left for the big city about 37 years ago."

Granted, the many possibilities detailed above concerning Gruba are a confusion of competing facts, considerable speculations, and possible motivating factors—most all of it suffering from *Conflation*. Only new pieces of evidence—ones that have yet to surface, or Andrew's now missing desk notes might provide more definitive answers, where they could either exonerate or accuse Gruba. Unfortunately, none of that is available.

Chapter Forty-Four

Simultaneous Undercurrent of Events

Over the last one hundred years, numerous bits and pieces of fact discovered in Father Andrew's locked desk drawer and from other sources regarding the tragedy have been stitched together to provide *alternative context*—a nice way of saying *conspiracy theories*. Those theories have been crafted to point to an alarming level of Church knowledge *after-the-fact*. It seems that during the critical years between 1907 and 1920, there was widespread gossip among the clergy which seems to have been sourced from the leaked confession of Stella from the Archdiocese of Milwaukee. By consolidation of all available materials, it weaves a pattern of likely periodic communication between the entities of personnel in the Archbishop's office in Milwaukee, the Diocese of Detroit and the Bishop's office in Grand Rapids that would ebb and surge as the controversy played out.

Published in The Augustinian, Kalamazoo, Michigan, 5 October 1918

Quoted from a story concerning a reception to be held at the Kalamazoo Knights of Columbus Hall. The gathering was for the incoming Bishop of Detroit, Rev. Michael James Gallagher. Per the story, five-thousand men of the various Catholic religious societies were expected to attend along with *other dignitaries* of the Church.

*"...The welcoming address will be delivered by **Bishop Kelly**, (Auxiliary Bishop of Detroit) who will, after the installation, formally give over to the new bishop the affairs of the diocese...It is probable that **Archbishop Messmer**, metropolitan of the province of Milwaukee will also attend..."*

Note: There was quite a bit of confusion, *conflation* and shuffling of personnel at the Bishop level in the State of Michigan in the years 1918 and 1919. Per the above story, Auxiliary Bishop of Detroit, Edward D. Kelly, was serving as the *acting* Bishop of Grand Rapids during the *sede vacante*—or *vacancy* in the office after Rev. Gallagher, who had been serving as Coadjutor Bishop of Grand Rapids to assist its then aging Bishop Henry Richter. Richter died in early 1918. Gallagher then left to serve in the Detroit Diocese as Coadjutor Bishop after the death of its Bishop John Foley. According to the story in the Augustinian, Gallagher was installed as permanent Bishop of Detroit on 18 November 1918.

It seems that news reporters—even those reporting for religious publication like the Augustinian, sometimes had trouble following the personnel transfers in the Church. Their writings often confuse and/or conflate the terms, *appointed* as Bishop and *installation* as Bishop. There is also the unreliability of reporting in regard to that person's current title(s) and where they served in those positions. The terms, *Auxiliary* Bishop, *Coadjutor* Bishop, and *acting* Bishop were interchangeably used and uniformly perplexing to researchers. Then there is the frequent misuse of the term *Archdiocese* for the word *Diocese*. The former is the correct use for an *Ecclesiastical Province* which would cover all the individual Diocese within its territory and under its administrative umbrella.

With all that as muddying as it might be in one's mind, per the anonymous sources who reviewed Father Andrew's desk notes, they were fairly confident that the following meeting occurred between Rev. Eduard D. Kelly and Archbishop Sebastian Gebhard Messmer at the above-described event.

"So good to see you Archbishop Messmer. Glad you could make this auspicious occasion." Bishop Kelly graciously greeted the prelate from Milwaukee.

"Thank you…" Messmer struggled to recall the name of the man who was bowing deeply and kissing his ring.

The always present, charge d'affaires for the Milwaukee Archdiocese, Father Renault Alarie whispered in the patriarch's ear. "This is Auxiliary Bishop Edward D. Kelly of Grand Rapids, who has been filling in since the passing of Bishop Foley."

"Oh, yes, Edward. Nice to see you *again*. I've been *hearing* much about you lately." The amiable elder lifted the bowing man to upright and clasped both of his hands tightly around Kelly's—pumping them vigorously, while not allowing him to separate from the captive greeting and step back to a comfortable distance.

Kelly's brow furled with uncertainty. He had never met the Archbishop before. *Messmer has been hearing about me? Oh, God!* He dreaded. "What is to come next?" He thought.

"Father Alarie!" Messmer half-turned to his assistant. "Schedule a time— perhaps an hour or two with Bishop Kelly, sometime tomorrow before we take the ferry back across…"

Alarie interrupted. "Yes, your Holiness, but I believe we should do this tonight, as the weather forecast is predicted to have howling winds by

Thursday. So, to beat the storm, we should be heading back tomorrow morning at the very latest."

"Ah, *The Gales of November* are upon us a month earlier this year…Yes, yes, Bishop Kelly you will be available tonight around *ten-ish*?" Messmer asked in a manner more like an order.

"Well, I had made other plans, but yes. Yes, Of course, I'll make time for you later this evening. What may I ask is the subject of this meeting?" Kelly meekly inquired.

"Oh, let's not ruin the festive atmosphere. There'll be plenty of time later to inform you of the matter and instruct you on what you will be required to do…" Messmer's voice trailed off, but then he continued his run-on sentence to slowly draw out his explanation as to what the meeting would be focused. "… in your capacity as administrator of your—well, *soon* to be one of your former Pastors under your charge in your Diocese."

"Well, I am only the *interim* Bishop, Your Excellency." Kelly corrected.

"For now. For now! But I'm seeing a bright future for you!" The Archbishop cheerfully responded. The Bishop's stomach churned with tension. He was now sure what was to be discussed later that night.

Kelly could guess that in addition to attending the reception, Messmer was here to be fully briefed about his meeting with Gruba, Father Leo and the sexton. He was there to hear first-hand the involvement of Pastor Podlaszewski and his ill-advised actions. And he was here for a personal commitment from Kelly as to the level of cooperation expected of him in the next few months. Moreover, he wanted to reaffirm—for anyone who might think otherwise—who was now in charge of this sensitive issue.

Knowing how Church administration of this sort of thing had been historically handled, Kelly knew he had no real choice in the matter. But on the upside, if he dutifully followed along, he could potentially benefit. Upon a later review of the timeline of *conspiratorially offered facts* in the mystery, that would seem to be born out.

Bishop Kelly's subservient follow-through on Messmer's instructive meeting seems to have been rewarded. Kelly emerged as the front-runner as the next *permanent* Bishop of Grand Rapids, despite other qualified candidates reported to be next in line for the promotion.

On 16 January 1919, a sealed document from Pope Benedict XV *named* Kelly to be the third Bishop of the Diocese of Grand Rapids. Coincidentally, the Lipczynska trial began in March 1919. Kelly was then *installed* as Bishop on 20 May 1919.

Chapter Forty-Five

Historical Perspective: *Confedentia*, Vatican, Rome, circa mid-1918

"Our response to the complaints, Your Holiness? Should I draft a letter to the bishops?" Pressed the advisor to Benedict XV, Bishop Donato Sbaretti.

"Nothing in writing!" The Pontiff firmly stated. Despite his noticeable frailty and increased signs of dementia of late, Benedict still had the where-with-all to know he did not want any of his *thoughts put to paper* in response to the flood of complaints of *priestly misdeeds* that had been submitted to his office from the various Diocese and Archdiocese around the world. He was emphatic that none of his subsequent actions or inactions to mitigate the complaints should be reduced to writing, where they might be discovered by a future Pope or some authority in the secular society and thereby diminish his legacy. "Summon the Archbishops and/or Bishops of the affected Diocese to the Vatican for personal instructions." He ordered.

"All of them?" The Nuncio blanched.

"Yes, my young Bishop." The Pope condescended. "But you will draft a separate letter to all the Bishops in the Americas—where most of the problems seem to be occurring these days—that there will be an encyclical issued in the coming days regarding the vows of celibacy. That will require them to clear their schedules for a required reading of it by them *personally* as a Homily in a High Mass at the major parishes in their respective Diocese. The Sermons delivered by them for those Masses will be crafted in a way to be a reminder to the *laity* that *they* must refrain from highly sinful physical encounters of that nature with those bound by vows to abstain from it. Their Homilies should emphasize praying for the victims of the various wrongdoings, and a pledge of full spiritual support for them by the Church, etc. etc.

Additionally, and of most importance, there will be instructions to them which will be delivered orally *ONLY*—in *confidentia*. They are to expunge the *clergy offender's names* from the records, and they are not to be mentioned in the Homily. Those individuals will be given expedited—let's call them, *vacations*. In essence, they are to be *transferred* to other needy or remote parishes—depending on circumstances within the Diocese. They will remain on limited duties until such a time that calm, and stability returns to the affected parishes."

"No admissions of guilt?" Asked the Nuncio.

The Pope glared at Sbaretti without answering because of the audacity of his question. After an uncomfortable amount of time, The Nuncio responded as he feverishly took notes on a ledger. "Yes, Your Holiness."

"And Sbaretti, *my instruction* to you regarding these matters is NOT to be released—or *leaked* to the public—something that I suspect has been happening of late! Give me your notes!" The Pope demanded. "I hope you have memorized my dictates, Father." Benedict lectured and summarized with an afterthought. "And of course, for the benefit of the greater Church, before any of this transpires, first there must be successful Confessions that will take place throughout the Institution, followed by a heartfelt Act of Contrition and appropriate penance performed."

The Pontiff lowered his voice to achieve maximum seriousness. "To be perfectly clear, Bishop Sbaretti, those shall be a requirement of not only the *offenders*—the priests and Bishops, and Archbishops if need be. But we must also reach out to the victims, so they are included in the *confidentia* and receive the blessings of the Sacrament of Penance as well. I expect all of the accumulated confessions, absolutions and atmosphere of forgiveness will include an explanation to the laity and reemphasized instruction to the clergy the understanding of the seriousness of the veil of secrecy in the confessional."

"Understood." Sbaretti yielded, submitting his notes to the Pontiff and nodded his compliance with his decree. However, he knew the nature of humanly created bureaucracies—the many levels of them in the priesthood within the Institution notwithstanding. He knew how the Pope's instructions would be managed differently at each level of the hierarchy. From the College of Cardinals to the affected Religious Orders and monasteries, to the administration in each Archdiocese, Diocese, and finally at the parishes, Sbaretti doubted the Pope's wishes would be followed *to the letter*—since there would be none.

He personally knew certain Archbishops in the United States, with ambitions to join the College of Cardinals, would covertly ignore the

Pontiff's instructions to them—feigning that something was lost in translation from the Italian-only speaking Pontiff. The best Sbaretti could hope for was that they would follow the *spirit* of the orders—if it suited them.

As Sbaretti began his retreat from the office, he stopped and turned back to the aging Pope when he heard him begin to mutter to himself. Apparently, the Pontiff's episode of lucidness was over for the moment, and he was reverting to his norm of late—which was dwelling in his own world and immersed in his inward thoughts.

Sbaretti had noticed during his assignment in the office of the Holy See, that this *muttering* was something that had become more frequent for the Pope over the last few months. At first he had suspected it to be a quirk of Benedict's personality, but later he saw it as a sign of aging and advanced dementia induced babble.

During these episodes—lapses in Benedict's cognitive reality, Sbaretti observed that the Pope often seemed to be having a running dialogue with an unseen, unknown person, or entity in the room. Was it an argument with Satan and his demons? Were they explanations to his ancestral Papal predecessors? Was it Benedict arguing with his own guilt-laden conscience? Sbaretti was never sure at first.

However, after having observed the behavior for some time, Bishop Sbaretti soon recognized that Benedict's mysterious *discussions* were in fact, the Pope's short-term recollections of the things he had *most recently read*. He was recounting them aloud. Sbaretti knew this was the fact from his own thorough review of the most recent incoming paperwork to the Vatican, as he had painstakingly familiarized himself with each report before giving it to the Pontiff for his reviews.

Sbaretti recognized that the subject of Benedict's current disjointed diatribe was unmistakably from a follow-up disposition sent to the Vatican from the Archdiocese of Milwaukee, Wisconsin in the United States. It regarded the case of a nun, who in 1907 had disappeared from the parish where she served. The official posture of the Archdiocese and her home Diocese in Michigan was that the nun had abandoned her vows and left on her own. However, recent revelations had discovered her remains found buried in the church cellar.

Out of respect, Sbaretti lingered in the room and listened to the Pope as he ruminated in his fog. "A new church is a fine idea, Father." Benedict rambled. "First, move the bones, Father. I trust you will *first*, move the *bones* prior to construction. Will you hear my confession?"

The Pontiff then stopped and seemed to drift off into a state of palsy and trance momentarily before resuming his meanderings and picked up his monologue at a later point in the missing nun story.

"...Father, only after a good confession and Act of Contrition can I give absolution. Should I start you off? Yes, yes, even though the unfortunate death of a soul—or is that *two*? Well, *two* if you count the unborn infant—if there was one. Do we know? Yes, Father Andrew, you know as well as I that as a Church, we *do* count the unborn as a soul—from conception! Your penance shall be three Our Fathers and three Hail Marys and a good Act of Contrition...I will contact your Bishop—Bishop Kelly, or is it Richter, to approve your transfer to a different parish...a different parish...different parish..."

"Your Holiness?" Sbaretti finally approached the Pope in an attempt to infuse some reality into the room to interrupt his prattling. Benedict looked up from the Papal desk's surface and blankly stared at his advisor but said nothing—as if in the throes of a petty seizure. But then in a few seconds he blinked and fully returned from his mental abyss.

"Why are you still here?" Questioned Benedict. "You have been given your orders. That will be all."

Feeling that the Pontiff had again returned to some normalcy, Sbaretti responded. "Yes, Your Holiness." He turned away and left the office to administer to the Pope's earlier instructions. He did this not so much out of loyalty to him, but to the Office of the Papacy and for the continued sake of the Church.

Chapter Forty-Six

Unevenly Applied Suspicions: Benefit of the Doubt for *Clergy*. However, NOT for *Laity*

> **Cross-examination of Father Andrew at the Preliminary Hearing for Stanislawa Lipczynska:**

After the discovery of the bones, Father Andrew and Stella were each detained by law enforcement for questioning under suspicion of murder. As the prime suspects, it was during canvasing and questioning of potential witnesses, that Stella's overly close and protective relationship with Father Andrew, and talk of their suspected tryst resurfaced. However, after so many years and beyond the rumors at the time, most would now only speculate that it was Stella who was under the misguided assumption that she and the priest had a relationship that went beyond friendship.

Regardless of the depth of that relationship, for investigators, it hinted at the possibility they were partners in the crime of Sister Janina's murder. Yet only Father Andrew had a solid alibi the day of the nun's disappearance—his fishing trip. And that was confirmed by several townsfolk. On the contrary, all who were questioned regarding Stella, confirmed her to be a bit of a religious zealot and completely loyal to the Pastor and his wishes—a near worshipping status. All uniformly believed she would do anything to preserve the sanctity of his moral spirit—including committing murder—which ultimately worked to her detriment. And it was common knowledge in Isadore that Stella had often disparaged Sister Janina.

A number of those who attested to Stella's dislike of the nun, would later have their words submitted into the record—regardless of some of them only rising to the level of *hearsay*. In more than one account, they contained a variation on a specific phrase used as condemnation of Sister

Janina that was attributed to Stella and used to establish *motive: You have turned the head of the men,* or *you are turning the head of the priest.* There were also several confirmations of her saying something to the effect of, "That woman is no kind of nun." A few others recalled Stella's outbursts of anger when fruit or baked goods that she specifically made as a gift for Father Andrew had been shared by him with Sister Janina and the other two nuns of Holy Rosary. In all, it would be the very public expressions of Stella's displeasure toward the nun that would lead to the severest of consequences for her.

Thus, to hear the Church tell it, the priest was completely exonerated and was properly released from culpability. As far as the legal authority was concerned, his alibi *for that day* was enough to exclude him from further investigation. Though, their focus and inferences of blame on the housekeeper was intensified and she would be charged with a Capital crime based on nothing more than circumstantial evidence.

Chapter Forty-Seven

Second Meeting/Confession with the Archbishop. Andrew Summoned to Milwaukee, circa, November 1918

"Thank you for making yet *another* arduous trip across the big lake to meet with me." Archbishop Messmer joyfully extended his hand with its ostentatious index finger ring waving in front of the demure Father Andrew.

"It is my pleasure." Andrew replied with politeness, if not sincerity.

"Is it?" Messmer question. "I'm surprised. I understand the wind and waves are frightful on the water today. Hopefully, the brewing storm will not be greater than the one in Scripture when our Lord walked on the water and calmed the seas to *save Peter.*" Messmer provided the perfect analogy. "I'm quite sure I *cannot* walk on water, Father. I may not be able to save *you.*" He looked over the top of his spectacles at the priest to make his point and glanced at his assistant who was also in attendance, Father Renault Alarie, who nodded in agreement. Messmer's point was not lost on Andrew.

"Well, it is good that you have a strong constitution for such upsetting situations!" The Archbishop stated with a hint of carefully worded sarcasm. "Please be seated. Sherry?" Messmer offered.

Although he would have liked to down the entire contents of the bottle from which Messmer poured to calm his anxiety, Andrew declined. "Thank you—no!"

"I suppose—being that you are of Polish descent, you would probably like a mug of beer, or as *your kind* calls it, a *kubek piwa*." Messmer laughed at his comparative stereotype."

"Thank you, *again*. No, your Excellency." Andrew squirmed.

"Shall I start you off—*again?*" The Archbishop mimicked and prodded. Andrew well knew he was being played by Messmer like a cat torturing a mouse—cornered—with no way to escape.

"Bless me father, for I have sinned..." Father Andrew began his portion of the Confession from rote memory. And while he verbally prefaced the ritual, he internally strategized what his potential answers might be to the Archbishop—in essence, his adversary in this stressful interaction. He plotted his rebuttals carefully and quickly came to the realization that his spiritual superior and *confessor* would again be in total charge of what was to transpire. He had no real options.

While the priest waited for Messmer's first foray of difficult queries, he also summarized Messmer's authority. Andrew knew from the *priestly grapevine* that the Archbishop had always had a complicated relationship with his majority Polish Archdiocese. Messmer, being of Swiss heritage—born in Goldach, Switzerland—he had often been criticized for not appointing a Polish bishop to his area until a full ten years after becoming the *Metropolitan* of the region. Bowing to pressure from the community, at long-last, Reverend Edward Kozlowski was named to the Bishop's post in January 1914. Many say this was Messmer's attempt to curtail the persistent criticism aimed at him by the local Polish newspaper, *Kuryer Polski*. In an editorial, they had suggested he was "Pro Germanic" in the buildup to WWI which began officially a few months earlier on 28 July of that year.

Thus, Andrew also imagined Messmer was somewhat enjoying his *third-degree* taunting of his Polish heritage under the guise of administering the Sacrament of Penance. However, in terms of the norms of a penitent informing a cleric their sins in a traditional Confession, Andrew was surprised this second episode would turn out to be more of a limited interrogation followed by a counseling session.

"Let's start at the beginning to refresh my memory. Tell me about the disappearance. Were there witnesses to that?" The Archbishop inquired. "Now, with this new discovery of the bones in *your* former church basement, how many years has it been since the nun's disappearance?" He attempted to clarify.

"Over ten." Father Andrew admitted as a matter of fact, with a relatively low degree of emotion.

"Were the remains reinterred?" Messmer asked even though he already knew that they had been by Father Podlaszewski from the word-of-mouth reports he had received from his well-placed informants in the clergy. "Who else was involved in that?" Messmer pressed.

For the second time he could ever remember—this time also in the company of the Archbishop—Andrew was not the one controlling the conversation. He felt the full weight of being on the receiving end of a lecture wrapped in condemnation. He fought the urge to establish his prowess. He knew he had no *cards to play* in this high-stakes game. If he and Messmer had been playing partners in the card game of Euchre, the Archbishop was going to *play this hand alone*. Andrew knew that his survival as a priest required him to remain completely subservient.

"Were the bones interred in the church basement the entire time after Sister Janina perished?" Asked Messmer. Then before Andrew could answer, the Archbishop digressed in a purposeful manner to *flex his muscles*, as it were, to show the priest that he had a far greater knowledge of the complete situation than Andrew would have guessed. "Father, you called the dearly departed *only* by her first name, Janina, in private, did you not? Or perhaps, Josephine? That was her given name, wasn't it?"

"I called her by *chosen* name, *Sister* Janina." Andrew responded with a bald-faced lie.

"Hmm, that's interesting." Ruminated the Archbishop. He said nothing beyond that, but turned and raised an eyebrow to his assistant, Father Alarie, indicating he suspected Andrew's answers were being crafted. "Father Bieniawski, what does law enforcement know of any of this?" The Archbishop delved deeply into the particulars.

"I…I'm not sure." Andrew could tell that his guarded responses were unsatisfying to the Archbishop and that they had started to annoy him.

"If the body was in the church cellar the whole time, how was it not discovered earlier? Messmer continued. "Surely there would be a smell! Or have you re-discovered the ancient Egyptian practice of mummification?

As Messmer continued to pepper him with questions, Andrew searched his mind and conscience for sufficient answers to satisfy the Archbishop and he was forced to recall some of the tragic events in the autumn of 1907.

Andrew's mind drifted back to his last conversation with his chore boy when he told him he was no longer able to provide money to him—a conditional stiped for his continued cooperation. That was several weeks after Janina's disappearance. He remembered that after he had given him the news, he observed the boy's suspicious last second addition of a canvas tarp and shovel to his horse drawn cart as he drove away from the parish. He relived his confrontation with him after he had sought him out at the hunting cabin. It did not go well. The boy had left the cabin in a huff and bolted into the woods. The priest had no recourse at the time but to return to the parish.

Later that same night, when Andrew traveled across the parish grounds to lock up the church, as he passed by the basement service entrance on the west side of the building, he noticed a flickering light through the transomed window of the cellar. Pausing, he then heard what he believed to be the repeated sound of a shovel being thrust into the earth.

Quietly, rounding the building and entering the church at the first-floor sacristy doorway, he saw debris scattered on the floor. Andrew recognized it as the black smudges of burnt incense— incense that had been used at High Mass for Benediction. He observed that the large metal ash bucket that was used to hold the spent ash was missing from its station. Though, he could see some of the incense's grime had spilled from the bucket and lay in clumps across the floor. The trail led to a trap door in the room that covered the steep, inside staircase that provided access down to the cellar. The trap door was open.

Andrew paused at the top of the stairs to listen. More shoveling below. It had to be Grubi. Swiftly but quietly moving down the stairs and reaching below grade, he was shocked to see the boy dumping an armload of putrid, rotting green canvas, brown wool, and a dark organic matter into a shallow excavated depression. Unable to speak out, Andrew stood in horror as the chore boy then tossed a layer of the still fragrant ash from the incense bucket onto the mass of decaying debris. The priest noticeably shuddered.

"Do you know if the Sacrament of Extreme Unction was performed upon the remains of the deceased Sister in the aftermath of the discovery as it should have been?" The Archbishop's voice pierced Andrew's disturbing memory and brought him back to the present.

"I do not know what Father Podlaszewski did. I was in Manistee." Again, Andrew's response was insufficient for someone so involved.

"I see." The Archbishop placed the index finger of his right hand to his lips and tapped them lightly to contemplate his next query. Andrew couldn't help but think that the ornate ring on Messmer's finger—with its amethyst center stone—was meant to impress him with the seriousness of the situation. At the same time, it offered a warning to the priest not to make the slightest hint of any more false statements to his superior.

"Father Andrew." Messmer leaned forward in his chair—maintaining a steely-eyed contact. "I now have some *general* questions about your *personal interactions* with the deceased. And only *general* answers will you need to provide me. The questions I will pose come to me from Auxiliary Bishop Kelly of Detroit who made a visit to Isadore and Holy Rosary a while back with a person knowledgeable of the situation. The questions are deeply concerning. Though, we can discuss them as men, and *informally*—just the two of us. Oh, and my administrative secretary. I almost forgot about you, Father Alarie."

Father Andrew had almost forgotten about the Archbishop's assistant as well. As was his intended duty, Alarie blended in. But when reminded of his shadowy presence, Andrew was chilled by the great potential of repercussions resulting from Alarie's eyes and ears being a witness to this meeting and perhaps his lips spreading its contents within the clergy.

In reality, Messmer's orchestrated discussion with Andrew was pure theatre. By the time of this second confession, the Archbishop was already well aware that a rudimentary examination of the sets of bones had been conducted at the time of their discovery by the current Pastor and sexton of Holy Rosary. Although highly unscientific and speculative—not a forensic medical examination, their findings held the belief that the nun had potentially *been with child* at the time of her death. This had been the conclusion passed up through the *priestly grapevine* to Messmer's office from priests in his own Archdiocese and through Bishop Kelly and then onto him. For the church, this additional element of the scandal had now risen to the level of consideration and treatment under the guidelines of the Vatican's *Ineditos Secredito Encyclios*—the *Secret Encyclical*—the highest level of confidentiality.

Keep in mind that at the time of his meeting with the Archbishop, Father Andrew was still unaware of the possibility of Sister Janina's pregnancy. That discussion between him and the nun or confirmation of the suspected fact had never taken place in either their oak grove discussion outside the church or during their last meeting in his rectory office.

Additionally, and troubling, the calculating Archbishop also did not inform Andrew of that critical possibility during this second confession. The possibility of such was only reportedly revealed to the priest while he sat in the gallery of the courtroom at the trial of Stella Lipczynska. According to several witnesses in the courtroom at the time, that new information was a shock of immeasurable proportion to the priest.

Why did the Archbishop withhold that detail during their second discussion? It is unknown. But perhaps he desired to retain the information as an additional *leverage point* with the priest—should he need it in the future.

After nearly an hour, Father Andrew could tell that he was near the conclusion of his discussion with Archbishop Messmer. He waited to hear his wise but also calculating judgement. He knew Messmer's ultimate decision on the matter would be weighted heavily toward the Institution's well-being—not his.

"Father, for the greater benefit of the Church, I'm sure you will agree that a series of transfers will be appropriate for you." Stated the Archbishop—sounding more like he was planning the seating arrangement for a dinner party rather than determining a fellow-clergy's fate. "Yes, I think it will be best for all. It will distance you from this scandal that has yet to be resolved, and it will serve the needs of the Church which are always evolving with retirements and other *situations*—let's call them, like yours that surface rather regularly, it seems."

Father Andrew was deflated by what he knew was the direction of the Archbishop's impending decision and reluctantly nodded his head in the affirmative.

"I understand your earlier request—or is that *requests?"* Messmer asked. Not receiving an answer from the priest, he proceeded. *"Your requests* to be transferred to my own Archdiocese in some capacity will be set aside for further review. Yes, I feel at this time that would not be in the best interest of the Church or my area of administration." Messmer flatly stated. "This was not my responsibility, I'm sure you can agree. Although, it seems to have been placed in my lap by you—and to be frank, your housekeeper! Thus, for you, staying in the remote parishes of the Grand Rapids Diocese, where this all transpired, would seem to be more appropriate. I understand they are in dire need of priests, and unfortunately a dwindling number of nuns in the *Isadore wilderness*—as you have stated." Again, the submissive priest nodded—fully realizing that nothing ever evaded the Archbishop's purview. Even the slightest comment by him, like referring to *Isadore as wilderness* had somehow gotten back to Messmer.

Messmer rose from his chair. He extended his right hand toward Andrew and performed the Sign of the Cross, which indicated the end of the meeting.

Andrew left the Archbishop's office and immediately made his way back to the passenger ferry at Manitowoc for return home. He had mixed feelings about the effectiveness of his *confession*—both in terms of preventing any immediate legal problems for him, and for his longer-term spiritual and career well-being. He knew he would be mistaken in assuming complete exoneration in either.

As the waves on Lake Michigan gently rocked, Andrew nestled into his deck chair on the starboard side of the ship. He was bathed in a brilliant late afternoon sunshine–even for this November day. Feeling like a man without a home—alone in the world, the swaying motion and warmth worked as a form of self-soothing—a comforting embrace in lieu of those he used to plentifully receive in his daily interaction with parishioners during his time at Holy Rosary. The nurturing gave him needed comfort and considerable clarity to review what had just occurred in the Archdiocese.

Andrew reasoned. He had been able to avoid discussing many of the problematic aspects of the mystery and was surprised that Messmer had essentially *let him off the hook*. He felt relieved about that, but he suspected that the Archbishop would now direct his considerable allotment of facts, suspicions, and rumors to further implicate someone else in the murder—someone not essential in the Church. He was sure it would be his housekeeper, Stella.

Overall, as he mentally reviewed the last few hours of his time in Milwaukee, Andrew understood and had seen firsthand, the tried-and-true, centuries-old Church practice of addressing internal problems. Both participants in the *confessional* operated on the assumption that the details of *their* conversation would not be shared with the community or law enforcement. It had been orchestrated and documented for a different audience—an audience of *one*. That *one,* being the person at the highest position of the Institution.

Administratively within the Church, there was to officially be only a single transcription of Andrew's and Messmer's encounter. It had been documented on official parchment, by one lone witness—Father Alarie. It would be carried by special courier to Europe and then on to Rome. There, it would *eventually* be read by the Pontiff, and perhaps by an Administrative Nuncio of the Vatican. Ultimately, regardless of action taken or not, the report would find its way to the accumulated documents of similar nature—arranged in chronological order, that were held in an ancient calfskin dossier. That dossier was the one locked away in the perpetually guarded desk at Castel Gandolfo.

However, for the meticulous Archbishop Messmer, in breaking with the prescribed protocol for things of this seriousness, he would also retain a contemporaneous, *unauthorized* copy of the events with Father Andrew. Additionally, further down the administrative line, there would also be at least one additional outline and summary generated for the Bishop of Grand Rapids—just for good measure.

In a state of half-sleep on the ship's deck, Andrew mulled the final portion of his discussion with the Archbishop.

> *"But Father, you should be assured of relative anonymity and sufficient confidentiality." Messmer concluded.*

The assurance gave little comfort to Andrew—but it was not supposed to. As stated by the Archbishop, it had been deliberately presented to him in this manner to keep Andrew looking over his shoulder for the extended future.

"And, for me?" Messmer added. "Now recite a good Act of Contrition—to cover the extent of your knowledge of the matters that we have discussed."

During the Contrition, the Archbishop concluded in Latin. "...abslovo a peccatis tuis in nomine Patris, et Filii, et Spiritus Sancti. Amen."

In Andrew's mind, the word, **absolvo**—*meaning absolution, felt hollow.*

Chapter Forty-Eight

The Atmosphere in Isadore: Enough Blame to go Around, circa 1907-1919

Transcribed from a *shorthand* note. The note, thought to be penned by a newspaper reporter from the Suttons Bay Courier, was retrieved from the documents found in Father Andrew's desk after his death. It is regarding the testimony of Mary Fleis, nee Lipczynska at the Preliminary Hearing for her mother, Stanislawa Lipczynska in 1919.

There is no record of the contents of the note ever having been published as written.

"She was nervous and difficult witness—often not understanding the nuances of the attorneys in questioning. Much explanation of terminology and translation from Polish to English was needed. Prosecutor unsuccessful in establish last time daughter saw mother and last time anyone saw the nun."

At this juncture, in attempting to establish Stella Lipczynska's whereabouts during the critical hours of Sister Janina's disappearance on 23 August 1907, it is important to place in context what was *next* said in her testimony with an extensive conversation. Mary's next answer under oath would be what we in a modern society would think of as racially offensive language. However, at the time of the story's setting, her open, unfiltered, and bigoted language was common—especially in segregated societies like Isadore.

For the Holy Rosary Polish Catholic community, it was common for ethnic slurs to be directed at *outsiders*—including the nearby Czech settlement to the northwest near Good Harbor, and to the northeast in Suttons Bay— despite the fact that the groups they were referencing were also Catholics.

Anecdotal evidence of that widespread practice was also documented in Father Andrew's own contemporaneous desk notes. A review of them in the 1970's showed he regularly espoused derogatory rhetoric for those *outsiders*. He was especially condemning of those of the Czech-Bohemian culture who were members of St. Wenceslaus Parish which was located only a few miles to the northeast of Holy Rosary. Pastor Andrew held a uniformly unfavorable view of their allotment of *chore boys,* who in his estimation during his interactions with them, were not receiving a strict enough education in the Faith.

The Poles of Isadore also frequently disparaged anyone *not* of their Faith. Reciprocally, there was considerable anti-Catholic sentiment throughout the country in the late 19th and early 20th centuries. Thus, the parishioners of Holy Rosary were also the target of frequent negative commentary. This sentiment could be traced to Protestant Christians and was a holdover from the Reformation of centuries earlier.

Anti-Catholic rhetoric was also prevalent among non-religious Americans who worried that a strengthening Church might attempt to take over the country politically. Though, the Church fought back with their own campaigns of propaganda including buying advertising space to spread their message.

Provemont Courier, 25 February 1916. (Public Domain)

Regularly appearing was this advertisement for a Catholic publication known for its continual efforts to refute anti-Catholic sentiment.

*"Catholics, **'Menace'** Readers, and others,*

should subscribe for the 'Sunday Visitor.'

and know the truth.

Subscription 50 cents per year.

SUNDAY VISITOR, Huntington, Indiana."

Cited as some of the specifics of the above contentions, at the time, there were plenty of other disrespectful and hateful terms that were common in conversation among the faithful whom they felt were those of the "Menace" types.

Terms like, *Honyock,* referred to the increasing population of mostly immigrant farmer and homesteaders from central or southeastern Europe— a large contingent of them from places like Hungary and the Balkans. Although a great number of them were also Christian, they were not quite acceptable to the Roman Catholic Poles as they were Eastern Orthodox. The slur of *Honyock* first appeared in print in the latter 1800's in the United States and was widespread in use throughout the time period of the tragedy in Isadore.

Bohunks—another ethnic slur, labeled the generally unskilled laborer from the European Province of Bohemia. (At the time, a part of the Austro-Hungarian Empire, later Czechoslovakia—now the Czech Republic). Although, Bohemian Catholics were also a majority Roman Catholics, the distance of around three hundred miles between the nations of Poland and Bohemia in Europe, and not speaking the same language, had created the rift in their interactions in the old country. That carried over to America.

In turn, those ethnic groups coined a term for the Polish of Isadore and elsewhere throughout Leelanau County and across the waters in Wisconsin. The insulting term, *Polack,* became a definition for ignorance, silly behavior, or a person with low I. Q.

Unfortunately, there was *one* area of agreement among these strictly segregated groups. They all used the "N" word for African Americans. With the area populated by an overabundance of what can be termed *white segregationists*—only a generation or so after the end of Reconstruction, they were universally suspicious and held unwarranted hatred for *blacks.* This was despite the fact that most residents of the Leelanau Peninsula had never interacted with that racial group. They were a rare sight in the remote areas of northern Michigan away from the larger cities of Grand Rapids, Saginaw, Flint, and Detroit.

For the community at large and the parishioners of Holy Rosary who were uninitiated in the difference, it was common for them to also apply the "N" word to the darker-skinned Hispanic migrant workers who appeared and left the area with the changing of the various harvest seasons on the surrounding farms and orchards. It seems the only area of agreement among the different local settlements, was the disparaging comments they used about others who were *non-white.*

That being explained, let's return to the Mary Fleis (Lipczynska) Preliminary Hearing testimony.

The following exchange is a textbook example of the above-described atmosphere around the Holy Rosary Parish. The crude language even made its way into cultured society as well as the courtroom. Here, under questioning, Mary revealed a shameful truth.

*Defense Attorney Glassmire addressing the disappearance of Sister Janina: "Didn't your mother also say to you, that the sisters had said "A little *igger stole her away?"*

As the nature of her testimony sinks in, also consider the possibility that an *outsider* may have had something to do with the disappearance of Sister Janina.

When it became apparent that Sister Janina was missing on the afternoon of the 23rd of August, the first reaction among many—apparently including the two remaining Sisters at Holy Rosary, was that most likely someone had *"stolen"* her away. In fact, it was Father Andrew's initial contention that "a drifter or other not of the community" was probably to blame for Janina's disappearance. He maintained this belief—at least in public, until his death.

Mary's insensitive testimony notwithstanding, one should also consider the possibility of *conflation* regarding Mary's confirmation of the utterance of Stella's *joke*; "A little *igger stole her away." It might have derived from *some* factual basis.

Per her later testimony, it was revealed that there was a resident of Isadore who lived fairly close to the parish. He had a *dog* that frequently roamed the grounds.

Take a moment to dwell upon or re-read the above.

Mary's testimony was that according to her mother, as told to her by the other two nuns of the parish, a *dog* had something to do with Janina's disappearance. That seems unlikely. More likely, Stella's meaning was that someone referred to as a *igger may have been the culprit.

To examine this further; Mary's drawn-out testimony served to expose to the outside world the temerity of the Isadore community to commonly think and talk in this racially insensitive way—even to the point of naming a resident's pet something so offensive. Additionally, if Stella's story, portrayed as a joke, was factual, that mindset even existed among Janina's fellow Felician Sisters.

And as it turned out, no matter which way one understands Mary's testimony, it was an unconvincing alibi to exonerate Stella, who would subsequently be bound over for trial. The only thing it did establish was a lesson in systemic racism.

Chapter Forty-Nine

Opening Statements in the Trial of Stanislawa Lipczynska. Difficulty in Finding an Unbiased Jury. Leland Courthouse, Leelanau County, Michigan, March 1919

"Gentlemen of the jury." Lead Prosecuting Attorney, C. L. Dayton, addressed the panel of twelve seated in the jury box. "This is a simple case. Sister Mary Janina was murdered, and we know who did it. It has unfortunately taken over a decade for it to be prosecuted."

The men selected as jurors—among the many summoned, listened intently. They were comprised of individuals who wanted to—once and forever—put the now highly publicized and terrible stain on their community behind them. They would *not* get their wish.

Attorney Dayton was confident that his presentation would easily sway the jury to convict. "And the murder was committed by none other than the defendant, Stanislawa Lipczynska—known as *Stella*." He turned to point his finger at the pitiful and aged looking woman seated at the oak table for the Defense. "We will prove this beyond a reasonable doubt—which is the requirement to convict any defendant in criminal court."

Turning away from the defendant and jury to address the gallery, Dayton continued his opening statement. "We will establish motive for the murder, opportunity to commit the murder, and they will be supported by irrefutable evidence—including a *confession by the defendant.* Let's continue…"

The People of the State of Michigan v. Stanislawa Lipczynska had met the first of the pre-trial requirements in the American Judicial system. The jury was made up of Stella's peers. Many of them had interacted with her on a daily basis when she was a fixture at Holy Rosary as the Pastor's housekeeper. Though, historians and observers would later debate whether a change of venue for the trial to another part of the state—perhaps downstate to a larger city, where indifferent jurors could have been chosen, would have been more appropriate for justice.

In retrospect, since it had been so long between the disappearance of Sister Janina and discovery of the bones—during the years 1907 to 1919, deep convictions and prejudices mixed with disinformation taken as fact about Father Andrew and his *entourage* had taken deep root in the jurisdiction. In fact, over the span of the ten-odd years since the nun's disappearance to the date of the trial, there was no one in the community who hadn't on at least one occasion discussed, spread salacious rumors, or offered conspiratorial opinions on who, why and when. Thus, opinion would be unlikely to change in this courtroom—even if exonerating circumstances or evidence was revealed.

Almost immediately after the disappearance, and increased national press coverage of it, wild speculations and beliefs had sometimes pivoted on charlatans who came to Isadore to hold seances and visits from traveling mystics who claimed they possessed powers to reveal the truth. More than one amateur detective showed up to lead groups of interested and sometimes amused citizens on treks through the swamps and fields around Carp Lake like a "pied piper." Fame seekers descended upon Isadore and orchestrated themselves with all manner of theatrics. Like dowsers divining for water with a forked stick, they used pseudo-science props in their failed attempts to solve the mystery. One even organized an excursion to the nearby community of Glen Lake searching for the truth based on his recurring visions of a basement.

Then, there was the consistent influx of anonymously penned letters coming into Isadore from 1907 up to 1919 when the murder case came to trial. Thought to be written by cruel pranksters, they attempted to see how many in the community they could fool with their specious claims. They maintained Sister Janina was still alive, to give up looking for her, or to drop the charges against Stella and inferred guilt upon the Pastor.

By the time of the trial, a flood of falsehoods had saturated the region.

Despite anyone's efforts or wishes to sweep the mystery under the rug and move on, it would turn out that no one had the where-with-all to make the publicity go away. A mélange of fact, fiction and opinion would fill the courtroom in Leland.

The above became apparent early on during jury selection. The prosecuting attorney asked the usual questions for the empaneled. "Are you already predisposed to a verdict?" If so, they were dismissed. But there were few that would answer that way. "Will you consider *only* the evidence presented in court—not hyperbole? All agreed that they could in their rote mechanical responses—although many did not know what *hyperbole* even was.

"Could you judge the defendant strictly upon the preponderance of innocence until proven guilty?" Shockingly, this standard question or a version of it, and subtle warning to the jury panel of the legal standard was *never* posed to any of the jurors by Stella's lead Attorney, Howard Campbell. One wonders why. Also troubling, there were no challenges to dismiss any of the obviously opinionated individuals in the jury pool by Stella's defense team.

During jury selection, more than one observer would attest to a hushed conversation that took place in the hallway outside the courtroom during a break. It was between Campbell and his associates, Attorneys Smurthwaite and Glassmire. The eavesdropped details were that they should more strenuously object to several potential jurors. However, for still unexplained reasons, when court reconvened, Campbell did not exercise his right under *voir dire*—to ferret out biased jurors, and the selection process finished in an orderly and surprisingly *dispassionate* way. The twelve were chosen.

After the trial, it was reported that at least two jurors commented that they had wished the Defense had taken more time in trying to empanel an *unbiased* jury.

"It's like they wanted to get it done and over with." Said Juror #7.

"You'd think they would at least make a show of it, so it didn't look like we was railroadin' her." Added Juror #3.

However, in retrospect, it appears early on the Defense conceded that coming up with a dozen men without pre-conceived notions in the same jurisdiction as the crime was impossible. So, they didn't expend any energies in trying.

From a newspaper reporter's notes: Overheard during a recess in the trial, circa March 1919

Mr. G. S., Juror #7, in conversation with another juror. (Speaking of Father Bieniawski) "He's awful charming on the stand. I just don't see how he didn't get arrested and charged too!"

Overheard conversation between two women in the gallery, Leland Courthouse, March 1919.

"I always thought there was something to the rumors. Who didn't know that Father Andrew was a little too cozy with the women?"

"And now Father Podlaszewski with a teenager? What's this church coming to?"

Chapter Fifty

The Trial's Opening Statements Continue – Establishing Motives - Tactics to Confuse

"Why would Sister Mary Janina's bones be found buried in the basement of the old church?" Prosecuting Attorney, C. L. Dayton asked the rhetorical question to the jury. "Per the testimony you will hear, and the affidavits you will read, that is an undisputable truth. But why? *Why* would this nun's remains be placed in a location where one would think that under ordinary circumstances, they would never be found? However, eleven years after interment, after everyone had long ago given up hope to find her alive, the bones *were* found. But only by happenstance. By a one in a million chance."

"That one in a million chance was pure coincidence." Dayton belabored his point. "The Sister's bones were discovered when a proposed new church would be built over the old and construction would likely uncover what had been buried for nearly 11 years. I know that the murderer, Stella, never imagined they'd be found!"

"Objection." Attorney Glassmire rose and strenuously announced.

"Your Honor!" Protested Dayton. "He's not allowed to *object* during my opening statement!"

"Your Honor—under normal circumstances, no!" Responded Glassmire. "But he's interjecting his own personal *belief*—he said so himself. He is not a witness or expert! In addition, he's attempting to introduce evidence that does not exist. It hasn't even been established by law enforcement investigators that the bones are even those of the missing nun. No one has ever even confirmed she is dead."

"Attorney Dayton, he's got you there—at least the first part of his objection! Leave your personal opinion out of it." Ordered presiding Judge Frederick Mayne.

"A verbal faux pau, Your Honor—won't happen again."

"Uh, huh." Mayne was unconvinced of his sincerity. He then addressed Glassmire. "It is true that under normal circumstances, opposing attorneys cannot object during opening statements. However, that rule is waived if the Prosecutor is mentioning evidence in his statement that he is never going to include in the trial." Mayne turned to Dayton. "I assume you will attempt to include evidence supporting your claim, Mr. Dayton—otherwise, you are flirting with a *mistrial*."

"Yes, your honor." Dayton assured.

The lecture to the litigants over, Mayne spoke to the jury. "I will warn you folks, that the questions Mr. Glassmire brings up will have to be considered by you at some point—based on evidence—not anyone's personal beliefs. Likewise, you will also get a chance to weigh Mr. Dayton's claims by the same standard."

"So, objection overruled!" Responded Judge Mayne. "Oh, and refrain from the dramatics, Mr. Dayton. Just present your opening statement."

"Sorry, Your Honor." Attorney Dayton laid the groundwork for his conclusion. "Who would have chosen the crawl space cellar of the church to dispose of the body? It had to be done by someone who had access to the church—at any time of the day or night. They had to have access to the keys to the building. They had to be someone who wouldn't be noticed as *out of place* in the space. They had to be someone who might be—say, I don't know, a cleaning woman! Someone like that! Someone who perfectly fits the description of the *defendant*." Dayton again pointed his finger at Stella—this time without looking at her. Stella, understanding little of the Prosecutor's nuances of his dissertation, showed no reaction.

"But motive—*motive?*" Dayton emphasized. "Why? Why would she do that? The attorney paused for effect. "Well, it seems that several witnesses have confirmed that the defendant had sufficient *motive* to commit the crime. In the days just before Sister Janina's disappearance, Mrs. Lipczynska was heard to complain that someone should *do something* about her. To politely state it, that the defendant was convinced that Sister Janina had an untoward effect on the men of the parish—impure, base, male-female interactions. *Something* needed to be done about that! We will show that several witnesses heard her say things to that effect. The State contends that the *something* that needed to be done—that Mrs. Lypczynska spoke about, was to *kill* Sister—in cold blood—and then cruelly bury her the basement of the church—stuffed into a shallow grave."

The courtroom loudly exhaled in unison at the grizzly description. Attorney Dayton heightened the drama of his oration. "But in a further self-righteous perversion of justice, in the defendant's mind, her overarching motivation to do *something* about Sister Janina was her religious obsession—arbiter of piety—monitor of morality." Dayton's performance continued. "The rest of her motivation is the fact that she was convinced that the Sister wasn't upholding *her* religious vows of chastity— as if that were any of her business. It was as if she had appointed herself as the *moral cop* of the parish. Imagine that! She was worried that Sister Janina might be making romantic advances toward the Pastor of the Parish. She couldn't stand by and let that happen!"

Stella well understood *that* accusation and turned and looked toward Father Andrew who was seated in the gallery behind her. Her telling glance was followed by twelve sets of eyes of the jury and a majority of the others in the courtroom turning in their seats to look at him. Father Andrew, normally cool under pressure, anxiously fidgeted and adjusted his collar. A rosy flush crept up his neck as the collective noise of the assembled shifting in their seats, along with a disrupting murmur brought a gavel from Judge Mayne. "Quiet! You all have a right to be here, but if you are disruptive, every one of you will be out on the street. And again, Mr. Dayton—*dramatics?*"

"Yes, Your Honor, I apologize." Dayton meekly acquiesced but knew in a minute he would have to take the chance to upset the judge again. But for the moment, he needed to tread lightly in order to be able to reach for the crescendo he had scheduled at the peak of his oration at the conclusion.

Judge Mayne peered suspiciously at the Prosecutor over the top of his glasses—gavel in his hand at-the-ready.

Attorney Dayton lowered his voice an octave and spoke in measured cadence as he continued. "The defendant is personally so obsessed, with a religious conviction so deep within her, that it compelled her to act in a violent manner—even *taking a life*—if it meant that she was doing it out of an overarching love of Church. By doing so she would preserve the vows of a member of the clergy—Father Andrew, over that of an individual life—Sister Janina's. The defendant decided herself that she would be some sort of modern Crusader—defeating her foe—Sister Janina—for the greater glory of the Faith."

"But this is a case of facts—not emotion." Dayton nodded to the Judge to show compliance with his earlier directive. "So, we'll look at those corroborating facts. We have the testimony of a jailhouse informant. By chance, that person was incarcerated in the same cell with Mrs. Lipczynska while awaiting trial. That informant will state under oath that Stella admitted to her that she killed Sister Janina."

Another gasp escaped the gallery. The Judge again banged his gavel, issuing a warning to several of the more animated near the back door of the courthouse, that if they could not control themselves that they would be expelled from the room.

"Why would she admit to the crime in jail?" Then Dayton posed the *devil's advocate* query. "Why would she admit that to an informant? Well, here is perhaps the most important element that you in the jury will consider."

Dayton slowly walked to the rail at the front of the Jury box and leaned against it—the palms of his hands spread wide and firmly on the railing of the well-polished mahogany to provide the "lynchpin" of his argument. "Stanislawa Lipczynska, a religious zealot, had no qualms about admitting to the crime, because she had been given *forgiveness*. She had been given *forgiveness* by her revered Church in her *confession to them!* The office of the Bishop of Milwaukee—Bishop Kozlowski himself admitted on his deathbed to another priest and a mother superior that one of his priests had *heard* her confession."

Judge Mayne needed to bang his gavel several more times. He did so not only to restore order, but because of Dayton ignoring his earlier instructions—submitting hearsay as some sort of fact in his opening statement. The Judge was in jeopardy of losing control of the proceedings. "Ten-minute recess!" He angrily ordered. "I'll see both attorneys in my chambers. Now!" He dropped the gavel, stormed off the bench and out of the courtroom.

The courtroom again collectively gasped. Though they reacted for different reasons. Most did so because of the display of histrionics. However, more than a few were appalled—most of them Catholics, because of the mention of *confession*—meaning the Sacrament of Penance.

After the recess, both attorneys and the judge reentered the courtroom. The Prosecution resumed their opening statement. "I have an affidavit from Mother Superior Veronica and a Father Lempke of the Archbishop's office in Milwaukee attesting to the veracity of Bishop Kozlowski's deathbed revelation. They *will* be presented as evidence." Attorney Dayton confidently stated—obviously having won the battle for its admission in the Judge's chambers. He held the affidavit high above his head. "Submitted as evidence—proof!" He waved it under the noses of the men in the front row in jury box as he slowly paced by. "Yes! He!..." Then he lowered his voice and breezed past the technicality of his next phrase. "...or one of the priests in his diocese..." Then he raised his voice again for dramatic effect. "...*heard her confession!*"

The entire courtroom again reacted loudly despite the Judge's earlier warnings. However, this time, Judge Mayne surprisingly did not admonish them.

Provemont Courier, 16 October 1919 (Public Domain)

"The Isadore case is progressing nicely. The bones were positively identified as those of the missing Sister. The trial will last about 2 weeks more as per indications."

Chapter Fifty-One

Defense Rebuttal in Opening Statements – Missed Opportunities. Mixed Result for the Prosecution

At this early point in the trial during the Defense's opening statements, a discussion of the *semantics* of a *confession* as the word is understood in the secular world of the law and *hearing* a *confession* as it is understood in the religious world of Catholicism, should have been warranted. In lieu of a clarification by the Judge or defense attorney at the beginning, at a minimum, during the Prosecution's later oral arguments in the trial, a strenuous objection should have been lodged by the Defense to point out the distinction to the jury and to the gallery. While a few in the courtroom—the ones who were more familiar with the investigation, documents, and evidence, anticipated some motion to rule out the hearsay nature of a Catholic Confession being admitted in trial, surprisingly, that never occurred. This would turn out to be a significant triumph for the Prosecution, and a self-inflicted "gut punch" to the Defense.

An explanation to compare and contrast the term *Confession* in order to underline the significant distinctions for the jury's benefit—the one never presented by any of Stella's Defense team, could have sounded like the following:

"Confession is not an unusual concept for a Catholic. It is a regular occurrence for a priest or even a bishop to hear a confession. Most practicing Catholics also receive Confession— this Sacrament of Penance on a regular basis—every few weeks at a minimum. This is a centuries-old practice that was mandated by the Vatican. Thus, on this point, you Catholics on the jury understand the word Confession to mean the above definition and do not understand it as admitting to committing a crime!"

"To both Catholics and non, in the courtroom gallery and for the benefit of you newspaper reporters, the way the Prosecutor is presenting the terminology of confession—whether it be to a priest in a church confessional, or in a jail cell to an informant, is being purposely presented in this way to confuse you—meant to infer that Stella had confessed to the murder—to make you think that it has already been established and is now a moot issue. It is not!

Granted, something to the effect of the above, albeit a complicated explanation from the Defense, and potentially difficult for the jury to follow, should have been attempted. But unfortunately, that kind of rebuttal never happened.

This lack of clarification was also alarmingly missing in any affidavits and/or testimony at trial from any source in the clergy. One would think at least one of them—Father Andrew, the Bishop, the nuns—would raise a question or submit an amendment to their affidavit to the Judge to emphasize the difference. Or in lieu of that, make a concerted effort to point out the dishonesty of the Prosecution's claims to Stella's attorneys so they could object. They surely knew how bad either alleged *confession* looked for the woman's case. But they too were lax in this area.

In fact, at least one person did object to the scenario playing out in the courtroom. There was a report that one disgruntled man from the gallery shouted out to Defense Attorney Campbell as he walked out of the building. "Subpoena the Bishop! Subpoena the Bishop! Put him on the stand! She's being railroaded!" A couple of others shouted their agreement to that suggestion to the quickly exiting lawyer. The men knew that a *subpoenaed* Bishop would be compelled to give authoritative testimony that would offer an explanation in the difference or point out the obfuscating tactic of the Prosecution. The Bishop would also have to come clean on how anything from a Sacrament based on privacy was allowed to leak out into the public discussion and how long they knew about it. However, none of that would ever occur because Bishop Kozlowski—the one who had leaked the contents from the confessional, had passed away.

Additionally, upon close examination of the affidavits submitted by Father Lemke or sister Veronica regarding the deathbed confession of Bishop Kozlowski, neither one ever specifically mentioned Lipczynska as the person who *confessed* to the crime in their Confessional. It only stated that a *woman*—speaking Polish, had confessed to having *knowledge* of a nun *disappearing* and *feared* dead. Later, again by method of *interpolation*, the confession now contained the added details of Stella being the woman who confirmed that she killed a nun and that she had buried her in a church basement in Michigan.

Then there is the legal concern from the Judge's viewpoint. How was a third-hand account of someone's confession—from someone who was no longer alive, allowed into evidence? That is legally *amazing*, and potentially, legally *contemptable*. But again, there would be no explanations forthcoming, no attempt to justify the dubious legality of it by Judge Mayne. It was simply allowed without commentary. The tainted evidence would stand, and not even substantially considered later by the Appellate Court during Stella's appeal in 1920.

At this juncture, it should be asked: What was the result of the Prosecutions' devious presentation to the jury—with intentional play on words and conflated meaning and interpolated additions within of the realm of *Confession*? At first observation, it seems to have succeeded. But as the trial wore on, it would also work against them. It would actually sway those on the jury who were practicing Catholics to initially advocate for acquittal in deliberations.

That group of fervently faithful on the jury were uniformly galvanized in their abhorrence of the Prosecutor for presenting as evidence what was alleged in the affidavits of the Bishop and Priest—suggesting Stella made *confession of the crime* to them. As presented in opening statements, the Catholics were distressed to think that those church authorities leaked the private contents of Stella's sacred *Sacrament* to either the Prosecution or law enforcement investigators. They became terribly dismayed that their religious mentors would violate that long-established norm of secrecy in the confessional.

Some jurors would later gather at a local *watering hole*. A series of statements categorized their displeasure at the trial's outcome.

"Can you imagine being betrayed by the Bishop or their Pastor?" Someone exasperated.

"Both the Bishop and the Pastor says there was a confession! Must be! No one said it didn't happen!" Added another.

"I feel bad for Stella. She told them in secret." Whispered yet another.

"No matter what she did or didn't do, how can we hold that against her if she'd been givin' absolution by the Church? If them priests are the closest thing to God on this earth—and that's what we been taught to believe—and they gave her forgiveness, who are we to punish her?" A patron questioned.

Another loudly spouted off. "Maybe the priests and bishops should be prosecuted as accessories to the crime. Sounds like they knew about it for a long time and covered it up. How long has Father Andrew been gone from Holy Rosary—five-six years?"

Each Catholic on the jury panel, and virtually every Catholic in the courtroom gallery now wondered how secure any of *their* confessions would be if the lips of the religious were that loose. Based on what they heard in the courtroom, few of them would ever participate in the Sacrament of Penance again. That sentiment also spread to the community in Isadore and church attendance plummeted. Those that weren't completely disgusted by the trial revelations or had totally renounced their Faith, started making the trip to other nearby communities for Sunday Mass.

So, the end result would turn out to be a mixed outcome for the Prosecution. On one hand, the misunderstanding of semantics in C. L. Dayton's presentation generated another layer of guilt heaped upon Stella. That was intended. But an unintended consequence of that ploy was that among some—the Catholics—the betrayal of Stella by the Church leadership created much sympathy for her.

Additionally, unintended animosity was also created by law enforcement's placement of a jail-house informant in the cell with Stella while she awaited her trial date. To a man, they felt any statements from the Defendant were probably secured through fraud and/or coercion.

Attorney Glassmire of the Defense focused on the occult-like mental and emotional torture allegedly placed upon Stella while incarcerated. They contended that the tactics of taunting her with the bones of the deceased in her jail cell, under what law enforcement called the "third degree" was particularly cruel and any confession obtained by it could not be reliable. The jury saw it that way too.

In retrospect, pressure tactics by investigators—ones coordinated with the Prosecution would spectacularly backfire. There was uniformity in thought among the jury that found the informant's testimony to be a *much too polished yarn*. They did not believe that Stella would—with impunity— openly confess to a paid law enforcement plant. No one believed that Stella would be that naïve.

Imagine, someone who was also fluent in Polish, supposedly incarcerated for a misdemeanor, placed in a jail cell with a suspected murderer? Even Lipcznyska would find that suspicious. In post-trial interviews, most in the jury believed the Prosecution needed to conjure up this additional *confession* to increase the likelihood of conviction. They could sense that the Catholics on the jury would reject the idea of *confession* being obtained through the Church, so they needed to double-down. However, Stella's own wild account of torture and coercion while in jail also sounded a bit too fantastical and improbable—although she was denied legal representation for quite some time while incarcerated. And the alleged mental torture described by her would certainly affect anyone, they thought.

Based on these troubling irregularities, the Government's case wavered. Though, the Defendant's shoddy representation was also riddled with unbelievability. Many speculated that a hung jury and subsequent mistrial was very possible.

Historians would later speculate, that Stella's defense team was guilty of malpractice—that they had already accepted as verbatim that Stella had indeed confessed to murder at some point—or at many points to Church clergy, and possibly also to the jailhouse informant—albeit under the claims of duress. Campbell's flaccid defense of Stella seemed to lay solely on two areas.

The first was his claim that the bones discovered were not the bones of Sister Janina at all—although accompanying materials from the gravesite tended to make one believe they were. The second, that even after a decade, it hadn't been established that she had actually died. These were not believable to the jury. Those contentions were quickly undermined in the view of several jurors and completely dispelled by others. Even lacking modern forensic evidence, the nun's reinterred bones exhumed from the adjacent cemetery and the unique ring found in the shallow grave under the church—identified as Sister Janina's, were circumstantially linked together to act as confirmation of the identity of the bones.

As far as Stella herself, on the witness stand, she seemed composed and never cracked under intense questioning by the Prosecution. She calmly denied every accusation against her. She was a solid witness. But in the end that was not enough.

In all, the jury ignored the Defense's two main contentions and Attorney Campbell failed to offer any other *reasonable doubt* to acquit Stella of the crime.

Some later historians would also float another troubling idea. The reason for Stella's inadequate defense, was that her attorney was complicit with the Prosecution for some unknown reason. Possibly he was also in league with the Church, and that he had agreed to only offer a passive defense to expedite the proceedings. Still others would argue that especially, lead Attorney Campbell was continually distracted throughout the trial—going through his own papers and doodling rather than listening to the evidence being submitted by Prosecution to then present any plausible rebuttals.

There was one area of total agreement. The empaneled jury wanted to quickly move past the community's decade of embarrassment, which had now spread statewide, nationally, and even internationally to Rome, the Vatican and across the European continent. They were evenly split as to why. Some believed the quickest way to expedite the end and move on, would be *to acquit.* The rest thought it would be quicker *to convict* to achieve the same end.

Chapter Fifty-Two

Public Sentiment. April-August 1919

As the Lipczynska trial progressed, updates continued to funnel back to
Manistee. The community sentiment of anger and disappointment there
and especially at Father Andrew's parish of St. Joseph's boiled over. The
Grand Rapids Diocese was worried that demonstrations could occur in
church during Mass. Reports at the time suggested that the Diocese had
requested law enforcement be on site to quell any trouble that might erupt.
Based on fallout from the proceedings in the Leland courthouse, a church
group—likely the Ladies Auxiliary, then formally requested that Father
Andrew be removed as Pastor.

Chapter Fifty-Three

The Defense Rests. Stella's Fate in the Hands of the Jury

> **The Northport Gazette, 26 October 1919, EXTRA!** (Public
> Domain)
>
> **Murder Trial Goes to Jury. Comes back with Conviction**
>
> *"On the same day of closing arguments, the Jury in the murder
> trial of Stanislawa Lipsnski (sic) counted twelve men to convict.
> Those willing to speak after released from duty say they had no
> other choices that seemed apparent. Some had wished to hear
> more evidence. 'Three in the room were unconvinced, blame to be
> shared elsewhere, but voted in the majority.' Recalled one juror, a
> Mr. G. S."*

In the end, after a long day of deliberations, where the possibility of a hung
jury loomed large, surprisingly, the twelve came back with a guilty verdict.
Their decision was not based on anything of real substance they had heard
in the courtroom. It was mostly based—not on actual forensic evidence
linking Stella to the crime, but on their gut feelings.

The only real expert to testify was a medical examiner who inspected the bones. His observations from the post-mortem examination of the remains showed a blunt force injury to the skull that eventually caused death. That lined up neatly with the jailhouse informant's testimony—as uniform as if choreographed. But that was not a determining factor in the jury's decision. Nothing else was offered to the jury to seriously deliberate. Despite many other plausible theories that could have been put forth for the causes of Sister Janina's demise, or who else could have committed the murder, they were noticeably absent from consideration.

Thus, three jurors—later identified as jurors #3, a Mr. G. S., reported to be #7 and #11, who each had serious problems with the State's presentation, simply relinquished their substantive doubts about the *tainted testimony* and *circumstantial evidence* put forth by the Prosecutor. But when it was weighed against the lack of any substantive exculpatory theories provided by the Defense, it tipped the scales of justice toward a guilty verdict.

In the wrangling of impressions that took place behind closed doors, the doubters in the jury finally voted in favor of the Prosecution's version of events and settled on the conviction of the only person from which they had to choose. They had abandoned their sworn duty to only find guilt if it was beyond a reasonable doubt—which seemed to be in abundance—and settled for a majority opinion on the criteria that Stella had made it publicly clear she did not like Sister Janina.

However, to the majority on the panel, Stella did have a plausible motive for the killing. She was assumed to be in the vicinity at the time of disappearance. She had no alibi—unlike Father Andrew's conveniently planned fishing trip. Those who testified on her behalf were less than enthusiastic. The majority opinion made her out to be the logical and convenient sacrificial lamb. She could be that because Stella, a simple housekeeper, was admittedly the one person who's absence from the Manistee parish, where she now resided, would least disrupt *that* religious community going forward. They could easily find another cleaning woman for the Pastor.

Stella was also an easy choice to convict because after so many years, her presence and any importance had faded to the status of a *stranger* to the residents of the Isadore community. Strangers are easier to convict than friends. Without another suspect to consider, it made it easier to condemn their old *church lady*.

Finally, those with compassion for Sister Janina—and there were many, felt that *any* conviction would finally secure the modicum of justice she deserved. It was long past time for that.

In the end, there was simply no other course of action to be taken that would provide a conclusion to this painful saga. The trial ended in the conviction of Stanislawa "Stella" Lipczynska on 26 October 1919.

Chapter Fifty-Four

A Second Cache of Unanswered Questions and Possibilities

> **26 October 1919, Heard Outside Leland Courthouse After Conviction.**
>
> *"I'm telling ya, that's the last time I go to confession if'n they can't keep it to themselves."*
>
> Mr. G. S., Juror #7, People of the State of Michigan vs. Stanislawa Lipczynska

Now the drama was over, and peace had returned to Isadore—albeit an uneasy one.

In her lengthy trial, at one point it had been suspended when Stella had shown signs of having a mental breakdown. During the pause, over the spring and summer of 1919, she was sent to a psychiatric hospital for evaluation. But medical examinations had shown that she was feigning insanity and she was returned to her incarceration, then convicted, and was now serving time in the State Prison. She awaited her appeal, but that too would be denied by the end of 1920. Time passed. But unsettling questions remained around the entire 11-year period of the mystery.

Per the official public record, Stella was *solely* responsible for the heinous deed. But were others involved? And if so, who were they?

Would Stella have committed the crime on her own as the self-appointed moral compass of the religious community and the unofficial arbiter of punishment? Or had someone used her willingness to act in that capacity as a *pawn* to accomplish *their* aims, while they remained outside any direct accusations and above reproach?

After the disappearance of Sister Janina and the level of the gossip abated over the next few years, Father Andrew's service at Holy Rosary returned to a kind of *normal*. Though, eventually the situation around Isadore would continue to spiral downward. There was a steady loss of parishioners attending Mass and fewer children enrolled in the school as a direct result of the Sister Janina incident—as the residents had a fear of the school building being secure or possibly haunted. That, coupled with a loss of parish revenue and consequential reduction in his effectiveness as Pastor would end up in Andrew's transfer to a parish in Manistee, Michigan in 1913.

Between the time of Sister Janina's disappearance and Andrew's departure from Holy Rosary, and then again soon after the discovery of the bones in the church cellar in 1917 or 1918, there are many accounts pieced together along a murky timeline by interested members of the public and private researchers. None of them have been independently verified, but they seem to lock in place with the timeline of events.

Foremost among them was an overwhelming number of accounts from within the clergy that Father Andrew attempted to or actually embarked upon perhaps two or three trips across Lake Michigan to Milwaukee for interaction with the Archbishop of that domain. This is something he would not ordinarily do in his normal capacity. Those meetings have never been independently verified by any authority as having taken place. And the initial stories about them by anonymous individuals claiming such meetings, have over time been refuted and/or documentation of them destroyed.

If accounts of a conspiracy between the Archdiocese of Milwaukee and the Grand Rapids Diocese to manage the situation and deflect criticism away from the Church are true, it would most certainly have been a closely guarded procedure directed by the hierarchy of the Church. To date, there are missing elements of the above suspicion that may never be confirmed. But those that anecdotally exist, by cross-referencing small town newspaper stories of the time, and tracking key players, tend to infer some coordination of the Church entities as accurate. The other anonymous sources who initially rediscovered evidence of Church involvement and spoke of it in the 1970's, maintain it was mentioned in the documents found in Father Andrew's desk after his death.

If some combination of the above is accurate, how did the knowledge of Stella's alleged culpability escape the sanctity of the confessional against long-standing Church policy? Was it done by gossiping priests in the

Milwaukee Archdiocese who passed the story back to Michigan? Was it passively-aggressively leaked by the Archdiocese under orders of the Archbishop, who by doing so would whitewash any blemish on at least the portion of the Institution under his control? If so, this would place the burden of the post-trial negative publicity and effects back onto the Grand Rapids Diocese, and its lead prelate at the time, Bishop Eduard D. Kelly, and onto St. Joseph's parish where Father Andrew still served.

The following statement appeared in several Michigan publications, circa 15 November 1919, and announced in church bulletins published by the Manistee parish around that time without further explanation.

Church News

"Father A. Bieniawski, Pastor of St. Joseph's Catholic Church, has been granted a short vacation by the Bishop of Grand Rapids, Rev. E. Kelly."

There is much evidence pointing an accusatory finger directly toward Bishop Kelly. Those would be the various newspaper reports of him visiting Isadore with the sexton Gruba, prior to or around the time of the discovery of the bones, attending functions where Archbishop Messmer was also scheduled to attend, and his suspiciously timed promotion to Bishop. Additionally, there is his action of granting a *vacation* to Andrew immediately after the trial, showing to investigators and the considerable numbers in the doubting public, that he sought to lay blame on Father Andrew, and distance himself and his Diocese from the continued criticisms from the public produced by the trial—even though in the course of it they officially exonerated the Church.

Rather than point to the official conclusions of the State, the ill-timed granting of Father Andrew's *vacation* in late 1919 by the Bishop seemed to show a knee-jerk reaction to insulate his Diocese from the unabating scandal. After all, there was still the appeals process to complete. And that would extend throughout 1920. Thus, by the Bishop suddenly making Father Andrew *incommunicado*, it showed a much deeper Institutional involvement than anyone had suspected and guilt after the fact.

Another curious aspect that tends to point to guilt or at least a guilty conscience, was Father Andrew's post-trial behavior over the next several years. There is ample evidence that he spent much of his time and a considerable amount of his or someone's financial resources in efforts to have the convicted Stella released from jail as he *knew* she was innocent.

This brings up the discussion by some of where a priest, with a simple salary, would acquire the substantial amount of capital needed to spend on these legal efforts. The math would never add up. There was no evidence to support any private donations to his cause as public sentiment was largely against him post-trial. He was considered *persona non grata* to most Catholics. Some would speculate that it was the greater Church who funded his campaign. Unfortunately, the public will never get a look at the Vatican's books.

But why would the Church fund Andrew's campaign to clear Stella? Looking at this in another way, with the pressure now off the Church as far as legal culpability, but not in the public's opinion, it was still considered to be a supreme embarrassment for the Church. They might have been forced to supply funds to those-in-the-know—and there were many in the Institution—to keep *them* quiet. The prime candidate for that would be the person nearest the heart of the matter, Father Andrew.

The suspected undercurrent of funding activity between Church and priest occurring post-conviction for Lipczynska's legal appeals could also show a *continuing leverage* placed on the Archdiocese and/or Diocese by the resourceful Andrew. It could be a financial response from the Church because they feared that if they did not help Father Andrew in his campaign, his sorrow over the mystery might compel him to publicly confess out of guilt. The resulting *conspiracy of funding and silence* benefitted all parties.

Additional aspects post-trial show that there were countless letters of appeal and requests for mercy on Stella's behalf penned by Andrew and sent to various governmental and court entities. Eventually, those—along with the passage of time—and *time served* by Stella, were the things that worked to get her paroled by Michigan's outgoing Governor Alex Groesbeck in 1927.

Some would later say that Andrew's ardent defense of Stella was simply motivated because she was his loyal friend who had been in his service for years. He was properly returning the loyalty—regardless of her guilt or innocence. They point to the fact that she also served as his housekeeper during his time in Manistee after the nun's disappearance as proof. Others would argue that because his *old friend* was more than just that—based on the hushed scandal and rumors between the two—that he owed her not out of a moral contract, but out of love.

However, some say that it was only Andrew's own supreme guilt buried deep within him that drove him to help the old woman after her conviction. At some depth within him, human decency would not allow another to serve punishment for *his* sin—*his* crime.

Still others—those that did not have the highest regard for the priest, were convinced Andrew was worried that Stella—showing signs of mental breakdown—away from his direct influence—might reveal details of his alleged affair with the nun, or that she somehow knew of his efforts to permanently eliminate the looming *problem* he was facing with Sister Janina. Andrew could have been deeply concerned that Stella would implicate him out of desperation. Thus, he put his maximum effort to work on her behalf to keep her quiet—lest there would be a reemergence of the scandal that for the time had ceased to follow him.

Chapter Fifty-Five

The Second Major Incident of Possible *Conflation*

A major contention that has been misreported, enriched into the legend, but disputed by some, is the element of the story—that if true—makes the mystery even more intriguing and tragic. That is the unconfirmed contention that Sister Janina was pregnant at the time of her death.

Various versions of the story report this based on nothing more than speculation. Medical examination(s) of the retrieved bones never say that bones or material remains of an unborn infant were also discovered.

In the courtroom, there was also no physical evidence presented identifying *two* skeletal remains—although there was a verbal accusation of it. A side comment that suspected it, caused Father Andrew visible distress when hearing it. The bones displayed on a table before Stella in the trial were described as nothing more than *adult human bones*.

Forensically, most likely an unborn infant's remains would have never survived from the date of Janina's death in 1907 to the trial in 1919. With it being a non-embalmed burial, in direct contact with soil, the small and delicate bones—if they even had developed at that point, would have likely disintegrated over that time. One must also take into consideration the unknown number of times that the nun's remains had been interred, excavated, and reburied. Any materials could have been lost during those moves.

Thus, with the uncertainty over Sister Janina being pregnant, this part of the saga could be another case of *conflation* with another closely related story.

By sheer coincidence, we know there was a Pastor who did in fact impregnate a woman at Holy Rosary some eleven years after Janina disappeared, and roughly four years after Andrew was reassigned to Manistee. We know this to be a fact from the documented story—from both inside the Church and in the public—of Father Edward Podlaszewski and his tryst with a young woman which did create a child.

Since it cannot be confirmed without modern DNA forensics, or even attempted because no one is sure of the exact location of Janina's reinterment, it appears that Father Podlaszewski's story and Father Andrew's story seem to have merged over time. Thus, *conflation!* But in the many versions of the mystery, a pregnancy for Janina certainly made for a more captivating aspect for storytellers.

Chapter Fifty-Six

Life in Isadore Returns to Normal. Holy Rosary Finally Moves Forward. Justice Served—But Was It?

At long last, after Stella's appeal had failed, in early 1921, the long-ago approved plans for the new Holy Rosary Church of Isadore were bid out to contractors. With the help of volunteers in the community in the various trades—especially stonemasons, work began and continued in earnest while the weather cooperated in 1921 and 1922. However, final completion of the building would be delayed as the parish waited for the delivery of thirteen resplendent stained-glass windows that had been commissioned and created years earlier in Munich, Germany. But due to shipping interruptions to the United States during the conflict of WWI, they had to be stored in a hidden underground warehouse somewhere in Europe— buried in a heavy layer of sawdust to protect them from bombing. After years, they had finally been cleared to ship. They arrived in Isadore and were quickly installed to complete the project.

Finally, scheduled for Sunday, 12 December 1923, Bishop Kelly of Grand Rapids would bless the completed Holy Rosary Church in a High Mass. A new era for the beleaguered parish could now begin over three years after the official determination of guilt at the end of the appeals process in the *Sister Janina* mystery. But there was one more aspect to this story.

On Saturday 11 December 1923, Father Andrew made his way back to Isadore for a visit with a few old friends. He would also attend the long-delayed dedication Mass for the new church the following day.

Father Andrew had not visited the parish in years. In the years after the nun's disappearance, he was strategically transferred regularly by Church authority to serve at other parishes in Michigan. It was believed this strategy would decrease the amount of scrutiny of him by parishioners in those locations.

For Andrew, none of those transfers would ever be consider a *promotion* within the hierarchy of the Church. His youthful driving force concerning career goals had predictably waned. He well knew, after the controversy and scandal at Holy Rosary that occurred during *his* tenure, not to expect any special treatment going forward. He was no longer on the fast-track or politically connected to affect anything regarding his career. And he was painfully aware he was on a *tight leash* regarding any of his future actions and was well-monitored.

Andrew was now simply a common priest existing to honor his vows and to serve the faithful. Additionally, with his relative advance in age, his human desires were also beginning to decline. Not surprisingly, his stopover in Isadore would be a short one. And he would not be given the honor of being one of the assistant officiants of the Dedication Mass. He would simply be a spectator.

Physically, Father Andrew now had a slightly slower step, a little grayer at the temples, and was far more introspective about things—less ebullient, less open with those he met—less optimistic. Scandal and suspicion can do that to a person.

The priest entered the nave of the new Holy Rosary. He walked slowly down the center aisle toward the main altar. Stopping before the altar, he remembered the hundreds of times in the old church where from that spot he had consecrated the host and wine into Body and Blood. He stood silently, taking in the impressive structure with its large but welcoming space. He marveled over the beautiful stained-glass windows depicting major Bible scenes that splashed brilliant colors of light over the interior.

Walking further up the aisle, Andrew ran his right hand over the ornately carved ends of each pew made of sturdy oak as he passed them. Missing from each touch was a once familiar tap-tapping sound that would have accompanied it. The sound would have been emitted from his gold ring with amethysts stone on his index finger as it made contact.

It had been a long time since he had been emboldened to wear the ring. He was not even sure of where it was—probably in his old desk. That was in storage somewhere in the Grand Rapids Diocese.

Andrew spent little time dwelling on that. None of that really mattered to him anymore. Wearing the ring would only serve as a distant reminder of his demotion, confession, and humiliation at the hands of the Archbishop of Milwaukee. Relinquishing that ring was Andrew's acquiescence to the Church's authority and to its traditions in exchange for acquiring the absolution he had sought and his continued existence as a priest. However, Andrew knew that the absolution he *did* receive was for *only* what he had admitted to Archbishop Messmer.

Returning to the present, Andrew continued to survey his surroundings. "Yes, this new Holy Rosary Church will serve the community for at least another century." He spoke to the empty space. His voice echoed. The hollowness of the sound depressed him. He would not be the one at the helm to guide the parish in their new church building. Ironically, he had been the one with the initial idea to replace the old church.

Remembering, he drifted back in his mind as best he could to those early days. With difficulty, Andrew recalled when he first performed Mass in the old Holy Rosary, with its clapboard structure, its creaky wooden floors of old growth white pine. As celebrant, his Masses were performed to an audience of hearty Polish homesteaders with intents to tame the primitive environment.

The priest summoned up the unique sounds that the old structure rhythmically made, as if it were able to breathe. He especially reminisced on the breezes that used to flow along the nave of the church when the windows were swung wide open on a warm August day. The refreshing air would wind its way from the oak grove that stood on the church's north side.

Then he remembered how those oaks had failed in their discretion. In his mind, they had willingly breached the privacy they should have afforded, and they had allowed the witnessing of his most scandalous secret—the heartfelt conversation he had with Sister Janina. Reliving that evening vividly, it gave him a slight shudder.

Moreover, he blamed that overheard conversation in the oak grove as not only responsible for his decline, but overall, it had contributed greatly to the decline of the parish. There had been a great reduction in church attendance, collections, enthusiasm, and widespread loss of Faith since the scandal. Some would also say he was unilaterally responsible for the decline of the Isadore community. The great potential for and steady growth of the settlement had stopped because of his actions. He shamefully had to admit. From his future parish assignments, he would watch the steady decline of Isadore. By the middle of the 20th Century, it would start to be listed on area maps as a *ghost town*.

Andrew sighed with disappointment in how things had changed for him. His priestly mission was so simple back then and he knew he was solely responsible for straying from it. With the reconciliation, the encumbrance of guilt had finally visited him at the time of its choosing—just as he had been warned in the writing of a fellow priest many years ago.

Andrew reached the front of the nave of the church. He crossed the aisle of the *transept* and past the communion rail. Unsteadily, he shuffled across the *chancel* toward the *sacristy*—the room behind the altar where a priest dresses in his vestments and prepares himself for the important duties he is about to perform in the stead of Christ during the Catholic Mass. Stopping at the entrance door, Andrew suddenly felt a sense of not belonging—not being worthy to be there. Though, he forced himself to step into the space.

He was surprised to find a young woman on her hands and knees scrubbing the polished Carrera marble floor—her vigorous action gently swaying her feminine form. The view stirred something within him—deep from within his suppressed libido. He had seen this sight before. It rekindled a fond memory which triggered a dementia of sorts in him and overcame the current reality.

"You are doing a fine job, Stella." Andrew interrupted the soft, rhythmic *sweep-sweep* sound created by the bristles of the wooden brush the woman worked. "Perhaps later you could join me for a glass of…"

The young woman was startled by the priest and immediately stood up and turned to him. "Monsignor?" She timidly questioned.

Immediately recognizing his error in mistaken identity, Andrew did a self-correction to regain his composure and place. He silently admonished himself for the confusion, as incidents like this had become increasingly frequent. Mentally for him, the mix of reality and distant memories had been increasingly *conflated* over the last few months and had now crossed the line from jumbled memories to clinical early dementia.

Embarrassed, Andrew immediately corrected himself. "I mean, I'm sorry. You reminded me of someone I knew a long time ago. You can continue." He then added an unusual assurance. "I won't bother you. I am not allowed." However, the alarmed woman remained standing—her brush dripping soap and water on the floor.

Andrew stepped back a few paces toward the oak hewn kneeler in the sacristy where an officiating priest would kneel to recite his before-Mass prayers. He did not bend his knees at it but steadied himself against it with his left hand. He then bowed his head and looked down. Regaining his balance, he slowly folded his hands—seemingly to say prayers.

Out of deference to the Priest, the young woman, who remained standing, also bowed her head, and clasped her hands—still holding the wet brush. She would silently pray with him. But in reality, Andrew was not about to pray—not yet. He was contemplating what lay *below* him.

Known only to him—and his God—and maybe to Father Podlaszewski and the Sexton, Jake, Andrew knew that directly below his feet—some fifteen feet under the sacristy, was the exact previous location of the reinterred bones of Sister Janina. He knew he stood directly over the location from his many reviews of the blueprints for the new church of brick and fieldstone that was to be built over the same spot as the old wooden church, and from his encounter with his chore boy that one night.

He remembered how he had purposely kept up with the news of the demolition of the old structure by volunteer townsfolk. Filled with anxiety at the time, he waited for someone—law enforcement or church authority to come to him with new questions upon an *additional revelation* coming from the cellar of the old church. But weeks and then months passed. Construction of the new building progressed without incident to its completion. No one had ever reached out to him. He wondered if that additional revelation *had* occurred during the excavation, but it had been handled in the same way as it had been for the initial discovery of Sister Janina's bones? Had it been suppressed in the Church's traditional way and thereby insuring another scandal for some future generation of Holy Rosary and Isadore?

Andrew continued to look down, as if he could peer through the marble floor and into the sub-structure of the building to where at one time, from under dirt, ash and a stack of lumber, Sister Janina's bones had been unearthed by the new pastor of Holy Rosary, Father Edward Podlaszewski and his sexton.

Father Andrew remained focused on the floor of the sacristy in the throes of his pseudo-prayer. The young cleaning woman had grown uncomfortable of the odd situation and had quietly slipped out the side door. Andrew did not notice as he continued to mull over his recollections.

He myopically lamented. If not for the new pastor's insistence on building a new Holy Rosary—without that incident of fate, he might still be a Pastor of *some* parish—even if not in that capacity at Holy Rosary. Father Andrew expelled a deflating sigh.

The priest had barely escaped official implication in the crime and had avoided any secular punishment. He was relieved in that. But he accepted that the name of Andrew Bieniawski would perpetually go forward from that troubling time determined as guilty in the public realm of innuendo, rumor and ill-will by former parishioners and Catholic faithful. His name would join a list of others archived in the same bureaucratic way as it had been done for centuries.

Regardless, of *official* outcomes exonerating him and the Church, Father Andrew knew that the responsibility of definitive guilt was his alone. It was he who had begun the controversy, pressed the extent of his priestly vows to their limits, and succumbed to their predictable and horrible ends by his errant actions. Those included his nefarious and ill-conceived attempts—born out of self-righteousness, to assuage his own guilt and preserve his priestly status. He should have known he would not win in a battle with the bureaucracy of the two-thousand-year-old institution or in the eye of public opinion.

Father Andrew continued to engage in his *faux prayer* of contemplation in the church sacristy over the spot of what had been the temporary grave of

Sister Janina. He muttered them drawing on a rote memory which was now fringed with dementia.

The priest then did the extraordinary in terms of *psychological projection*. Andrew then proceeded to perform his own form of *confession*. He administered the Sacrament of Penance to himself. It included an absolution for yet another instance of his *sin*—another of his *crimes*. Evidence of both lay below his feet. Because, to date, no one had ever questioned him about it, he believed this was a fact unbeknown to any other human—even to his superiors in the Church.

"It is known only to me and to you, God." Andrew whispered. After *sixteen years* being held a secret, his hushed admission now deepened his own substantial guilt.

Andrew's first *sin* was well known. The bones from it had been discovered years earlier. Though, a trial had convicted someone else of it. However, the evidence of his *second sin*—his *secret sin* could be found if one were looking for it, just a few feet further into the interior of the structure's cellar. Now inaccessible, as far as he could tell, it had *not* been discovered by construction workers excavating for the new church foundation. It had also amazingly not been unearthed by Father Podlaszewski and his sexton, or even later by law enforcement combing the crime scene. Andrew believed the oversight must have occurred when in their zeal to arrest someone after investigators exhumed the reinterred bones of Janina in the cemetery, they curtailed any further investigation under the old church.

Father Andrew, still hovering in the church sacristy mulled the possibilities. If only law enforcement investigators, or Sister Regina of the Felician Order, when she had visited the parish to investigate, had explored deeper into the old church cellar to an area immediately behind a center support column—probing the dirt only another eight to ten feet further under the old building, she would have discovered a *fuller truth*.

The crushing full weight of guilt now settled onto Father Andrew as he stood in the holy space. In *truth*, had anyone only searched the ground a little more, they would have found *another set of bones*. They were not some of those left in the haphazard disinterment of Sister Janina, or any fetal remains within her skeletal remains, but they were those *of a man—a young man—a boy, really—a chore boy.*

The bones were those of someone who in life, was by his nature unkempt. Even Father Andrew referred to him, not by name, but often in derogatory fashion based on his human condition, *grubi*. Ironically, in life, he was quietly mysterious, submissive, and loyal *to a point*. It was the bones of a young man who spoke few words in the flesh during his relatively short life and he would forever remain silent under a layer of sandy loam to conceal him and a bucket of fragrant spent ash from Benediction to cloak the senses.

However, it is ironic that his bones, even to this day—if discovered—if they have not already been—would speak the volumes he never did in life. They would be the definitive words still missing from the public record, as to the ultimate *truth* of who was responsible for the disappearance and death of Sister Janina and potentially her unborn child. This *additional* set of bones and its truth would point to the person who likely masterminded the crimes and who was solely responsible for *his* death.

Out of rote habit, Andrew now stood and prayed his insincere prayer for the repose of *three* souls. Not knowing what else to do, he decided in his convoluted thought, that he should at least complete his offer to hear the confession of the young man—his protégé, who had angrily refused it years earlier—as if that was somehow still possible. But he reasoned that there was no need for the penitent to verbally confess his sins—a requirement for the living, as Father Andrew already knew every detail. So, he proceeded—determined that, in absentia of the young man's long-ago departed soul, he could do so on his behalf.

Even though there was no historical precedent of post-death formal confession rituals in any Church historical accounts—albeit they are covered in the Sacrament of the Last Rites for the living, Andrew forged ahead with the confession for the remains in the dirt grave a level below his feet. He continued. "…Ego te absolve ab omnibus censurius, et peccatis…" Though, he was not completely sure that the Almighty would grant absolution for the deceased due to Andrew being the one who was administering the Sacrament.

Andrew knew the possibility existed that God might just negate his whole effort, if he felt that the priest was but a *tainted* instrument of His Grace. Still, undeterred by logic, the Priest concluded. "…in nominee Patris, et Filli, et Spiritus Sancti. Amen."

With his hands still clasped in prayer, Andrew noticed where his once large and protruding index finger ring had once been worn. Though it had been discarded since his interaction with the Archbishop of Milwaukee, it had left permanent marks on his hand. The phantom impression left on the adjoining fingers would be his constant reminder that his previous choices had been for himself, for his career within the Church, and to the detriment of Sister Janina, a possible child, and for a chore boy he barely took the time to know. For the rest of his life, it would remind him that his personal desires took precedent over the human dignity and compassion for those under his stewardship and over a woman who loved him.

In the absence of any physical discoveries under the new church during construction, Andrew knew there would always be another way for others to find the *truth*. It would be detailed in a one-hundred-forty-three-page, handwritten account on college-ruled notebook paper which would represent his final and complete *confession*. Andrew would plan that his words in that document would only be discovered by chance well after his own death when his estate was liquidated.

For the moment, the critical piece from it—his desk, was now in storage in the Grand Rapids Diocese. But he figured in a few more years, after the deaths of two of his superiors familiar with his controversy, he would request it be returned to him. Then he could be sure the desk would secure his admissions over the rest of his life and would only give up his secrets when, per his will, it was donated to charity. And then that document, well hidden behind the lower-left hand drawer of the desk and secured by lock with key broken off in it, would only be found if the desk were disassembled at some point. He also understood that there was also the great possibility it would never be found. He hoped that if it were, it would be years—perhaps decades, or even a century or two, after he was gone. Regardless, he reasoned that his document would finally bring closure to the entire mystery.

The aging priest had now completed his reconciliation of the tragic events. He shook his head at the terrible choices he had made. But what could he do beyond his own self-admission? No. Another confession by him to a priest hardly seemed pertinent at this point. He knew his final judgement before the Lord would be what he anticipated to be in a relatively few short years anyway.

Exhaling deeply, the priest made the Sign of the Cross to end his prayers. He turned and shuffled back down the main aisle of the new church and out the back vestibule. He had decided that he would not stay to attend the new church's dedication Mass the next day out of his overwhelming burden of shame. Even Andrew, in his normal self-righteousness, could not do that to the parish and parishioners he once loved and served with pride. Compassionately, he knew his attendance would taint the celebration of the new building for the many who still remembered him. His presence would only serve to distract and rekindle the horrible grief for them. Bishop Kelly would wonder about his absence, but only for a short while. He would be able to guess the reason.

Exiting the atrium at the back of the church and descending the stairs to the street, Andrew looked back and up to the steeple of the new Holy Rosary as the gathering clouds in the overcast, that had earlier threatened to become a storm, showed signs of dissipating, but not completely going away. They lingered with their *cognitive dissonance*—their contradictory nature. Despite the beliefs of many who felt the mystery and tragedy had passed, others like Father Andrew knew that the full truth—like the storm clouds, with their true nature, would reassemble at some point, and shed their contents on Isadore, Holy Rosary, and the faithful. But he did *not* know when. Both the truth about Sister Janina and the inevitable storm would be like the guilt that had descended upon him. They would do so at the time of their own choosing.

As Andrew continued to stare into the indeterminate sky, he thought of the uncertain possibilities that lay ahead for Holy Rosary, the parish faithful, and for him. While he did, he fingered the key that dangled from the leather lanyard around his neck. The one that was concealed by his high white collar and lay beneath his black shirt. He knew that at least for the near future, his key and those like it held by others throughout the hierarchy of the nearly two-thousand-year-old institution, would likely preserve—for a time—the secrecy of the *Sister Janina Mystery,* and others like it—both great and small.

Andrew also knew that for the remainder of his days, he would never again return to Holy Rosary—the site of his sins for which *he* was solely responsible but was only partially absolved. The priest would slowly fade from the headlines to a simple life in another remote parish, and the *Mystery of Sister Janina* would recede into the hidden archives. But years later, its hidden *truth* would have yet another opportunity to be revealed.

Chapter Fifty-Seven

Historical Perspective: Serious Effort to Expose Files of the *Ineditus Secredito Encyclios*, circa 1939

Ambrogio Ratti, always a measured statesman, had remained a diplomatically neutral Cardinal during the years in the aftermath of WWI—occurring during the reign of his predecessor, Benedict XV.

Following The Great War, drastic changes in borders and governments had created great uncertainty in the direction of the Church.

Now under the leadership of Ratti, who had been elevated to be Pope Pius XI, the Roman Catholic Church was facing an even more dangerous threat. This time it would be posed by Hitler—with help of the Italian fascist, Mussolini. Should they complete their hostile takeover of the continent, it would surely be the death knell of Pius' Institution that had survived for 1900 years. There was no doubt in his mind that the Third Reich would decimate the religion's power and confiscate every financial resource they held.

Complicating matters at this critical time in history, most knew that the days of Pius XI were numbered due to his failing health and two recent heart attacks. The next Pontiff must be able to thread the needle of diplomacy with any future secular leaders to secure the Church's existence.

However, by the years-long persistent vacillation in its position, the Church ultimately compromised its function as the preeminent arbiter of spiritual and moral justice. This was culminated in the signing of an agreement of understanding between the German Weimar government and Reich factions. That agreement, called the Reichskonkordant, effectually eliminated the Vatican's objections to Nazi persecution of peoples they deemed inferior. It gave the Reich legitimacy, while the promises contained in it by Hitler, allowed the Church to operate as normal.

That aspect of the agreement was tentative at best. The document had been finalized with the full knowledge of the atrocities that were occurring under the Reich—specifically to the Jewish populations. Shamefully, it ignored some of the Church's own conciliations in this regard. Factions of its Faith, like Father Josef Tito of the Slovak Republic, a priest turned politician, was accused of openly coordinating with Nazis in exporting Jews from his region to concentration camps. This complicated things for the Vatican and was an endless source of embarrassment which was difficult to politically explain to the free world. However, the Vatican was determined to continue to negotiate some sort of path forward with the Reich for its own well-being.

Sadly, the most troubling aspect of the agreement that satisfied both signatories was that it patently ignored the plight of the Jews of Europe and was devoid of any mention of their future. Viewed by many historians as the Church's abdication of moral leadership, it implied that Hitler could do with them what he wished without objection.

Interestingly, the negotiated agreement was championed on the Church's side by Eugenio Cardinal Pacelli, who at the time was the Vatican Secretary of State under Pius XI.

However, major factions of the Church, along with most of the free world, clamored for the Institution to boldly speak out against Fascism and the Reich and their record of crimes against humanity—not cooperate with them. Meanwhile, behind the scenes maneuvering was underway at some of the highest levels in the Vatican to expose its inactions and appeasements leading up to WWII. But this effort would also go much deeper to reveal how the Church had also acted in the same cavalier manner going back centuries in regard to persecuted groups of peoples and even toward individual victims.

"The question remains." Began Cardinal Michael von Faulhaber, provisional nuncio from Bavaria to Pope Pius XI. "How do we get to the official reports that the Holy See has suppressed for centuries under the *Ineditus Secredito Encyclios*—the *unpublished secret encyclical?*" He mouthed in a barely audible volume several yards down the hall from the hospice room of Pius XI.

In reality, the *Encyclical* Faulhaber mentioned, did not actually exist. But it had become a catch-all phrase for reformers within the Institution to categorize all manner of either applied controversial doctrine or the suppression of certain circumstances and incidents that the Vatican historically had set aside for inaction. No one in the higher levels of authority in the Church would ever admit that such a policy or practice existed, as there was no corroborating documentation. This was unusual for anything in the highly bureaucratic organization of learned and literate administrators. But in practice, all above the level of Bishop and many in the simple priesthood could cite a plethora of current and historical examples where the unwritten encyclical had been employed. To Faulhaber, this Encyclical—published or not, needed to be exposed as the horrible stain on the Church it was. And more importantly, anything derived from the unwritten policy, or archived under its dictates, needed to be exposed as well.

In a marble lined alcove that jutted off the vestibule, Faulhaber huddled under a well-worn marble bust mounted on a tall granite pedestal. Supposedly, the statuary was that of St. Stephen, the first Christian Martyr.

The choice of that statue by Faulhaber for his clandestine meeting would turn out to be a foreboding of the reformer's coming fate.

Cardinal Faulhaber, a native of the Bavarian state, had firsthand knowledge of the eroding political landscape in his region and was incensed when the Vatican had gone ahead and signed the *Koncordant*. He had prepared several briefs for the Vatican Secretary of State advising against the treaty of cooperation as it had been proposed. He documented in detail several known atrocities committed by the Reich. He was sure the Secretary of State would use his citations in negotiations, but he did not. Ostensibly, he purposely ignored everything Faulhaber had prepared and against his advice, had approved the agreement.

In addition, Faulhaber had personal knowledge, that those briefs he had prepared—the verified records of those crimes against humanity committed by the factions of the growing Reich, were sent back from negotiations and were archived where most all records of this kind had been housed since the 1600's—in the Papal desk in the inner office at the summer residence of the Pope at Castel Gandolfo.

Nuncio Faulhaber, along with his co-conspirator, who would soon be Pius XI's outgoing *Under*-Secretary of State, Bishop Evaristo Lucidi, discussed their options in English with some difficulty understanding each other based on their pronounced German and Italian accents, respectively.

"You could actively campaign to become Camerlengo—the interim administrator of the Vatican!" Lucidi offered. "This is the most feasible option."

"How so?" the Nuncio was unsure.

"Due to the authority—albeit a temporary one given to you during the *Sede Vacante*—or *empty seat* period of time when the Church is between Popes." Urged the Bishop. "Although as Camerlengo, you will be under restriction from making major decisions and will only be certified to run the day-to-day affairs, you *would* have unlimited access to all official files and be able to withdraw the select the ones from the cadre—the ones we know to be scandalous."

"Unworkable!" Faulhaber shot back. "The information we need is housed forty miles away at the Papal summer retreat. Just this last summer, I saw Pius stash a fistful of such recent reports in the bottom drawer of his desk in the Papal office. He was so consumed with writing and completing his encyclical denouncing antisemitic and fascist thought before his Papacy ended, he showed little time for what he saw as lesser internal offences. I have read them. They are many—some even resulting in death at the hands of *our* clergy. But because they only involve one or possible two or three people per *priestly transgression,* they have been ignored by the Church." Faulhaber was saddened. "They are none-the-less serious and should be exposed to the light of criticism, as each of the individual victims also deserves closure, Ya?"

Bishop Lucidi nodded. "Scripture says each soul is important to Our Lord. Yes, I agree. Why should we only speak out for those who are currently being persecuted in large numbers? Names of those who have been *transgressed*—who have been lost to history, should also be vindicated. At minimum, we should advocate for the surviving families to offer them closure. We owe them that. But even the records for those—how you say—*priestly transgressions*, are *also* under the same lock and key? As far as I know, the only key to the Castel Gandolfo desk, is on the person of the dying Pontiff!"

The two muffled their conversation, as a team of doctors accompanied by aids passed them in the hall as they headed for the Pontiff's room.

After they were out of earshot, Lucidi resumed. "On second thought, you are right. Vying for Camerlengo is no good for you. You will be confined to Rome immediately following the elevation of the new Pontiff to ease his transition into the job."

"We must remain anonymous for the interim as the Vatican's focus is on the Pontiff's health. But we must act between Popes—in the *sede vacante*, otherwise the opportunity will be lost." Anguished Faulhaber.

In ancient times, the interim between Popes could take months. It was a real possibility that this next transition—which should be upon the Vatican very soon based on the Pontiff's rapidly failing health could also take weeks or even months. Coupled with the current serious rift in the College of Cardinals and their sharply divided loyalties caused by the political pressures placed on them by the Nazi regime, the *sede vacante* would most likely be an extensive deliberation.

Faulhaber determined he must take the calculated risk to launch his now-or-never plan. Both men took one more look around to see if there conversation had been eavesdropped upon and then each went their separate ways.

Adding to the complications for Faulhaber's success in his plan, but in another way aiding it, were the heavy travel restrictions throughout the continent at every border due to the buildup of the impending war. He could also count on at least a couple weeks for a quorum of Cardinals to get to the Vatican for any vote.

That would be just enough time for Faulhaber to clear time in his schedule of duties to make an anonymous trip to Castel Gandolfo to access the Papal Office. He hoped for ample time, in private, to sort through the volume of files stored in the papal desk there—some dating back to the 13th Century, to retrieve the ones he found to be the most salacious to publish to make the maximum statement for reform within the Church. If enough time were left before unveiling his work, he would also continue as a ghost writer of Pius XI's unfinished Encyclical regarding the dangers of fascism and antisemite thought, and then publish it with the rest of his *expose.'*

To Faulhaber, this was equally important and of urgency. He was sure that the Pope's successor—likely the *current* Secretary of State for the Vatican, Cardinal Pacelli, would never publish it and simply set aside the Encyclical, and more likely also lock it away at Castel.

However, for Faulhaber to accomplish anything, he first needed the Pope's key—the one to access the Papal desk at the summer retreat—the one on a leather lanyard around the Pontiff's neck. He would never get *that* key as Pius was now under constant monitoring. Then the Cardinal had an idea. "Perhaps I can have a duplicate made?" For that, Faulhaber decided he must make a hazardous trip to his home region.

From his knowledge of Church and his local history, he knew the desk at Gandolfo was crafted there by the ancient guild of woodcarvers—the Zunft in the early 1600's. The original lock mechanism of the desk and key were also forged there. He even knew the exact shop where that occurred. Amazingly, the shop was still in business.

Luckily, travel throughout the continent was still possible. Cardinal Faulhaber told others in the Vatican that he was making a quick trip—categorized as a *vacation*, to southern Germany.

Among a small group of brave tourists who dared to take holiday in the politically charged atmosphere in Europe, Faulhaber, in plain clothes, followed a tour guide in sheep-like demeanor on the brisk winter afternoon. The talkative guide led them into a shopping district for groups like his. Although many of the shops had been closed due to either the winter weather or because the owners of Jewish ancestry had fled the country, a few were still open. With Nazi soldiers stationed every couple of blocks, the guide, whose livelihood was based on commissions from the shop owner's sales, took the risk to lead his tourists through the open shops selling cuckoo clocks, carvings, and other wooden trinkets.

Finally, Faulhaber and his group entered the shop for which he had specifically made the trip. Its history dated back centuries under the same family. The Lienberger family legacy included producing commissioned items for kings and dignitaries in past centuries—including the ornate desk at Castel Gandolfo for Pope Urban VIII. Cardinal Faulhaber lingered behind the rest of the group and asked to speak to the elder proprietor.

The Cardinal knew that Frau Lienberger had worked in this shop since he was a boy. He also knew that the now elderly man was well versed in the shop's history. His family had a long legacy of staunch Catholicism—including offering stiff resistance to the persecution by Calvinists in the 1600's. The story was that during those times the patriarch of the family had remained loyal to the traditional Church despite limited help from the Pope. The lack of support from the Vatican had resulted in the death of three family members.

The old man emerged from the back of the shop.

"I am Cardinal, er, Michael von Faulhaber—the one who called you in confidence regarding *the key*." He extended his hand.

"Ah yes! Come with me." Motioned the old man. "We will check to see if it can be done."

To the back corner of the cluttered workshop, they entered a separate storeroom—the walls lined with woodworking tools. Lienberger pointed up to a shelf and dragged over a stepstool for the Cardinal to access something from it. Unsteadily reaching the top step, Faulhaber saw two blocks of heavy aggregate tied together with heavy twine. From his own knowledge of the process of casting molten bronze, he determined that the stones must be the outer molds. Wedged in between them he could see a folded and fragile piece of parchment. As Faulhaber pulled the blocks off the shelf, the dust of hundreds of years rained down upon the pair and danced in the dim sunlight penetrating the space from the room's only window. As gently as he could, he dropped the heavy load on a workbench.

To be sure that this was the mold to the key he needed, Faulhaber stepped back into the light to better read the parchment that accompanied the stones. Gingerly folding it open, the iron gall ink written on it had decayed the paper. However, some of the writing on it was still legible. The Cardinal could clearly read the letter *U*, followed by the roman numeral *VIII*. A notation dated 14 May 1640 confirmed these two stones were the outer forging mold for the key to the desk at Castel Gandolfo.

As he watched the elder Lienberger cut away at the twine that held the stones together, the Cardinal knew that his trip here to Bavaria could still be all for naught.

If inside the stones, the carved original wooden model of the key were missing, or if the blank were reduced to a pile of sawdust due to powder post beetle infestation, they would not be able to replicate the Papal desk key with its unique multitude of cuts of the key's pins.

After cutting away the last of the twine, with difficulty, Frau Lienberger flipped over the top stone. In the cavity, perfectly preserved, was the beautifully carved wooden original of the key—still completely intact. The Cardinal admired the detailed craftsmanship. "Marvelous. Can you make a copy of it?" Faulhaber urgently asked.

"As you know already know it is one of a kind!" The old man dithered. "We will make a new clay impression of the wooden original and then use the lost wax method for the molten bronze…" Frau Lienberger then paused his explanation of the creative method. "I see you are not interested in the process, only the results. Yes, I am confident we can create an exact match of the Pope's key—even after four hundred years. So, the original has finally worn out, Ya?" Frau inquired.

"No, it's, uh, an *additional* key!" Faulhaber lied. "It's for the incoming Pope. You are aware that Pius XI is seriously ill, and it is only a matter of time. I want to make the new Pontiff's job easier. He is likely to delegate responsibilities. Thus, the extra key." The Cardinal prattled. "Here is payment. That is 10,000 German Marks?"

The old man—unconvinced by the explanation, raised an eyebrow toward the Cardinal. "Delegation of responsibility *by a Pope?* My, my, times have changed in the Vatican." The old man commented. "The key should be done by the end of the week. The work performed by me alone—by no others in the shop. In Latin, how you say, done in *secredito*." He assured Faulhaber. "To whom should I mail it when it is done?"

"Parcel post it to it to Michael von Faulhaber—Visiting Papal Nuncio,

Vatican City, Italy. Mark CONFIDENTIAL in bold writing—TO BE OPENED BY ADDRESSEE ONLY.

"As you request." Frau Lienberger re-mated the blocks of stone, dragged them off the workbench and shuffled to the forging room to begin his work. The Cardinal left the shop—his first critical step of his mission complete. Faulhaber decided to cut short his *vacation*, and hurry back to Vatican City.

On the train back to Italy, Faulhaber evaluated his plan thus far. It could still fail if the key did not arrive in a timely manner. It needed to get to his Vatican office through the now highly censored mail and with enough time to act. Without that small piece of bronze, it would be pointless to make the trip to access to the Papal desk at Gandolfo. The key also needed to fit the lock.

If those elements went well, he could then select some from the most egregious examples of *inhumanity* stored in that desk drawer—especially the most recent ones still in the public's memory from the 20th Century. His plan was to release the stories to the world's wire services. Those would be ones where the Church could then officially apologize to the victims, or at least to their living relatives. The perfect example of one that fit that description was a report from the Archdiocese of Milwaukee in the United States that had been submitted to the Vatican some three decades earlier. He remembered hearing about it at the time and discussing it with other Bishops at a dinner party shortly after the story broke in the press.

That report was about the disappearance of a nun. Years later, her bones had been found buried in her own church's cellar. Faulhaber recalled that the Parish priest at the time was under tremendous suspicion for her disappearance, but never legally charged with anything. However, his housekeeper *was* and was later convicted of her murder. The Cardinal knew the mystery had never been sufficiently explained to the local community's satisfaction. Though, the Vatican report about it, known to be stored in the desk at the Castel Gandolfo Papal office, was complete, and it left out no detail or names. It would be one of the more prominent reports Faulhaber would publish as an example.

Returning his thoughts to the present, Cardinal Faulhaber was not naive about what his scheme would accomplish. He fervently believed that his faction's mission would no doubt create upheaval but make a bold statement—a Church statement of solidarity regarding *moral justice*. As a keen historian, he agreed with theologians who often referenced a mid-19th Century Unitarian minister, Reverend Theodore Parker. That cleric, in

1883 was the first to pen the idea of a *moral arc that eventually bends toward justice.*

Thus, Faulhaber took it upon himself to be the one who would begin the long process of *bending* righteousness for the world's nations who were still in the throes of *isolation politics* in the late 1930's. He would do this in order to galvanize them to push back at this critical point in history to defeat the grave threat to human liberty posed by the Third Reich. As the train rumbled over the European countryside, Faulhaber continued to pray for his plan's success.

If it succeeded, the incoming Pontiff would be blindsided by it and have to acknowledge the entirety of those historical incidents. He would also be politically forced to release his predecessor, Pius XI's encyclical denouncing the Nazi's and the Reichskoncordant of cooperation—despite him earlier giving it the "green-light." No doubt, Hitler would respond by dissolving it and increase his threat to the Church. But the moral leadership shown by the Vatican—albeit coerced, would rally Allied support against the Reich. That would prevent more of the indiscriminate loss of life and persecution that Hitler was beginning to inflict on an unimaginable scale. In the long game of Faulhaber's plan, the Church would emerge stronger.

There was one final caveat in order for Cardinal Faulhaber's plan to successfully break into the Papal desk inside the office at the Pope's summer retreat. It would require a defection from within the Swiss Guard—the staunchly loyal protection detail that surrounded the Pope and all Vatican offices—including the one at Castel Gandolfo. Outside the Papal office there, a guard was on duty 24-hour-a-day, 365 days a year. Breaking that code of ethics in the Swiss Guard would be difficult, but Faulhaber reasoned, that there would only need to be one small *schism* in their ranks—and then for just a brief amount of time to allow him to access the desk with his newly made key. The most likely scenario to achieve the defection, would be accomplished by either simple bribery, or cooperation leveraged via the personal circumstances of the subject Guard.

As nuncio and aide to whom would likely be named the Camerlengo upon the Pontiff's passing, Faulhaber had convenient access to all Swiss Guard personnel files to identify the most likely candidate for his scheme. Faulhaber did his hasty homework and chose one. With the offer of a substantial *stipend*, the Guard agreed to cooperate.

Then it was just a matter of choosing the window of opportunity for retrieval of documents from Castel. The Cardinal would coordinate the time to when his marked subject would be stationed on guard duty outside the Castel Papal office. In his temporary position, Faulhaber also had the authority to make out their work schedules without raising any suspicions during the time of the interim Pontiff. He had the power and means to coordinate every aspect. He just needed for the current Pope to pass.

A few days later, the duplicate key to the Castel Gandolfo desk arrived in the mail at Cardinal Faulhaber's temporary Holy See office. However, he was concerned because the package looked as if it had been opened and resealed as some point, or at many points during its journey across the continent. The question was by whom? Whether by Reich postal inspectors in Bavaria, or by curious border guards stationed along their expanding territories, or even at the Vatican Post Office itself by unauthorized assistants or by counter-reformationists, he could not tell.

A whole new set of complications swirled in Faulhaber's head. Was the package at this very moment being tracked by the Gestapo to reveal its final recipient? Or more troubling, was it being tracked by elements within the Vatican structure to discover its purpose? He did not have the time to dwell on any of it at this point, because all the elements of his plan were now in place and must go forward. Though, the prospects of failure had now grown to ones that were terrifyingly problematic.

On 10 February 1939, Pope Pius XI died.

Chapter Fifty-Eight

Northern Michigan, circa 1939

Father Andrew read the familiar details of the story about him that had appeared on the front page of the local weekly newspaper. The paper had been printed some 20 years earlier. Someone had mailed it to him in a manila envelope with no return address.

Lake County Star, Friday, 28 February 1919 (Public Domain)

ARRESTED FOR MURDER OF NUN 11 YEARS AGO

"A murder mystery 11 years old was revived in Traverse City by discovery that the body of the missing nun Sister Mary Johns, also

The anonymous sender had also included two other newspapers with stories about the recent passing of Pope Pius XI.

Courier-Northerner, 24 February 1939 (Public Domain)

"...the entire world has for the past week been in mourning over the passing of the Pope Pius XI head of the Roman Catholic church who passed away several days ago..."

Palladium, 16 February 1939 (Public Domain)

"The death of Pope Pius XI was a shock to the whole world..."

The sender had even highlighted the news article by circling them in pencil, so Father Andrew was sure to read them. It had been several years since the priest had received something like this in the mail. As he read, his anxiety rose. The submissions were surely meant to taunt him.

Andrew had been carefully following the recent news headlines and had grown increasingly worried. The priest knew a Papal transition was imminent. His concerns were that moderate and reformist factions in the Vatican within the College of Cardinals would win-out and one of their own would be installed as the next Pontiff.

He was also well aware of the discussions within the Church that if a *progressive* were elected the new head of the Holy See, there was a good chance he would release documents from its secretive archive that had been under restricted access for centuries. They would be published as a way for the Church to *come clean* on its history on human rights. The thought was that the Church would take a moral stance against the threat posed by the Third Reich to rally support from isolationist countries as the European continent moved closer to war.

Andrew also knew that Pius XI had been well-along in completing an encyclical regarding the dangers of Naziism, Fascism and Anti-Semitic thought when his health began to fail. He knew from insiders in the Vatican, that Pius' writings also took some responsibility for the Church's own failings in regard to human liberty. An early draft of it referenced several examples that had occurred during recent Papacies since the turn of the century. Andrew had been informed from the *priestly grapevine* that his own salacious case file regarding Sister Janina had been discussed among the document's drafters and would likely be among those cited in the finalized document. Andrew feared that the new administration—one in the same mindset as that of Pius XI, would no longer protect clergy like him. And moreover, he could be the scapegoat—the face of the Church's shame. The thoughts of his scandal reemerging after all these years, chilled him.

Andrew re-read the articles. He pulled at his starched white collar. It had suddenly gotten very tight. The awful circumstances again flooded his guilty conscience.

Andrew refolded the papers and tucked them back into the manila envelope. He dropped it into the lower drawer of his rectory office desk. It was his old desk from Holy Rosary.

After years in storage, he had been reunited with the desk and its locked contents. That was in 1930 after the death of Archbishop of Milwaukee, Sebastian Messmer. The desk then had accompanied him on each of his succeeding assignments over the last nine years.

Filled with a wave of panic, Andrew slammed the drawer shut with a trembling hand. He then pulled off his collar, unbuttoned the top button of his shirt and withdrew the leather lanyard that hung around his neck. Struggling to grasp the brass key that dangled from it, he quickly locked the drawer with a firm twist. Then in an obsessive-compulsive behavior— not completely satisfied that the mechanism was locked—he gave the drawer pull an extra two firm shakes, to insure the contents were inaccessible.

Chapter Fifty-Nine

Rome, 10 February 1939

Upon hearing the news of the passing of Pius XI, Nuncio Cardinal Faulhaber immediately took out pen and paper to make out the schedule for the Swiss Guard—stationing his chosen compromised individual at Castel Gandolfo the day after next. He then made a call to the Vatican motor pool and reserved an inconspicuous sedan for early on that day. He would make the drive to the Castel alone. Without unforeseen complications, he expected to pass to the Pope's inner office unchallenged by his hand-picked Swiss Guard, unlock the desk, retrieve the needed documents, and return to the Vatican later that morning. He would then quickly begin the first of his dispatches from the cache to the international news organizations for publication. Now he was even more determined that what he was doing was the right thing to do. His actions would be for the preservation of freedom for people in Europe, and a righteous, overall strengthening of Christianity. Though, at least at first, his actions would not necessarily benefit the Institution of the Church.

Two days later, Faulhaber entered the compound at Castel Gandolfo. He briskly paced down the hallway toward the inner complex. Reaching the door of the Pontiff's office, he nodded and winked at his chosen Swiss Guard posted outside the door. Both surveyed the hallway to make sure no one else was around. The guard winked back and let the Cardinal pass.

Quickly going to the desk, he pulled at his starched collar and retrieved from under his shirt a leather lanyard with its newly cast bronze key hanging from it and thrust it into the lock. He wryly grinned when the key turned without resistance and crisp tumblers in the mechanism responded. It performed flawlessly. Pulling back on the overstuffed drawer, he took no time to select anything specific—hastily grabbing two fistfuls of documents from the top of the stack. A few fell to the floor. One happened to be the Diocesan report from the Archbishop of Milwaukee in the United States, *re: Death of Sister Mary Janina, et al.*

As he bent over to retrieve the fallen pages, a strong hand grasped him by the wrist. Faulhaber looked up to see his Swiss Guard holding him tight. The Cardinal dropped several documents from his armload due to the force of his grip.

"What are you doing?" Faulhaber forcefully whispered.

"I can't let you have them." The guard calmly stated.

"What do you mean? We had a deal, Adolphus—an *arrangement*. There was compensation.*" Pleaded Faulhaber.

"I'm sorry, Cardinal Faulhaber. I have taken a solemn oath to the Pontiff and to my Apostolic service to him unto death. You should have known I would not betray that trust." The guard informed. "Moreover, you should have known I could never dishonor my family name."

"Family name?" Faulhaber faltered.

The Cardinal's righteous plan had failed. He would not be able to take the needed documents from the Castel desk archive. He would not be publishing his expose. Pius XI's Encyclical denouncing Nazi atrocities and antisemitism would also never be published.

Still bent over and being held by the wrist, Faulhaber peered up into the determined Swiss Guard, Adolphus' eyes for an explanation. He then realized he had made one critical mistake. He had failed in his due diligence in one area for selecting a member of the Guard in which to compromise.

It is true, Faulhaber had reviewed Adolphus' personnel file. He saw that he had some serious debts from a pending lawsuit against him in the courts and determined that a large influx of money would sway him to the Cardinal's service. It was unfortunately the only criteria he used to make his selection. He should have dug deeper into the background of his Guard.

Had Faulhaber had more time to do his research—to learn of his guard's family lineage—his family's association with the greater Church and their political connections, he would have chosen someone else to be on guard the day he was to breach the Papal office and desk.

Had he done a more thorough review, Faulhaber would have made a *name connection* of this Swiss Guard to another with the same *surname* who had a deep connection to the Church. Only a few years back, that person held a prominent position. Faulhaber had even recently read about and discussed him. That individual had served as an Archbishop in the United States. He also happened to be the Swiss Guard, Adolphus' favorite great uncle. In fact, in 1930, Adolphus had taken a leave from the Guard to attend his funeral after the elderly Archbishop had died while visiting his hometown in Goldach, Switzerland. Ironically, at birth, in honor of his great uncle, Adolphus had also been named after him.

Faulhaber's Swiss Guard, of the rank of a Halberdier—a common soldier, would turn out to be ill-chosen. Adolphus Kaufmann—Adolphus *Sebastian Messmer* Kaufmann, had still not released his grip on Faulhaber's wrist. Holding firm, he reached down and retrieved the several reports that had fallen to the floor, including the one, re: Death of Sister Mary Janina, et. al., and gently placed them back on top of the removed documents. One handed, he settled all of them back into the drawer and closed it firmly. Confiscating Faulhaber's new bronze key by roughly snapping the leather lanyard from his neck, he locked the drawer with it and then led the bewildered Cardinal out of the Papal office.

Chapter Sixty

Vatican City, 2 March 1939

A puff of white smoke billowed from the small chimney on the Sistine Chapel signaling that a new Pope had been elected. In St. Peters Square, the gathering multitudes cheered wildly as they waited for the new Pontiff to make his first appearance at the traditional window above the square and give his first official blessing.

Inside the Papal quarters, Eugenio Cardinal Pacelli, soon to become known as Pius XII, was receiving instructions about the procedure for his appearance above Vatican Square while being measured for his new vestments. "Cardinal Faulhaber—my Nuncio—where is he?"

A group of three in attendance from the College of Cardinals looked at each other as if to decide how they should answer. Finally, one of them stepped forward. "Your Holiness, Cardinal Faulhaber has been given..." He paused to select a word to provide obfuscation to his answer. "...given *vacation*—for an unspecified time and then to be reassigned or perhaps enter retirement." One of the other Cardinals then spoke up. "Here is your man. Your Holiness, let me introduce you to your new Under-Secretary, Bishop Cappeletti."

A nondescript cleric emerged from behind the three Cardinals. He deeply genuflected and kissed the new Pontiff's sleeve. Cappeletti had been negotiated into his new position by the same powerful caucus of Cardinals in the Papal enclave who had pushed for the elevation of their choice, the former Secretary of State, Eugenio Cardinal Pacelli to be the new Pope. With both selections, the faction of Cardinals would maintain a status quo for the Church's direction.

The details of their successful negotiations to install Pacelli and Cappeletti was the direct result of not only intense political infighting, but the discovery of a specific act of intrigue and internal espionage they had recently uncovered and successfully quashed in the last several days. They knew Cappeletti to be a fiercely loyal Bishop to their conservative caucus—one with an impressive *traditionalist* lineage from the line of the Gandolfo family of vintners and clerics. He would make sure the new Pope would follow the steady course of neutrality that had been established with the Nazi regime and not sway to the calls for human dignity for the Jewish populations—which would surely jeopardize the survival of the Institution of the Church. And for now, the late Pope Pius XI's *Encyclical on the Evils of Fascism and Antisemitism* would be set aside.

While the three Cardinals receded from the room, Cappeletti remained and then escorted the new Pontiff into the antechamber of the Chapel. Known as the *Room of Tears,* the new Pope, Pius XII, would be dressed in his regal vestments there by his waiting entourage of valets, and then be left alone with his thoughts for a time to ponder the weight of his office.

The new Pontiff—clearly having a moment of nervousness, shivered as he was reverently and ceremoniously laid bare by the valets. A cassock made of pure white, adorned with gold embroidery was dropped over his slight frame and a pair of red slippers were fitted to his feet.

Before the *pallium*—a liturgical vestment unique to the Pope—a woolen sash that makes a circle around the neck and hangs down in the front and back was lowered onto him, Cappeletti, placed an ancient leather lanyard around his Pontiff's neck. The browned and heavily oiled and tanned calf-skin string secured a bronze key. It was the same key that had been used to lock the Papal desk at Castel Gandolfo as it had been for nearly four centuries. But for this new Pope, the Under-Secretary had also tied on another key—a new one. Each told a story.

The original key to the desk at Castel Gandolfo was highly tarnished, with a rich patina of brown and tinged with green due to chemical reaction from the proximity of if to the skin of the dozens of Popes that had worn it before Pius XII. The *second* key, also in bronze, was an exact copy of the much older one, was devoid of patina, indicating it had only recently been created.

After Pius XII had been completely dressed, the ever-obedient Cappeletti stepped back two paces and followed the new Pontiff toward the portico above Vatican Square. Two paces behind Cappeletti, was an accompanying contingent of Swiss Guards led by the *Oberstleutnant* or vice-commandant of the Papal Guard—the newly commissioned, Lieutenant-Colonel, *Adolphus Sebastian Messmer Kaufmann.*

When Pius XII indicated he was ready, the procession of *traditionalists* triumphantly opened the portico doors and dutifully followed him as he stepped out toward the window above Piazza San Pietro above Vatican Square to greet thousands of the faithful and begin his Papacy of *neutrality.*

Chapter Sixty-One

Northern Michigan, 3-7 March 1939

For the last month, Father Andrew had been getting a series of anonymous packages in the mail delivered to his parish. Each contained disturbing and incriminating stories from Michigan newspapers dating from 1907 to 1919 regarding the Sister Janina Mystery. The mentions of his name and involvement were highlighted in each article. There were also additional news clippings with blurbs about the recent death of Pope Pius XI the previous month. It was evident to him that the collection of news stories were meant to send a *message.* He understood what that message was. If a less-traditional Pontiff were elected, he would once again, after two decades be the talk of the nation. Surfacing would be the stories of his alleged sordid relationship with the nun, her disappearance, death, and discovery of her bones in the basement of *his* church. It would re-dredge up every aspect of his time at Holy Rosary.

However, today Father Andrew was relieved to read the front-page headlines of the major newspapers that had been delivered in that day's mail.

WORLD HAILS NEW POPE

"...worldwide approval is given with the election of Eugenio Cardinal Pacelli, papal secretary of state as the new Pope Pius XII..."

New Pope Elected

"Pius XII greets crowd in St. Peters square..."

The New Pope

"Vatican Elevates Pius XII as Church Leader..."

Andrew breathed a sigh of relief. The new Pope was, indeed, Eugenio Cardinal Pacelli. He was a pacifist and had already demonstrated that he was an advocate for neutrality for the Church in dealing with the threat of Naziism. He had already placated the Nazi Regime in 1933 with signing a Koncordant with the Fuhrer rather than confront their record on human rights. He was not about to expose his own Church's history of much of the same sorts of indifference to humanity and the individual. Thus, Father Andrew was confident that the new Pius XII would maintain traditions of Institutional *secredito*. The priest was reassured to know that *his* transgressions would remain that way as well.

Chapter Sixty-Two

North Lake Leelanau, Labor Day Weekend, 1974

It was time to close the vacation season at the lake cottage. But first, there would be one more get-together to wrap up what had been a busy summer. It had unexpectedly provided intrigue and entertainment for the owner of the property—a teacher named Ann. During her summer break, rather than immersing herself in what the book industry calls *a summer read* in her favorite genre, *true crime* novels, she had spent a majority of her *off time*— days when the northern Michigan weather didn't cooperate for sunbathing or taking the boat out to waterski or fish, by poking around in local libraries, historical societies and reading from dusty newspaper archives.

Her focus was a true local saga that had always fascinated her. Tonight, and tomorrow she would contribute to it.

Ann smiled as she remembered reading an advertisement in one of the old newspapers clippings she had come across during her summer of research. The quaint nature of the language of the time had amused her. She quoted from the ad in her mailed-out party invitations.

"Dance...Don't Fail to Come."

She checked her watch. Her friends would begin arriving within the hour. She expected eight to twelve of her closest friends from her college days to attend the Labor Day weekend beach party and sleepover at her family's cottage on the east side of North Lake Leelanau. Each guest would bring a dish to pass, wine and beer. A few of her *4-20 friendly* guests would bring their diversion of choice. To encourage dancing in the moonlight, she pointed her stereo speakers out toward the beach from the cottage's screened-in porch. As the evening progressed and everyone mellowed, additional entertainment would be provided by her old platonic "dorm brother" who was expected to bring his guitar. She took a moment to fantasize and said aloud. "Maybe the *platonic* aspects of our relationship might just evaporate this weekend!"

Ann continued her preparations by dragging a big cardboard box from the boathouse toward the beach. This was her third trip to fill the firepit with fuel—mostly well-seasoned oak. She had decided after careful consideration, that the occasion called for a fire—a huge bonfire to drive off the night chill and any insects. It would be constructed with something of personal significance—an office desk.

The desk *and its contents* were the only thing she had requested from her Grandpa John's estate. He had passed earlier that summer. For the last few years, the desk, along with a trove of items that he found hidden in it, had sat on his sunroom porch at his summer residence in the Bay View Association neighborhood in Petoskey in Emmet County. The *contents* concerned the legend of the *Missing Nun of Isadore* from 1907.

As Ann pulled more wood from the box and stacked it within the large stone circle, she thought in some way it sad that she had felt the need to cut up what was the still-serviceable office desk into manageable pieces with a reciprocating saw. She had done so as a visceral response to the desk, and from what she had discovered over her summer of research, others like it that had helped to shroud the mystery of the missing nun for over six decades and others for centuries. She surmised that by burning the desk and its contents it would bring some closure.

Ann tossed the final piece of wood—she believed it to be the desk's lower drawer face—onto the pile and then pulled the large handful of papers from the box—the ones that had been archived in the desk's drawer. She would use them as dry tinder to start the fire. But then she paused.

She reconsidered her options that might satisfy her commitment to her Catholic Faith and to preserve some of the contents of the trove for posterity and for future historians and investigators like her. She decided that someone—someday might be able to come up with the definitive facts and provide the ultimate answers to the mystery. She determined that process should also involve participation of her Faith—the Church itself.

Yes, she concluded. It would be wrong to destroy *everything*. Rather, it would be prudent for her to peruse the papers at least one more time and save the most important ones.

At the top of the stack was a *copy* of an original document of several pages once stapled together from the Archdiocese of Milwaukee. The subject line of the cover page read, *re: Death of Sister Mary Janina, et. al.* After reviewing it she decided *she* would *not* add it to the firepit. She folded it and tucked it into the back pocket of her jeans.

Ann continued to work her way down the stack of papers. They included a hundred or so pages of what was a transcript from the Leland Courthouse from the State of Michigan v. Stanislawa Lipczynska murder trial in 1919. Her best guess was that this was just a copy and therefore expendable. Had she known that this was likely the only remaining copy of the proceedings, she would have held onto it. However, she felt that there must be another official transcript of the same in some county or State archive. So, it went into the firepit.

Following that, Ann thumbed through several office files. They were pages concerning reprimands for work behavior and personnel transfers that had occurred at the parish of Holy Rosary Catholic Church in Isadore, Michigan in the early 1900's. She could find no reason to keep those, so they too went into the pit.

Next, Ann came upon a college-ruled, spiral-bound notebook with faded blue cover. It was moisture damaged and many of the pages were stuck together. However, she flipped through the undamaged ones—stopping to read certain passages. She found them to be as fascinating as when she had first read them at her grandfather's cottage. They were the highly personal recollections and revealing contemporaneous notes about the mystery of Sister Janina penned by a Father Andrew. She dwelled on the notebook's historical, potentially legal, and personally appealing nature.

Perhaps someday—maybe in her retirement years—she'd write a book about its contents. The notebook had great potential for intrigue and romance. Or in lieu of her composing a manuscript herself, she could give it to one of her old college friends with a penchant for writing. A couple were expected to attend the beach party. She knew they would find it fascinating and jump at the chance to write the novel for her. Though, for tonight during the beach party, she would refrain from the discussion of it with her potential storytellers as she believed it might ruin the festive mood. She would instead save the notebook from the blaze and place it in a box of memorabilia. The box would be stored in the back of a bedroom closet at the cottage where it would remain untouched for the next forty-five years.

Nearing the bottom of the stack of papers, Ann came upon newspaper clippings recounting the Sister Janina saga. There were also several letters that had been sent to the town of Isadore and Holy Rosary Parish at the height of the mystery during the years 1907 to 1919. Some offered their services to conduct *seances* or were from traveling mystics who promised to solve *the mystery*. The rest were mostly penned by anonymous sources—thought to be from pranksters. They told authorities to give up their investigations or gave false leads and made spurious claims.

Ann knelt at the edge of the pit, struck a match, and held it near a single yellowed sheet of letter stationary. Before touching the corner of it with the flame, she read the verbiage. It's text seemed to taunt the recipient, Father Andrew—and the greater Catholic church.

Remembering back to when this letter had been displayed prominently on top of her grandfather's desk in his Petoskey home, it had always galled her the most. Being a devout and still practicing Catholic, she was going to particularly enjoy eliminating it. She wondered what kind of person would seek to minimize the tragedy by drafting something like this. Was it done to divert attention away from the murder? Maybe it was written by the culprit to throw off investigators. Those would always be open questions.

Ann's belief is that the letter was mainly produced to ridicule the Catholic Faith. A read of the available documents concerning the Sister Janina case shows that the Church had created the controversy, suppressed elements of it, and had appropriately been saddled with the aftermath of ill-will since its occurrence—a self-inflicted wound. Conflicted on what were the ultimate facts, she impulsively lit the edge of the brittle page with the ignited match. The flame slowly crept across the paper to the signature line. She smiled as she watched the words, *A Protestant Pup*, turn to blackened ash. Tossing the page to the base of the wood, it ignited the pyre.

Stepping back from the growing heat from the now established bonfire, Ann knew she needed to do something else. She dragged the box to the edge of the dock. Reaching into it, she lifted out the heavy brass locking mechanism that had once secured the lower desk drawer. Unbuttoning the top two buttons on her blouse, she reached under it and pulled out a leather lanyard with a brass key dangling from it. It was the key her grandfather had commissioned to be made by a locksmith to replace the original that had been broken off in the lock. She edged closer to the end of the planks of the dock and paused to take in the calm and beauty of the placidly flat lake in the rapidly approaching dusk.

Without looking, Ann pulled the lanyard up over her head, removing it from around her neck and inserted the key in the mechanism—giving it a half-twist. Then, taking a step backward and a quick step forward, with all the strength she could muster, she launched the heavy lock out over the water. It smacked through the dead calm surface, causing a heavy splash. The sound from it reverberated across the lake and returned to her in a second as an echo from the other side. A wave of concentric ripples pushed out from the center of the impact.

Finally, Ann reached into the box and retrieved the only thing left in it—a man's ring made of gold with a large amethyst stone at its center. She wouldn't think of tossing the expensive jewelry. Perhaps she would have the gold melted down for value content and use its pale violet stone in one of her silversmithing projects—pairing it with one of the Petoskey stones she had gathered from the beaches in Glen Arbor that summer. But then she determined that would not be fair to the legend she had researched. Repurposing the important item would not urge her Faith to confront the story of Sister Janina in an open manner. She would do something else with it that might prompt them to action. She slipped the ring into the front pocket of her jeans just as the last glimmer of the brilliant burnt-orange sunset dropped behind the pines that rimmed the western side of the lake. The scene and her decided resolve gave her a *partial* sense of closure.

Turning back to the bonfire on her beach—now fully engulfed, she continued to formulate a plan to play her part in the missing nun story.

Tomorrow morning—Sunday, while most of her overnight guests were still sleeping in, she would drive south from her cottage, then west through the town of Lake Leelanau at the narrows between North and South Lake Leelanau. Then she would turn south on French Road—Co. Road 645, to the intersection of Schomberg and E. Gatzke to the Four Corners and Holy Rosary Church in Isadore to attend Mass.

Still conflicted, in some ways, Ann was determined to do her part to finally end the embarrassment for the community of Isadore, the decades of slander by outsiders, and help to mitigate the ill-will that was felt within her Faith which was caused by the Sister Janina tragedy. But in another way, as a history teacher, she believed debate about it should continue for future historians. Based on her summer of research, she was convinced there was still more to discover. However, her overarching concern was the disenchantment she felt as a result of her discoveries of how *her* Church— *her* Faith, had handled the tragedy. She considered how she might reconcile her swirling unease and prompt their full disclosure.

Awake early the next morning, Ann decided what would be her protocol at the 11 o'clock Mass—a High Mass with Benediction at its completion. After the Homily, when the priest would ask for additional Intercessory Prayers for individuals, she would reply to his; *We pray to the Lord* with *Lord hear our prayer.* But her responses would be for an additional group of souls not mentioned by the priest. Ann had decided that based on her observation of human behavior in the Sister Janina mystery, her prayers would be for those who had been disparaged over the course of the last three-quarters of a century.

"Lord hear our prayer." Ann murmured for those of the Sisters of the Felician Order. In her estimation, throughout her summer of study, those educators had often been treated as *chattel*—beneath worthiness, believability, or ability as administrators to create educational policy. Being a teacher herself, she had difficulty extending the sincerity of her prayer to those who had looked down on the Sisters.

"Lord hear our Prayer." Ann then implored for the repose of the souls of *six* individuals. They were key individuals in Isadore at the time in question. She had never met them, and all had passed away long ago. Though, *four* of whom she now knew by name. Over the course of her investigations, she now felt she knew them intimately.

The first prayer would be a begrudgingly offered one for a Father Andrew, the former Pastor of Holy Rosary, and for his suspected central role in the tragedy. In the spirit of forgiveness, she decided he needed prayers too.

The second would be for Sister Mary Janina—born Josephine Mezek—a victim who's life of purpose was cut short, and the circumstances surrounding her demise never fully known.

The third prayer by Ann was for Stanislawa "Stella" Lipczynska—the pastor's housekeeper—who in her estimation—fueled by a gut feeling and discovered anecdotal evidence, had been wrongly convicted of murder.

Ann's fourth prayer would be for the official Sexton-Groundskeeper of Holy Rosary at the time of Janina's disappearance, a young man known by the name of Theodore Gruba—aka, Teddy, Ted, Gus, Fred, and possibly others. To date, his behind-the-scenes role and knowledge of the events have never been fully revealed—only discussed with speculation. Over the decades, local small-town newspaper mentions of him were few but intriguing and never pursued to discover the potential truth of his involvement or knowledge of this tragedy.

There would also be extensive prayers for a *fifth*—another young man. He was, according to what Ann's research had revealed from her review of Father Andrew's faded blue notebook, one whom she was now *literally* praying *over*.

Though, from the time she had read Father Andrew's contention, her judgement of its validity had been tempered with considerable speculation. She viewed his claim in his narrative as just as likely the product of his imagination as fact. She knew from her study of the justice system, there were always a high percentage of criminals who had the mental capacity to proclaim and firmly believed they *did not do it! It had to be someone else*—despite overwhelming evidence to the contrary.

None the less, Ann continued her prayers extended to the boy as if he *had* existed. She knew he was likely one of the transient and nameless other chore boys or orphans of Holy Rosary produced from the Church's antiquated orphanage and foster home system for its male youth. Sadly, he would remain an anonymous soul—real or not—who in life was generally ignored and entirely dominated by authority to do what he was told to do when he was "whistled for."

For this fifth soul, Ann had discovered that most never attempted to know him. Many in Isadore had marginalized him and his ilk. This fifth soul was probably from outside the Isadore Polish ethnic community. The quiet, mysterious, and perpetually unkempt young man was either jokingly—but more often disparagingly—referred to by the interchangeable name-derogatory term of *gruba* or *grubi—dirty* or *filthy,* or by the collective *"N" word* by the community for lack of another readily available ethnic slur.

Finally, Ann's last prayer would be for a soul she did not know by name or if had ever actually existed. But she would make her supplication anyway. It was for the unborn infant of Father Andrew and Sister Janina.

While Ann prayed her final, *Lord Hear Our Prayer*, she retrieved an offering envelope from the pocket attached to the back of the pew in front of her. In it she would place two items. One would be the cover page of the Diocesan Report from the Archdiocese of Milwaukee—the subject line: *re: Death of Sister Mary Janina, et. al.* In it she wrapped the large men's ring of gold with its amethyst stone and Crucifix engraved on one side and the initials *A. B.* on the other.

With a wave of hesitation due to the difficulty of sealing the bulky envelope, she finally managed to provide enough saliva from her nervously parched mouth onto the glued flap and pressed it closed. On the front of the envelope, in the space after NAME: she wrote in large letters, *A Catholic Pup.*

During the offering, when the usher passed the collection basket in front of her, the elderly man took note of the heft of the envelope as it dropped into the green velvet lined wicker. He paused a moment as he read Ann's unusual identification scrawl upon it. Then he briefly glanced at her with a noticeable scowl.

Ann had achieved her limited goal. She had piqued the usher's curiosity. Her hope was that he and/or the officiating priest would inspect the offering later when counting money in the collection and wonder its nature. She was sure they would discuss it with the authorities in the parish—perhaps the Diocese—and recall its significance. The odds were long, but she envisioned there would then be serious internal discussion taking place in the hierarchy of the Church about her revival of the Sister Janina story and her chiding of them with her submission. If the modern leadership was forthcoming, then subsequent appropriate action would be taken. She determined that this was the best she could hope for from the Institution from her anonymous position.

At the end of Mass, Ann exited the vestibule at the back of the church and descended the steps. Like Father Leo and Father Andrew had done decades earlier, she too paused and turned to look up to the steeple and beyond it to building storm clouds rolling in from the west. Ann contemplated the significance of what the old wooden structure had played in the mystery. But she also recognized the irony that the newer structure would also continue to figure prominently in any truth—should it ever be discovered.

Ann continued to search the skies until large rain drops and hail started to pelt her. With a sense of relief, she made a solemn vow. While she would keep and practice her Christian ethics—not necessarily her *Catholic* ones—going forward she would only occasionally attend Mass on the major holidays and be more of a *follower of Jesus*, rather than ascribe to any particular religion. And she was fairly sure she would never again *go to confession*.

Holding the printed church program over her head to shield her from the cloudburst, she ran to her vehicle and started the drive back to her cottage. A short distance from the Four Corners, the storm suddenly dissipated. She thought that perfectly symbolic. The dark cloud had remained over Isadore and would continue to do so until the turbulent *atmosphere* there was settled—by whom, or what, and at what time, she could not predict.

Ann then drew from verbiage she had read in the collection of documents from the desk to express her feelings on the uncertainty of it all. She paraphrased. "It will resolve itself at the time of its own choosing, not mine." She accepted the fact that to her and others, there would always be more questions than answers on what had occurred in Isadore.

As Ann continued to mull all the possibilities, inside her vehicle, she also noticed that the lingering faint scent of burnt incense from the Benediction after Mass had remained with her. To her, that too was symbolic in an insidious way. From what she had read, the properties of incense had helped to cloak the truth, but by its nature it also lingered as a faint clue and reminder of what had happened. The mystery of Sister Mary Janina would also linger *with her*—occasionally resurfacing in her memory in the years to come.

Brilliant sunshine of the new day now penetrating the windshield of Ann's vehicle. Her thoughts began to turn to the rest of the holiday weekend with her friends—and since last night, her now *special* friend. Cresting the large hill on the road just north of the parish, in her review mirror, Holy Rosary and Isadore finally dropped from sight and thought—at least for her—at least for now.

The End.

Lawrence D. Yaklin is an American writer and broadcast professional. His voice is heard on countless radio and television commercials in the United States as well as being the Narrator of over 50 audiobooks.

Larry got his start in authoring comedic content with his early efforts and thought-provoking art applied to the cars of slow-moving freight trains with cans of spray paint with the intent that it be appreciated by drivers stuck at railroad crossings.

From there he progressed to 8-1/2x11, 20# bond on Smith-Coronas and eventually to IBM PC Juniors. Along the way, he received discipline from strict educators in the English Department at Central Michigan University who enjoyed and encouraged his creative style but gave him split grades on his compositions, i.e., A+/C- for his "questionable uses of grammar and punctuation."

In his defense, Larry maintains he learned his "bros-prose" on the streets of the north end of Flint, Michigan during the 1960's—where it was taught to him that it was more important to express oneself rather that cross t's, dot i's or restrain himself from the excessive use of .... Those had always afforded him the needed time to come up with the advertising copy's "call to action" but ultimately failed to curtail run on sentences like this one.

FIRST, MOVE THE BONES: A NOVEL is his third work of fiction. It follows DESIRE TO WALK IN LONG ROBES – A Mystery and Transformational Love Story and DONE FOR THE GREATER GOOD. All three of these stories are serious in nature. *Whooda thunk* that was possible?

Lawrence's writings—both the serious and humorous—share either one of two principals.

One; to advocate for the ideals of the Ancient Roman Poet, Virgil, who said: ***Amor Vincit Omnia*—Love Conquers All.**

Two; to apply the 'ol adage, **Laughter is the Best Medicine**...But he refuses to get that new Laughter Vaccine! He did his own research online and saw that it's made with snake venom and makes you magnetic. He personally knows three people who took the Vaccine and when they went to the Post Office to buy some stamps, they got stuck to the mailbox.